KEN SANCHEZ

Twisted Fate (Major Arcana Book One)

An Enemies to Lovers Gay Urban Fantasy

Contents

Author's Acknowledgement

Hi there! Thanks for picking up this book. If you're enjoying my work, you can find more stories like this if you scan the QR code below. While you're there, consider leaving a review once you've finished reading the book – it really helps a writer out!

1

Luck Be a Lady Tonight

Ethan

Ethan Hawke stood before the mirror, meticulously adjusting his tailored suit, his crystal green eyes gleaming with anticipation. "Looking sharp, Hawke," he smirked at his reflection, his fingers deftly securing the hidden gadgets within his sleeves. "Time to show this casino what The Arcana is made of."

"Ready to rock and roll, boss?" Zoe's voice crackled through his earpiece, her tone laced with excitement.

"Always," Ethan replied, a grin spreading across his face. "Marcus, you in position?"

"Affirmative," came the gruff response. "Got eyes on the floor and the security feeds. You're good to go."

The casino was a glittering oasis amidst the gritty, neon-soaked streets of the city. As Ethan stepped inside, he was immediately assaulted by the cacophony of slot machines, the clinking of glasses, and the laughter of high rollers. The air hummed with an undercurrent of magic, a reminder that in this world, nothing was quite as it seemed.

Ethan scanned the room, his enhanced senses picking up on the subtle tells of the players and the watchful eyes of the security staff. He had to be careful, had to blend in with the crowd while still maintaining his edge. But this was what he lived for - the thrill of the hunt, the rush of putting his skills to the test against the shadows that threatened the innocent.

"Alright, team, let's find our mark and get this done," Ethan murmured, his lips barely moving as he spoke into his hidden mic.

As he approached the bar, a sultry voice purred in his ear, "Well, well, what do we have here? A handsome stranger in our midst."

Ethan turned, his gaze falling upon a stunning figure draped in a shimmering silk dress. Her eyes, a mesmerizing shade of amber, locked with his, and he felt a spark of intrigue ignite within him.

"Handsome? You're too kind," Ethan replied, his tone playful. "I'm just a man looking for a little excitement. Care to join me?"

The mysterious woman smiled, her ruby lips parting to reveal a row of perfect teeth. "Excitement is my specialty, darling. But be careful what you wish for in a place like this."

Ethan raised an eyebrow, his interest piqued. "Oh? And why's that?"

She leaned closer, her breath hot against his ear. "There are secrets hidden beneath the glitz and glamour, secrets that could swallow a man whole."

Ethan's heart raced, his mind whirling with possibilities. "Secrets, you say? Now you've got my attention."

The woman chuckled, her eyes sparkling with mischief. "That's all you're getting for now, handsome. But if you play your cards right, maybe we'll meet again."

With a wink, she turned and melted into the crowd, leaving Ethan grinning like a Cheshire cat.

"Ethan, focus," Marcus's voice cut through his thoughts. "We've got a job to do."

"Right, right," Ethan replied, shaking his head to clear the distraction.

"Zoe, any sign of our target?"

"Negative," Zoe responded. "But I'm picking up some chatter on the security channels. Something's got them spooked."

Ethan's eyes narrowed, his instincts on high alert. "Keep monitoring, Zoe. Marcus, watch my back. I'm going to take a closer look."

As Ethan made his way through the casino, his eyes darted from table to table, searching for his target. Then, he spotted him—the notorious mutant crime lord, sitting at the high-roller poker table, surrounded by a group of wealthy-looking men.

"Bingo," Ethan muttered under his breath, a smirk playing on his lips. "Zoe, Marcus, I've got eyes on our guy. I'm going in."

"Be careful, Ethan," Zoe's voice crackled through his earpiece. "This guy's no joke. He's got a reputation for making people disappear."

"Well, let's hope he doesn't make me disappear before I get what we need," Ethan quipped, his tone light despite the seriousness of the situation.

Ethan approached the table, his posture relaxed and his smile easy. "Room for one more?" he asked, his eyes meeting the crime lord's in a silent challenge.

The crime lord, a large man with a shaved head and a scar running down his cheek, regarded Ethan with a calculating gaze. "If you think you can handle it, pretty boy," he rumbled, his voice like gravel.

Ethan grinned, taking a seat at the table. "Oh, I can handle anything you throw at me," he replied, his tone laced with innuendo.

As the game began, Ethan focused his powers, using his ability to manipulate the cards to his advantage. He could feel the emotions of the other players, their excitement, their fear, their greed. It was a heady mix, and Ethan reveled in it.

"So, what brings a guy like you to a place like this?" Ethan asked casually, his eyes never leaving his cards.

The crime lord chuckled, a humorless sound. "Business, of course.

Just like everyone else here."

Ethan nodded, his expression neutral. "I hear you're the man to talk to about certain…disappearances," he said, his voice low and conspiratorial.

The crime lord's eyes narrowed, his posture stiffening. "I don't know what you're talking about," he growled, his tone warning.

Ethan shrugged, a picture of nonchalance. "My mistake. I must have heard wrong."

He knew he needed an edge to gain the upper hand and extract the information he sought.

Discreetly, Ethan focused his mind, summoning the power of his Wheel of Fortune tarot card. The ethereal card materialized in his hand, glowing faintly with an otherworldly energy. He channeled its power, manipulating probability and turning luck in his favor.

"I raise," Ethan declared, pushing a stack of chips forward, his eyes never leaving the crime lord's face.

The crime lord studied Ethan for a moment, his gaze calculating. "You've got guts, pretty boy," he growled, matching Ethan's bet.

As the dealer revealed the final card, Ethan felt a surge of energy coursing through him. The Wheel of Fortune was working its magic, and he knew the odds were in his favor.

"All in," Ethan said, his voice calm and confident as he pushed his remaining chips into the middle of the table.

The crime lord's eyes widened, surprise flickering across his face. He hesitated for a moment, glancing down at his own cards before making his decision. "Call," he grunted, revealing his hand.

Ethan smiled, laying his cards on the table. "Straight flush," he announced, his tone triumphant. "Looks like luck is on my side tonight."

As Ethan collected his winnings, he could feel the crime lord's eyes boring into him, a mixture of suspicion and grudging respect. The ethereal tarot card in Ethan's hand faded away, its power spent.

"That was quite a run you had there," the crime lord remarked, his voice low and menacing. "Almost too good to be true."

Ethan shrugged, his expression nonchalant. "What can I say? I've always been a lucky guy."

He could feel the tension mounting as the crime lord's bodyguards began to close in, their hands hovering near their weapons.

"Boss, you need to get out of there," Marcus urged through the earpiece. "Those guys look like they mean business."

Ethan nodded almost imperceptibly, his mind already formulating an escape plan. He knew he had to act fast, before the situation escalated beyond his control.

In a flash, Ethan was on his feet, his chair clattering to the floor behind him. He vaulted over the poker table, sending chips and cards flying in his wake. The bodyguards lunged for him, but Ethan was faster, his reflexes enhanced by his mutant abilities.

He ducked and weaved through the chaos of the casino floor, his heart pounding in his chest as he sought a way out. Patrons screamed and scattered, adding to the confusion and mayhem.

"Zoe, I need an exit strategy!" Ethan panted, his eyes scanning the room for a way out.

"There's a service corridor to your left," Zoe replied, her voice calm and focused. "It should lead you to the back alley."

Ethan nodded, sprinting towards the corridor, his feet pounding against the plush carpet. He could hear the shouts of the bodyguards behind him, their footsteps growing louder as they closed in.

He sprinted down the corridor, his mind raced, searching for a way to turn the tables on his pursuers. Suddenly, a flash of movement caught his eye—the crime lord, slipping through a side door, alone and unguarded.

"Gotcha," Ethan muttered, a fierce grin spreading across his face. He quickly summoned the power of The Hermit card, cloaking himself in invisibility as he slipped through the door behind his target.

Inside, Ethan found himself in a private back room, dimly lit and lined with shelves of antique books and strange artifacts. The crime lord stood at the far end, his back turned, seemingly unaware of Ethan's presence.

"Well, well, well," Ethan drawled, allowing his invisibility to fade as he stepped out of the shadows. "Fancy meeting you here."

The crime lord whirled around, his eyes widening in surprise and anger. "You! How did you—"

"Oh, I have my ways," Ethan smirked, his hand casually brushing against the hilt of his concealed weapon. "Now, let's talk about those disappearances, shall we?"

The crime lord's face darkened, his posture shifting into a defensive stance. "I told you, I don't know anything about that."

Ethan sighed, shaking his head in mock disappointment. "You know, for a guy with your reputation, you're a terrible liar."

He focused his mind, summoning the power of The Lovers card. A wave of emotional energy surged through the room, and Ethan could feel the crime lord's resolve beginning to waver.

"Come on," Ethan coaxed, his voice smooth and persuasive. "We both know there's more to this than meets the eye. Just give me a hint, a clue, anything to point me in the right direction."

The crime lord hesitated, his eyes darting around the room as if searching for an escape. "I... I can't. They'll kill me if I talk."

Ethan's eyebrows shot up, his interest piqued. "They? Who are they?"

The crime lord shook his head, his face pale and sweaty. "I've already said too much. You have no idea what you're up against."

Just then, the door burst open, and a group of heavily armed men poured into the room, their weapons trained on Ethan.

"Shit," Ethan cursed, his mind racing as he assessed his options. He was outnumbered and outgunned, but he wasn't about to go down without a fight.

With a flick of his wrist, Ethan summoned the power of The Tower card, sending a blast of fiery energy towards his attackers. The men scattered, ducking for cover as the room erupted into chaos.

Ethan leaped into action, his body moving with superhuman speed and agility as he dodged bullets and delivered devastating blows. He could feel the power of his tarot cards surging through him, enhancing his strength and reflexes.

One by one, Ethan cut down his opponents, his hands and feet striking with brutal precision. He summoned the power of The Emperor card, channeling its energy into a bone-shattering punch that caved in a man's skull. Another attacker fell to The Hanged Man, his neck snapped by an impossible twist of Ethan's wrist.

Ethan stood over the fallen bodies of his enemies, his chest heaving with exertion and emotion. He knew that some would call his actions brutal, even monstrous. But in a world where the innocent suffered and the guilty went unpunished, Ethan knew that sometimes, the only justice was the kind you made for yourself.

As the adrenaline slowly faded, a sense of weariness settled over him. The weight of his actions, the lives he had taken, pressed heavily upon his shoulders. He was no stranger to violence, but each time he took a life, it chipped away at a piece of his soul.

Ethan stalked towards the crime lord, his steps slow and deliberate, he couldn't help but feel a twinge of uncertainty. The information he had gathered so far pointed to a larger conspiracy, one that threatened to unravel everything he had fought for.

He knew that his actions carried consequences, and the deeper he delved into this mystery, the more likely it was that those consequences would come back to haunt him.

The crime lord, cowering in the corner, watched in horrified fascination as Ethan tore through his men like a whirlwind of death. "W-wait!" he stammered, holding up his hands in a gesture of surrender. "I'll tell you everything! Just let me live!"

Ethan paused, his breathing heavy and his eyes blazing with righteous fury. He stalked towards the crime lord, his steps slow and deliberate. "You had your chance," he growled, his voice low and menacing. "But you chose to side with evil. And now, you'll pay the price."

He couldn't help but wonder if his crusade had strayed too far from the ideals that first motivated him. But each time doubt crept in, Ethan reminded himself of the innocent lives at risk, the victims whose cries for help went unanswered by a system too corrupt or inept to protect them.

That was why he had to keep fighting, keep pushing forward no matter the personal cost. He was their last line of defense against the shadows that threatened to consume them all.

As Ethan raised his blade, poised to strike down the crime lord, he steeled his resolve. This was the life he had chosen, the burden he carried. He was The Arcana, and he would see justice done, even if he had to walk through hell itself to achieve it.

With a swift motion, Ethan plunged the blade into the crime lord's heart. The man's eyes widened in shock and pain, a gurgling cry escaping his lips as he slumped to the ground.

He knew that some would call his actions brutal, even monstrous. But, Ethan knew that sometimes, the only justice was the kind you made for yourself.

"Zoe, Marcus, I need an exit strategy, now!" Ethan barked into his earpiece, his voice strained with urgency.

"On it, boss," Zoe replied, her fingers flying over her keyboard. "There's a window on the north wall. If you can make it there, we'll have a car waiting for you in the alley."

Ethan nodded, his jaw clenched with determination. He summoned the power of The Chariot card, channeling its energy into a burst of speed as he raced towards the window.

Glass shattered as Ethan leaped through the opening, his body twisting in midair as he landed in a crouch on the pavement below. He could hear the distant wail of police sirens, but he didn't dare look back.

"I'm out," Ethan panted, sprinting towards the waiting car. "But we've got a problem. The crime lord let slip that there's a larger conspiracy at play here. Someone powerful is behind these disappearances."

As Ethan slid into the backseat, he took a moment to catch his breath, his mind reeling from the implications of what he had just learned. He could feel the adrenaline still pumping through his veins, the thrill of the fight slowly fading into a dull ache in his muscles.

Glancing down at his hands, Ethan noticed a few cuts and bruises, the marks of his brutal confrontation with the crime lord's men. These physical injuries were nothing compared to the toll that this case was taking on his mind and soul.

"Boss, are you okay?" Marcus asked, his voice tinged with concern as he eyed Ethan from the rear view mirror.

Ethan nodded, his expression grim. "I'm fine. But this is bigger than we thought. The crime lord was just a small fish in a much larger pond. Someone powerful is pulling the strings behind these disappearances."

Zoe, her laptop balanced on her knees as she typed furiously, looked up with a frown. "I've been digging into the files we retrieved from the casino's servers. There are mentions of a shadow organization, but nothing concrete. Whoever they are, they know how to cover their tracks."

Ethan sighed, rubbing his temples as he tried to piece together the fragments of information they had gathered. "We need to keep digging. If there's a way to find these people, we'll find it. Even if I have to call in every favor that this 'shadow organization' will be brought to justice."

As the car sped through the neon-lit streets, Ethan couldn't shake the feeling that this was just the beginning of a much larger and more dangerous game. He had always known that his work as a vigilante would come with risks, but this felt different. The scale of the conspiracy, the power of the players involved… it was like nothing he had ever faced before.

"We'll need to be careful," Ethan said, his voice low and serious. "If these people are as powerful as they seem, they won't hesitate to come after us. We need to watch our backs and keep our guard up at all times."

Marcus and Zoe nodded, their expressions mirroring Ethan's own determination and resolve. They knew that they were in for the fight of their lives, but they also knew that they had each other's backs, no matter what.

As the car pulled up to Ethan's penthouse, he took a deep breath, steeling himself for the battles to come. He knew that he would need all his skills and resources to unravel the mystery and protect the innocent lives at stake.

"Get some rest, both of you," Ethan said, his hand on the door handle. "We'll regroup in the morning and plan our next move. And Zoe, keep digging. If there's a way to find these bastards, I know you'll find it."

With a final nod to his team, Ethan stepped out of the car and made his way into his building, his mind already racing with the implications of what he had uncovered.

Once inside his penthouse, Ethan made a beeline for the bar, pouring himself a generous glass of whiskey. He stood by the floor-to-ceiling windows, staring out at the glittering city skyline, the weight of the world seeming to rest on his shoulders.

But as he sipped his drink, Ethan felt a flicker of something else beneath the worry and the fear. It was a sense of purpose, a burning desire to see justice done, no matter the cost. He had always known that this was his calling, his reason for being. And now, more than ever, he knew that he would stop at nothing to protect the innocent and bring the guilty to their knees.

With a determined smile, Ethan raised his glass in a silent toast to the challenges ahead. He didn't know what the future would bring, but he knew one thing for certain. He would win.

2

Into the Inferno

Liam

Liam Quinn's heart raced as the fire truck sped through the city streets, sirens blaring and lights flashing. He'd responded to countless emergencies in his career as a firefighter, but the call that had just come in sent a chill down his spine. A mutant shelter, engulfed in flames, with dozens of lives hanging in the balance.

As the truck screeched to a halt outside the burning building, Liam leaped out, his senses immediately assaulted by the chaos and panic surrounding him. Terrified residents fled the shelter, their faces streaked with soot and their eyes wide with fear. The heat from the flames was intense, and Liam could feel the sweat already beading on his forehead beneath his helmet.

"Alright, team, listen up!" Liam barked, his voice cutting through the din of the screams and the roar of the fire. "We've got a full-scale evacuation on our hands. Martinez, O'Neill, you're with me on search and rescue. Davis, coordinate with the paramedics and get triage set up. And for God's sake, everyone, watch your backs in there."

His team nodded, their expressions grim but determined. They knew the risks, but they also knew that every second counted when lives were on the line.

Liam turned to face the burning building, his mind already racing as he assessed the situation. The flames were intense, licking at the walls and windows with a hungry ferocity. He could see the roof starting to sag, and he knew that they didn't have much time before the whole structure came down.

"Martinez, take the west side. O'Neill, you're on east. I'll take the center," Liam commanded, his voice steady despite the adrenaline pumping through his veins. "We go floor by floor, room by room. Check every corner, every closet. We don't leave anyone behind."

With a final nod to his team, Liam charged forward, his axe gripped tightly in his gloved hands. He could feel the heat of the flames as he pushed through the front door, the smoke immediately stinging his eyes and filling his lungs.

"Fire department! Call out!" Liam shouted, his voice muffled by his oxygen mask. He strained his ears, listening for any cries for help over the crackling of the flames.

Liam ventured deeper into the heart of the inferno, he could feel the intensity of the heat bearing down on him like a physical weight. Despite his protective gear, the sweat poured down his face, stinging his eyes and making his grip on the hose slick. But he pushed forward, his jaw set with determination. He had a job to do, and he wouldn't rest until every last soul was safe.

"Fire department! Call out!" Liam shouted again, his voice muffled by his oxygen mask. The crackling of the flames and the groaning of the weakening structure made it hard to hear anything else, but Liam strained his ears, desperate for any sign of life.

Suddenly, he heard it - a faint cry, barely audible over the roar of the fire. Liam's heart leaped into his throat. There was someone still trapped inside, and they needed his help.

With renewed urgency, Liam pressed on, using his pyrokinetic abilities to push back the flames and clear a path. He could feel the heat of the fire licking at his skin, but he gritted his teeth and focused his mind, channeling his power to redirect the flames away from him.

As he rounded a corner, Liam came upon a scene that made his blood run cold. A group of mutant children, huddled together in a corner, their faces streaked with tears and soot. They were cut off from the main evacuation route, trapped by a wall of flames that threatened to consume them at any moment.

"Hey there, little ones," Liam called out, his voice gentle despite the urgency of the situation. "I'm here to help you. We're going to get you out of here, okay?"

The children looked up at him with wide, frightened eyes, but Liam could see a glimmer of hope in their faces as well. They knew that help had arrived, and that they weren't alone anymore.

Using his powers, Liam created a shield of energy around the children, protecting them from the searing heat and choking smoke. He could feel the strain on his mind and body as he maintained the shield, but he pushed through the pain, knowing that their lives depended on him.

"Stay close to me," Liam instructed, reaching out to take the hand of the smallest child. "We're going to move quickly, but I won't let anything happen to you. I promise."

With the children huddled close behind him, Liam began to make his way back through the burning building, retracing his steps towards the exit. The fire seemed to be growing more intense with every passing moment, and Liam knew that time was running out.

As they neared the main hallway, Liam heard a sickening crack from above. He looked up just in time to see a section of the ceiling give way, sending a cascade of flaming debris tumbling towards them.

"Watch out!" Liam cried, throwing up his hands and channeling all his power into reinforcing the weakened structure. He could feel the strain on his mind and body as he held the ceiling in place, his muscles trembling with the effort.

But even as he fought to keep the ceiling from collapsing, Liam knew that he couldn't maintain it forever. The fire was too intense, the damage too severe. They had to get out, and fast.

"Liam, what's your status?" The voice of his chief crackled over the radio, barely audible over the roar of the flames.

"I've got a group of kids with me, chief," Liam replied, his voice strained with the effort of maintaining the shield and the ceiling. "But the way out is blocked. I need backup, and I need it now."

"Copy that," the chief responded, his voice tense but calm. "Martinez and O'Neill are on their way to your location. Just hold on a little longer, Liam. You're doing great."

Liam gritted his teeth, his mind racing as he tried to come up with a plan. He knew that he couldn't wait for backup - every second counted, and the children's lives were in his hands.

With a deep breath, Liam made a decision. He would have to use his powers to clear a path through the flames, to carve a way out for the children. It would be risky, and it would take every ounce of his strength and control. But it was their only chance.

"Listen up, kiddos," Liam said, his voice calm and reassuring despite the fear that gnawed at his gut. "I'm going to need you to be brave for just a little bit longer. We're going to make a run for it, okay? But I need you to stay close and do exactly what I say."

The children nodded, their faces pale but determined. They trusted Liam, and they knew that he would do everything in his power to keep them safe.

With a nod to the chief over the radio, Liam began to gather his power, feeling the heat of the flames bending to his will. He took a deep breath, and then, with a cry of effort, he pushed forward, the children huddled close behind him.

The fire fought him every step of the way, the heat and smoke threatening to overwhelm him at any moment. But Liam refused to give in, refused to let the flames win. He pushed back with all his strength, carving a path through the inferno with sheer force of will.

As they neared the exit, Liam could hear the sound of sirens outside, the shouts of his fellow firefighters as they worked to contain the blaze. Just a little further, he told himself. Just a little further, and they would be safe.

And then, finally, they burst through the doors and into the cool night air, gasping and coughing as they stumbled to safety. Liam could feel his knees buckling beneath him, his vision swimming as the adrenaline began to fade. But he forced himself to stay upright, to make sure that each and every child was accounted for and reunited with their loved ones.

As Liam basked in the glow of their successful rescue, he couldn't help but feel a sense of unease niggling at the back of his mind. The fire had been intense, the damage severe, and something about the whole situation just didn't sit right with him.

But before he could dwell on those thoughts for too long, a frantic shout from one of his teammates snapped him back to attention.

"Liam!" Martinez called out, his voice strained with urgency. "We've got a problem. There's an elderly couple trapped on the top floor, and they can't make it out on their own."

Liam's heart sank. The top floor had been the most heavily damaged by the fire, and he knew that reaching the couple would be a daunting task. But he also knew that he couldn't leave them behind, not when every life counted.

"I'm on it," Liam said, his jaw set with determination. "Martinez, you and O'Neill keep working on the fire. I'll handle the rescue."

With a nod to his teammates, Liam turned and raced back into the building, his mind already racing as he tried to map out the quickest route to the top floor. The smoke was thicker now, the heat more intense, but Liam pushed forward, his senses heightened by the adrenaline pumping through his veins.

As he climbed the stairs, Liam could feel the strain on his muscles, the fatigue threatening to overtake him. But he gritted his teeth and pushed on, determined to reach the couple before it was too late.

Finally, he reached the top floor, the smoke so thick that he could barely see his hand in front of his face. But Liam didn't hesitate. He called out, his voice hoarse from the smoke and the exertion.

"Fire department! Is anyone up here?"

For a moment, there was nothing but the crackling of the flames and the creaking of the weakening structure. But then, faintly, Liam heard a response.

"Over here! Please, help us!"

Liam's heart leaped with relief. He had found them, and now all that was left was to get them out safely.

With renewed energy, Liam pushed forward, using his powers to clear a path through the debris and flames. And there, huddled in the corner of a small apartment, he found them - an elderly mutant couple, their faces lined with fear and exhaustion.

"It's okay," Liam said, his voice gentle but urgent. "I'm here to help you. We're going to get you out of here, but I need you to trust me."

The couple nodded, their eyes wide with gratitude and relief. And so, with great care and skill, Liam helped them to their feet, supporting their weight as he guided them back towards the stairs.

It was a treacherous journey, the flames licking at their heels and the smoke choking their lungs. But Liam never wavered, his focus laser-sharp as he used his powers to shield the couple from harm.

Step by step, they made their way down the stairs, Liam's muscles screaming with the effort of supporting the couple's weight. But he pushed through the pain, determined to see them to safety.

And then, finally, they emerged into the cool night air, gasping and coughing but alive. Liam handed the couple off to the waiting paramedics, his heart swelling with relief and pride.

"You did it, Liam," Martinez said, clapping him on the shoulder. "You saved their lives."

Liam nodded, too exhausted to speak. But even as he caught his breath, his mind was already racing ahead, trying to make sense of the night's events.

As the fire was brought under control and the survivors were tended to, Liam began to investigate the scene, his instincts telling him that something wasn't right. He noticed scorch marks on the walls that didn't match the pattern of the fire, and debris that seemed out of place.

"Hey, Martinez," Liam called out, his brow furrowed with concern. "Does something seem off to you about this fire?"

Martinez frowned, studying the scene with a critical eye. "Now that you mention it, yeah. The way it spread, the intensity of the flames… it's not like any accidental fire I've ever seen."

Liam nodded, his suspicions confirmed. "I think there's more to this than meets the eye. We need to start asking some questions."

And so, as the night wore on, Liam and his team began to gather information, speaking with the shelter's staff and residents to try to piece together a picture of what had happened.

What they learned was disturbing. In the weeks leading up to the fire, the mutant community had been targeted by a series of threats and acts of vandalism, each one more violent than the last. There were whispers of an anti-mutant hate group that had been growing in power and influence, and some even suspected that they might be behind the recent disappearances.

As Liam listened to the stories of fear and persecution, he felt a deep sense of anger and injustice welling up inside him. How could anyone target innocent people simply because of who they were? How could they spread such hate and violence in a world that was already so broken?

But even as he grappled with those heavy thoughts, Liam knew that he couldn't let his emotions cloud his judgment. He needed to stay focused, to follow the evidence wherever it led.

And so, as the sun began to rise over the smoldering ruins of the mutant shelter, Liam made a promise to himself and to the survivors he had saved. He would not rest until he had uncovered the truth behind the fire and the disappearances, until he had brought those responsible to justice.

"Alright, team," Liam said, his voice ringing out clear and strong in the early morning light. "We've got work to do. Let's start digging into these leads and see where they take us. We're going to get to the bottom of this, no matter what it takes."

His team began their investigation into the suspicious fire at the mutant shelter, they quickly realized that their work would not go unnoticed. Within hours of the blaze being extinguished, the media descended upon the scene like vultures, hungry for a story of heroism and tragedy.

Liam found himself thrust into the spotlight, his face plastered across every news channel and his name on the lips of reporters from all over the city. They clamored for interviews, for soundbites, for a glimpse into the mind of the brave firefighter who had risked everything to save the lives of the innocent.

At first, Liam was reluctant to speak to the press. He had never been one for the limelight, preferring to let his actions speak for themselves. But as he watched the footage of the fire on the news, saw the fear and pain etched onto the faces of the mutant survivors, he knew that he couldn't stay silent.

And so, with a deep breath and a determined set to his jaw, Liam stepped out in front of the cameras, ready to face the barrage of questions.

"Liam! Liam!" the reporters shouted, their voices overlapping in a cacophony of sound. "Can you tell us what happened in there? How did you manage to save so many lives?"

Liam held up a hand, waiting for the clamor to die down before he spoke. "What happened in there was a tragedy," he said, his voice steady and clear. "But it was also a reminder of the incredible resilience and strength of the mutant community. These people have faced so much adversity, so much hatred and fear, and yet they continue to fight for their right to exist, to live their lives in peace."

The reporters scribbled furiously in their notepads, their cameras flashing as they captured every word. Liam took a deep breath, his eyes scanning the crowd before he continued.

"But what happened last night was more than just a fire. It was a symptom of a much larger problem, one that threatens to tear our city apart. The hatred and bigotry that some people hold towards mutants, the fear and misunderstanding that divides us… it's not sustainable. We need to find a way to come together, to bridge the gap between our two communities before it's too late."

As Liam spoke, he could feel the weight of his words settling on his shoulders. He knew that he was stepping into a minefield, that his comments would likely be met with both praise and condemnation. But he also knew that he couldn't stay silent, not when so much was at stake.

"Liam, do you think that the fire was set intentionally?" one reporter asked, her eyes narrowing with suspicion. "Is there any evidence to suggest that this was a hate crime?"

Liam hesitated, choosing his words carefully. "It's too early to say for certain," he said, his voice measured. "But I can tell you that my team and I will not rest until we have uncovered the truth. We will follow every lead, investigate every angle, until we have brought those responsible to justice."

As the press conference wound to a close, Liam could feel the adrenaline beginning to fade, the exhaustion of the long night catching up with him. But even as his body ached and his mind raced, he knew that he couldn't stop, couldn't rest. Not until he had fulfilled his promise to the mutant community.

Stepping away from the cameras, Liam found a quiet corner to collect his thoughts. He leaned against the wall, his eyes closing as he tried to process everything that had happened.

"You did good out there," a voice said, startling Liam from his reverie. He looked up to see Martinez standing beside him, a look of pride and concern on her face.

"Thanks," Liam said, managing a weak smile. "I just hope it was enough."

Martinez shook his head, her gaze fierce. "It was more than enough. You gave those people hope, Liam. You showed them that they have allies, that they're not alone in this fight."

Liam nodded, his resolve hardening. "I just wish I could do more. Wish I could wave a magic wand and make all the hate and fear disappear."

"I know," Martinez said, his voice softening. "But that's not how it works. Change takes time, takes effort. And it takes people like you, willing to stand up and fight for what's right."

Just then, O'Neill came jogging over, a look of excitement on his face. "Guys, you're not gonna believe this. I just got a tip from one of my sources. They say they have information on the hate group that might be behind all this. But they'll only talk to you, Liam."

Liam's eyes widened, his heart racing with anticipation. "Me? Why me?"

O'Neill shrugged, a grin tugging at his lips. "Guess you made quite an impression with that little speech of yours. They say they trust you, that you're the only one who can help."

Liam took a deep breath, his mind spinning with the possibilities. He knew that this could be the break they had been waiting for, the key to unlocking the mystery of the disappearances and the rising tide of anti-mutant violence.

But he also knew that it could be a trap, a setup designed to lure him into a dangerous and unpredictable situation. He would have to be cautious, have to tread carefully if he wanted to make it out alive.

"Alright," Liam said, his voice steady with determination. "Set up the meeting."

3

Fancy Meeting You Here, Handsome

Ethan

The crisp lines of his tailored suit hugged his athletic frame, the deep burgundy fabric a stark contrast to his piercing green eyes. He looked every inch the successful businessman, a far cry from the masked vigilante who prowled the city's rooftops at night.

But appearances could be deceiving, and Ethan knew that better than anyone. Behind the polished veneer and charming smile, his mind was a whirlwind of thoughts and questions, all circling back to the cryptic clue he had uncovered and the larger conspiracy that threatened to engulf the city.

"Another night, another dog and pony show," Ethan muttered to himself, a wry smile tugging at his lips. "Let's just hope this one actually leads somewhere."

With a final glance in the mirror, Ethan strode out of his penthouse, his footsteps echoing through the cavernous space. He had a corporate event to attend, a room full of power players and influencers to charm and cajole. It was all part of the game, the delicate balancing act he had to maintain to keep his two worlds from colliding.

As he stepped into the glittering ballroom, Ethan was immediately swept up in a sea of designer suits and expensive perfume. He moved through the crowd with ease, his smile bright and his handshake firm as he greeted colleagues and competitors alike.

"Ethan, darling, so good to see you," a familiar voice purred, and Ethan turned to see a stunning woman in a shimmering gown gliding towards him.

"Vivienne," Ethan replied, his tone warm but guarded. "I didn't expect to see you here tonight."

Vivienne laughed, a tinkling sound that set Ethan's teeth on edge. "Oh, you know me, darling. I never miss a chance to rub elbows with the city's elite."

Ethan nodded, his eyes scanning the room even as he kept his attention on Vivienne. "Of course. And I'm sure it has nothing to do with the rumors of a certain business deal in the works."

Vivienne's eyes narrowed, her smile turning sharp. "Careful, Ethan. You know what they say about curiosity and cats."

"Good thing I'm more of a dog person," Ethan quipped, his grin widening at Vivienne's annoyed huff.

As Vivienne drifted away, Ethan made his way to the bar, his mind already racing with the implications of her presence. Vivienne was a notorious gossip, with her perfectly manicured fingers in every pie in the city. If she was here, it meant that something big was brewing, and Ethan needed to find out what.

Sipping his whiskey, Ethan let his gaze wander over the crowd, searching for any sign of the man he was here to meet. Marcus had tipped him off to a potential business partner, someone with connections to the city's underbelly and a reputation for getting things done. It was a long shot, but Ethan knew he couldn't afford to leave any stone unturned.

Just then, a hand clapped him on the shoulder, and Ethan turned to see a man with salt-and-pepper hair and a shark's smile standing beside him.

"Ethan Hawke," the man said, his voice smooth as silk. "I've been looking forward to meeting you."

Ethan raised an eyebrow, his grip tightening on his glass. "Is that so? And who might you be?"

The man chuckled, his eyes glinting with amusement. "Forgive me, where are my manners? Damien Blackwood, at your service."

"A pleasure," Ethan said, shaking Damien's hand. "I've heard great things about your work. Perhaps we could find somewhere more private to discuss a potential partnership?"

Damien's smile widened, his teeth gleaming in the low light. "I thought you'd never ask."

As they made their way to a secluded corner of the ballroom, Ethan's mind was already racing ahead, trying to anticipate Damien's moves and motives. He knew he would have to play his cards carefully, to use every ounce of his business acumen and charm to extract the information he needed without tipping his hand.

"So, Damien," Ethan said, leaning back in his chair with a casual air. "Tell me about your company. What sets you apart from the competition?"

Damien leaned forward, his elbows resting on the table. "We specialize in...unconventional solutions, shall we say. We have a unique set of resources and connections that allow us to tackle problems that others might find insurmountable."

Ethan nodded, his expression thoughtful. "Interesting. And have you ever encountered any problems related to the recent mutant disappearances?"

Damien's eyes flashed, and for a moment, Ethan thought he saw a flicker of something darker behind the polished facade.

"Mutants? No, I can't say that I have. Our focus is more on the corporate world, not the affairs of…individuals."

"Of course," he said, his smile never wavering. "Just thought I'd ask, given the current climate in the city."

Damien nodded, his own smile tightening. "Understandable. But I assure you, our partnership would be focused solely on business matters. Nothing more, nothing less."

As the conversation turned to negotiations and contracts, Ethan couldn't shake the feeling that he was dancing on the edge of a knife. Damien was smooth, almost too smooth, and Ethan knew he would have to watch his back every step of the way.

With a final handshake and a nod of agreement, Ethan sealed the deal, his mind already racing ahead to the next move in the game.

Just as he was about to make his exit, Ethan felt a familiar buzz in his pocket. He slipped his hand inside, his fingers curling around his phone as he glanced at the screen.

"Urgent message. Meet us at the usual spot in thirty."

Ethan's heart skipped a beat as he read the words, his mind already whirling with possibilities. Zoe and Marcus wouldn't have contacted him like this unless it was something big, something that couldn't wait.

With a final nod to the party goers, Ethan slipped out of the ballroom, his footsteps echoing off the marble floors as he made his way to the elevator. His mind was already miles away, focused on the meeting ahead and the information it might yield.

As he stepped out into the cool night air, Ethan tapped his earpiece, his voice low and urgent.

"Zoe, Marcus, what's the situation?"

"We've got a lead, boss," Zoe's voice crackled through the earpiece, her tone serious. "An informant with intel on the disappearances. They're willing to meet, but only on their terms."

Ethan's eyes narrowed, his mind already racing with the possibilities. "Where and when?"

"Abandoned warehouse on the outskirts of town. One hour."

Ethan nodded, his jaw clenching with determination. "I'll be there. Marcus, I need you to run recon on the location. Make sure it's not a trap."

"On it, boss," Marcus replied, his voice gruff but focused. "I'll have eyes on the place within the hour."

* * *

As Ethan sped through the city streets, his mind was a whirlwind of thoughts and emotions. He knew that this meeting could be the break they'd been waiting for, the key to unlocking the mystery of the disappearances and bringing those responsible to justice.

But he also knew that it could be a trap, a setup designed to lure him out into the open and take him out of the game. He would have to be careful, to trust his instincts and his team to watch his back.

As he approached the warehouse, Ethan killed the engine of his motorcycle, his eyes scanning the dark alleyways and shadowed corners for any sign of trouble. The place was desolate, a forgotten corner of the city where the only sounds were the distant hum of traffic and the skittering of rats in the shadows.

Ethan made his way to a nearby rooftop, his movements quick and silent as he scaled the fire escape and crouched low on the gravel-strewn surface. From here, he had a clear view of the warehouse entrance, his eyes sharp and focused as he watched for any sign of his informant.

Minutes ticked by, each one feeling like an eternity as Ethan waited, his muscles coiled and ready for action. And then, just as he was starting to wonder if the whole thing had been a wild goose chase, he saw it.

A sleek black car pulling up to the warehouse entrance, its windows tinted and its engine purring with power. Ethan watched as two heavily armed men emerged from the vehicle, their faces obscured by dark glasses and their movements sharp and precise.

They scanned the area, their hands resting on the guns at their hips as they checked for any sign of trouble. And then, apparently satisfied that the coast was clear, they moved to the back of the car, opening the trunk and removing a large, heavy-looking crate.

Ethan's heart raced as he watched them carry the crate inside the warehouse, his mind whirling with the possibilities of what it might contain. Weapons? Drugs? Something even more sinister?

He knew he needed to get a closer look, to find out what was really going on inside that warehouse. But he also knew that he couldn't just charge in blindly, not without backup and a plan.

"Marcus, you seeing this?" he murmured into his earpiece, his voice low and urgent.

"Affirmative," Marcus replied, his own voice tight with tension. "Looks like our informant wasn't kidding around. Something big is going down in there."

Ethan nodded, his mind already racing ahead to the next step. He tapped his earpiece, connecting with Zoe back at the headquarters. "Zoe, I need you to run a background check on those guys. See if you can find out who they are and who they work for."

"On it, boss," Zoe's voice crackled through the comm link. Ethan could hear the faint sound of rapid typing in the background as Zoe worked her magic.

As he waited for Zoe to get back to him, Ethan reached into his backpack, pulling out the sleek black armor that had become his second skin over the past few months. As he fastened the clips and tightened the straps, he could feel the familiar rush of adrenaline surging through his veins.

Just as Ethan finished suiting up, Zoe's voice came through the earpiece once more. "Ethan, you're not going to believe this. Those men? They work for Genexis."

Ethan's heart skipped a beat, a surge of adrenaline coursing through his veins. Genexis. The very company they had been investigating for their shady dealings and potential involvement in the mutant disappearances. If their hunch was correct, this could be the break they'd been waiting for.

"Are you sure, Zoe?" Ethan asked, his voice low and urgent.

"Positive," Zoe confirmed, her tone grim. "I cross-referenced their faces with the Genexis employee database. They're part of the company's private security team."

Ethan's mind raced with the implications. If Genexis was sending armed guards to a secret meeting in an abandoned warehouse, it could only mean one thing - they had something to hide. Something big.

With a grim smile playing at the corners of his mouth, Ethan slipped out of the shadows and made his way towards the warehouse, his footsteps silent on the cracked pavement. He could feel his senses sharpening with every step, his mind laser-focused on the task at hand.

But even as he moved forward, Ethan couldn't shake the feeling that something was different this time. The stakes were higher, the danger more palpable. And with the knowledge that Genexis was involved, he knew that he would have to be at the top of his game if he wanted to come out of this in one piece.

But just as he was about to slip through the side door, a voice rang out from the darkness behind him.

"Hold it right there, asshole."

Ethan spun around, his hand already reaching for the blade at his hip. But as his eyes adjusted to the gloom, he saw a figure stepping out from behind a stack of crates, a figure that he recognized all too well.

"Well, well, if it isn't the famous Liam Quinn," Ethan drawled, his voice dripping with sarcasm. "To what do I owe the pleasure of your company on this fine evening?"

Liam's eyes narrowed, his jaw clenching with barely contained anger. "Cut the crap, Arcana. You know damn well why I'm here. To bring you in and put an end to your reckless vigilantism once and for all."

Ethan couldn't help but smirk, his eyes glinting with amusement behind his mask. "Reckless? Moi? I prefer to think of it as proactive problem-solving."

But even as he bantered with Liam, Ethan's mind was racing. What the hell was a firefighter doing staking out an abandoned warehouse in the middle of the night? And how had he managed to track down the elusive Arcana?

"Listen, Quinn," Ethan said, his voice growing serious. "I know you think I'm just some reckless thrill-seeker with a chip on my shoulder. But the truth is, we both want the same thing - to find out what's behind these disappearances and put a stop to it. So why don't we just put aside our differences for one night and work together on this?"

Liam scoffed, his eyes flashing with contempt. "Work together? With a vigilante who thinks he's above the law? Not fucking likely."

Ethan's jaw clenched, frustration boiling up inside him. Why did this guy have to be so goddamn stubborn? Couldn't he see that they were on the same side?

"What were you doing here anyway?" Ethan asked, changing tack. "I doubt you were just out for a leisurely stroll in the warehouse district and there's no fire in here."

"Not that it's any of your business, but I received a tip that someone wanted to meet with me here tonight. Said they had information about the disappearances."

Ethan's eyes narrowed behind his mask, his mind whirling with the implications. Liam had received the same tip as him? That couldn't be a coincidence.

"I don't know who your source is, Quinn, but you're walking into a trap," Ethan said, his voice low and urgent. "I've been staking out this place, and I've seen some seriously shady shit going down. Whoever lured you here, they're not on your side."

But Liam just shook his head, his eyes hard with determination. "I don't need your advice, Arcana. I can handle myself just fine. And I sure as hell don't need some masked vigilante telling me how to do my job."

Ethan threw up his hands in frustration, his patience wearing thin. "Goddamn it, Quinn, will you just listen to me for one fucking second? I'm trying to help you here, even if you're too stubborn to see it."

But Liam wasn't having it. He stepped forward, his fists clenched at his sides. "I don't need your help, Arcana. I need you to step aside and let me do my job. The authorities will handle this, not some reckless vigilante with a savior complex."

Ethan's eyes flashed with anger, his own fists clenching in response. "The authorities? You mean the same ones who have been sitting on their asses for months while innocent people go missing? Face it, Quinn, the system is broken. Someone has to step up and take action, and if that someone has to be me, then so be it."

The two men stood there, face to face, their eyes locked in a battle of wills. The tension crackled between them like electricity, the air thick with the weight of their convictions.

Ethan knew that he should just walk away, that he had more important things to do than argue with some self-righteous firefighter with a stick up his ass. But something about Liam Quinn got under his skin, made him want to push back and prove him wrong.

"Fine," Ethan spat, his voice cold with disdain. "You want to go in there and play hero, be my guest. But don't come crying to me when you end up in over your head."

Ethan slipped through the warehouse door, his senses on high alert as he scanned the shadowy interior for any sign of trouble. He could feel Liam's presence behind him, the firefighter's stubborn determination practically radiating off him in waves.

"I can't believe I'm doing this," Liam muttered, his voice low and tense. "Working with a vigilante. If the chief finds out, I'll be on desk duty for a month."

Ethan smirked, his eyes glinting with amusement behind his mask. "Relax, Quinn. What happens in the creepy abandoned warehouse stays in the creepy abandoned warehouse."

But even as he joked, Ethan could feel a growing sense of unease settling in the pit of his stomach. Something about this whole setup felt off, like they were walking into a trap.

And then, as they rounded a corner and stepped into a pool of dim light, Ethan saw it. Lying there face down in a pool of his own blood a man that looked like he had better days.

"I am guessing that this person was our informant." Liam said grimly.

"Fuck," Ethan breathed, his heart hammering in his chest. "We're too late."

Liam rushed forward, his face pale and his eyes wide with shock. He knelt down beside the body, his fingers searching for a pulse that Ethan knew he wouldn't find.

And then, as Liam gently rolled the man over, Ethan saw it. A scrap of paper, clutched in the informant's hand, the edges stained with blood.

He snatched it up, his eyes scanning the cryptic message scrawled across the page. "The truth lies beneath the surface. Find the key to unlock the door."

Liam stood up, his jaw clenched with anger and frustration. "What the hell is that supposed to mean? And why did he have to die for it?"

Ethan shook his head, his mind racing with the implications. "I don't know. But whatever it is, it's big. Bigger than either of us realized."

He tucked the note into his pocket, his eyes meeting Liam's with a fierce intensity. "We need to get out of here, Quinn. Whoever did this, they'll be back to make sure they finished the job."

But Liam wasn't listening. He was staring at the note in Ethan's pocket, his eyes narrowed with suspicion. "Give me that note, Arcana. It's evidence, and it needs to be turned over to the authorities."

Ethan scoffed, his patience wearing thin. "The authorities? You mean the same ones who have been sitting on their asses while people go missing? No fucking way."

Liam stepped forward, his fists clenched at his sides. "Damn it, Arcana, this isn't a game! That note could be the key to solving this whole thing, and you want to keep it for yourself?"

Ethan's eyes flashed with anger, his own fists clenching in response. "I want to use it to actually make a difference, Quinn. To stop these disappearances and bring the bastards responsible to justice. And I sure as hell don't trust the cops to do that."

They stood there, face to face, their eyes locked in a battle of wills. The tension crackled between them like electricity, the air thick with the weight of their convictions.

But before either of them could make a move, a sound from outside the warehouse shattered the silence. The unmistakable sound of footsteps, heavy and purposeful, moving towards the door.

"Shit," Ethan hissed, his hand reaching for the blade at his hip. "We've got company."

Liam's eyes widened, his own hand reaching for his gun. "How many?"

Ethan shook his head, his mind racing to formulate a plan. "Too many to fight. We need to get the hell out of here, now."

He scanned the warehouse, his eyes landing on a small window high up on the wall. It was a tight squeeze, but it was their only chance.

"There," he said, pointing to the window. "We can boost each other up and slip out before they even know we're here."

Liam hesitated, his eyes darting between Ethan and the door. Ethan could practically see the gears turning in his head, the stubborn firefighter weighing his options.

But then, with a muttered curse, Liam nodded. "Fine. But this doesn't change anything between us, Arcana. I still think you're a reckless vigilante who's going to get himself killed one of these days."

Ethan grinned, his eyes sparkling with mischief. "Aw, Quinn, I didn't know you cared."

Liam rolled his eyes, his jaw clenching with barely contained frustration. "Don't flatter yourself, Arcana. I just don't want your death on my conscience."

But before Ethan could fire back with another witty retort, the sound of heavy footsteps and angry voices echoed through the warehouse. The armed pursuers were closing in, and they needed to move fast.

"Shit," Ethan muttered, his mind racing to formulate a plan. "We need to split up, Quinn. You take the left, I'll take the right. We'll meet up on the other side and make a run for it."

Liam hesitated, his eyes darting between Ethan and the approaching threat. Ethan could practically see the gears turning in his head, the stubborn firefighter weighing his options.

But then, with a muttered curse, Liam nodded. "Fine. But don't do anything stupid, Arcana. I'm not going to be the one to explain to the authorities why you got yourself killed."

Ethan smirked, his eyes glinting with amusement behind his mask. "Relax, Quinn. I've got more tricks up my sleeve than a magician. And besides, where's the fun in playing it safe?"

And with that, the two men split up, each taking off in opposite directions through the maze-like interior of the warehouse. Ethan's heart pounded in his chest as he ran, his senses on high alert for any sign of trouble.

He could hear the pursuers behind him, their heavy boots pounding against the concrete floor as they gave chase. But Ethan was faster, his lean body moving with the grace and agility of a panther.

He focused his mind, summoning the ethereal image of The Magician card. With a flick of his wrist, he channeled the card's power, creating an illusion of himself running in the opposite direction. The pursuers fell for the trick, their shouts of confusion and frustration music to Ethan's ears as he slipped away into the shadows.

On the other side of the warehouse, Liam was holding his own against the armed men. His firefighter training had given him an edge in close-quarters combat, and he moved with a fluid, almost balletic grace as he dodged and weaved around his attackers.

But even with his skills, Liam was outnumbered and outgunned. He needed a way out, and fast.

Just then, he heard a shout from above. Looking up, he saw Ethan perched on a catwalk, his hand outstretched in a beckoning gesture.

"Quinn! Up here!"

Liam hesitated for a split second, his instincts warring with his desire to take down the armed men. But then, with a muttered curse, he leaped for the ladder leading up to the catwalk, his powerful arms propelling him upward with incredible speed.

As he climbed, Liam focused his mind, channeling his pyrokinetic abilities to create a wall of flames behind him. The pursuers recoiled from the searing heat, their screams of pain and fear echoing through the warehouse as Liam made his escape.

He reached the top of the catwalk just as Ethan summoned another ethereal card, the image of The Tower shimmering in the air before them.

"Hold on tight, Quinn," Ethan said, his voice low and urgent. "This is going to be a wild ride."

And with that, he channeled the card's power, creating a massive explosion that rocked the warehouse to its foundations. The catwalk buckled and swayed beneath their feet, but Ethan and Liam held on tight, their eyes locked on the window at the far end of the warehouse.

They ran, their feet pounding against the metal grating as the catwalk began to collapse behind them. Liam could feel the heat of the flames licking at his heels, could hear the screams of the armed men as they were consumed by the inferno.

But he didn't look back, his eyes focused on the window ahead. With a final burst of speed, he and Ethan leaped, crashing through the glass and out into the cool night air.

They hit the ground hard, their bodies rolling to absorb the impact. Ethan was on his feet in an instant, his hand reaching down to help Liam up.

But Liam ignored the offered hand, his eyes narrowing with suspicion. "Give me the note, Arcana. It's evidence, and it needs to be turned over to the authorities."

Ethan scoffed, his patience wearing thin. "Not this again, Quinn. We've been over this. That note is the key to solving this whole fucking mess, and I'm not going to let it fall into the wrong hands."

Liam stepped forward, his fists clenched at his sides. "And what makes you think your hands are the right ones? You're a vigilante, Arcana. A criminal. Why should I trust you with something this important?"

Ethan's eyes flashed with anger, his own fists clenching in response. But then, slowly, he forced himself to relax, his voice dropping to a low, persuasive purr.

"Because, Quinn, whether you like it or not, we're in this together now. That note is the only lead we have, and we both know that the authorities aren't going to do shit with it. But if we work together, if we pool our resources and our skills, we might just have a chance of cracking this thing wide open."

Liam hesitated, his eyes searching Ethan's face for any sign of deception. Ethan could practically see the gears turning in his head, the stubborn firefighter weighing his options.

But then, with a muttered curse, Liam nodded. "Fine. But this is a temporary truce, Arcana. As soon as we decipher that note and stop these disappearances, I'm bringing you in. Understood?"

Ethan grinned, his eyes sparkling with mischief. "Understood, Quinn. But let's not get ahead of ourselves. We've got a lot of work to do before we start planning our happily ever after."

4

Unraveling the Threads

Liam

The problem was, he wasn't sure he could trust The Arcana. The man was a vigilante, a criminal who operated outside the law. How could Liam be sure that he wasn't just using him to further his own agenda?

And yet, as much as he hated to admit it, there was something about the man that drew Liam in. The man was infuriating, cocky, and reckless - but he was also brilliant, resourceful, and fiercely committed to his cause.

Liam groaned, pushing himself up from the bench and heading out into the main area of the firehouse. He needed to focus on his job, on the people who counted on him to keep them safe.

As he went about his duties, checking equipment and running drills with his team, Liam couldn't help but let his mind wander to his own past. He had always known that he was different, that his pyrokinetic abilities set him apart from other people.

At first, he had been afraid of his powers, afraid of what they meant and how people would react if they found out. But over time, he had learned to embrace them, to see them as a gift rather than a curse.

Still, it hadn't been easy. Liam had faced his fair share of discrimination and prejudice over the years, both in his personal life and in his work as a firefighter. There were those who saw his mutant abilities as a threat, who believed that he couldn't be trusted to do his job safely and effectively.

Liam gritted his teeth, feeling a familiar surge of anger and frustration welling up inside him. It wasn't fair, the way mutants were treated in this world. They were just people, trying to live their lives and make a difference in whatever way they could.

And now, with the disappearances, Liam couldn't shake the feeling that there was something bigger at play. Something that threatened not just the mutant community, but the entire city.

"Hey, Quinn!" a voice called out, jolting Liam from his thoughts. "You okay, man? You look like you're a million miles away."

Liam looked up to see his fellow firefighter, Jack, standing in front of him with a concerned expression on his face.

"Yeah, I'm good," Liam said, forcing a smile. "Just got a lot on my mind, you know?"

Jack nodded, his eyes sympathetic. "I hear you, man. This job can be tough, especially when you're dealing with all the shit that comes with being a mutant."

Liam raised an eyebrow, surprised. "You know about that?"

Jack chuckled. "Dude, everyone knows about that. You're not exactly subtle, what with the whole 'creating walls of fire' thing."

Liam felt a flush creep up his neck, but he couldn't help but grin. "Yeah, I guess I'm not the best at keeping a low profile."

"That's putting it mildly," Jack said, laughing. "But seriously, man, if you ever need to talk, I'm here. We're all in this together, you know?"

Liam felt a surge of gratitude for his friend, for the reminder that he wasn't alone in this fight.

"Thanks, Jack," he said, clapping the other man on the shoulder. "I appreciate it."

Liam strode into the firehouse kitchen, his mind still reeling from the conversation with Jack. He couldn't shake the feeling that there was more to these disappearances than met the eye, and he was determined to get to the bottom of it.

He grabbed a cup of coffee and settled down at the table, pulling out his phone and scrolling through his contacts. If he was going to uncover the truth, he needed to start gathering intel, and he knew just where to begin.

"Hey, Martinez," he said, his voice low and urgent as his colleague picked up on the other end. "I need a favor. Can you dig up any info on hate groups targeting mutants in the city? Anything that might be connected to the recent disappearances?"

There was a pause on the other end of the line, and Liam could practically hear the gears turning in Martinez's head. "I'll see what I can find," she said finally, his tone cautious. "But Liam, you know this isn't really our jurisdiction, right? We're firefighters, not cops."

Liam sighed, running a hand through his hair in frustration. "I know, I know. But I can't just sit back and do nothing, not when innocent people are being targeted like this."

Martinez was quiet for a moment, and Liam could sense his hesitation. "Just be careful, okay?" he said finally. "Don't go sticking your nose where it doesn't belong. You never know who might be watching."

Liam felt a chill run down his spine at the words, but he pushed it aside. He couldn't afford to let fear hold him back, not when there were lives on the line.

"Thanks, Martinez," he said, his voice steady. "I owe you one."

He hung up the phone and took a sip of his coffee, his mind already racing with the possibilities of what he might uncover. He knew he was taking a risk by getting involved, but he couldn't just sit back and watch as his community was torn apart.

As he sat there, lost in thought, a voice suddenly jolted him back to reality. "Hey, Quinn! What the hell do you think you're doing?"

Liam looked up to see his captain, a gruff, no-nonsense man named Roberts, standing in the doorway with his arms crossed over his chest.

"What do you mean, Cap?" Liam asked, trying to keep his tone casual.

Roberts fixed him with a stern look. "Don't play dumb with me, Quinn. I heard you on the phone just now. You're poking around in things that don't concern you, and I want to know why."

Liam felt a flicker of anger rise up inside him, but he forced it back down. He knew he needed to tread carefully here, or risk blowing his cover entirely.

"I'm just trying to help, Cap," he said, his voice even. "These disappearances, the hate crimes against mutants... it's not right. Someone has to do something."

Roberts shook his head, his expression a mix of exasperation and concern. "And you think that someone is you? Jesus, Quinn, you're a firefighter, not a fucking vigilante. Leave the heroics to the cops and focus on doing your job."

Liam gritted his teeth, biting back the retort that sprang to his lips. He knew Roberts was just looking out for him, but he couldn't help but feel a surge of frustration at the man's narrow-mindedness.

"With all due respect, Cap," he said, his voice tight, "I am doing my job. Protecting the innocent, standing up for what's right... that's what being a firefighter is all about. And if that means stepping outside my lane every once in a while, then so be it."

Roberts stared at him for a long moment, his expression unreadable. Finally, he let out a heavy sigh, shaking his head.

"Just be careful, Quinn," he said, his voice gruff but not unkind. "I don't want to see you get hurt, or worse."

With that, he turned and walked away, leaving Liam alone with his thoughts once more.

As he finished his coffee and headed back out into the firehouse, Liam couldn't shake the feeling that he was standing on the edge of something big. He knew he needed to be cautious, to cover his tracks and keep his head down.

But he also knew that he couldn't just sit back and do nothing. Not when there were lives on the line and a truth that needed to be uncovered.

And so, with a deep breath and a nod of determination, Liam got back to work, his mind already racing with the possibilities of what lay ahead. It was time to uncover the truth, to bring the disappearances to an end and the people responsible to justice.

* * *

He met with activists and community leaders, listening to their stories and gathering what information he could about the recent spate of hate crimes and disappearances. The more he learned, the more disturbed he became.

There was a pattern emerging, a sinister web of violence and discrimination that seemed to be targeting the most vulnerable members of the mutant community. Liam couldn't shake the feeling that there was something bigger at play, a conspiracy that went far beyond a few isolated incidents.

Liam leaned forward, his elbows resting on the small table as he fixed the community leader with an intense gaze. "Maria, I can't even begin to imagine what you and the others have been going through. It's fucking unacceptable, and I'm so sorry that you've had to endure this kind of hatred and violence."

Maria sighed, her fingers absently tracing the rim of her coffee cup. "It's not your fault, Liam. You're out there every day, putting your life on the line to keep people safe. But sometimes, it feels like the system is rigged against us, you know?"

Liam nodded, a wry smile tugging at the corner of his mouth. "Believe me, I know. I've been beating my head against that particular wall for years now. But I'm not about to give up, not when there are lives on the line."

Maria raised an eyebrow, a glimmer of amusement in her eyes. "You always were a stubborn one, Liam Quinn. Even back in high school, when you were just a scrawny little thing with a big mouth and an even bigger heart."

Liam clutched his chest in mock offense, his eyes widening in exaggerated shock. "Scrawny? Excuse you, I was a fucking Adonis. The ladies couldn't keep their hands off me."

Maria snorted, shaking her head. "Keep telling yourself that, hotshot. But seriously, Liam, I appreciate what you're doing. It means a lot to know that there are people like you out there, fighting for us."

Liam's expression sobered, his voice low and earnest. "I'm not going to lie to you, Maria. This isn't going to be easy. There are a lot of powerful people out there who have a vested interest in keeping things the way they are. But I promise you, I won't rest until I get to the bottom of this. I won't let them get away with it."

Maria reached out, her hand resting gently on top of Liam's. "I know you won't, Liam. Just promise me you'll be careful, okay? I don't want to lose another friend to this fight."

Liam's heart clenched at the words, a reminder of the toll that this struggle had already taken on the mutant community. But he forced a smile, his voice light and teasing. "Come on, Maria. You know me. I'm like a cat - I always land on my feet."

Maria rolled her eyes, but there was a hint of a smile on her face. "More like a bull in a china shop. But I'll take what I can get."

They sat in silence for a moment, sipping their coffee and lost in their own thoughts. Finally, Maria spoke again, her voice soft and hesitant. "Liam, there's something else you should know. Something that might help with your investigation."

Liam leaned forward, his eyes intense. "What is it, Maria? You can trust me, I promise."

Maria took a deep breath, her gaze darting around the room as if to make sure they weren't being overheard. "There's a group, a sort of underground network of mutants who have been tracking the disappearances. They have information, leads that the authorities don't know about. I can put you in touch with them, but you have to promise me that you'll be discreet."

Liam's heart raced with excitement, his mind already whirling with the possibilities. "Of course, Maria. You have my word. This could be the break we've been looking for."

Maria nodded, her expression grave. "Just be careful, Liam. These people, they're not messing around. They're desperate, and they're angry. They might not take kindly to an outsider poking around in their business."

Liam grinned, his eyes sparkling with mischief. "Well, lucky for them, I'm not just any outsider. I'm Liam fucking Quinn, and I always get my man. Or woman. Or non-binary individual."

Maria shook her head, a reluctant smile tugging at her lips. "You're incorrigible, you know that? But maybe that's just what we need right now. Someone who's not afraid to take risks, to do whatever it takes to get justice for our people."

Liam's expression sobered, his voice low and intense. "I won't let you down, Maria. I promise you that. I'll find out the truth, and I'll make sure that the people responsible for this pay for what they've done."

Maria nodded, her eyes shining with unshed tears. "I know you will, Liam. I have faith in you. Just remember, you're not alone in this fight. You have people who care about you, who are here for you if you need them."

Liam felt a lump rise in his throat, touched by the sincerity in Maria's words. "Thank you, Maria. That means more to me than you know."

They finished their coffee in companionable silence, each lost in their own thoughts about the challenges that lay ahead. But as Liam stood to leave, he felt a renewed sense of purpose, a determination to see this fight through to the end.

He had a lead now, a way forward. And with Maria's help and the support of his friends and allies, he knew that he could do this. He could uncover the truth and bring the people responsible for the disappearances to justice.

His mind was racing as he left the coffee shop, Maria's words echoing in his head. An underground network of mutants, tracking the disappearances and gathering information that the authorities didn't have access to. It was a lead, a potential breakthrough in the case that he couldn't afford to ignore.

But he also knew that he needed to be careful. These people were taking a huge risk by investigating on their own, and they had no reason to trust an outsider like him, even if he was a mutant himself.

He needed to approach this delicately, to find a way to gain their trust and convince them that he was on their side. And so, with a deep breath and a nod of determination, Liam set off to track down the contact Maria had given him.

* * *

It took some doing, and more than a few dead ends and false starts. But finally, after hours of searching and more than a few close calls with some unsavory characters, Liam found himself standing outside a nondescript building on the outskirts of the city.

He took a deep breath, steeling himself for whatever lay ahead. And then, with a final glance over his shoulder to make sure he hadn't been followed, he knocked on the door.

For a long moment, there was nothing. And then, just as Liam was starting to wonder if he had the wrong address, the door swung open, revealing a young woman with piercing blue eyes and a guarded expression.

"What do you want?" she asked, her voice sharp and wary.

Liam held up his hands in a gesture of peace, his voice low and earnest. "My name is Liam Quinn. I'm a friend of Maria Vasquez. She told me that you might have some information about the mutant disappearances that have been happening in the city."

The woman's eyes narrowed, her gaze flicking over Liam's face as if searching for any sign of deception. "And why should we trust you? How do we know you're not just another cop looking to shut us down?"

Liam sighed, running a hand through his hair in frustration. "Look, I get it. You have no reason to trust me. But I'm not a cop. I'm a firefighter, and I'm also a mutant. I've been investigating these disappearances on my own, and I keep hitting dead ends. I need your help."

The woman hesitated, her gaze still wary. But then, after a long moment, she nodded, stepping back to let Liam inside.

"Fine. But if you try anything funny, if you do anything to put my people at risk, I will personally make sure that you regret it."

Liam nodded, his expression serious. "I understand. I'm not here to cause trouble. I just want to find out the truth and stop these disappearances before anyone else gets hurt."

The woman led him down a dimly lit hallway, her footsteps echoing off the concrete walls. And then, as they stepped into a large, open room, Liam saw them.

A group of mutants, hunched over a table covered in maps and documents and computer screens. They looked up as Liam and the woman entered, their expressions guarded and wary.

"This is Liam," the woman said, her voice clipped and businesslike. "He's a friend of Maria's. He says he's been investigating the disappearances on his own, and he wants our help."

There was a moment of tense silence, the mutants exchanging glances and murmurs of conversation. And then, finally, one of them stepped forward, a tall, broad-shouldered man with a scar running down the side of his face.

"Alright, Liam," he said, his voice deep and rumbling. "You want our help? Then you need to prove that you're on our side. Tell us what you know, and we'll see if we can fill in the gaps."

Liam nodded, taking a deep breath as he gathered his thoughts. And then, slowly and carefully, he began to lay out everything he had uncovered so far - the mysterious disappearances, the lack of progress from the authorities, the cryptic clues that seemed to point to a larger conspiracy at work.

As he spoke, he could see the mutants exchanging glances, their expressions shifting from wariness to interest to a growing sense of excitement. And when he finished, the tall man with the scar nodded, a grim smile spreading across his face.

"You've done good work, Liam," he said, his voice filled with a grudging respect. "But you're right. There's more to this than meets the eye. And we might just have the piece of the puzzle you've been looking for."

He gestured to one of the other mutants, a wiry young man with a shock of bright green hair. "Tell him what you found, Jax."

The green-haired man nodded, his fingers flying over the keyboard of a nearby computer. "I've been monitoring the city's surveillance cameras, trying to track the movements of some of the missing mutants. And I think I might have found something."

He pulled up a grainy video feed, the image flickering and stuttering on the screen. But even through the static, Liam could make out the unmistakable shape of a large, industrial building on the outskirts of the city.

"I've seen vans coming and going from this place at all hours of the night," Jax said, his voice tight with excitement. "And I've cross-referenced the license plates with the city's vehicle registry. They're all registered to shell companies, with no clear owner or purpose."

Liam leaned forward, his heart pounding with a growing sense of anticipation. "You think this might be where they're taking the missing mutants?"

Jax nodded, his eyes shining with a fierce determination. "I'd bet my life on it. But we haven't been able to get close enough to confirm it. The place is locked up tight, with armed guards and security cameras everywhere."

Liam's mind was racing, the pieces of the puzzle starting to fall into place. A hidden base of operations, a well-funded and organized group with a sinister agenda. It all pointed to a conspiracy that went far beyond a few isolated hate crimes.

He turned to the tall man with the scar, his voice low and urgent. "I need to get inside that building. I need to see for myself what's going on in there."

The man hesitated, his expression torn. "It's too dangerous, Liam. If they catch you, if they find out what you're doing..."

But Liam just shook his head, a fierce determination burning in his eyes. "I don't care about the risk. I need to do this. For Maria, for all the mutants who have gone missing. For everyone who is counting on us to find the truth and bring these bastards to justice."

Liam crept through the abandoned factory, his heart pounding in his chest as he followed the lead Maria had given him. He knew he was taking a risk by coming here alone, without backup or support. But he also knew that he couldn't afford to wait, not when every moment counted in the race to uncover the truth.

As he made his way deeper into the building, Liam couldn't shake the feeling that he was being watched. The hairs on the back of his neck stood on end, and he found himself glancing over his shoulder every few seconds, half-expecting to see someone lurking in the shadows.

But he pushed on, his determination to see this through outweighing his fear. And then, as he rounded a corner and stepped into a large, open room, he saw it.

A makeshift command center, filled with maps and surveillance equipment and a wall covered in photos of missing mutants. Liam's breath caught in his throat as he took in the scene before him, his mind reeling with the implications of what he was seeing.

"Holy fuck," he breathed, his eyes wide with shock. "This is no ordinary hate group. This is a fucking military operation."

He stepped closer to the wall of photos, his gaze scanning the faces of the missing. Men and women, young and old, all of them mutants, all of them gone without a trace. Liam felt a surge of anger and disgust rise up within him, a fury at the cruelty and callousness of the people responsible for this.

But even as he stood there, taking in the evidence before him, Liam knew that he couldn't afford to get caught up in his emotions. He needed to document this, to gather as much information as he could before getting the hell out of there and sharing what he'd found with someone he could trust.

With shaking hands, he pulled out his phone and started snapping photos, his mind racing with the possibilities of what this could mean for the investigation. But just as he was about to take a final shot of the command center as a whole, he heard a noise from outside the room.

The unmistakable sound of footsteps and voices, approaching fast.

"Shit," Liam hissed, his heart leaping into his throat. He looked around wildly, searching for a place to hide. There, in the corner - a stack of crates, just tall enough to conceal him if he crouched down behind them.

He dove for cover just as the door to the room swung open, two men in dark suits striding in with purposeful steps. Liam held his breath, his body pressed flat against the dusty floor as he listened to their conversation.

"—telling you, we need to move fast," one of the men was saying, his voice low and urgent. "The authorities are starting to ask questions, and we can't afford to let them get too close."

"Relax," the other man replied, his tone dismissive. "We've got everything under control. The mutants we've taken, they're just the beginning. Once we have what we need from them, we'll be able to move on to phase two of the plan."

Liam's eyes widened, his mind reeling with the implications of what he was hearing. Phase two? What the hell did that mean?

He strained his ears, trying to catch every word of the conversation. But the men were already moving on, their voices fading as they made their way over to the command center.

"—need to send a message," the first man was saying. "Let them know that we're not fucking around. That we're willing to do whatever it takes to keep our city pure."

Liam felt a chill run down his spine at the words, a sickening realization of just how deep the hatred and bigotry ran. This wasn't just about fear or ignorance. This was about a twisted ideology, a belief that mutants were somehow less than human, that they needed to be eradicated for the greater good.

He clenched his fists, fighting back the urge to leap out from his hiding spot and confront the men directly. But he knew that would be suicide. He was outnumbered and outgunned, and he couldn't afford to blow his cover now, not when he was so close to uncovering the truth.

And so he waited, his heart pounding in his chest as he listened to the men discuss their plans, their casual cruelty sending shivers of revulsion down his spine. And then, after what felt like an eternity, they were gone, their footsteps fading into the distance as they left the room and disappeared down the hallway.

Liam let out a shaky breath, his body trembling with a mix of fear and adrenaline. He knew he needed to get out of there, to put as much distance between himself and this place as possible. But first, he needed to make sure he had everything he needed.

With a final glance around the room, he snapped a few more photos, his mind already racing with the possibilities of what he would do next. He needed to get this information to someone he could trust, someone who could help him make sense of it all and figure out their next move.

And he knew just the person.

5

Tarot-fic Twist

Ethan

His mind kept drifting back to his run-in with a certain infuriatingly handsome firefighter.

Liam Quinn. Even the thought of the man's name sent a strange mixture of irritation and intrigue coursing through Ethan's veins. He was stubborn, self-righteous, and utterly convinced of his own moral superiority.

And yet, there was something about him that Ethan couldn't quite shake. A spark of intelligence in those piercing eyes, a hint of vulnerability beneath that tough-guy exterior.

Ethan shook his head, trying to banish the distracting thoughts. He had more important things to worry about than some uptight do-gooder with a hero complex.

Just then, the door to the hideout burst open, jolting Ethan from his musings. He looked up to see Zoe striding in, a mischievous grin on her face and a large pizza box balanced precariously in her hands.

"What up, boss man?" she said, setting the pizza down on the desk and giving Ethan a playful punch on the arm. "Thought you could use some brain fuel. Can't solve the mystery of the universe on an empty stomach, right?"

Ethan couldn't help but smile, feeling some of the tension drain from his shoulders at Zoe's infectious energy. She had that effect on him - always able to cut through the bullshit and remind him of what really mattered.

He thought back to the day he first met her, all those years ago. She had been just a kid then, a scrawny little thing with a shock of bright pink hair and a defiant gleam in her eyes.

He had caught her trying to hack into his computer system, her fingers flying over the keyboard with a speed and skill that belied her young age. But instead of turning her over to the cops, Ethan had taken her under his wing, recognizing in her a kindred spirit and a valuable ally.

Over the years, Zoe had become more than just a teammate to him - she was family, the little sister he never had. And he knew that he would do anything to keep her safe, to protect her from the darkness that threatened to swallow them all whole.

"Thanks, Zo," Ethan said, grabbing a slice of pizza and taking a large bite. "You're a lifesaver, you know that?"

Zoe grinned, plopping down in the chair next to him and propping her feet up on the desk. "That's what I'm here for, boss. Saving your sorry ass, one pizza at a time."

Just then, the door opened again, and Marcus stepped into the room, his brow furrowed with concern. He gave Ethan a nod of greeting, his eyes flicking to the cryptic note on the wall.

"Any leads on that thing yet?" he asked, his voice low and serious.

Ethan shook his head, feeling the familiar frustration rising up inside him. "Not yet. It's like trying to decipher a fucking alien language. I swear, whoever wrote this thing must have been on some serious drugs."

Marcus cracked a rare smile, his eyes crinkling at the corners. "Maybe we should start hanging out in more dive bars, then. Might stumble across the key to the universe in between shots of tequila."

Ethan snorted, feeling a rush of affection for his old friend. Marcus had been by his side through thick and thin, ever since those early days when he was just a rookie detective trying to make sense of a string of murders that seemed to have ties to the mutant community.

Ethan had been wary of him at first, not trusting any cop as far as he could throw them. But Marcus had proven himself to be different - a man of integrity and compassion, who treated mutants with the same respect and dignity as anyone else.

Over time, he had become more than just an ally to Ethan - he was a true friend, a confidant who always had his back no matter how dangerous things got.

And right now, with the stakes higher than ever and the enemy closing in from all sides, Ethan knew that he needed Marcus more than ever.

Ethan leaned forward in his chair, his eyes intense as he looked at Zoe and Marcus. "Alright, listen up, because this shit is about to get real." He took a deep breath, running a hand through his tousled hair. "So, last night at the warehouse, things went sideways real fast. The informant we were supposed to meet? Dead as a fucking door nail."

Zoe's eyes widened, her mouth falling open in shock. "Holy shit, boss. What happened?"

Ethan shrugged, his expression grim. "Your guess is as good as mine, Zo. But whoever offed the guy left a little parting gift - a cryptic note that makes about as much sense as a drunk monkey trying to do calculus."

He pulled the note out of his pocket and tossed it on the table, watching as Zoe and Marcus leaned in to get a closer look.

"But that's not even the best part," Ethan continued, a wry smile tugging at the corner of his mouth. "Guess who else showed up to the party? None other than our favorite firefighting boy scout, Liam fucking Quinn."

Marcus raised an eyebrow, his expression skeptical. "The guy who's been trying to bring you in? What the hell was he doing there?"

Ethan shrugged, leaning back in his chair with a cocky grin. "Beats me, but I gotta say, the man knows how to make an entrance. We ended up having to work together to escape some heavily armed goons who crashed the party. It was like something out of a bad action movie."

Zoe snorted, shaking her head in disbelief. "Wait, wait, wait. You're telling me that you and the hot firefighter teamed up to take down some bad guys? That's fucking priceless."

Ethan rolled his eyes, but he couldn't quite hide the smile that tugged at his lips. "Yeah, yeah, laugh it up, Zo. But I'm telling you, there's something about Quinn that I can't quite put my finger on. He's not just some dumb jock with a hero complex."

Marcus frowned, his expression thoughtful. "What do you mean, Ethan? You think he knows something about all this?"

Ethan shrugged, his eyes distant as he turned the cryptic note over in his hands. "I don't know, Marcus. But my gut tells me that he's more than just a pretty face with a badge. There's something else going on here, and I think Quinn might be the key to figuring it out."

Zoe leaned forward, her eyes narrowing as she studied the note. "You know, boss, this thing kind of reminds me of a puzzle I used to play as a kid. It's like a code or something, but you have to look at it from a different angle to make sense of it."

Ethan's head snapped up, his eyes widening with realization. "Zo, you're a fucking genius. That's it - we need to approach this thing from a different perspective. Maybe there's a pattern or a hidden message that we're not seeing."

Marcus nodded, his expression grave. "That's a good idea, Ethan.

But we need to be careful. We don't know who we can trust right now, and that includes Quinn. He might be working his own angle, trying to get close to you for his own reasons."

Ethan bristled, feeling a surge of defensiveness rise up inside him. "I know that, Marcus. I'm not some naive kid who's gonna fall for a pretty face and a badge. But I'm telling you, my instincts are rarely wrong. And right now, they're telling me that Quinn is on our side, whether he knows it or not."

Zoe grinned, her eyes sparkling with mischief. "Aww, does someone have a little crush on the hot firefighter? That's adorable, boss."

Ethan glared at her, his cheeks flushing with embarrassment. "Shut up, Zo. It's not like that. I just think he could be a valuable asset, that's all."

Marcus sighed, running a hand over his face. "Alright, Ethan. I trust your judgment. But promise me you'll be careful, okay? We can't afford to let our guard down, not now."

Ethan nodded, his expression serious. "I know, Marcus. I'll be careful. But we can't just sit back and do nothing. We have to keep pushing forward, no matter how dangerous it gets."

He stood up, stretching his arms above his head and feeling the satisfying pop of his joints. "Alright, team. I think we've done enough damage for one night. Let's break and regroup in the morning, see what fresh hell awaits us then."

Zoe grinned, her eyes sparkling with mischief. "Aye, aye, captain. But don't think you're off the hook about the hot firefighter. I want all the juicy details, boss."

Ethan rolled his eyes, flipping her off with a smile. "In your dreams, Zo. My love life is strictly off-limits, even to nosy little sisters like you."

Just as he was about to turn and head for the door, Ethan's phone buzzed in his pocket. He frowned, pulling it out and glancing at the screen.

His heart skipped a beat when he saw the name flashing up at him: Liam Quinn.

"Well, speak of the devil," he muttered, his voice low and cautious. "Looks like the boy scout has something to say after all."

He stepped away from the others, moving into a quiet corner of the room before answering the call. "Quinn. To what do I owe the pleasure of your dulcet tones at this late hour?"

On the other end of the line, Liam's voice was tense and urgent, his words tumbling out in a rush. "Listen, I don't have much time. I need to talk to you, in person. It's important."

Ethan frowned, his mind racing as he tried to piece together the clues in Liam's tone. He sounded worried, almost afraid. And if there was one thing Ethan knew about Liam Quinn, it was that the man didn't scare easily.

"Whoa, slow down there, cowboy," he said, his voice low and soothing. "What's going on? What's got you so worked up?"

Liam took a deep breath, his voice shaking slightly as he spoke. "I can't tell you over the phone. But trust me, it's big. Bigger than anything we've seen so far. I need to show you what I've found, but it has to be in person. Somewhere private and secure."

Ethan's heart raced, his mind already whirling with the possibilities. If Liam was right, if he really had uncovered something that could blow the lid off the conspiracy...

But he also knew that he had to be careful. Liam was still an unknown quantity, a wild card that could just as easily be working against him as with him.

"Alright, Quinn," he said finally, his voice low and cautious. "I'll meet you. But it has to be on my terms. And if this is some kind of trap, if you're trying to play me..."

Liam cut him off, his voice fierce and insistent. "It's not a trap. I swear to you, on everything I hold dear. This is real, and it's big. And I need your help to figure out what the hell to do about it."

Ethan was silent for a long moment, weighing the risks and benefits of trusting Liam with this new information. But in the end, he knew that he didn't have a choice. If there was even a chance that Liam was right, that he had uncovered the key to the conspiracy...

"Alright," he said finally, his voice low and intense. "Meet me at the old abandoned warehouse on the edge of town. You know the one. Come alone, and make sure you're not followed. I'll be there in an hour."

As he hung up the phone and turned back to his team, Ethan could see the concern and skepticism written all over their faces. Zoe's brow was furrowed, her lips pursed in a worried frown, while Marcus had his arms crossed over his chest, his expression unreadable.

"Are you sure about this, boss?" Zoe asked, her voice hesitant. "I mean, I know you've got a thing for the hot firefighter, but can we really trust him?"

Ethan rolled his eyes, a cocky grin spreading across his face. "Please, Zo. I don't have a 'thing' for anyone. I'm just trying to get to the bottom of this conspiracy, and if Quinn has information that can help us do that, then I'm willing to take the risk."

Marcus shook his head, his expression grave. "I don't like it, Ethan. This whole setup feels off. What if it's a trap?"

Ethan sighed, running a hand through his tousled hair. "I know, Marcus. But what choice do we have? If Quinn really has uncovered something big, then we need to know about it. And I'm the only one who can get close enough to find out."

He grabbed his jacket and headed for the door, his mind already racing with the possibilities of what lay ahead. "Look, I know you guys are worried. But you have to trust me on this. I've got a gut feeling that Quinn is on the level, and I'm not going to ignore it just because it's risky."

Zoe and Marcus exchanged a glance, but they knew better than to argue with Ethan when he got like this. When the boss made up his mind, there was no changing it.

"Just be careful, okay?" Zoe said softly, her eyes shining with concern. "And if you need us, we'll be here."

Ethan nodded, a grateful smile tugging at the corner of his mouth. "I know, Zo. And I appreciate it. But this is something I have to do alone."

With that, he turned and strode out into the night, his heart pounding with a heady mix of anticipation and fear. He knew that he was taking a risk, trusting Liam with this new information. But he also knew that he didn't have a choice.

If there was even a chance that Liam was right, that he had uncovered the key to the conspiracy, then Ethan needed to hear him out. No matter how dangerous it might be.

As he made his way to the rendezvous point, Ethan couldn't shake the feeling of unease that settled in the pit of his stomach. He arrived early, his senses on high alert as he scanned the area for any sign of trouble.

The warehouse loomed in the darkness, its broken windows and crumbling walls a testament to years of neglect and decay. Ethan paced back and forth in front of the entrance, his mind racing with the possibilities of what Liam might have found and what it could mean for their investigation.

As the minutes ticked by, he began to feel a growing sense of doubt, a nagging fear that maybe he had made a mistake in trusting Liam. What if this was all just a ploy, a way for the firefighter to lure him out into the open and take him down once and for all?

But just as he was about to give up and leave, Ethan saw a figure approaching in the distance, a familiar silhouette that he would know anywhere. Liam stepped out of the shadows, his face grim and determined as he held up a folder stuffed with papers and photographs.

"Arcana," he said curtly, his voice tight with tension. "I wasn't sure you'd actually show."

Ethan smirked, crossing his arms over his chest. "What can I say, Quinn? I'm a sucker for a good mystery. And you've certainly piqued my interest with this little rendezvous of ours."

Liam shook his head, his expression serious. "This isn't a game, Arcana. What I've found… it's big. Bigger than either of us could have imagined."

Without another word, he handed the folder to Ethan, his eyes locked on the vigilante's face as he watched for his reaction. Ethan flipped through the pages, his eyes widening with each new revelation.

Surveillance photos of missing mutants, their faces haunted and afraid. Financial records linking the conspiracy to powerful corporations and government officials, their names and signatures stark against the white paper. Maps and blueprints of secret facilities where unspeakable experiments were being carried out, the very thought of which made Ethan's stomach turn.

He looked up at Liam, his voice hoarse with shock and anger. "Where the fuck did you get this?"

Liam shook his head, his expression grim. "It doesn't matter. What matters is what we do with it. We have to stop this, Arcana. We have to put an end to the conspiracy before it's too late."

Ethan nodded, his mind already racing with the possibilities. He knew that Liam was right, that they had to act fast if they wanted to save the missing mutants and bring the conspirators to justice.

And as much as he hated to admit it, Ethan knew that he was going to enjoy working with Liam Quinn. Even if it meant constantly butting heads with the stubborn, infuriatingly attractive firefighter.

Because in the end, they both wanted the same thing - to save the city they loved and the people they had sworn to protect. And if that meant putting aside their differences and working together, then so be it.

The game was on.

6

Forging an Alliance

Liam

He lay in bed for a moment, staring up at the ceiling and trying to make sense of the whirlwind that his life had become.

Finally, he dragged himself out of bed and stumbled into the bathroom, splashing cold water on his face in an attempt to clear the cobwebs from his mind. As he brushed his teeth and shaved, he couldn't shake the feeling that everything had changed, that the world he thought he knew had been turned upside down.

He made his way into the kitchen, starting a pot of coffee and rummaging through the fridge for something to eat. As he waited for the coffee to brew, he pulled out his phone and scrolled through his messages, his heart skipping a beat when he saw a text from an unknown number.

"Meet me at the docks tonight. Come alone. - A"

Liam felt a grin spreading across his face, a thrill of excitement coursing through his veins. He knew it was crazy, knew that he should be cautious and wary of any message from The Arcana. But he couldn't help himself. The man was intriguing, a puzzle that Liam couldn't resist trying to solve.

He typed out a quick reply, his fingers flying over the screen. "I'll be there. But if this is a trap, I'm going to kick your ass. - Q"

With a chuckle, Liam hit send and pocketed his phone, grabbing his coffee and heading out the door. He had a shift at the firehouse to get to, and he knew that he needed to keep up appearances if he wanted to avoid suspicion.

He drove and pulled into the firehouse parking lot, taking a deep breath and trying to clear his mind. He needed to focus on his job, on the people who were counting on him to keep them safe. He couldn't afford to let his mind wander, not when lives were on the line.

As Liam walked into the firehouse, he couldn't shake the feeling that he was carrying a huge secret on his shoulders. The weight of the conspiracy, the knowledge of the disappearances, and his unlikely alliance with The Arcana all swirled in his mind, threatening to overwhelm him at any moment.

He tried to focus on his duties, on the routine of checking equipment and running drills with his team. But every few minutes, Liam found himself reaching for his phone, checking for any new messages or updates from The Arcana.

He knew it was ridiculous, knew that he should be focusing on his job and the people who were counting on him. But he couldn't help it. The thrill of the chase, the promise of justice, was like a drug he couldn't quit.

"Hey, Quinn!" a voice called out, jolting Liam from his thoughts. "You okay, man? You seem a little distracted today."

Liam looked up to see Jack, standing in front of him with a concerned look on his face. He forced a smile, trying to brush off the question with his usual charm.

"Yeah, I'm good, man," he said, his voice a little too casual. "Just didn't get much sleep last night, you know how it is."

But Jack wasn't buying it. He crossed his arms over his chest, fixing Liam with a skeptical look. "Bullshit. I know you, Quinn. Something's up, and you're not telling me what it is."

Liam hesitated, torn between his loyalty to his friend and his need to keep the investigation under wraps. He knew that involving Jack could be dangerous, could put him in the crosshairs of the very people they were trying to take down.

But at the same time, he couldn't keep carrying this burden alone. He needed someone to talk to, someone who could understand the magnitude of what he was facing.

"Alright, fine," he said, his voice low and serious. "But not here. Let's take a walk."

He led Jack outside, away from the prying eyes and ears of the rest of the team. They walked in silence for a few minutes, Liam trying to gather his thoughts and find the right words to explain the insanity that had become his life.

Finally, he took a deep breath and started talking. He told Jack everything, from the mysterious disappearances to the cryptic clues to his unlikely partnership with The Arcana. He spoke of the conspiracy, the powerful forces that seemed to be working against them at every turn.

As he talked, he could see the skepticism and concern in Jack's eyes. He knew how crazy it all sounded, how hard it was to believe that something like this could be happening right under their noses.

But to his surprise, Jack didn't dismiss his claims outright. Instead, he listened intently, asking questions and offering his own insights. He seemed to understand the gravity of the situation, the importance of uncovering the truth no matter the cost.

"Damn, Quinn," he said when Liam had finished, his voice low and serious. "I knew something was up, but I never imagined it was something like this."

Liam nodded, feeling a sense of relief wash over him. It felt good to finally share his secret with someone, to have an ally in this fight.

"I know it sounds crazy," he said, his voice wavering slightly. "But I can't just sit back and do nothing, not when innocent people are being hurt. I have to see this through, no matter what."

Jack was silent for a moment, his expression thoughtful. Then, slowly, he reached out and clapped Liam on the shoulder, a grim smile spreading across his face.

"Well, you're not doing it alone," he said, his voice firm and resolute. "I'm in, Quinn. Whatever you need, whatever I can do to help, I'm there."

Liam felt a lump rising in his throat, a rush of gratitude and affection for his friend. He knew that involving Jack was a risk, that it could put him in danger. But he also knew that he couldn't do this without him, without someone who had his back no matter what.

"Thanks, man," he said, his voice rough with emotion. "I don't know what I did to deserve a friend like you, but I'm sure as hell glad I have you."

Jack grinned, punching Liam lightly on the arm. "Don't get all sappy on me now, Quinn. We've got work to do."

Liam laughed, feeling a sense of lightness wash over him. For the first time in days, he felt like he could breathe again, like he wasn't carrying the weight of the world on his shoulders.

"Damn straight," he said, a mischievous glint in his eye. "But first, we need to come up with a badass name for our little operation. Something like 'The Renegades' or 'The Vigilantes.'"

Jack rolled his eyes, but Liam could see the smile tugging at the corner of his mouth. "How about 'The Idiots Who Are Going to Get Themselves Killed'? That seems more accurate."

Liam clutched his chest in mock offense, gasping dramatically. "You wound me, Jack. I thought you had more faith in our skills than that."

Jack snorted, shaking his head in amusement. "Skills? What skills? You're a firefighter, not a detective. And I'm pretty sure The Arcana has more experience with this kind of thing than either of us."

Liam grinned, feeling a thrill of excitement at the mention of Ethan's alter ego. "Maybe so, but we've got something he doesn't have: rugged good looks and charming personalities."

Jack rolled his eyes again, but this time he couldn't hide his smile. "Alright, Quinn, you win. Let's do this. But if we die, I'm going to haunt your ass for all eternity."

Liam laughed, feeling a sense of camaraderie and purpose wash over him. He knew that the road ahead would be dangerous, that they were up against powerful forces that would stop at nothing to keep their secrets hidden.

"Alright, partner," he said, clapping Jack on the back as they headed back into the firehouse. "Let's go save the world, one conspiracy at a time."

The words had barely left his mouth when the alarm blared through the station, the urgent sound of the bell sending a jolt of adrenaline through Liam's veins. He and Jack exchanged a glance, their earlier levity forgotten as they raced to suit up and join the rest of the team.

As they sped through the city streets, sirens blaring and lights flashing, Liam couldn't shake the feeling that this was no ordinary call. The dispatcher's voice had been tight with tension, the details of the fire sparse and vague.

As the fire truck raced through the city streets, Liam could feel the tension in the air, the unspoken knowledge that this was no ordinary call. The dispatcher's voice had been tight with urgency, the details of the fire sparse and vague.

When they arrived on the scene, Liam's heart sank. The building was engulfed in flames, the heat so intense that he could feel it from a block away. And there, trapped on the upper floors, were the screams of civilians, their cries for help piercing the night air.

"Jesus Christ," Jack muttered, his eyes wide with horror. "This is bad, Quinn. Really fucking bad."

Liam nodded, his jaw clenched tight. "We've got to get in there, fast. Those people don't have much time."

He turned to his team, his voice steady and commanding. "Alright, listen up. Martinez, O'Neill, I want you on the hoses. Keep that fire contained and give us as much time as you can. Davis, you're with me and Jack. We're going in to get those civilians out."

The team nodded, their faces grim but determined. They knew the risks, knew that they were walking into the mouth of hell itself. But they also knew that this was what they had signed up for, the sacred duty that they had sworn to uphold.

As they made their way towards the building, the heat growing more intense with every step, Liam could feel the flames responding to his presence, the fire almost seeming to reach out and beckon to him.

He gritted his teeth, pushing back against the temptation to unleash his powers. He knew that he could control the flames, that he could bend them to his will and carve a path to safety for those trapped inside.

But he also knew the risks, the danger of exposing his mutant abilities to the world. Even though his team knew about his powers, he had always been cautious about using them in public, afraid of the consequences that could follow.

"Quinn!" Davis shouted, his voice muffled by his oxygen mask. "We can't get through! The flames are too high!"

Liam cursed under his breath, his mind racing as he tried to find another way. But there was no time, no other option. He could hear the screams of the civilians growing fainter, the precious seconds ticking away like grains of sand in an hourglass.

"Liam!" Jack yelled, his voice urgent and insistent. "You have to use your powers, man! It's the only way!"

Liam hesitated, his heart pounding in his chest. He knew that Jack was right, that his pyrokinesis was the only thing that could save those people. But he also knew the risks, the danger of exposing himself so publicly.

"Quinn!" Davis shouted, his voice desperate. "There's no time! You have to do it now!"

Liam closed his eyes, taking a deep breath and reaching deep within himself. He could feel the power surging through his veins, the flames responding to his call like loyal soldiers.

And then, with a roar of fury and determination, he unleashed his pyrokinesis, the flames bending and parting before him like the Red Sea. His team watched in amazement as he carved a path through the inferno, the fire seeming to dance and flicker around him like a living thing.

"Holy shit," Martinez breathed, his eyes wide with awe. "I've seen him use his powers before, but never like this."

Liam didn't respond, his focus entirely on the task at hand. He pushed forward, his power growing stronger with every step, until finally they reached the civilians trapped on the upper floors.

"It's okay!" he shouted, his voice raw and hoarse from the smoke. "We're here to help you! Just follow me!"

The civilians looked at him with a mix of fear and relief, their faces streaked with soot and their eyes wide with terror. But they did as he asked, following him back through the path he had carved, the flames licking at their heels like hungry wolves.

And finally, after what felt like an eternity, they emerged from the building, the cool night air hitting their faces like a balm. Liam collapsed to his knees, his body shaking with exhaustion and the aftershocks of his power.

His team surrounded him, their expressions a mix of pride and concern. "Quinn," Davis said, his voice low and urgent. "Are you okay?"

Liam looked up at them, his eyes blazing with a mix of defiance and fear. "I'm fine," he said, his voice rough and raw. "I had to do it. I couldn't let those people die."

Jack stepped forward, his hand outstretched and a grin on his face. "Damn, Quinn," he said, his voice filled with pride and admiration. "You never cease to amaze me. Those people owe you their lives."

Liam felt a rush of relief and gratitude wash over him, his heart swelling with the knowledge that his team had his back, no matter what. He took Jack's hand, allowing himself to be pulled to his feet and into a tight embrace.

And as they made their way back to the fire truck, the civilians safe and the fire contained, Liam couldn't shake the feeling that everything had changed. He had used his powers in a way he never had before, had exposed himself to the world in a moment of desperation and heroism.

He showered and changed back into his civilian clothes, Liam couldn't help but feel a sense of unease settling in the pit of his stomach. He checked his watch, his heart skipping a beat as he realized that it was almost time for his meeting with The Arcana.

He slipped away from the firehouse, making his way to the rendezvous point with a sense of purpose and determination. He knew that he was taking a risk, that he was putting his trust in a man who operated outside the law. But he also knew that he didn't have a choice, not if he wanted to get to the bottom of this mystery.

When he arrived at the meeting spot, a secluded alley on the outskirts of town, he was surprised to find The Arcana already waiting for him. The vigilante was leaning against the wall, his arms crossed over his chest and his expression grim.

"You're late," he said, his voice low and rough.

Liam raised an eyebrow, a smirk tugging at the corner of his mouth. "Well hello to you too, sunshine. I was a little busy saving lives and putting out fires, you know how it is."

The Arcana snorted, but Liam could see a flicker of amusement in his eyes. "Excuses, excuses. Let's just get down to business, shall we?"

Liam nodded, sobering up as he remembered the gravity of the situation. "What have you got for me?"

The Arcana pushed himself off the wall, reaching into his pocket and pulling out a crumpled piece of paper. "I've been following up on some leads, trying to connect the dots between the disappearances and the larger conspiracy at play. And I think I might have found something."

He handed the paper to Liam, watching carefully as the firefighter unfolded it and scanned the contents. Liam's eyes widened as he took in the information, his mind racing as he tried to fit the pieces of the puzzle together. The word Genexis stood out the most.

"If this is true, then we're dealing with something much bigger than we ever could have imagined. I've heard the name Genexis before but never really thought of them to do something like this."

The Arcana nodded, his expression grim. "Exactly. And that's why we need to move fast, before they catch on to what we're doing and shut us down for good."

As he spoke, Liam found himself studying the vigilante's face, taking in the sharp angles and chiseled features that were only partially obscured by his disguise. Despite himself, he felt a flicker of appreciation for the man's rugged good looks, a thought that he quickly pushed away before it could fully manifest.

He reminded himself that The Arcana was still a criminal, a wild card who operated outside the law. He couldn't afford to let his guard down or be swayed by something as superficial as physical attraction.

And yet, as they stood there in the alley, their heads bent together over the crumpled piece of paper, Liam couldn't shake the feeling that there was something more between them, a connection that went beyond the simple necessity of their partnership.

He shook his head, pushing the thought aside. He had more important things to worry about than his own misguided hormones.

"So what's our next move?" he asked, focusing his attention back on the task at hand.

The Arcana's eyes glinted with a mix of determination and mischief. "Well, my dear Watson, I thought you'd never ask. Let's just say that things are about to get a whole lot more interesting."

Liam groaned, rolling his eyes at the vigilante's theatrics. "Please don't tell me you're going to start wearing a deerstalker hat and smoking a pipe. I don't think my fragile ego could handle being relegated to sidekick status."

The Arcana laughed, the sound rich and warm in the cool night air. "Wouldn't dream of it, darling. I look terrible in hats."

Despite the playful banter, Liam could feel the tension simmering just beneath the surface. They had a lot of ground to cover, and not a lot of time to do it in. The fate of countless innocent mutants hung in the balance, and every second they wasted was another second their enemies had to cover their tracks.

"We can't just go in guns blazing, Ethan. We need a plan, a strategy." Liam asked, his voice turning serious.

Arcana raised an eyebrow, a smirk playing at the corner of his mouth. "Why, Liam Quinn, are you suggesting we play it safe? Where's your sense of adventure?"

Liam huffed out a breath, trying to ignore the way his heart skipped a beat at the sound of his name on The Arcana's lips. "My sense of adventure is just fine, thank you very much. But I also have a sense of responsibility. We can't afford to fuck this up. Too many lives are at stake."

Arcana's expression sobered, his eyes turning serious. "I know that, Quinn. But we also can't afford to sit back and do nothing. Every day we wait, every moment we hesitate, is another chance for those bastards to slip away and disappear into the shadows."

Liam sighed, running a hand through his hair in frustration. He knew that The Arcana had a point, but he also knew that they needed to be smart about this. They needed evidence, proof that would stand up in a court of law and bring the conspirators to justice.

"Look," he said, his voice low and intense. "I get where you're coming from, Ethan. I really do. But we have to be careful. We can't just go off half-cocked and hope for the best. We need to gather more evidence, build a case that even the most corrupt judge can't ignore."

Arcana's eyes flashed with something that Liam couldn't quite read. Anger? Frustration? Or maybe something else entirely? And how long is that going to take, Liam?" he asked, his voice tight with barely controlled emotion. "Weeks? Months? Years? How many more innocent mutants are going to disappear while we're busy dotting our i's and crossing our t's?"

Liam felt his own temper flare, his fists clenching at his sides. "Damn it, that's not fair. You know I want to stop these bastards just as much as you do. But we have to do it the right way, the legal way. Otherwise, we're no better than the criminals we're trying to catch."

For a moment, the two men stared at each other, their eyes locked in a silent battle of wills. The tension between them was palpable, the air crackling with unspoken emotions and unresolved feelings.

And then, just as quickly as it had begun, the moment passed. Arcana's shoulders slumped, his head dropping forward in a gesture of resignation.

"You're right," he said, his voice soft and weary. "I know you're right. I just... I can't stand the thought of those bastards getting away with it. Of all those innocent lives being lost because we were too slow, too cautious."

Liam felt his heart clench at the pain in his voice. He knew how much this meant to the vigilante, how deeply he cared about the mutant community and the people he had sworn to protect.

"Hey," he said, his voice gentle as he reached out and laid a hand on The Arcana's arm. "We're going to get them. I promise you that. But we have to do it the right way, the smart way. We have to be better than them, or else what's the point of all this?"

Arcana looked up at him, his eyes searching Liam's face for something that neither of them was quite ready to acknowledge. And then, slowly, he nodded, a small smile tugging at the corner of his mouth.

"Alright, Boy Scout," he said, his voice teasing. "We'll do it your way. But if we get stuck filling out paperwork and attending court hearings, I'm holding you personally responsible."

Liam couldn't help but laugh, the tension draining from his body like water from a sieve. "Deal," he said, his eyes sparkling with mirth. "But only if you promise to behave yourself and not go rogue on me. I don't want to have to explain to my captain why I'm bailing your sorry ass out of jail."

The Arcana grinned, his eyes crinkling at the corners in a way that made Liam's heart skip a beat. "No promises, darling. You know how much I love a good jailbreak."

They fell into a comfortable silence then, the banter and the tension fading away into something softer, more intimate. Liam could feel the warmth of Ethan's skin beneath his hand, the steady thrum of his pulse beating in time with his own.

It was a dangerous thing, this attraction he felt for the vigilante. He knew that now was not the time for distractions or complications, that they had a job to do and a mission to complete.

But he also couldn't deny the way his heart raced whenever The

Arcana was near, the way his skin tingled with electricity at the slightest touch. It was a force of nature, a tidal wave of emotion that threatened to sweep him away if he wasn't careful.

7

Masks and Mayhem in the City That Never Sleeps

Ethan

As he stared at his reflection in the mirror, he couldn't help but smirk. Even with bags under his eyes and stubble on his chin, he still looked damn good. It was a gift, really. One of the perks of being Ethan fucking Hawke.

He went about his morning routine, showering and dressing in one of his signature tailored suits. To the outside world, he was just another successful businessman, a rising star in the cutthroat world of finance. But beneath the surface, he was so much more.

Ethan made his way to the kitchen, where Zoe and Marcus were already waiting for him. Zoe was hunched over her laptop, her fingers flying over the keys as she dug deeper into the financial records of the companies involved in the conspiracy. Marcus, meanwhile, was on the phone, his brow furrowed as he spoke in low, urgent tones.

"Please tell me you two have some good news for me," Ethan said, pouring himself a cup of coffee. "Because I could really use a win right about now."

Zoe looked up from her screen, her eyes bleary from lack of sleep. "I've been digging into the financials of Genexis," she said, her voice hoarse. "And let me tell you, boss, there's some shady shit going on there. Money moving in and out of offshore accounts, shell companies popping up like weeds… it's a fucking mess."

Ethan raised an eyebrow, a smirk playing at the corner of his mouth. "Sounds like my kind of party," he said, taking a sip of his coffee. "What about you, Marcus? Any luck with your contacts in the force?"

Marcus hung up the phone, his expression grim. "Nothing good," he said, shaking his head. "The DMA is ramping up their efforts to track you down, Ethan. They've got their top agents on the case, and they're not pulling any punches. We need to be careful."

Ethan felt a thrill of excitement run through him, his eyes sparkling with mischief. "Careful? Where's the fun in that?" he said, grinning. "If the DMA wants a piece of me, they're welcome to try. But they better bring their A-game, because I'm not going down without a fight."

Zoe rolled her eyes, but Ethan could see the hint of a smile tugging at the corner of her mouth. "You're an idiot, you know that?" she said, her voice fond. "One of these days, that ego of yours is going to get you killed."

Ethan shrugged, his grin widening. "Maybe," he said, his voice teasing. "But what a way to go, right?"

He drained the rest of his coffee, his mind already racing with the possibilities of the day ahead. He had a cover to maintain, a persona to uphold. But beneath the surface, he was already planning his next move as The Arcana.

"Alright, team," he said, clapping his hands together. "Let's get to work. Zoe, keep digging into those financials. If there's a money trail, I want to know where it leads. Marcus, I need you to keep your ear to the ground. If the DMA makes a move, I want to know about it."

As Ethan made his way out of the apartment, his mind kept drifting back to Liam. The way the firefighter's eyes had blazed with determination, the way his jaw had clenched with barely controlled anger. There was a fire in him, a passion that Ethan couldn't help but admire.

And if he was being honest with himself, there was something else there too. A spark, a connection that he couldn't quite explain. It was dangerous, he knew that. Liam was a wild card, a variable that he couldn't control.

But Ethan had never been one to play it safe. He lived for the thrill, for the rush of adrenaline that came with taking risks and pushing boundaries. And if that meant getting a little too close to a certain stubborn, infuriating, drop-dead gorgeous firefighter?

Well, that was a risk he was willing to take.

And if along the way, he got to spend a little more time with Liam Quinn? Well, that was just icing on the cake.

Ethan grinned to himself, his eyes sparkling with mischief. Oh, this was going to be fun. The DMA thought they could take him down?

They had no idea who they were fucking with.

He was just getting started. And heaven help anyone who stood in his way.

* * *

As the day wore on, Ethan went about his usual business, attending meetings and schmoozing with clients. But all the while, his mind was racing, his senses on high alert for any sign of trouble.

It wasn't until later that evening, as he was preparing to head home, that he received the message. It came from one of his most trusted informants, a mutant with the ability to sense danger from miles away.

"Arcana," the message read, "there's been a spike in mutant disappearances in Hell's Kitchen. You need to check it out, now."

He quickly typed out a response, thanking the informant for the tip and promising to look into it right away.

As he stepped into his hidden base of operations, he couldn't help but feel a sense of pride wash over him. This was his domain, the place where he could shed his daytime persona and become something more. Something powerful, something dangerous.

He quickly donned his Arcana outfit, the sleek black material clinging to his muscular frame like a second skin. He could feel the power thrumming through his veins, the ethereal energy of his tarot cards just waiting to be unleashed.

As Ethan raced through the streets of Hell's Kitchen, his mind was a whirlwind of thoughts and emotions. He couldn't help but reflect on the history of mutants and the M-Gene, the genetic quirk that had shaped the lives of so many individuals like himself.

He knew that the existence of the M-Gene could be traced back several generations, with the earliest known cases of mutation occurring in the late nineteenth century. But it wasn't until the mid-twentieth century that the mutant population began to grow significantly, as the gene became more prevalent in the general population.

Scientists believed that the activation of the M-Gene was triggered by a combination of environmental factors and intense emotional or physical stress. When activated, the gene caused a dramatic shift in an individual's DNA, leading to the manifestation of their unique mutant abilities.

Ethan thought about his own powers, the way he could summon ethereal constructs and manipulate energy with just a thought. He knew that his abilities were just one example of the countless forms that mutant powers could take, ranging from enhanced physical attributes to exotic abilities like telekinesis and shapeshifting.

But as the mutant population grew, so too did the fear and prejudice that followed them. Ethan knew all too well the struggles that mutants faced, the discrimination and persecution that forced so many of them to hide their true nature.

He thought about the rise of mutant communities, hidden enclaves where they could live and thrive among their own kind. And he thought about the government agencies that had been established to regulate and control mutants, like the Department of Mutant Affairs.

The DMA. Just the thought of the agency made Ethan's blood boil. He knew that they operated under the guise of registering and regulating mutants, but he also knew that their true purpose was far more sinister.

Behind closed doors, the DMA was a ruthless and efficient machine, tasked with maintaining human supremacy and neutralizing any mutant threats. They employed advanced technology, propaganda, and covert operations to keep the mutant population in check, all under the leadership of the hardline anti-mutant extremist known only as Director Thorne.

Ethan gritted his teeth, his fists clenching at his sides as he thought about the DMA and their twisted agenda. He knew that they saw him as a threat, a dangerous vigilante who operated outside the law to protect mutant rights.

As he turned down a darkened alley, his senses on high alert, Ethan couldn't shake the feeling that he was being watched.

And then, without warning, all hell broke loose.

A group of heavily armed DMA agents emerged from the shadows, their weapons trained on Ethan with deadly precision. He could see the cold determination in their eyes, the ruthless efficiency with which they moved.

"Arcana!" one of the agents barked, his voice harsh and commanding.

"Stand down and surrender immediately. You are interfering with an official DMA investigation."

Ethan felt a smirk tug at the corner of his mouth, his eyes sparkling with mischief. "Well, well, well," he drawled, his voice dripping with sarcasm. "If it isn't my favorite group of government lapdogs. Tell me, boys, how does it feel to be on the wrong side of history?"

The agents bristled at his words, their fingers tightening on the triggers of their weapons. Ethan knew he had to act fast, before they had a chance to take him down.

With a flick of his wrist, he summoned the power of The Magician card, the ethereal construct materializing in his hand like a glowing ball of energy. He hurled it towards the agents, watching with satisfaction as it exploded in a blinding flash of light and sound.

The agents scattered, their formation broken by the sudden attack. Ethan took advantage of the chaos, leaping into action with a feral grin on his face.

He raced through the streets, his heart pounding in his chest as he dodged and weaved through the pursuing agents. He could hear their shouts of anger and frustration, the sound of their boots pounding against the pavement.

But Ethan was in his element, his body moving with a fluid grace that was almost superhuman. He summoned the power of The Chariot card, the ethereal construct wrapping around him like a shield of energy.

He could feel the bullets bouncing off the shimmering barrier, the agents' weapons useless against his mutant abilities. He laughed, the sound wild and reckless in the night air.

"Is that all you've got?" he taunted, his voice echoing through the streets. "I thought the DMA was supposed to be the best of the best. Looks like you're nothing but a bunch of second-rate thugs with fancy toys."

He could see the anger burning in the agents' eyes, the frustration etched into every line of their faces. They knew they were outmatched, that they had underestimated his power.

But Ethan knew he couldn't let his guard down, not even for a moment. The DMA was ruthless, and they would stop at nothing to bring him in.

He summoned the power of The Tower card, the ethereal construct exploding outwards in a wave of destructive energy. The agents were thrown back, their weapons clattering to the ground as they struggled to regain their footing.

Ethan took advantage of the momentary respite, racing down a narrow alleyway and out of sight. He could hear the agents regrouping behind him, their shouts of anger and frustration echoing through the night.

He had bought himself some time, a precious few moments to catch his breath and plan his next move. He leaned against the wall, his chest heaving with exertion as he tried to calm his racing heart.

"Fuck me," he muttered, a grin spreading across his face. "That was a close one. Guess the DMA is stepping up their game."

He couldn't stay in the alleyway for long, not with the DMA agents hot on his trail. He could hear their shouts and footsteps drawing closer, the sound echoing off the narrow walls like a pack of hungry wolves closing in on their prey.

But he had a job to do, a mission to complete. He couldn't let the DMA's interference stop him from uncovering the truth behind the mutant disappearances.

With a muttered curse, Ethan pushed himself off the wall and reached out with his mind, summoning the power of The Hermit card. He felt the ethereal energy wrap around him like a cloak, rendering him invisible to the naked eye.

He slipped out of the alleyway and into the bustling streets of Hell's

Kitchen, his footsteps silent and his presence undetectable. He could feel the thrum of the city's energy pulsing through him, the chaos and the noise fading into the background as he focused on his goal.

His pursuit led him to an abandoned tenement building on the outskirts of the neighborhood, a place that seemed to be the epicenter of the recent disappearances. Ethan could feel the hairs on the back of his neck standing up as he approached the building, his senses on high alert for any sign of danger.

He slipped inside, the power of The Hermit still cloaking him in invisibility. The building was dark and musty, the air thick with the stench of decay and neglect. Ethan wrinkled his nose in disgust, his eyes scanning the shadows for any sign of life.

As he made his way deeper into the building, he stumbled upon a hidden room, its door concealed behind a stack of rotting crates. Ethan's heart raced with anticipation as he pushed the door open, his mind already whirling with the possibilities of what he might find inside.

What he saw made his blood run cold.

The room was filled with high-tech equipment and medical supplies, all bearing the DMA's logo. There were computers and monitors, their screens glowing with complex algorithms and data streams. And there, in the center of the room, was a large metal table, its surface stained with the unmistakable rust-brown of dried blood.

Ethan felt a wave of nausea wash over him as he realized the implications of what he was seeing. The DMA had been using this place as a base of operations, likely to investigate the disappearances and gather evidence. But at what cost? What kind of twisted experiments had they been conducting here, in the name of national security?

He was just about to step further into the room, to gather more evidence of the DMA's wrongdoing, when a voice rang out behind him.

"Don't move, Arcana."

Ethan froze, his heart pounding in his chest as he slowly turned around. Standing in the doorway was a woman with a stern demeanor and an air of authority, her hand resting on the gun at her hip.

"Agent Reyes, I presume?" Ethan said, his voice dripping with sarcasm. "To what do I owe the pleasure of your company?"

Reyes narrowed her eyes, her expression hard and unyielding. "You're interfering with a DMA investigation, Arcana. I'm going to have to ask you to come with me."

Ethan laughed, the sound harsh and bitter in the cramped confines of the room. "And why would I do that? So you can lock me up and throw away the key? I don't think so, sweetheart."

Reyes took a step forward, her hand tightening on her gun. "This isn't a game, Arcana. The DMA has been tracking your activities for some time now. We know about your involvement in the mutant disappearances case."

Ethan felt a flicker of unease run through him at her words, but he pushed it aside. He couldn't let the DMA intimidate him, couldn't let them bully him into submission.

"And what exactly do you think you know, Agent Reyes?" he asked, his voice low and dangerous. "Because from where I'm standing, it looks like the DMA is the one with something to hide."

Reyes sighed, her expression softening slightly. "Look, Arcana. I know our methods may seem harsh, but they're necessary. We're trying to maintain order, to protect both mutants and humans alike. And sometimes, that means making difficult choices."

Ethan scoffed, his eyes flashing with anger. "Difficult choices? Is that what you call kidnapping and experimenting on innocent mutants? Is that what you call using fear and intimidation to keep us in line?"

Reyes shook her head, her voice tinged with frustration. "It's not that simple, Arcana. The world is changing, and we have to change with it. The DMA is doing the best it can to navigate these new waters, to find a balance between freedom and security."

Ethan was silent for a moment, his mind racing as he tried to process her words. As much as he hated to admit it, he could see the complexity of the situation, the difficult position the DMA was in. But that didn't mean he had to like it, or accept it.

"So what now?" he asked, his voice weary. "Are you going to arrest me? Throw me in some secret DMA prison and throw away the key?"

Reyes studied him for a long moment, her expression unreadable. Finally, she spoke, her voice low and serious.

"I'm going to give you a choice, Arcana. You can either work with us to solve this case and bring the perpetrators to justice, or you can face the consequences of your vigilante actions. It's up to you."

Ethan felt a surge of anger at her ultimatum, his fists clenching at his sides. He couldn't believe the audacity of the DMA, thinking they could just waltz in and demand his cooperation after everything they had done.

"You've got to be fucking kidding me," he snarled, his voice dripping with venom. "You think I'm just going to roll over and play nice with the same people who have been oppressing and persecuting my kind for years? Not a chance in hell, Reyes."

Reyes's expression hardened, her hand tightening on her gun. "Don't be foolish, Arcana. You can't take on the DMA alone. We have resources, connections, information that you could never hope to access on your own. Working with us is your best chance of solving this case and keeping the mutant community safe."

Ethan laughed, the sound harsh and bitter in the cramped confines of the room. "Safe? You call this safe? Look around you, Reyes. Look at the blood on that table, the equipment, the files. The DMA isn't interested in keeping anyone safe. They're interested in control, in maintaining their power at any cost."

He took a step forward, his eyes blazing with defiance. "I'll find another way to solve this case, Reyes. I'll work with people I trust, people who actually give a damn about the mutant community. But I will never work with the DMA. Not now, not ever."

Reyes's jaw clenched, her eyes flashing with anger. "You're making a mistake, Arcana. The DMA will not tolerate your interference. If you continue down this path, there will be consequences."

Ethan grinned, the expression sharp and dangerous. "Bring it on, Reyes. I've been dealing with the DMA's 'consequences' my whole life. I'm not afraid of you or your little club of fascist assholes."

With that, he summoned the power of The Tower card, the ethereal construct exploding outwards in a wave of destructive energy. Reyes was thrown back, her gun clattering to the ground as she struggled to regain her footing.

Ethan didn't waste a second, his mind already racing with escape plans and contingencies. He could hear the shouts of the DMA agents getting closer, their footsteps pounding against the crumbling concrete like a stampede of angry bulls.

"Looks like it's time for a little disappearing act."

He reached out with his mind, summoning the power of The Magician card. The ethereal construct shimmered into existence, a glowing orb of pure energy that pulsed with an otherworldly light.

With a flick of his wrist, Ethan sent the orb hurtling towards the far end of the hallway, where it exploded in a dazzling burst of light and sound. The DMA agents cried out in surprise and confusion, their attention momentarily diverted from their pursuit of The Arcana.

Ethan seized the opportunity, racing down the hallway in the opposite direction. He could feel the adrenaline pumping through his veins, the thrill of the chase setting his nerves on fire.

He burst out of the building and into the night, his boots pounding against the pavement as he ran. He could hear the shouts of the DMA agents behind him, their voices getting fainter with every step he took.

But Ethan didn't stop, didn't look back. He weaved through the shadows and alleyways of Hell's Kitchen, his mind already racing ahead to his next move.

He needed to regroup with his team, to fill them in on everything that had happened and start piecing together the clues they had gathered.

8

Echoes of the Past

Liam

He went about his morning routine, trying to push the thoughts of The Arcana and the mutant disappearances out of his mind. But as he brushed his teeth and shaved, he found himself overwhelmed by memories of his parents.

He remembered the way his mother used to hum as she cooked breakfast, the smell of bacon and eggs filling the tiny apartment. He remembered the way his father used to ruffle his hair and call him "sport," even after he'd grown taller than the old man.

They had always been there for him, always supported him, even after his mutant abilities had manifested. Liam felt a lump form in his throat as he thought about the day they died, the day his world had shattered into a million pieces.

It had been a car accident, a stupid, senseless tragedy that had taken them both from him in an instant. Liam had been at the fire academy, training to follow in his father's footsteps and become a firefighter. He remembered the moment he got the call, the way his heart had stopped and his blood had run cold.

"Fuck," he whispered, gripping the edge of the sink as the memories threatened to overwhelm him. "I miss you guys so much."

He took a deep breath, trying to steady himself. He knew that his parents would have been proud of him, proud of the man he'd become. They had always taught him to use his powers for good, to help those in need and make a difference in the world.

And that's what he'd done. He'd become a firefighter, dedicating his life to saving others and protecting his community. It hadn't been easy, being a mutant in a profession that often feared and misunderstood them. He'd had to work twice as hard, prove himself twice as capable, just to earn the respect of his colleagues.

But he'd done it. He'd become one of the best damn firefighters in the city, earning a reputation for bravery and selflessness that few could match. And he knew that his parents would have been proud of him for that, too.

As he finished getting ready for the day, Liam couldn't shake the feeling of unease that had settled in the pit of his stomach. The confrontations with The Arcana, the secrets that seemed to be lurking around every corner… it all felt like pieces of a puzzle that he couldn't quite put together.

He knew that he needed to keep digging, to find out the truth behind the mutant disappearances and the mysterious vigilante who seemed to be at the center of it all. But he also knew that he couldn't do it alone.

With a sigh, he grabbed his phone and scrolled through his contacts until he found the one he was looking for. He hesitated for a moment, his thumb hovering over the call button.

But then, a sudden realization hit him like a ton of bricks. He needed a break, a chance to step back from the chaos and confusion of his life and reconnect with his roots. With a determined nod, he put his phone back in his pocket and headed for the door.

"Sorry, Jack," he muttered under his breath. "But this is something I need to do on my own."

He made his way to the fire station, his mind already racing with the possibilities of what the day might bring. As he walked through the doors, he was greeted by the usual hustle and bustle of the morning shift.

"Hey, Quinn!" a voice called out from across the room. "You're looking chipper this morning. What's the occasion?"

Liam grinned, shaking his head as he made his way over to his locker. "No occasion, Martinez. Just taking a little personal time today. Gotta recharge the old batteries, you know?"

Martinez raised an eyebrow, a knowing smirk on his face. "Personal time, huh? Does that have anything to do with a certain vigilante who's been making headlines lately?"

Liam rolled his eyes, trying to ignore the way his heart skipped a beat at the mention of The Arcana. "Don't know what you're talking about, man. I just need a day to myself, that's all."

He quickly changed out of his uniform and into a pair of jeans and a t-shirt, feeling a sense of relief wash over him as he shed the weight of his responsibilities. With a final wave to his colleagues, he headed out the door and into the bright morning sun.

As he walked through the city streets, Liam couldn't help but feel a sense of excitement building in his chest. It had been too long since he'd taken a day for himself, since he'd had a chance to reconnect with the people and places that mattered most to him.

And there was one person in particular that he knew he needed to see.

His brother, Dylan, lived on the other side of the city, in a small apartment that he shared with his girlfriend. Liam and Dylan had always had a complicated relationship, their bond strained by the differences in their abilities and their outlooks on life.

Dylan was not a mutant, and he had always struggled to understand and accept Liam's powers. He couldn't wrap his head around why Liam felt such a strong need to use his abilities to help others, to fight for the mutant cause.

And if Liam was being honest with himself, he knew that he hadn't always made it easy for Dylan to understand. He had been so focused on his own struggles, on the weight of his responsibilities, that he had often neglected the one person who had always been there for him.

But today, he was determined to change that.

As he made his way through the city, Liam couldn't help but think about all the memories he and Dylan had shared over the years. The summers spent playing in the park, the late-night movie marathons, the heart-to-heart talks that had helped them both through some of their darkest moments.

Despite their differences, Dylan had always been there for him. And Liam knew that he needed to be there for his brother now more than ever.

When he finally arrived at Dylan's apartment, Liam felt a sense of nervousness wash over him. It had been months since he'd last seen his brother, and he wasn't sure what kind of reception he would get.

But as soon as Dylan opened the door, all of Liam's fears melted away. His brother's face broke into a wide grin, his eyes lighting up with surprise and joy.

"Liam!" he exclaimed, pulling him into a tight hug. "What the hell are you doing here, man? I thought you were too busy saving the world to come visit your lowly civilian brother."

Liam laughed, feeling a sense of warmth and comfort wash over him as he hugged his brother back. "What can I say? Even superheroes need a day off every now and then."

They made their way into the apartment, the smell of coffee and toast filling the air. Dylan's girlfriend, Sarah, greeted Liam with a warm smile and a quick hug before heading off to work, leaving the two brothers alone to catch up.

As they sat at the kitchen table, sipping their coffee and munching on slightly burnt toast, Liam felt a sense of nostalgia wash over him. It reminded him of the mornings they had spent together as kids, giggling over cartoons and fighting over the last piece of bacon.

But as much as he wanted to bask in the memories of the past, Liam knew that he needed to address the tension that had been building between them for years.

"Listen, Dylan," he said, his voice serious. "I know that things haven't always been easy between us. I know that my powers, my work with the mutant community… it's a lot to take in."

Dylan sighed, his eyes flickering with a mix of emotions. "It's not just that, Liam. It's the fact that you're always putting yourself in danger, always taking on these crazy risks. I worry about you, man. I don't want to lose you like we lost Mom and Dad."

Liam felt a lump form in his throat, his heart clenching at the mention of their parents. He reached out and placed a hand on his brother's arm, his voice gentle.

"I know, Dylan. And I'm sorry for not being there for you like I should have been. But you have to understand… this is who I am. This is what I was meant to do."

He took a deep breath, trying to find the right words to explain the fire that burned within him, the unshakable sense of purpose that drove him forward.

"When I use my powers to help people, to save lives… it's like I'm honoring Mom and Dad's memory. It's like I'm doing something that matters, something that makes a difference in the world."

Dylan was quiet for a moment, his eyes searching Liam's face. Then, slowly, he nodded, a small smile tugging at the corner of his mouth.

"I get it, Liam. I really do. And I'm proud of you, even if I don't always show it. I just… I just want you to be safe, you know? I want you to be happy."

Liam grinned, feeling a sense of relief wash over him. "I am happy, Dylan. I mean, sure, things are a little crazy right now, what with the mutant disappearances and the whole Arcana situation. But I'm doing what I love, and I'm making a difference. That's all I've ever wanted."

Dylan leaned back in his chair, a thoughtful expression on his face. "You know, Liam, I think I'm starting to get it. I mean, I've always known that you were a hero, but hearing you talk about it like this… it's like I'm seeing a whole new side of you."

Liam felt a warmth spreading through his chest, a sense of gratitude and love for his brother that he hadn't felt in a long time. "Thanks, man. That means a lot, coming from you."

Dylan shook his head, a rueful smile tugging at the corner of his mouth. "I just wish I'd been more supportive over the years, you know? I mean, here you are, putting your life on the line every day to help people, and what have I been doing? Bitching and moaning about how hard it is to be a normal human in a world full of mutants."

Liam reached out and placed a hand on his brother's arm, his voice gentle. "Hey, don't be so hard on yourself, Dylan. We've both made mistakes, both said and done things we regret. But the important thing is that we're here now, together. And I promise, from now on, I'm going to be more open with you about what's going on in my life. No more secrets, no more holding back."

Dylan grinned, his eyes crinkling at the corners. "I'm gonna hold you to that, little brother. And who knows, maybe one of these days I'll even tag along on one of your crazy vigilante adventures. I may not have any powers, but I've been known to throw a mean right hook when the situation calls for it."

Liam laughed, feeling a sense of joy and lightness that he hadn't experienced in longer than he could remember. "I don't doubt it,

Dylan. But let's maybe start with a few more family dinners and movie nights before we jump straight into the crime-fighting, yeah?"

As they continued to talk and laugh, the conversation eventually turned to their parents, and the legacy they had left behind. Liam felt a bittersweet pang in his heart as he remembered the love and guidance his mom and dad had provided, the way they had always encouraged him to be true to himself and stand up for what he believed in.

"Do you remember the time Dad caught us sneaking out of the house in the middle of the night to go to that underground mutant rave?" Liam asked, a mischievous grin spreading across his face.

Dylan groaned, burying his face in his hands. "Oh god, don't remind me. I thought for sure he was going to ground us for life. But instead, he just sat us down and gave us this long, serious talk about being responsible and staying safe."

Liam chuckled, shaking his head. "Yeah, and then he made us promise to call him if we needed a ride home, no questions asked. I think that was the moment I realized just how lucky we were to have parents who loved and supported us unconditionally, even when we fucked up."

Dylan nodded, his eyes shining with unshed tears. "They would be so proud of you, Liam. Of both of us, really. I know we've had our struggles and our differences, but at the end of the day, we're still family. And that's what matters most."

Liam reached out and pulled his brother into a tight hug, feeling a sense of peace and contentment wash over him. "You're damn right, Dylan. And I promise, from now on, I'm going to do a better job of showing you just how much you mean to me. No more letting work or the mutant cause come between us."

They held each other for a long moment, the years of tension and misunderstanding melting away in the warmth of their embrace. When they finally pulled apart, Liam could see a new sense of determination and purpose in his brother's eyes.

"I'm gonna hold you to that, Liam. And I promise, I'm going to be there for you too, no matter what. Whether you need someone to talk to, or just a place to crash after a long night of fighting crime, I've got your back."

Liam grinned, feeling a surge of affection and gratitude for his brother. "Thanks, man. That means more to me than you know."

They spent the rest of the afternoon reminiscing and catching up, the conversation flowing easily between them in a way it hadn't in years. By the time the sun began to set and Liam reluctantly acknowledged that it was time for him to head home, he felt like a weight had been lifted from his shoulders.

He hugged his brother one last time, savoring the feeling of connection and understanding that had blossomed between them. "I love you, Dylan. And I promise, we'll do this again soon. No more letting life get in the way of what really matters."

Dylan nodded, a soft smile on his face. "I love you too, Liam. Now go out there and save the world, you crazy bastard. And don't forget to call me if you need anything, okay?"

Liam chuckled, giving his brother a playful salute. "Aye aye, captain. And the same goes for you, you know. If you ever need a dashing mutant firefighter to come to your rescue, you know who to call."

With a final wave and a grin, Liam headed out into the evening air, feeling more grounded and connected to his roots than he had in longer than he could remember. He took a deep breath, savoring the cool breeze on his face and the sense of purpose that thrummed through his veins.

9

The Scientist

Ethan

Ethan leaned against the wall of the abandoned warehouse, his heart pounding with a heady mix of anticipation and adrenaline. He couldn't help but feel a thrill of excitement at the thought of seeing Liam again, of working together to unravel the mystery of the mutant disappearances.

But he also knew that the stakes were higher than ever, that the information they uncovered could blow the lid off the entire conspiracy. And as much as he hated to admit it, he needed Liam's help to see this through.

The sound of footsteps echoing off the concrete walls jolted Ethan out of his thoughts, and he looked up to see Liam striding towards him, his expression grim and determined.

"Alright, Arcana," Liam said, his voice low and urgent. "What's so important that you had to drag me out here in the middle of the night?"

Ethan grinned, pushing himself off the wall and sauntering towards the firefighter with a cocky swagger. "Oh, you know me, Quinn. I just couldn't resist the chance to see your pretty face again."

Liam rolled his eyes, but Ethan could see the hint of a smile tugging at the corner of his mouth. "Cut the crap. What's going on?"

Ethan sobered, his expression turning serious. "I've got a new lead on the disappearances."

He reached into his pocket and pulled out a crumpled piece of paper, handing it to Liam with a flourish. "Take a look at this. It's a list of names, all mutants who have gone missing in the last few months. And guess what they all have in common?"

Liam scanned the list, his brow furrowing in concentration. "They were all patients at Genexis."

Ethan grinned, his eyes sparkling with excitement. "Yes. My team and I did some digging, and it turns out that Genexis has been conducting secret experiments on mutants, trying to unlock the secrets of their powers. And guess who's leading the charge?"

He tapped the paper, his finger landing on a name at the bottom of the list. "Dr. Elise Novak. She's a top researcher at Genexis, and she's scheduled to present her latest findings at a scientific conference and coincidentally it is tomorrow. I think that's our best chance to get some answers."

Liam frowned, his expression skeptical. "You want us to crash a scientific conference? Are you out of your mind?"

Ethan laughed, the sound rich and warm in the cramped confines of the warehouse. "Oh, come on, Quinn. Where's your sense of adventure? Besides, we won't be crashing anything. We'll be attending as interested investors, eager to learn more about the exciting world of mutant biotechnology." He waggled his eyebrows, his grin turning suggestive. "And who knows, maybe we'll even get to share a hotel room. You know, for the sake of our cover."

Liam groaned, burying his face in his hands. "You're impossible, you know that? This is serious. We're talking about people's lives here."

Ethan sobered, his expression turning serious once more. "I know,

Quinn. And believe me, I want to find those missing mutants just as much as you do. But we have to be smart about this. We can't just go charging in guns blazing, not without more information."

Liam sighed, running a hand through his hair in frustration. "I know, I know. It's just… the thought of those innocent people being experimented on, being treated like lab rats… it makes me sick to my stomach."

Ethan reached out and placed a hand on Liam's shoulder, his touch gentle and reassuring. "And we're going to stop it, I promise. But we have to do this right, or we'll just end up putting more people in danger."

Liam nodded, his jaw clenching with determination. "Alright, I'm in. But we're going to need a plan, and a damn good one at that. Dr. Novak is sure to be heavily guarded, and we can't afford to blow our cover."

Ethan grinned, his eyes sparkling with mischief. "Oh, don't worry about that, Quinn. I've got a few tricks up my sleeve. And with the two of us working together, there's nothing we can't handle."

He leaned in closer, his breath hot against Liam's ear. "Besides, I've always had a thing for men in suits. And something tells me you clean up real nice."

Liam shivered, his heart pounding with a mix of anticipation and desire. "You…"

But Ethan was already pulling away, his expression turning serious once more. "We'll need to do some recon first, scope out the conference center and see what we're up against. And we'll need to come up with some solid cover identities, something that will hold up under scrutiny."

Liam nodded, his mind already racing with possibilities. "I can talk to some of my contacts in the industry, see if I can dig up any dirt on Genexis or Dr. Novak. And maybe we can use your tech skills to create some fake credentials, something that will get us past security."

Ethan grinned, his eyes sparkling with excitement. "I like the way you think, Quinn. This is going to be one hell of a ride."

They spent the next few hours planning and strategizing, their heads bent together over a makeshift desk covered in papers and blueprints. And despite the seriousness of the situation, Ethan couldn't help but feel a thrill of excitement at the thought of working side by side with Liam, of taking on the world together.

Because as much as he hated to admit it, there was something about the firefighter that got under his skin in all the right ways, that made him want to be a better man, a better hero.

And as they finally parted ways in the early hours of the morning, Ethan couldn't shake the feeling that this was just the beginning of something big, something that would change both of their lives forever.

* * *

As they prepared for the conference, Ethan couldn't help but feel a sense of excitement buzzing beneath his skin. This was the kind of mission he lived for - high stakes, deep cover, and the chance to unravel a mystery that could change the world.

He checked his reflection in the mirror, adjusting his tie and smoothing back his hair with a cocky grin. Damn, he looked good. The sharp cut of his suit accentuated his lean, muscular frame, and the deep green of his eyes seemed to glitter with mischief and promise.

"Zoe, Marcus, tell me you've got something for me," he said, tapping his earpiece as he strode out of his apartment and into the waiting car.

Zoe's voice crackled over the comm, her tone playful and teasing. "I've hacked into the conference center's security system and I'll have eyes on you the whole time. Just try not to do anything too stupid, okay?"

Ethan chuckled, shaking his head as he slid into the driver's seat. "No promises, Zo. You know how I love a good challenge."

"Just be careful, Ethan," Marcus chimed in, his voice gruff and serious. "Dr. Novak is a big fish, and she's sure to have some serious security. Don't let your guard down for a second."

"I need to talk to you guys about something." Ethan said hesitantly. He knew what he was about to do was a big deal so he wanted the input of his friends and trusted companions.

"What's up, boss?" Zoe's voice crackled over the comm, her tone curious.

Ethan took a deep breath, steeling himself for what he was about to say. "I'm going to tell Liam who I am. Who I really am."

There was a moment of stunned silence, then Marcus's voice cut in, sharp and concerned. "Ethan, are you sure about this? You've always kept your identity a secret, even from us. Why reveal it now?"

Ethan sighed, running a hand through his hair. "Because if Liam and I are going to work together, really work together, he needs to know the truth. He needs to trust me completely, and I need to trust him."

He could practically hear Zoe's grin over the comm. "Aww, boss, that's so sweet. You're catching feelings for the hunky firefighter, aren't you?"

Ethan rolled his eyes, but he couldn't quite suppress the smile tugging at his lips. "Shut up, Zo. This is serious."

"We know, Ethan," Marcus said, his voice softening. "And we trust your judgment. If you think this is the right move, then we've got your back. Always."

Ethan felt a surge of affection for his team, a warmth that spread through his chest like a physical thing. "Thanks, guys. I don't know what I'd do without you."

The doorbell rang, and he felt his heart skip a beat.

It was time.

He slipped on his mask, the familiar weight of it settling over his features like a second skin. Then, with a final deep breath, he opened the door.

Liam stood on the other side, his eyebrows raising in surprise as he took in Ethan's appearance. "You look… adequate." Liam said.

Ethan faked being hurt. "Adequate, you hurt my ego." Ethan laughed and sobered before he stepped aside, motioning for Liam to come inside. "There's something I need to show you," he said, his voice steady. "Something important."

Liam's brow furrowed, but he stepped over the threshold, his eyes widening as he took in the opulent surroundings of Ethan's penthouse.

Ethan took a deep breath, then reached up and removed his mask.

Liam's jaw dropped, his eyes widening in shock. "Ethan Hawke?" he said, his voice barely above a whisper. "You're… you're the Arcana?"

Ethan nodded, his expression serious. "I am," he said, his voice firm. "And before you say anything, I want you to know that I didn't keep this from you to deceive you. We didn't know each other on a personal level before, and I had my reasons for keeping my identity a secret."

Liam shook his head, his expression still stunned. "I can't believe it," he said, his voice filled with awe. "Ethan Hawke, the billionaire philanthropist, is secretly a vigilante fighting for mutant rights. It's like something out of a comic book."

Ethan allowed himself a small smile, feeling a flicker of pride. "I know it's a lot to take in," he said, his voice gentle. "But I needed you to know the truth, Liam. If we're going to work together to uncover the truth behind the disappearances, we need to trust each other completely."

Liam was silent for a long moment, his eyes searching Ethan's face.

Then, slowly, he nodded, his expression resolute.

"Alright, Hawke," he said, his voice steady. "I'll admit, I'm still processing all of this. But I understand why you kept your identity a secret, and I respect your principles. If you say we need to trust each other to get the job done, then I'm in."

Ethan felt a surge of relief, a warmth spreading through his chest. "Thank you, Liam," he said, his voice sincere. "I know this isn't easy, but I promise you, I won't let you down. We're going to get to the bottom of this, no matter what it takes."

Liam grinned, his eyes sparkling with determination. "Damn straight, we are. Genexis won't know what hit them."

Ethan couldn't help but smirk, feeling a thrill of excitement at the thought of taking on the shadowy corporation. With Liam by his side and his team at his back, he felt invincible, like he could take on the world and win.

Speaking of his team…

"Zoe, Marcus," he said, tapping his earpiece. "You there?"

"Always, boss," Zoe's voice crackled over the comm, her tone playful. "Just waiting for you to stop flirting with the hunky firefighter and get down to business."

Ethan rolled his eyes, ignoring the way Liam's eyebrows shot up in amusement. "I don't flirt, Zo. I seduce. There's a difference."

Marcus's gruff chuckle echoed over the line. "Whatever you say, Casanova. Now, what's the plan? How are we going to infiltrate this conference and get close to Dr. Novak?"

Ethan grinned, his mind already racing with possibilities. "We'll pose as investors," he said, his tone confident. "Rich, eccentric types with more money than sense, looking to get in on the ground floor of the next big thing in mutant research."

Liam frowned, his expression skeptical. "You really think they'll buy that? These are some of the smartest people in the world we're talking about here."

Ethan shrugged, his smirk widening. "You'd be surprised what people will believe when you flash a little cash and a lot of charm. Besides, with my powers, we'll have an edge they won't see coming."

He summoned a tarot card with a flick of his wrist, the ethereal image of The Magician hovering in the air before him. "Illusion, persuasion, misdirection… all tools of the trade for a master of the arcane arts."

Liam snorted, shaking his head. "More like tools of the trade for a master bullshit artist."

Ethan clutched his chest in mock offense. "You wound me, Liam. And here I thought we were partners, united in our noble quest for truth and justice."

"Partners, yes," Liam said, his tone dry. "But that doesn't mean I have to like your methods. Or your ego."

Ethan grinned, feeling a flicker of heat in his belly at the challenge in Liam's eyes. "Careful, Quinn. Keep talking like that and I might start to think you're flirting with me."

Liam's cheeks flushed, but he held Ethan's gaze, his own smirk tugging at the corner of his mouth. "In your dreams, Hawke. Now, are we doing this or what?"

Ethan nodded, his expression turning serious. "We're doing this. Zoe, Marcus, I want you to run background checks on everyone attending the conference. If there's even a hint of a connection to Genexis or the disappearances, I want to know about it."

"On it, boss," Zoe said, the sound of rapid typing echoing over the comm. "We'll have dossiers on every attendee by the time you walk through those doors."

"Good," Ethan said, feeling a surge of pride in his team. "Then let's get to work."

* * *

The conference center was a buzzing hive of activity, the air thick with the hum of conversation and the clink of champagne glasses. Ethan and Liam moved through the crowd with purposeful strides, their sharp suits and confident demeanors blending seamlessly with the sea of wealthy investors and cutting-edge researchers.

As they mingled and schmoozed, Ethan kept one ear on the conversations around them, his mind whirring with the implications of what he was hearing. Dr. Novak's research was the talk of the conference, her groundbreaking discoveries on the genetic basis of mutant abilities sparking both excitement and trepidation among the attendees.

"I heard she's found a way to isolate the M-gene," one man whispered to his companion, his eyes wide with awe. "If that's true, it could change everything. Imagine being able to turn mutant powers on and off at will."

"Or weaponize them," the other man murmured, his expression grim. "In the wrong hands, that kind of knowledge could be catastrophic."

Ethan exchanged a glance with Liam, seeing his own concerns mirrored in the firefighter's eyes. If Genexis really had found a way to control mutant abilities, the implications were staggering. And terrifying.

Just then, a hush fell over the room, the conversations dying away as all eyes turned to the stage. Dr. Elise Novak had arrived, her presence commanding and magnetic as she took her place behind the podium.

"Good evening, everyone," she said, her voice clear and confident. "Thank you for joining me tonight to discuss the exciting developments in mutant genetic research. I believe that we are on the cusp of a new era, one in which the secrets of the M-gene will be unlocked and the full potential of mutant abilities will be realized."

As she spoke, Ethan found himself drawn in by her passion and intelligence, her evident dedication to her work. But he also couldn't shake the feeling that there was something more going on beneath the surface, a hidden agenda that she was carefully concealing behind her polished facade.

He glanced at Liam, seeing the same suspicion and unease in the firefighter's eyes. They needed to get closer, to find out what Dr. Novak was really up to.

As the presentation drew to a close and the floor opened up for questions, Ethan seized his chance. He raised his hand, feeling the weight of Dr. Novak's gaze settle on him as she called on him to speak.

"Dr. Novak," he said, his voice smooth and confident. "Your research is truly groundbreaking. But I can't help but wonder about the potential risks involved. How can you ensure the safety and well-being of your mutant test subjects?"

Dr. Novak's smile was polished and practiced, her answer equally so. "I assure you, we take the utmost precautions to ensure the safety and comfort of our volunteers. Every experiment is carefully monitored and controlled, and all participants are fully informed of the risks and benefits before consenting to take part."

Ethan nodded, his expression skeptical. "And what about the long-term effects? Have you considered the possibility that your research could be used to exploit or manipulate mutants, rather than help them?"

Dr. Novak's eyes flashed with something like annoyance, but her smile never wavered. "Of course, we have considered those risks. But I firmly believe that the benefits of this research far outweigh the potential drawbacks. Imagine a world where mutants can fully control and harness their abilities, where they are no longer feared or marginalized but celebrated for their unique gifts."

Ethan opened his mouth to respond, but Liam beat him to it. "And what about consent?" he asked, his voice hard. "How can you be sure that your volunteers are truly informed and willing, and not just desperate for the money or the promise of a cure?"

Dr. Novak's smile turned brittle, her eyes narrowing. "I assure you, Mr...?"

"Roy," Liam said, his jaw clenched. "Gary Roy."

"Mr. Roy," Dr. Novak continued, her tone icy. "I assure you that we take consent and autonomy very seriously at Genexis. Every one of our volunteers is carefully screened and counseled before being accepted into the program, and they are free to leave at any time if they feel uncomfortable or unsure."

Ethan could feel the tension crackling between Liam and Dr. Novak, the air thick with unspoken accusations and barely-contained hostility. He knew they were treading on dangerous ground, that they needed to be careful not to tip their hand too soon.

But he also knew that they couldn't back down, not when the stakes were this high. The lives of countless mutants hung in the balance, and they were the only ones who could uncover the truth and bring Genexis to justice.

As the Q&A session drew to a close and the attendees began to disperse, Ethan caught Liam's eye, a silent message passing between them. They needed to regroup, to compare notes and plan their next move.

But before they could slip away, Ethan felt a sudden surge of inspiration. He summoned The Magician card, feeling its power thrumming through his veins like an electric current.

"Follow my lead," he murmured to Liam, a mischievous grin tugging at his lips. "And try not to look too impressed, won't you? I'd hate for you to stroke my ego any more than necessary."

Liam snorted, rolling his eyes. "Trust me, Hawke, your ego doesn't need any more stroking. It's already the size of a small planet."

Ethan just smirked, reveling in the way Liam's barbs always seemed to have an undercurrent of reluctant admiration. He knew the firefighter was just as drawn to his confidence and charm as he was infuriated by it.

With a flick of his wrist, Ethan sent The Magician's power out into the room, a subtle wave of influence and persuasion that had Dr. Novak turning towards them, her expression curious.

"Dr. Novak," Ethan said, his voice smooth as silk. "We were wondering if we might have a moment of your time. My associate and I are very interested in your work, and we'd love the opportunity to discuss some potential investment opportunities."

Dr. Novak's eyes widened, a flicker of surprise passing over her face before she schooled her features into a polite smile. "Of course, Mr. Hawke. I would be happy to discuss my research with you further. Perhaps we could continue this conversation in my lab? I can give you a more in-depth look at our facilities and the projects we have underway."

Ethan exchanged a glance with Liam, seeing the same flicker of excitement and trepidation in the firefighter's eyes. This was it, their chance to get close to Dr. Novak and uncover the truth behind Genexis and the missing mutants.

"That would be wonderful," Ethan said, his smile all charm and confidence. "Lead the way, Dr. Novak."

As they followed Dr. Novak out of the conference center and towards the Genexis lab, Ethan could feel Liam's tension radiating off him in waves. He knew the firefighter was on edge, his instincts screaming at him that something wasn't right.

"Relax, Quinn," Ethan murmured, his voice low and teasing. "You're wound tighter than a spring. If you don't loosen up, you're going to pull something."

Liam shot him a glare, his jaw clenched. "This isn't a game, Hawke. We're walking into the lion's den here. We need to be on our guard."

Ethan sighed, his expression turning serious. "I know that, Liam. But we can't let Dr. Novak see us sweat. We have to play this cool, keep her talking until we can figure out what the hell is going on."

Liam nodded, his posture relaxing slightly. "You're right. I just… I don't trust her, Ethan. There's something off about this whole situation."

Ethan reached out, his hand brushing against Liam's in a fleeting moment of reassurance. "I know. But we've got this, Liam. Together, we can handle anything."

Before Liam could respond, they arrived at the Genexis lab, a sleek, state-of-the-art facility that buzzed with activity. Dr. Novak led them inside, her heels clicking against the polished floors as she gave them a tour of the various labs and research areas.

As they walked and talked, Ethan kept a careful eye on Dr. Novak, looking for any signs of deception or malice. But the woman was a master at hiding her true intentions, her smile never faltering as she explained the intricacies of her work.

"As you can see, we are making great strides in unlocking the secrets of the M-gene," she said, gesturing to a bank of computer screens displaying complex genetic sequences. "With the right funding and support, I believe we could make significant breakthroughs in the treatment and understanding of mutant abilities."

Ethan nodded, his expression thoughtful. "And what about the rumors of mutant disappearances? Have you heard anything about that, Dr. Novak?"

For a moment, Dr. Novak's smile flickered, a hint of unease passing over her face. But then she shook her head, her expression smoothing back into one of polite concern.

"I have heard the rumors, yes. And I can assure you, Genexis is doing everything in its power to investigate and put a stop to any unethical practices."

Liam frowned, his eyes narrowing. "But how can you be sure that someone within your own organization isn't responsible? With the kind of research you're doing here, it would be all too easy for someone to take advantage of vulnerable mutants."

Dr. Novak sighed, her expression turning grave. "You're right, Mr. Roy. And that is why I have been conducting my own investigation into the matter. I have reason to believe that someone within Genexis is indeed using my research for nefarious purposes, experimenting on mutants without their knowledge or consent."

Ethan and Liam exchanged a glance, their pulses quickening with a mix of excitement and dread. This was it, the confirmation they had been looking for. But the implications were staggering, the potential for abuse and exploitation too horrifying to contemplate.

"Dr. Novak," Ethan said, his voice low and urgent. "If what you're saying is true, then we need to act fast. We need to find out who is behind this and put a stop to it before any more innocent lives are lost."

Dr. Novak nodded, her expression determined. "I agree, Mr. Hawke. And that is why I am asking for your help. With your resources and connections, I believe we can uncover the truth and bring those responsible to justice."

Liam frowned, his eyes flicking to Ethan's in a silent question. Could they trust Dr. Novak? Was she truly an ally, or just another piece in a much larger and more sinister puzzle?

But Ethan knew they had no choice. They needed Dr. Novak's knowledge and access if they were going to get to the bottom of this. And so, with a deep breath and a nod of agreement, he extended his hand to the doctor, sealing their partnership with a firm shake.

As they left the Genexis lab and made their way back to Ethan's penthouse, he could feel the weight of their new alliance settling heavy on his shoulders. He summoned The High Priestess card, feeling its energy swirling around him like a cool mist, offering clarity and insight in the face of uncertainty.

"Zoe, Marcus, what do you guys have?," he said, tapping his earpiece as he poured himself a drink from the bar.

"We've been digging into Dr. Novak's background," Zoe's voice crackled over the comm, "and so far, everything seems to check out. She's got a stellar reputation in the scientific community, and there's no indication that she's been involved in anything shady."

Liam frowned, his brow furrowed with doubt. "That doesn't mean she's innocent, though. She could be really good at covering her tracks."

Ethan sighed, running a hand through his hair. "Or she could be telling the truth. Maybe she really is trying to do the right thing, and someone else at Genexis is using her research for their own fucked up purposes."

Marcus's gruff voice cut in, his tone skeptical. "Or maybe she's playing us, trying to gain our trust so she can stab us in the back later."

Ethan felt a flicker of irritation at the suggestion, but he couldn't deny that it was a possibility. He'd been burned before, had trusted the wrong people and paid the price. He couldn't afford to make that mistake again, not when the stakes were this high.

"We need more information," he said, his voice firm. "Zoe, keep digging. See if you can find anything that might point to Dr. Novak's involvement in the disappearances or the experiments. Marcus, I want you to put out feelers to your contacts in the mutant community. See if anyone's heard anything about Genexis or Dr. Novak that might give us a lead."

"On it, boss," Zoe said, the sound of rapid typing echoing over the comm.

"I'll do what I can," Marcus said, his tone grudging. "But I'm telling you, Ethan, this whole thing stinks. I don't trust that doctor as far as I can throw her."

Ethan bit back a retort, knowing that arguing with Marcus would only make things worse. Instead, he turned to Liam, his expression serious.

"What do you think, Quinn? You've been awfully quiet over there."

Liam sighed, his eyes conflicted. "I don't know, Ethan. I want to believe that Dr. Novak is on our side, but I can't shake the feeling that something's off. It's like my gut is telling me not to trust her, but my head is saying we need her help."

Ethan nodded, feeling a pang of sympathy for the firefighter. He knew how hard it was to reconcile instinct with logic, to make a decision when the stakes were this high and the lines between right and wrong were so blurred.

"I get it, Liam. Believe me, I do. But we can't let our doubts paralyze us. We have to keep moving forward, keep digging until we find the truth. And right now, Dr. Novak is our best shot at doing that."

Liam's jaw clenched, his eyes flashing with frustration. "And what if she's playing us, Ethan? What if we're walking into a trap and we don't even know it?"

Ethan stepped forward, his hand coming up to rest on Liam's shoulder. He could feel the tension thrumming through the firefighter's body, the barely-contained anger and fear that threatened to boil over at any moment.

"Then we'll deal with it," he said, his voice low and intense. "We'll fight our way out, just like we always do. But we can't let our fear control us, Liam. We have to take the risk, or we'll never find out what's really going on."

For a long moment, Liam just stared at him, his eyes searching Ethan's face for some sign of deception or doubt. But Ethan held his gaze, his own expression open and honest, willing Liam to trust him, to believe in him.

Finally, Liam nodded, his shoulders slumping with resignation. "Alright, Hawke. We'll do it your way. But if this goes sideways, I'm holding you personally responsible."

Ethan grinned, the tension breaking like a spell. "Wouldn't have it any other way, Quinn. Now, let's get to work. We've got a conspiracy to unravel and some missing mutants to save."

10

Blurred Lines and Burning Desires

Liam

Liam had found himself starting to question his initial judgment. Ethan was brilliant, there was no denying that - a master strategist with a mind like a steel trap and a knack for seeing connections that others missed. And for all his bravado and recklessness, there was a deep sense of compassion and justice that drove him, a fierce determination to make the world a better place.

And then there was the other thing, the thing that Liam had been trying so hard to ignore. The attraction, the pull he felt towards Ethan that went beyond mere physical desire. It was like a force of nature, a gravitational pull that drew him in even as he tried to resist it.

He thought back to all the moments of tension and flirtation between them, the way Ethan's eyes would linger on his just a little too long, the way his heart would race and his skin would tingle whenever they were close. Liam had tried to brush it off as nothing, just a byproduct of the adrenaline and the high stakes of their mission. But deep down, he knew it was more than that.

He stood up, pacing the length of his living room as he tried to clear his head. He needed to focus, needed to keep his eye on the prize and not get distracted by his own damn feelings. The lives of countless mutants were hanging in the balance, and he couldn't afford to let his guard down for even a second.

But even as he tried to push his feelings aside, Liam couldn't help but wonder what it would be like to give in to them. To let himself fall, to surrender to the pull of Ethan's gravity and see where it might lead. He imagined what it would feel like to kiss Ethan, to feel the heat of his skin and the pressure of his lips, to lose himself in the sensation of being touched and wanted and needed.

"No," he said out loud, his voice firm and resolute. "I can't. I won't. I have to stay focused, have to keep my head in the game. Ethan is my partner, my ally in this fight. Nothing more."

Liam knew they were a lie. Ethan was so much more than just a partner, so much more than just an ally. He was a force of nature, a whirlwind of charisma and power and raw, unbridled energy that threatened to sweep Liam away if he let it.

And damn it, how he wanted to let it.

Liam groaned as he tried to push away the images that flooded his mind. Ethan's cocky grin, the way his eyes sparkled with mischief and challenge. The heat of his skin, the pressure of his lips, the feeling of his hands roaming over Liam's body…

"Fuck," he muttered, his voice muffled by his palms. "I can't do this. I can't think about him like that, not now. Not when everything is so fucked up and complicated."

He needed to clear his head, needed to talk to someone who could help him make sense of the tangled mess of emotions that swirled inside him like a hurricane. And there was only one person he trusted enough to bare his soul to, one person who had always been there for him through thick and thin.

Jack.

Liam grabbed his phone, scrolling through his contacts until he found his best friend's name. He hit the call button, his heart pounding in his chest as he waited for Jack to pick up.

"Liam?" Jack's voice was groggy, like he'd just woken up from a nap. "What's up, man? Everything okay?"

Liam took a deep breath, trying to steady the tremor in his voice. "Not really, no. I need to talk to you, Jack. Can you meet me at O'Malley's in like, an hour?"

There was a pause, a moment of hesitation that made Liam's stomach clench with anxiety. But then Jack's voice came through again, warm and reassuring as always.

"Of course, man. I'll be there. Just hang tight, okay? Whatever it is, we'll figure it out together."

Liam felt a rush of gratitude, a warmth that spread through his chest like a balm. "Thanks, Jack. You're the best."

He hung up the phone, his mind already racing with the words he needed to say, the confession that he knew he couldn't keep bottled up inside any longer.

An hour later, Liam was sitting at the bar, a cold beer in his hand and a knot of tension in his gut. He heard the door open behind him, felt the rush of cool air that signaled Jack's arrival.

"Hey, man," Jack said, sliding onto the stool next to him with a grin. "What's the emergency? You sounded like you were about to have a fucking aneurysm on the phone."

Liam cracked a smile, but it felt strained and brittle on his face. "It's complicated," he said, his voice low and rough. "I've been working with this guy, Ethan, on something. And I've started to develop feelings for him, feelings that I know I shouldn't have."

Jack's brow furrowed, his expression turning serious. "Okay, I'm listening. What's the problem? Is he a criminal or something?"

Liam shook his head, taking a long swig of his beer before answering.

"No, nothing like that. He's a businessman, a billionaire actually. But he's also… he's not what he seems, Jack. There are things about him that I can't tell you, things that could get us both in a lot of trouble if anyone found out."

Jack's eyes widened, his mouth falling open slightly. "Damn, Liam. That's heavy. Are you sure you can trust this guy? I mean, if he's got secrets like that…"

Liam sighed, running a hand through his hair in frustration. "That's the thing, Jack. I don't know if I can trust him, not completely. But I also can't deny the connection I feel with him, the way he makes me feel alive and excited and fucking terrified all at the same time."

Jack was silent for a long moment, his expression thoughtful as he sipped his own beer. Then he leaned forward, his eyes locking with Liam's in a steady gaze.

"Liam, listen to me. I can't tell you what to do here, because honestly, I don't know the whole story. But what I can tell you is this: you have to trust your gut, man. If something feels off about this guy, if you have doubts about his intentions or his secrets… then maybe it's not worth the risk."

Liam felt a flicker of doubt, a tiny voice in the back of his mind that whispered that Jack was right. But then he thought of Ethan's smile, the way his eyes lit up when he talked about the things he was passionate about. The way he made Liam feel like he could take on the world, like anything was possible as long as they were together.

"I know you're right, Jack. I know I should be careful, that I shouldn't let my feelings cloud my judgment. But I can't help it, man. There's just something about him, something that makes me want to take that risk and see where it leads."

Jack nodded, his expression sympathetic. "I get it, Liam. Believe me, I do. But you have to remember what's at stake here. You're in the middle of something and you can't afford to let your guard down, not even for a second."

He fixed Liam with a steady gaze, his voice low and serious. "Just… be careful, okay? Take things slow, and don't let your feelings for this guy compromise what you're fighting for. You have a job to do, and people are counting on you to see it through."

Liam felt a rush of gratitude and affection for his best friend, a sense of clarity and purpose settling over him like a warm blanket. Jack was right. He couldn't let his conflicted feelings for Ethan distract him from the mission at hand, couldn't let his desire for the man cloud his judgment or put them both at risk.

But he also couldn't deny the connection that had been growing between them, the spark of something deeper and more profound than just physical attraction. And maybe, just maybe, if they could learn to trust each other and work together…

Liam drained the last of his beer, setting the bottle down on the bar with a decisive thunk. "Thanks, Jack. I needed to hear that. And I promise, I'll be careful. I won't let my feelings for Ethan get in the way of what needs to be done."

Jack grinned, clapping Liam on the shoulder with a strong hand. "I know you won't, man. You're one of the best damn firefighters I know, and an even better friend. Just remember, I've got your back, no matter what happens."

Liam smiled, feeling a sense of warmth and camaraderie wash over him. "I know you do, Jack. And I've got yours, too. Always."

They talked for a while longer, catching up on old times and swapping stories about life at the firehouse. But eventually, Jack had to head home to his wife and kids, and Liam knew he needed to get some rest before the next phase of the investigation began.

As he walked out of the bar and into the cool night air, Liam felt a sense of determination and purpose settle over him like a mantle. He still didn't know what the future held, still didn't know if he could fully trust Ethan or if their growing feelings for each other would survive the trials ahead.

But he did know one thing for sure.

He was ready to face whatever challenges lay ahead with courage, determination, and just a touch of reckless bravado.

And if Ethan Hawke wanted to come along for the ride?

Well, he'd just have to prove that he was worthy of Liam's trust, one dangerous mission at a time.

Liam chuckled to himself as he made his way back to his apartment, his mind still buzzing with the conversation he'd had with Jack. It felt good to have gotten some of his fears and doubts off his chest, to have talked through the tangled mess of emotions that Ethan stirred up inside him.

But even as he got ready for bed, brushing his teeth and changing into his pajamas, Liam couldn't shake the sense of unease that had been growing in the pit of his stomach ever since he'd learned the truth about Ethan's identity.

It wasn't that he didn't trust Ethan, exactly. He knew that the man was brilliant and resourceful, and that he had a deep commitment to justice and doing what was right. But he also knew that Ethan had a dark side, a reckless streak that sometimes led him to take unnecessary risks and put himself in danger.

And then there were Liam's own feelings to contend with, the undeniable attraction and connection that he felt towards Ethan, despite his better judgment. He knew that getting involved with a colleague, especially one as complicated and enigmatic as Ethan, was a recipe for disaster.

But try as he might, Liam couldn't seem to shake the hold that Ethan had on him. Every time they were together, whether they were arguing or flirting or working side by side, Liam felt a spark of something electric and irresistible, a pull that he couldn't seem to escape.

As he lay in bed, staring up at the ceiling and trying to quiet his racing thoughts, Liam couldn't help but wonder what the future held for him and Ethan.

Liam sighed, rolling over and burying his face in his pillow. He knew that there were no easy answers, no clear path forward. But he also knew that he wasn't going to give up, not on the investigation and not on Ethan.

Because despite everything, despite the risks and the uncertainties and the constant push and pull of their personalities, Liam knew that there was something special about Ethan Hawke. Something that made him want to fight for what they had, to see where this crazy, dangerous, exhilarating ride might take them.

11

Shadows and Secrets

Ethan

He took a long sip of coffee, letting the bitter liquid scald his tongue and jolt him into full wakefulness.

A few hours later, Ethan was pacing the floor of his penthouse, his mind whirring with the details of the new information he'd uncovered. Zoe and Marcus were already there, hunched over their laptops and murmuring to each other in low, urgent tones.

"Boss, this is some seriously shady shit," Zoe said, her eyes never leaving her screen. "I've been tracking the money trail, and it's like a fucking labyrinth. Shell companies, offshore accounts, encrypted transactions… whoever's behind this knows how to cover their tracks."

Marcus nodded, his expression grim. "And my contacts in the mutant community are reporting more disappearances every day. It's like they're being picked off one by one, and no one knows who's behind it or why."

Ethan felt a surge of anger and determination, his fists clenching at his sides. "That's what we're going to find out," he said, his voice low and intense. "And when we do, there's going to be hell to pay."

Just then, the doorbell rang, and Ethan felt his heart skip a beat. He knew who it was without even looking, could feel the electric charge of Liam's presence even through the thick steel of the door.

"I'll get it," he said, trying to keep his voice casual as he strode across the room. "Zoe, Marcus, try not to scare him off, okay? We need him on our side."

Zoe smirked, her eyes twinkling with mischief. "No promises, boss. You know how much I love to play with the new kids."

Ethan rolled his eyes, but he couldn't quite suppress the grin that tugged at the corner of his mouth. Zoe and Marcus were more than just his team, they were his family. And as much as they might tease him about his growing feelings for Liam, he knew that they had his back no matter what.

He opened the door, his breath catching in his throat as he took in the sight of Liam standing there, his expression a mix of anticipation and apprehension. The firefighter was dressed in his usual off-duty attire of jeans and a t-shirt, but Ethan couldn't help but notice the way the fabric clung to his muscular frame, the way his blue eyes seemed to sparkle with a hint of something dangerous and alluring.

"Quinn," he said, his voice a little rougher than he'd intended. "Glad you could make it."

Liam nodded, his jaw clenching slightly as he stepped inside. "Wouldn't miss it for the world, Hawke."

Ethan grinned, the tension between them crackling like electricity. "All in good time, Quinn. First, there's some people I want you to meet."

He led Liam into the living room, where Zoe and Marcus were waiting, their expressions curious and slightly wary. Ethan could feel the tension in the room, the slight hesitation as his two worlds collided for the first time.

"Liam, this is Zoe and Marcus," he said, gesturing to his team.

"They've been helping me track down leads on the Genexis case, and they're the best damn hackers and informants in the business."

Zoe grinned, her eyes raking over Liam's form with a hint of appreciation. "So, you're the famous Liam Quinn," she said, her voice teasing. "I've heard a lot about you, handsome. Mostly from Ethan, who can't seem to shut up about your dreamy eyes and your heroic deeds."

Ethan felt his cheeks flush, and he shot Zoe a warning glare. "Ignore her," he said to Liam, his voice tight. "She's just trying to get a rise out of me."

But Liam didn't seem to be listening. His eyes were locked on Zoe and Marcus, his expression a mix of curiosity and something else, something that Ethan couldn't quite put his finger on.

"Nice to meet you both," Liam said, his voice cool and polite. "I've heard a lot about you too, mostly from the police reports and criminal databases."

Marcus raised an eyebrow, his expression amused. "Well, we all have our hobbies," he said, his voice dry. "Some people collect stamps, others hack into government servers for fun. To each their own, right?"

Ethan could feel the tension in the room growing, the unspoken rivalry between Liam and his team simmering just beneath the surface. He knew that he needed to get the meeting back on track, needed to focus on the task at hand before things got out of hand.

"Alright, enough with the pleasantries," he said, his voice firm. "We've got work to do. Zoe, Marcus, why don't you fill Liam in on what we've found so far?"

Zoe nodded, her expression turning serious as she pulled up a series of files on her laptop. "So, here's the deal," she said, her voice low and urgent. "We've been tracking the money trail behind Genexis and Dr. Novak's research, and it's a fucking mess. There's shell companies, offshore accounts, encrypted transactions… it's like they're trying to hide something big."

Marcus chimed in, his expression grim. "And my contacts in the mutant community are reporting more disappearances every day. It's like they're being targeted, picked off one by one for some kind of twisted experiment."

Liam's eyes widened, his expression a mix of horror and anger. "Jesus," he muttered, his voice rough. "We have to stop this."

Ethan nodded, his heart swelling with pride and admiration for the man beside him. Liam might be stubborn and infuriating at times, but he was also brave and compassionate, a true hero in every sense of the word.

"That's the plan, Quinn," he said, his voice low and intense. "But we need to be smart about this. We need to gather more evidence."

He turned to Zoe and Marcus, his expression determined. "Keep digging," he said, his voice firm. "Follow the money, track down every lead, no matter how small. We're going to crack this thing wide open, and we're going to make sure that the people responsible pay for what they've done."

Zoe and Marcus nodded, their expressions grim but resolute. They knew the stakes, knew the danger that they were facing. But they also knew that they had each other's backs, that they were a team in every sense of the word.

As the meeting broke up and Zoe and Marcus went back to their work, Ethan turned to Liam, his expression softening slightly. "Thanks for coming," he said, his voice low and sincere. "I know this isn't easy for you, working with me and my team. But I want you to know that I appreciate it, more than you know."

Liam nodded, his jaw clenching slightly. "I'm not doing this for you, Hawke," he said, his voice cool. "I'm doing it for the mutants who are suffering, for the people who need our help. But if we're going to work together, you need to be straight with me. No more secrets, no more lies. Got it?"

Ethan felt a flicker of frustration, a spark of the old animosity that had always simmered between them. But he also knew that Liam was right, that they needed to trust each other if they were going to have any chance of succeeding.

He took a deep breath, pushing down the urge to snap back at Liam's accusation. Instead, he summoned The High Priestess card, feeling its energy wash over him like a cool, calming breeze.

"Alright," he said, his voice steady. "Let's go."

Zoe looked up from her laptop, her brow furrowed in concentration. "I've been digging deeper into the financial records, boss, and I think I might have found something. There's a pattern of coded transactions that keep popping up, linked to specific dates and locations."

Ethan leaned over her shoulder, his eyes scanning the screen. "Coded transactions? What kind of code are we talking about here?"

Marcus chimed in, his expression thoughtful. "It's not like anything I've seen before. It's almost like a language of its own, with symbols and patterns that don't make any sense."

Ethan felt a thrill of excitement, a spark of the old thirst for knowledge that had always driven him. "A language, huh? Sounds like we need a translator."

Liam snorted, his arms crossed over his chest. "And where exactly are we going to find someone who speaks financial gibberish?"

Ethan shot him a cocky grin, his eyes sparkling with mischief. "Oh, ye of little faith. You're looking at the master of all languages, my friend. The Arcana knows no bounds."

Liam rolled his eyes, but Ethan could see the hint of a smile tugging at the corner of his mouth. "Right. How could I forget? The great and powerful Arcana, fluent in bullshit and bravado."

Ethan clutched his chest, feigning a look of wounded pride. "You wound me, Quinn. And here I thought we were partners, equals in every sense of the word."

Liam's expression softened, just a fraction. "We are partners, Hawke. But that doesn't mean I have to stroke your ego every five minutes."

Ethan waggled his eyebrows, his grin turning suggestive. "Oh, I can think of a few other things you could stroke instead."

Zoe cleared her throat, her expression amused. "If you two are done flirting, maybe we could get back to the task at hand? You know, the whole saving the world thing?"

Ethan felt a flush creep up his neck, but he quickly pushed it down. "Right. Sorry, Zo. What were you saying about the code?"

Zoe sighed, her fingers flying over the keyboard. "I'm saying that we might need some inside information to crack it. Someone who knows Genexis and Dr. Novak's operation from the inside out."

Ethan nodded, his mind already racing with possibilities. "Dr. Novak. She's the key to all of this. If we can get close to her, maybe we can find out what these transactions are really about."

Liam frowned, his expression skeptical. "And how exactly are we going to do that? It's not like we can just waltz into her office and start asking questions."

Ethan grinned, a plan already forming in his mind. "Leave that to me, Quinn. I have a few tricks up my sleeve."

He summoned The Magician card, feeling its energy crackling through his fingertips. With a flick of his wrist, he sent a pulse of power out into the room, a subtle suggestion that would make anyone who saw him forget his face, his name, his very existence.

Liam's eyes widened, his mouth falling open in shock. "What the hell did you just do?"

Ethan smirked, feeling a rush of pride at the look of awe on Liam's face. "Just a little something to help me blend in. Now, if you'll excuse me, I have a doctor to see."

He turned to leave, but Liam's hand shot out, gripping his arm. "Wait. You can't just go in there alone. What if something happens to you?"

Ethan felt a warmth spreading through his chest, a flicker of something that he didn't quite want to name. "Aw, Quinn. I didn't know you cared."

Liam's jaw clenched, his eyes flashing with something that might have been anger, or might have been something else entirely. "Don't be an idiot, Hawke. You're no good to anyone if you get yourself killed."

Ethan sobered, his expression turning serious. "I know. But someone has to do this, and I'm the best equipped to handle it. Trust me, Liam. I know what I'm doing."

For a long moment, Liam just stared at him, his eyes searching Ethan's face for some sign of deception, of ulterior motive. But Ethan held his gaze, willing Liam to see the truth in his eyes, the sincerity in his words.

He could feel the tension crackling between them, the electric charge of something unspoken and undeniable. It was always like this with Liam, a push and pull of attraction and animosity that set Ethan's nerves on fire.

But before either of them could say anything more, a breaking news alert flashed across the screen of Zoe's laptop, catching their attention.

"Guys, you need to see this," Zoe said, her voice tight with concern. "A prominent mutant rights activist has gone missing, and the authorities are barely lifting a finger to investigate."

Ethan felt a chill run down his spine, a sinking feeling in the pit of his stomach. He exchanged a glance with Liam, seeing the same realization dawning in the firefighter's eyes.

"Fuck," Liam muttered, his jaw clenching. "This can't be a coincidence. Not with everything else that's been going on."

Ethan nodded, his mind already racing with possibilities. He summoned The Hierophant card, feeling its energy pulsing through his fingertips, granting him insight and understanding.

"You're right," he said, his voice low and intense. "This disappearance could be the key to everything we've been trying to uncover. We need to investigate, and fast."

Marcus frowned, his expression skeptical. "But what about Genexis and Dr. Novak? We can't just drop that lead, not when we're so close to finding out the truth."

Ethan grinned, a cocky glint in his eye. "Who says we have to choose? We're the fucking dream team, remember? We can handle both cases at once."

Liam snorted, rolling his eyes. "Right. Because we're just that good, aren't we? The Arcana and his merry band of misfits, saving the world one conspiracy at a time."

Ethan's grin widened, a challenge sparking in his gaze. "Damn straight, Quinn. And you're one of us now, whether you like it or not. So why don't you put your money where your mouth is and help us crack this case wide open?"

For a moment, Liam looked like he might argue, his stubborn pride warring with his desire to see justice served. But then he sighed, his shoulders slumping in defeat.

"Fine," he said, his voice gruff. "But I still think you're a reckless idiot who's going to get us all killed one of these days."

He turned to Zoe and Marcus, his expression turning serious. "Alright, team. Here's the plan. Zoe, Marcus, I want you to dig into this missing activist case. Find out everything you can about their background, their associates, any potential enemies or threats they might have faced."

Zoe nodded, her fingers already flying over the keyboard. "On it, boss. We'll have a full dossier on your desk by morning."

Ethan turned to Liam, his eyes sparking with mischief. "As for you and me, Quinn? We're going to keep pursuing the Genexis angle. We need to find out what the hell is going on at that secret facility, and we need to get close to Dr. Novak to do it."

Liam's jaw clenched, his expression wary. "And how exactly do you propose we do that, Hawke? It's not like we can just waltz in there and start asking questions."

Ethan's grin turned sly, a wicked glint in his eye. "Oh, I have a few ideas. But first, we need to do a little recon. Scope out the facility, see what kind of security they've got in place."

He summoned The Chariot card, feeling its energy thrumming through his veins, granting him speed and agility. With a flick of his wrist, he sent a pulse of power out into the room, a subtle suggestion that would sharpen their focus and heighten their senses.

"Alright, team," he said, his voice ringing with authority. "We've got a lot of ground to cover, and not a lot of time to do it in."

As Zoe and Marcus set to work on their respective tasks, Ethan turned to Liam, his expression softening slightly.

"Hey," he said, his voice low and sincere. "I know this isn't easy for you, working with me and my team. But I want you to know that I appreciate it, more than you know."

Liam's eyes widened, surprise flickering across his face. For a moment, Ethan thought he might brush off the sentiment, might retreat back behind his walls of stubborn pride and cool detachment.

But then Liam smiled, a small, hesitant thing that made Ethan's heart skip a beat.

"Yeah, well," he said, his voice gruff. "Someone's got to keep you in line, Hawke. Might as well be me."

Ethan grinned, feeling a rush of warmth and affection that he couldn't quite explain. "Careful, Quinn. Keep talking like that and I might start to think you actually like me."

Liam snorted, but there was no real heat behind it. "Don't flatter yourself, Hawke. I'm just in it for the heroics and the glory."

Ethan laughed, feeling a sense of camaraderie and purpose wash over him. This was what he lived for, the thrill of the hunt and the rush of working alongside people he trusted and respected.

And as much as he hated to admit it, he was starting to realize that Liam Quinn might just be one of those people.

The team continued to discuss their plan of action, the question of involving the DMA or other authorities arose once again. Liam, ever the skeptic, expressed his doubts about the agency's effectiveness and trustworthiness.

"I'm telling you, Hawke," he said, his voice tight with frustration. "The DMA is about as useful as a screen door on a submarine. They've had plenty of chances to step up and do the right thing, but they've failed at every turn."

Ethan sighed, running a hand through his hair. He knew that Liam had a point, that the DMA's track record was far from stellar. But he also recognized the risks of operating entirely outside the law, especially as the stakes continued to rise.

"I hear you, Quinn," he said, his voice low and serious. "But we can't just go rogue and expect to come out on top. We need to be smart about this, and that means keeping our options open."

Liam's jaw clenched, his eyes flashing with anger. "Options? What options? The option to sit back and let the DMA fuck everything up like they always do? No thanks, Hawke. I'd rather take my chances on my own."

Ethan felt a flicker of irritation, a spark of the old animosity that had always simmered between them. But he pushed it down, knowing that they needed to find a way to work together if they were going to have any chance of success.

"Alright, look," he said, his voice firm but not unkind. "I'm not saying we should trust the DMA blindly. But if we uncover evidence that requires official action, we need to be ready to reach out and make our case. Otherwise, we're just pissing in the wind."

Liam was silent for a long moment, his expression torn. Ethan could practically see the gears turning in his head, the stubborn pride warring with the pragmatic need to get results.

Finally, he nodded, his shoulders slumping in resignation. "Fine. But we do this on our terms, Hawke. The moment the DMA starts to screw us over, we walk away and handle it ourselves. Deal?"

Ethan grinned, feeling a rush of relief and admiration for the man in front of him. Liam might be a pain in the ass sometimes, but he had a heart of gold and a will of steel.

"Deal," he said, extending his hand. "Partners?"

Liam hesitated for a moment, then reached out and clasped Ethan's hand in a firm shake.

12

Unmasking the Truth

Liam

A sudden knock at the door jolted Liam . He opened it to find Ethan standing there, a mischievous grin on his face.

"Rise and shine, Liam," Ethan quipped. "We've got a missing activist to find and a conspiracy to unravel. No time for beauty sleep."

"How did you even know where I lived?" Liam groaned. "Don't answer that."

"Hello? Vigilante, remember?" Ethan teased. It was too early for this.

Liam frowned, confusion etched on his face. "Wait a minute, I thought we agreed to focus on Dr. Novak and Genexis. Why are we suddenly chasing after this missing activist?"

Ethan's grin widened, his eyes sparkling with excitement. "Why not kill two birds with one stone? If we can find the activist, we might uncover some new leads that tie back to Genexis and the good doctor herself."

Liam considered this for a moment, then shrugged. "Fuck it, you're right. Let's do this."

As they made their way to the missing activist's last known location, Liam found himself studying Ethan's profile, the way his brow furrowed in concentration as he scanned the area for clues. There was a grace to his movements, a fluidity that spoke of years of training and experience.

"Take a picture, Liam," Ethan smirked, catching his gaze. "It'll last longer."

Liam felt his cheeks heat up, but he quickly covered it with a scowl. "Don't flatter yourself, Ethan. I was just trying to figure out how someone with such a big head can fit through doorways."

Ethan laughed, the sound rich and warm in the cool morning air. "It's a gift, really. Along with my dashing good looks and rapier wit."

They continued their investigation, interviewing witnesses and searching for any sign of the missing activist. Liam had to admit, working with Ethan was starting to feel natural, like they were two pieces of a puzzle finally clicking into place.

Liam couldn't shake the feeling that they were on the cusp of something big. Every witness they interviewed, every scrap of evidence they uncovered, seemed to point towards a larger, more sinister picture.

"Check this out," Ethan said, handing Liam a stack of papers. "Looks like our missing activist was doing some serious digging into Genexis before they vanished."

Liam flipped through the pages, his eyes widening with each new revelation. "They were onto something, something that Genexis clearly didn't want anyone to know about."

Ethan nodded, his brow furrowed in concentration. "And look at this," he said, pointing to a scribbled note in the margin. "It's some kind of code, a message that only makes sense if you know what you're looking for."

Liam felt a thrill of excitement run through him, the pieces of the puzzle finally starting to fall into place. "Like that piece of paper that the informant left. We need to crack this code, Ethan. It could be the key to everything." He then turned to Ethan. "Have you ever figured out what the message meant?"

Ethan sighed. "No, but I suspect it was just to bring us together because no one seemed to be looking for it."

Liam nodded and focused on the the task at hand.

As they pored over the cryptic message, Liam couldn't help but steal glances at Ethan, marveling at the intensity of his focus. There was something magnetic about the way he approached the investigation, a relentless determination that bordered on obsession.

"So, how's life at the fire department?" Ethan asked suddenly, catching Liam off guard. "I mean, when you're not busy chasing after devilishly handsome vigilantes, that is."

Liam scoffed, rolling his eyes at Ethan's shameless self-flattery. "Don't think for a second that I'm here because of your so-called charm, Hawke. I'm just trying to get to the bottom of this mess."

Ethan chuckled, the sound warm and genuine. "Sounds like a tough gig. I don't know how you do it, Liam. Risking your life every day to save others... it's pretty fucking heroic."

Liam felt a flush creep up his neck, unused to such sincere praise from the usually snarky vigilante. He quickly brushed it off, not wanting to give Ethan the satisfaction of seeing him flustered. "Yeah, well, someone's gotta do it. And I'd rather it be me than some rookie who doesn't know his ass from his elbow."

Ethan grinned, but there was a seriousness in his eyes that Liam hadn't seen before. "I mean it, Liam. What you do... it matters. Don't ever forget that."

Liam swallowed hard, a lump forming in his throat. Despite his outward dismissal of Ethan's compliments, he couldn't deny the warmth that spread through his chest at the vigilante's words. It was rare for anyone to acknowledge the sacrifices he made as a firefighter, let alone someone like Ethan, who seemed to thrive on sarcasm and snark.

"You know, I never really understood why you do it as well," Liam said suddenly, the words spilling out before he could stop them. "The whole vigilante thing, I mean. What drives you to put on that mask every night and risk your life for people you don't even know?"

Ethan was quiet for a long moment, his expression unreadable. Then, with a sigh, he set down the papers and leaned back in his chair, his eyes distant.

"When I was a kid, my parents were murdered," he said softly, his voice heavy with old pain. "Gunned down in the street by a bunch of anti-mutant thugs who thought they were doing the world a favor."

Liam felt his heart clench, a wave of sympathy washing over him. He'd known that Ethan had a tragic past, but to hear him speak of it so openly, so rawly... it was like seeing a whole new side of the man.

"I'm sorry, Ethan," he said, his voice barely above a whisper. "I can't even imagine what that must have been like."

Ethan shrugged, a bitter smile twisting his lips. "It was hell. But it also lit a fire inside me, a burning need to make sure that no one else ever had to go through what I did. To fight back against the hatred and the bigotry and the fucking injustice of it all."

Liam nodded, a newfound understanding dawning in his eyes. "So that's why you became The Arcana. To give a voice to the voiceless, to protect the innocent and punish the guilty."

Ethan met his gaze, something raw and vulnerable in his expression. "Yeah. But it's more than that, Liam. It's about doing what's right, no matter the cost. It's about being the change you want to see in the world, even if it means sacrificing everything you have."

Liam felt a lump form in his throat, his heart swelling with a sudden, fierce admiration for the man in front of him. He'd always seen Ethan as a cocky, arrogant bastard, but now… now he was starting to see the depth of his conviction, the strength of his character.

"Well, for what it's worth," Liam said, his voice rough with emotion, "I think you're doing a pretty fucking amazing job. And I'm honored to be fighting by your side, Ethan. Even if you are a pain in the ass sometimes."

Ethan grinned, the moment of vulnerability passing as quickly as it had come. "Aw, Liam. And here I thought you were just in it for my stunning good looks and sparkling wit."

Liam rolled his eyes, but he couldn't stop the smile that tugged at the corners of his mouth. "You're an idiot."

As they delved deeper into the cryptic message, Liam found his mind wandering back to their earlier conversation. Ethan's revelation about his past, the pain and guilt that drove him to become The Arcana, had struck a chord deep within Liam's heart.

He'd always seen Ethan as a reckless vigilante, a man who played by his own rules and damn the consequences. But now, he was starting to realize that there was so much more to the cocky, infuriating bastard than met the eye.

Ethan wasn't just fighting for the thrill of the chase or the glory of the spotlight. He was fighting for something deeper, something more profound. He was fighting for justice, for the innocent lives that had been lost and the ones that still hung in the balance.

Liam felt a newfound respect for his Ethan, a sense of understanding that he'd never had before. He could see the heavy burden that Ethan carried, the weight of responsibility that came with donning the mask of The Arcana.

It couldn't be easy, living a double life, constantly putting himself in danger for the sake of others. Liam wondered how Ethan managed to keep it all together, how he found the strength to keep going in the face of such overwhelming odds.

"I think I've got something," Ethan said suddenly, his voice cutting through Liam's thoughts. "This code, it's not just random gibberish. It's a set of coordinates, leading to a location on the outskirts of the city."

Liam leaned in closer, his heart racing with anticipation. "You think that's where they're keeping the missing activist?"

Ethan nodded, his eyes gleaming with determination. "It's our best lead so far. We need to check it out, see if we can find any clues that might tie this whole thing back to Genexis."

Liam couldn't argue with that. They had to follow every lead, no matter how dangerous or unlikely it might seem. The lives of countless mutants depended on it.

They made their way to the coordinates, a sense of unease growing in the pit of Liam's stomach with every passing mile. Something about this felt off, like they were walking into a trap.

As they approached the location, Liam's instincts screamed at him to turn back. But he couldn't, not when they were so close to the truth.

Suddenly, a hail of gunfire erupted from the shadows, forcing Liam and Ethan to dive for cover. They were outnumbered and outgunned, facing off against a group of armed thugs who clearly meant business.

"Fuck!" Ethan cursed, his eyes wide with panic.

They were trapped, backed into a corner with no way out.

But then, out of nowhere, Ethan was there, his eyes glowing with an otherworldly light as he summoned the power of his tarot cards. Liam watched in awe as ethereal constructs burst forth from Ethan's mind, each one imbued with a different power.

The Magician, a glowing figure wreathed in arcane energy, cast a shimmering shield around them, deflecting the hail of bullets with ease. The Tower, a construct of pure destructive force, blasted through the ranks of the thugs, sending them flying like ragdolls.

Ethan moved with inhuman speed and grace, his powers flowing through him like a conduit. He was a force of nature, a whirlwind of psychic energy and raw, unbridled power.

He summoned his own powers, feeling the heat of the flames coursing through his veins. Together, he and Ethan unleashed a devastating barrage of fire and psychic energy, driving the thugs back and clearing a path to freedom.

They ran, their hearts pounding and their lungs burning as they raced through the twisting corridors of the warehouse. Bullets whizzed past their heads, the sound of gunfire echoing in their ears.

But somehow, miraculously, they made it out alive, bursting through the doors and into the cool night air. They collapsed onto the ground, their chests heaving as they gulped in lungfuls of precious oxygen.

For a long moment, neither of them spoke, too overwhelmed by the sheer magnitude of what had just happened. They had come so close to death, so close to losing everything they had fought so hard for.

Finally, Liam turned to Ethan, his eyes shining with gratitude and something else, something deeper and more profound. "You saved our lives back there," he said softly, his voice rough with emotion. "I... I don't know how to thank you."

Ethan just shrugged, a small smile playing at the corners of his mouth. "You would have done the same for me. That's what partners do, right?"

Partners. The word sent a thrill through Liam's heart, a warmth that spread through his chest like wildfire. He had never thought of Ethan as his partner before, had never allowed himself to see the man as anything more than a necessary evil.

But now, in the aftermath of their brush with death, he realized that Ethan was so much more than that. He was a friend, a confidant, someone who understood the sacrifices and the risks that came with the life they had chosen.

Liam reached out, his hand finding Ethan's in the darkness. He squeezed it gently, feeling the warmth of the other man's skin against his own. "Thank you," he said again, his voice barely above a whisper. "For everything."

Ethan's eyes widened, a flicker of surprise crossing his face. But then he smiled, a real smile, not the cocky smirk that Liam had grown so used to. "Anytime, Liam. Anytime."

Liam felt a warmth spreading through his chest at the sound of his name on Ethan's lips. Not "Quinn," not "Firefighter," but "Liam." It was a small thing, but it felt like a step forward, a sign that the walls between them were slowly starting to crumble.

As they made their way back to the main room of the headquarters, Liam's mind was racing with the new information they had uncovered. The missing activist, the secret research facility, the shady dealings of Genexis… it was all starting to paint a picture, and it wasn't a pretty one.

"Fuck me," Liam muttered under his breath as he stared at the evidence board they had set up on the wall. "This is some seriously messed up shit."

Ethan chuckled, his eyes sparkling with mischief. "You know, Quinn, if you wanted me to fuck you, all you had to do was ask."

Liam rolled his eyes, but he couldn't quite suppress the grin that tugged at the corner of his mouth. "In your dreams, Hawke. Now, can we focus on the task at hand? Or do I need to get a spray bottle to keep you in line?"

Zoe looked up from her laptop, her expression amused. "Boys, boys. Can we keep the sexual tension to a minimum while we're trying to unravel a massive conspiracy here?"

Liam saw Ethan's cheeks heat up, but he tried to play it off with a laugh. "Sorry. You know how Hawke gets when he's on a roll."

Marcus shook his head, a small smile playing at the corner of his mouth. "Alright, let's break this down. What do we know so far?"

Ethan nodded, his brow furrowed in concentration. "We know that Genexis has been conducting shady experiments on mutants, and that they have some kind of secret research facility outside the city. We also know that they've been funneling money through shell companies and offshore accounts to cover their tracks."

Liam felt a chill run down his spine as the pieces started to fall into place. "And now we have a missing activist who was last seen investigating Genexis. It can't be a coincidence."

"But what about Dr. Novak?" Zoe asked, her expression troubled. "We still don't know for sure if she's involved in the disappearances or not."

Ethan sighed, running a hand through his hair. "That's the million-dollar question, isn't it? She's definitely hiding something, but we need more proof before we can make any accusations."

Liam started pacing the room, his mind whirling with the implications. "So, what's our next move? We can't just sit around and wait for another mutant to go missing."

Marcus leaned forward, his eyes narrowed in thought. "We need to keep digging. Follow the money trail, see where it leads us. And we need to find out more about that secret research facility. If Genexis is hiding something, that's where we'll find it."

Ethan nodded, his expression determined. "Agreed. Zoe, Marcus, you two keep working on the financial angle. See if you can find any more connections between Genexis and the missing mutants."

He turned to Liam, his eyes softening slightly. "Quinn, you and I will focus on the research facility. We need to find a way to get inside and see what they're really up to."

Liam felt a thrill of excitement mixed with trepidation at the thought of going undercover with Ethan. It was a dangerous game they were playing, but he knew that they had no choice. Too many lives were at stake.

"Alright, Hawke," he said, his voice rough with emotion. "Let's do this. But we need to be careful. We can't afford to tip our hand too soon."

Ethan grinned, that infuriating, irresistible smirk that never failed to get under Liam's skin. "Careful is my middle name, Quinn. Well, that and 'devastatingly handsome.'"

Liam groaned, but he couldn't help the laugh that bubbled up in his throat. "You're impossible, you know that?"

But even as he said it, he knew that he wouldn't have it any other way. Because despite their differences, despite the danger and the uncertainty that lay ahead, Liam knew that he trusted Ethan with his life.

And maybe, just maybe, with his heart as well.

13

Matters of the Heart

Ethan

The truth was, he was distracted. Distracted by the way Liam's smile made his heart skip a beat, by the way his skin tingled every time they accidentally brushed against each other.

It was a feeling he wasn't used to, a vulnerability that he had spent his entire life trying to avoid. Ethan Hawke was the Arcana, the cocky, confident vigilante who always had a plan and always got the job done. He didn't do feelings, didn't do attachments.

But with Liam, everything was different. The firefighter had gotten under his skin in a way that no one else ever had, had made him question everything he thought he knew about himself.

As he entered the headquarters, still lost in thought, he was immediately confronted by Zoe and Marcus. They were waiting for him in the main room, their arms crossed and their expressions serious.

"We need to talk," Zoe said, her tone leaving no room for argument.

Ethan raised an eyebrow, trying to play it off with his usual cockiness. "If this is about the coffee, I promise I'll start bringing enough for everyone."

But Zoe wasn't having it. "Cut the crap, Ethan. We know what's going on with you and Liam."

Ethan felt his heart skip a beat, a flicker of panic rising in his chest. "I don't know what you're talking about," he said, his voice tight.

Marcus sighed, his expression softening slightly. "Ethan, we're not blind. We've seen the way you look at him, the way you act around him. It's okay to have feelings for someone."

But Ethan shook his head, his jaw clenching with stubborn denial. "I don't have feelings for Liam," he said, his voice rough. "He's just a colleague, a partner in this investigation. Nothing more."

Zoe snorted, rolling her eyes. "Right. And I'm the Queen of England. Come on, Ethan. You can't fool us."

Ethan felt a surge of anger rising in his chest, a defensive wall slamming into place. "Look, even if I did have feelings for Liam, which I don't, it wouldn't matter. We're in the middle of a dangerous case here, and I can't afford to be distracted by personal bullshit."

Marcus frowned, his expression concerned. "Ethan, we're not saying you can't have feelings for Liam. We're just worried about what it might mean for the investigation, and for you."

Ethan ran a hand through his hair, frustration and confusion warring in his chest. "I appreciate the concern, guys. But I've got this under control. Liam and I are just friends, and that's all we'll ever be."

Zoe raised an eyebrow, her expression skeptical. "Friends? Really, Ethan? You expect us to believe that?"

She leaned forward, her eyes boring into his with an intensity that made him squirm. "I've known you for years, and I've never seen you light up the way you do when Liam's around. It's like he flips a switch in you, brings out a side of you that I didn't even know existed."

Ethan scoffed, trying to play it off. "You're imagining things, Zo."

Zoe shook her head, a knowing smile playing at the corners of her mouth. "You know, I saw Liam talking to that cute firefighter the other day. The one with the dimples and the killer abs. They looked pretty cozy, if you know what I mean."

Ethan felt a sudden surge of jealousy, hot and sharp in his chest. The thought of Liam flirting with some other guy, laughing at his jokes and letting him get close… it made his blood boil in a way that he couldn't quite explain.

"What the fuck are you talking about?" he snapped, his voice coming out harsher than he intended.

"Just what I thought, you're smitten." Zoe smirked.

"Liam can talk to whoever he wants. It's none of my business."

The idea of Liam with someone else made him feel like he was being stabbed in the gut, like he was losing something precious that he hadn't even realized he wanted.

Marcus sighed, his expression sympathetic. "Ethan, listen to me. I know you're scared. I know you're used to being the lone wolf, the guy who doesn't need anyone else. But maybe this thing with Liam… maybe it's not a weakness. Maybe it's a strength."

Ethan frowned, confused. "What do you mean?"

Marcus leaned forward, his eyes intense. "Think about it. All your life, you've been fighting for something bigger than yourself. Justice, freedom, the chance to make a difference in the world. But what if Liam is the thing that makes it all worth it? What if he's the reason you keep going, even when things get tough?"

Ethan felt a lump forming in his throat, a sudden rush of emotion that he couldn't quite contain. Because as much as he hated to admit it, Marcus was right. Liam Quinn had become more than just a partner, more than just a friend. He was the reason Ethan got up in the morning, the reason he kept fighting even when the odds seemed insurmountable.

"Fuck," he muttered, running a hand over his face. "I don't know what to do, guys. I've never felt like this before. It's like he's in my head, under my skin. I can't shake him, no matter how hard I try."

Zoe reached out, placing a hand on his shoulder. "Ethan, it's okay to be scared. It's okay to feel vulnerable. But don't let your fear hold you back from something that could be really special."

She grinned, a mischievous glint in her eye. "Besides, have you seen the way Liam looks at you? That boy is thirsty as hell. You'd have to be blind not to see it."

Ethan felt a flush creeping up his neck, a sudden warmth spreading through his chest. Because as much as he tried to deny it, he knew that Zoe was right. He had seen the way Liam looked at him, the heat in his gaze and the hunger in his touch. It was like a live wire, a current of electricity that crackled between them every time they were in the same room.

"Alright, fine," he said, throwing up his hands in defeat. "You win. I have feelings for Liam. Are you happy now?"

Zoe grinned, punching him lightly on the arm. "Ecstatic. Now we just have to figure out how to get you two idiots together without blowing up the city in the process."

Ethan groaned, burying his face in his hands. "Fuck my life. I'm never going to hear the end of this, am I?"

As much as he hated to admit it, it felt good to finally say the words out loud. To acknowledge the depth of his feelings for Liam, and to know that his friends had his back no matter what.

But even as relief washed over him, Ethan felt a new fear gripping his heart. The fear of losing Liam, either to the dangers of their mission or to the complications of a romantic relationship.

"What if I fuck this up?" he asked, his voice barely above a whisper. "What if my feelings for him cloud my judgment, make me take stupid risks that put us both in danger?"

Zoe's expression softened, her eyes filled with understanding. "Ethan, you can't let fear control you. Yes, there are risks, but there are also rewards. And I've never seen you back down from a challenge before."

Ethan sighed, his mind drifting back to a past he'd tried so hard to forget. A past where he'd let himself be vulnerable, let himself fall deeply in love, only to have his heart shattered into a million pieces.

He could still remember the pain of that betrayal, the way it had felt like his entire world was crumbling around him. He had been young and naive, so sure that he had found the one, the person he wanted to spend the rest of his life with.

Ethan's mind drifted back to a time he'd tried so hard to forget, a memory that still haunted him in his darkest moments.

He had been young and in love, so sure that he had found the one person he wanted to spend the rest of his life with. His fiancé, Alex, had been everything he'd ever wanted - smart, funny, kind, and utterly gorgeous.

They had been planning their wedding, dreaming of a future together filled with laughter and love. Ethan had never been happier, never felt more complete.

But there was one secret he had kept from Alex, one truth he had been too afraid to reveal. Ethan was a mutant, born with powers that set him apart from the rest of the world.

He had always been careful to hide his abilities, to keep that part of himself locked away from prying eyes. But as his love for Alex grew deeper, so too did the guilt and shame he felt at keeping such a huge part of himself hidden.

One night, after a particularly close call with a group of anti-mutant protesters, Ethan had finally worked up the courage to come clean. With shaking hands and a pounding heart, he had revealed his secret to Alex, waiting with bated breath for his reaction.

But the response he got was not the one he had been hoping for.

Alex's face had twisted with shock and disgust, his eyes filling with a hatred that Ethan had never seen before. "You're one of them," he had spat, his voice dripping with venom. "A freak, a monster. How could you keep this from me? How could you lie to me all this time?"

Ethan had tried to explain, had begged Alex to understand that his powers didn't define him, that he was still the same person he had always been. But Alex wouldn't listen, his mind already made up.

"I can't be with a mutant," he had said, his voice cold and unfeeling. "I can't marry someone who's been lying to me, someone who's not even human. It's over, Ethan. We're done."

With those words, Alex had walked out of Ethan's life, leaving him shattered and alone. Ethan had felt like his entire world was crumbling around him, like he would never be whole again.

It had taken him years to recover from that betrayal, to rebuild the walls around his heart and learn to trust again. And even now, the scars of that heartbreak lingered, a constant reminder of the pain that came with opening himself up to love.

As Ethan pulled himself out of the memory, he felt a renewed sense of fear and hesitation. If Alex, the person he had loved more than anything, couldn't accept him for who he was, then how could he ever expect Liam to be different?

But even as the doubts swirled in his mind, Ethan knew that he couldn't let his past control him forever. He had to be willing to take that leap, to trust that what he and Liam had was real and worth fighting for.

The firefighter had snuck past his defenses, had wormed his way into Ethan's heart without him even realizing it. And now, the thought of losing him, of opening himself up to that kind of pain again, was almost too much to bear.

"I've been hurt before," Ethan said, his voice rough with emotion.

"Badly. And I swore I would never let it happen again. But with Liam… it's different. He makes me want to take that risk, to put my heart on the line one more time."

Marcus leaned forward, his expression serious. "Ethan, I know you're scared. And I know your past has made it hard for you to trust, to let yourself be vulnerable. But you can't let that define you forever. You have to be willing to take a chance, to open yourself up to the possibility of love again."

Ethan felt a lump forming in his throat, a sudden rush of emotion that threatened to overwhelm him. Because as much as he wanted to deny it, Marcus was right. He couldn't let his past dictate his future, couldn't let his fear of getting hurt keep him from something that could be truly special.

"You're right," he said, his voice barely above a whisper. "I can't let my past control me anymore. I have to be willing to take that leap, to trust that what Liam and I have is real and worth fighting for."

Zoe grinned, her eyes sparkling with mischief. "Damn right, it is. And if you don't make a move soon, I might just have to step in and play matchmaker myself."

Ethan groaned, burying his face in his hands. "Please, Zo, I'm begging you. Let me handle this my own way, in my own time. The last thing I need is you meddling in my love life."

But even as he said it, he couldn't help but feel a flicker of warmth in his chest. Because as much as Zoe's teasing drove him crazy sometimes, he knew that it came from a place of love, of genuine concern for his happiness.

"Alright, fine," Zoe said, throwing up her hands in mock surrender. "I'll back off. For now. But don't think I won't be watching you like a hawk, Hawke. If you don't make a move soon, I might just have to take matters into my own hands."

Ethan rolled his eyes, but he couldn't quite suppress the smile tugging at the corners of his mouth. "I'd like to see you try, Zo. I'm the master of evasion, remember? You'll never catch me."

Marcus chuckled, shaking his head in amusement. "Alright, you two, enough bickering. We've got work to do. Ethan, just promise us that you'll think about what we said, okay? Don't let your fear hold you back from something that could be really great."

Ethan nodded, his expression turning serious. "I promise, Marcus. I won't let my past define me anymore. And I won't let my feelings for Liam compromise our mission, either. We're going to take down Genexis and save those mutants, no matter what it takes."

As they settled back into their work, poring over the evidence and planning their next move, Ethan couldn't help but feel a new sense of determination washing over him. Yes, he was scared. Yes, the thought of opening himself up to love again was terrifying.

14

Trial by Fire

Liam

Standing outside his boss's office, his heart pounding in his chest as he tried to quell the rising tide of anxiety that threatened to overwhelm him. He had been called in for a meeting, and he had a sinking feeling that it had something to do with his involvement in the Genexis investigation.

Taking a deep breath, he knocked on the door, his knuckles rapping against the wood with a sharp, staccato rhythm.

"Come in," a gruff voice called from inside.

Liam stepped into the office, his posture rigid and his jaw clenched with tension. Chief Johnson sat behind his desk, his expression stern and his eyes hard as he motioned for Liam to take a seat.

"You wanted to see me, Chief?" Liam asked, his voice carefully neutral.

Chief Johnson leaned forward, his elbows resting on the desk as he fixed Liam with a piercing stare. "Quinn, I'm going to cut right to the chase. It has come to my attention that you've been involved in some extracurricular activities, specifically related to the disappearing mutants."

Liam felt his stomach drop, a sense of dread washing over him like a cold wave. Someone had ratted him out, but who? And why?

"Chief, I can explain—" he began, but Chief Johnson held up a hand, cutting him off.

"I don't want to hear it, Quinn. What I want to know is what the hell you were thinking, getting involved in something like this without going through the proper channels. You're a firefighter, not a goddamn vigilante or a cop."

Liam felt a surge of anger rising in his chest, hot and fierce. He had dedicated his life to protecting the innocent, to fighting for what was right. And now, he was being reprimanded for doing just that?

"With all due respect, Chief," he said, his voice tight with barely controlled fury, "I couldn't just sit back and do nothing. Not when innocent lives were at stake. Not when there was a chance to uncover the truth and bring those responsible to justice."

Chief Johnson sighed, leaning back in his chair with a weary expression. "I understand your motivations, Quinn. But you have to understand the position this puts me in. If word gets out that one of my firefighters is involved in an unauthorized investigation, it could have serious consequences for the entire department."

Liam's jaw clenched, his hands balling into fists at his sides. He knew that the Chief was right, but that didn't make it any easier to swallow. He had worked too hard, sacrificed too much, to let this setback derail him now.

"So what happens now?" he asked, his voice low and rough. "Am I being suspended? Fired?"

Chief Johnson shook his head, his expression softening slightly. "No, Quinn. You're too valuable an asset to the department to let go over something like this. But I am putting you on notice. If you continue to pursue this investigation without proper authorization, there will be consequences. Serious consequences."

Liam nodded, his heart heavy with the weight of the reprimand. He knew that he should be grateful for the second chance, but all he could feel was a sense of frustration and betrayal.

"I understand, Chief," he said, his voice flat and emotionless. "It won't happen again."

With that, he stood up and walked out of the office, his shoulders hunched and his jaw clenched with barely contained rage. He needed to blow off some steam, needed to channel the anger and frustration that coursed through his veins like molten lava.

He made his way to the gym, his mind whirling with the implications of what had just happened. Someone had betrayed him, had revealed his involvement in the Genexis investigation to the Chief. But who? And why?

As he stepped onto the treadmill, his feet pounding against the belt with a steady rhythm, Liam's mind raced with possibilities. It couldn't have been Ethan or his team; they had too much to lose themselves to risk exposing him like that. But then who?

He thought back to the confrontation with the armed thugs, the way they had seemed to know exactly where to find them. Could there be a mole within the department, someone working with Genexis to undermine their investigation?

The thought made Liam's blood boil, his fists clenching at his sides as he pushed himself harder, faster. He couldn't believe that someone he trusted, someone he worked with every day, could betray him like that.

But then again, in a world where mutants were hunted and persecuted simply for being different, was it really so hard to believe?

As the miles ticked by and the sweat poured down his face, Liam's mind continued to race, his thoughts jumbled and chaotic. He knew that he couldn't let this setback stop him, couldn't let the betrayal and the reprimand deter him from his mission.

He had come too far, risked too much, to turn back now. He had to see this through, had to uncover the truth and bring those responsible to justice, no matter the cost.

And if that meant going against the Chief's orders, defying the very institution he had sworn to serve?

Then so be it.

Liam stepped off the treadmill, his chest heaving and his heart pounding with a fierce, unrelenting rhythm. He grabbed his towel, wiping the sweat from his brow as he made his way towards the locker room.

He had a job to do, a mission to complete. And he wouldn't let anything, not the Chief's warning, not the betrayal of a colleague, stand in his way.

As Liam made his way towards the locker room, his mind still reeling from the reprimand and the implications of the betrayal, he caught sight of a familiar figure across the gym. It was Jack, his teammate and supposed friend, the one person he had confided in about his involvement with investigation.

A sudden realization hit Liam like a punch to the gut, stealing the breath from his lungs and making his blood run cold. It was Jack. Jack was the one who had ratted him out to the Chief.

Fury, hot and uncontrollable, surged through Liam's veins. He stormed over to where Jack was standing, his fists clenched at his sides and his eyes blazing with anger.

"You fucking bastard," Liam growled, his voice low and menacing. "How could you do this to me? I trusted you, man. I thought you had my back."

Jack's eyes widened, a flicker of guilt and shame crossing his face. "Liam, listen, I can explain—"

But Liam wasn't in the mood for explanations. He shoved Jack, hard, sending him stumbling back against the wall. "Explain what, exactly? How you stabbed me in the back? How you betrayed my trust and sold me out to the Chief?"

Jack's expression hardened, his own anger rising to the surface. "I was trying to protect you, you ungrateful prick. You have no idea the kind of danger you're putting yourself in, the risks you're taking by getting involved with this shit."

Liam laughed, a harsh, bitter sound that echoed through the gym. "Protect me? By ratting me out and jeopardizing everything I've worked for? Some fucking friend you are."

The two men stared at each other, the tension between them crackling like electricity. Liam's heart was pounding, his blood roaring in his ears as he fought to control the rage that threatened to consume him.

"You know what? Fuck this," he spat, turning on his heel and stalking towards the boxing ring. "You want to settle this like men? Then let's settle it. Right here, right now."

Jack hesitated for a moment, his expression conflicted. But then he nodded, a grim determination settling over his features as he followed Liam into the ring.

They faced off against each other, their fists raised and their eyes locked in a silent challenge. Liam could feel the adrenaline coursing through his veins, the thrill of the fight mingling with the anger and betrayal that still burned in his chest.

"Come on, then," he taunted, his voice rough and mocking. "Show me what you've got, you traitorous piece of shit."

Jack's jaw clenched, his eyes flashing with fury as he lunged forward, his fist connecting with Liam's jaw in a sickening crack. Liam staggered back, his vision swimming as he shook his head to clear the stars that danced before his eyes.

But he didn't stay down for long. With a roar of rage, he launched himself at Jack, his own fists flying in a flurry of jabs and hooks. They traded blows, the sound of flesh on flesh echoing through the gym as they poured out their anger and frustration in a brutal, primal display of aggression.

"You don't get it, do you?" Jack panted, his face contorted with pain and exertion. "I was trying to save your fucking life, Liam. You have no idea what you're up against, the kind of people you're dealing with."

Liam snarled, his eyes blazing with a fierce, unwavering determination. "I know exactly what I'm up against, Jack. And I'm not going to back down, not when innocent lives are at stake. Not when there's a chance to uncover the truth and bring those responsible to justice."

Jack shook his head, a sad, weary expression settling over his features. "You're a fucking idiot, Liam. You're going to get yourself killed, and for what? Some misguided sense of heroism? Some naive belief that you can make a difference?"

Liam's heart clenched, a flicker of doubt and uncertainty creeping into his mind. Was Jack right? Was he being reckless, putting himself and others in danger for a cause that he barely understood?

But then he thought of Ethan, of the unwavering dedication and fierce determination that burned in the vigilante's eyes. He thought of the innocent mutants who had been taken, experimented on, their lives forever changed by the cruel machinations of Genexis.

And he knew, with a certainty that he had never felt before, that he couldn't turn his back on this fight. Not now, not ever.

"You're wrong, Jack," he said, his voice low and steady. "I'm not doing this for some misguided sense of heroism. I'm doing this because it's the right thing to do. Because someone has to stand up and fight for what's right, even if it means risking everything."

Jack's expression softened, a flicker of understanding and respect crossing his face. He opened his mouth to speak, to say something that might bridge the gap between them and heal the rift that had torn their friendship apart.

But before he could utter a word, the shrill, piercing wail of the fire alarm cut through the air, shattering the moment and jolting them both back to reality.

"Shit," Liam cursed, his eyes wide with sudden realization. "That's the alarm for Times Square. Something big must be going down."

He turned to Jack, his expression grim and determined. "We'll finish this later. But right now, we've got a job to do."

Jack nodded, his own face set in a mask of professionalism as they both raced towards the locker room, their fight forgotten in the face of the greater emergency that demanded their attention.

As Liam and his team sped towards Time Square, the wail of the sirens and the flashing of the lights a constant reminder of the urgency of the situation, he couldn't shake the feeling of unease that had settled in the pit of his stomach. Something about this call felt different, felt wrong in a way that he couldn't quite put his finger on.

When they arrived on the scene, the chaos that greeted them was unlike anything Liam had ever seen before. Time Square, usually a bustling hub of activity and life, was now a scene of panic and destruction. A massive fire engulfed one of the buildings, the flames licking at the sky and casting an eerie, flickering glow over the crowds of people who rushed to evacuate.

But it wasn't just the fire that caught Liam's attention. As he scanned the area, his eyes fell on a group of DMA agents, their dark suits and grim expressions a stark contrast to the bright lights and colorful billboards of Time Square. They seemed to be focused on something else entirely, their attention drawn away from the blaze and towards a shadowy corner of the square.

"What the hell are they doing here?" Liam muttered to himself, his brow furrowed in confusion and suspicion. The DMA's presence at a fire scene was unusual, to say the least, and he couldn't shake the feeling that there was more going on here than met the eye.

But there was no time to dwell on that now. The fire was spreading rapidly, and every second counted if they were going to save the lives of those trapped inside the burning building.

"Alright, team, let's move!" Liam barked, his voice cutting through the chaos and panic like a knife. "We've got people to rescue and a fire to put out. Let's show these bastards what we're made of!"

With a roar of determination, Liam and his team sprang into action, battling their way through the smoke and flames with a fierce, unwavering courage. Liam could feel the heat of the fire on his skin, could taste the acrid tang of smoke in the back of his throat, but he pushed forward, his mind focused solely on the task at hand.

As he made his way deeper into the building, the sound of screams and cries for help echoing in his ears, Liam's heart raced with a mixture of fear and adrenaline. He knew that every second counted, that every moment he wasted could mean the difference between life and death for those trapped inside.

And then he saw it. Through the haze of smoke and the flickering flames, he caught a glimpse of a small, huddled figure, cowering in the corner of a room. It was a child, no more than six or seven years old, her eyes wide with terror and her face streaked with tears.

But she wasn't alone. Standing over her, a dark, menacing figure loomed, his face obscured by a mask and his hands wrapped around the child's arm in a vise-like grip.

"Hey!" Liam shouted, his voice hoarse and ragged from the smoke. "Let her go, you son of a bitch!"

The figure turned slowly, his eyes glinting with a malevolent amusement that sent a chill down Liam's spine. He seemed to regard Liam with a sort of detached curiosity, as if he were nothing more than a mildly interesting insect that had crossed his path.

"Well, well, well," the figure drawled, his voice low and mocking.

"If it isn't one of New York's finest, come to play the hero. How very predictable."

Liam's jaw clenched, his fists tightening at his sides as he fought to control the rage that boiled up inside him. Who the fuck did this guy think he was, taunting him like this while a child's life hung in the balance?

"I'm not going to ask you again," Liam growled, his voice low and dangerous. "Let the girl go, or I swear to God, I'll make you regret the day you were born."

The figure laughed, a cold, mirthless sound that echoed through the burning building like a death knell. "You're welcome to try, little hero. But I'm afraid you're out of your depth here. This is bigger than you, bigger than all of us."

And then, before Liam could even blink, the figure was gone, vanishing into thin air like a wisp of smoke on the wind. The child, too, had disappeared, leaving no trace of their presence behind.

"No!" Liam screamed, his voice raw with desperation and fury. "Fuck, no! Come back here, you cowardly piece of shit!"

But it was too late. They were gone, vanished into the ether like ghosts in the night. Liam stood there, his chest heaving and his mind reeling with the shock of what had just happened. How could he have let this happen? How could he have failed that child so completely?

The sound of the fire roaring around him snapped Liam back to reality, the heat and smoke a searing reminder of the danger that still lurked in the burning building. He couldn't give up now, couldn't let his failure consume him. There were still lives to be saved, still a job to be done.

With a growl of determination, Liam focused his mind, summoning the power of his pyrokinetic abilities. He could feel the flames responding to his will, bending and twisting to his command as he fought to clear a path through the inferno.

But the fire was too strong, too intense. Liam could feel his strength waning, his powers pushed to their limits as he poured every ounce of his energy into controlling the blaze. His vision swam, his lungs burning with every breath as the smoke and heat threatened to overwhelm him.

"Liam!" he heard a voice call out, distant and muffled through the roar of the flames. "Liam, where are you?"

It was Jack, his teammate and friend, searching for him amidst the chaos. Liam tried to call out, to let him know where he was, but his voice was little more than a hoarse whisper, drowned out by the crackling of the fire.

He stumbled forward, his legs feeling like lead as he fought to stay upright. But it was no use. His strength had finally given out, his body and mind pushed beyond their limits. With a final, gasping breath, Liam felt himself falling, the world around him fading into darkness as he collapsed to the ground.

Through the haze of smoke and heat, he saw a figure emerge, a silhouette wreathed in flames. For a moment, he thought it was the kidnapper, come back to finish the job. But then he heard Jack's voice, closer now, shouting his name with a desperate urgency.

"Liam! Fuck, Liam, hold on! I'm coming!"

Liam felt strong arms wrap around him, dragging him back from the brink of oblivion. He tried to speak, to tell Jack to leave him, to save himself. But the words wouldn't come, his tongue thick and heavy in his mouth as the darkness closed in around him.

The last thing he heard before the blackness claimed him was the sound of Jack's voice, pleading with him to stay awake, to hold on just a little longer. And then, with a final, shuddering breath, Liam let go, surrendering himself to the void as the world around him faded away.

15

Unmasking the Heart

Ethan

Ethan sat at the head of the conference table, his eyes sharp and focused as he listened to the latest financial reports from his team. The numbers were good, the projections even better, and he couldn't help the small, satisfied smirk that tugged at the corner of his mouth.

"Excellent work, everyone," he said, his voice smooth and confident. "It seems our latest acquisitions are already paying off. At this rate, we'll be dominating the market in no time."

His team nodded and murmured their agreement, their faces alight with the glow of success. Ethan leaned back in his chair, his fingers steepled in front of him as he savored the moment. This was what he lived for - the thrill of the hunt, the rush of victory, the knowledge that he was the best at what he did.

"So, what's next on the agenda?" he asked, his voice crisp and businesslike. "I assume we have some new investment opportunities to discuss?"

His CFO nodded, shuffling through a stack of papers in front of her.

"Yes, sir. We've identified a few promising startups in the biotech and renewable energy sectors. With the right funding and guidance, they could be real game-changers."

Ethan nodded, his mind already racing with the possibilities. This was what he was good at - spotting potential, seizing opportunities, making bold moves that others were too afraid to even consider. It was what had made him one of the most successful businessmen in the city, and it was what would keep him on top, no matter what challenges lay ahead.

But just as he was about to dive into the details of the new investments, a sudden buzz from his phone interrupted his train of thought. Ethan frowned, glancing down at the screen to see Zoe's name flashing urgently.

"Excuse me for a moment," he said, rising from his chair and stepping out of the conference room. "I need to take this."

As soon as the door closed behind him, Ethan answered the call, his heart suddenly pounding with a sense of dread. Zoe never called him during business hours unless it was an emergency, and the tone of her voice when she spoke only confirmed his worst fears.

"Ethan," she said, her words rushed and breathless. "It's Liam. He's been hurt."

Ethan felt his blood run cold, his grip tightening on the phone until his knuckles turned white. "What happened?" he demanded, his voice raw and ragged. "Is he okay?"

There was a pause on the other end of the line, a moment of hesitation that made Ethan's stomach twist with fear. "There was a fire," Zoe said finally, her voice trembling slightly. "At Time Square. Liam and his team were called in to help evacuate the building, but something went wrong. He collapsed, Ethan. They had to rush him to the hospital."

Ethan felt like he had been punched in the gut, the air rushing out of his lungs in a single, painful exhale. Liam, hurt? In the hospital? It didn't seem possible, didn't seem real. Liam was strong, invincible, a force of nature that nothing could touch. The thought of him lying broken and vulnerable in a hospital bed made Ethan's heart ache with a pain he had never known before.

"How bad is it?" he asked, his voice barely above a whisper. "Is he going to be okay?"

Zoe hesitated again, and Ethan could almost see the pained expression on her face. "They don't know," she said softly. "He inhaled a lot of smoke, and there was some kind of explosion… Ethan, it's not looking good."

Ethan felt a wave of nausea wash over him, his eyes stinging with sudden, hot tears. This couldn't be happening, couldn't be real. Liam was supposed to be invincible, unbreakable, a constant presence in Ethan's life that he could always count on. The thought of losing him, of never seeing that crooked smile or hearing that warm, rich laugh again… it was too much to bear.

"I'm on my way," he said, his voice hard and determined. "I'll be there as soon as I can."

He hung up the phone, taking a deep breath to compose himself before stepping back into the conference room. His colleagues looked up at him expectantly, their expressions curious.

"Gentlemen, I apologize," Ethan said, his voice tight with barely controlled emotion. "I have to leave. There's been an emergency, and I'm needed elsewhere."

He began gathering his papers and laptop, his hands shaking slightly as he shoved them into his briefcase. "I'll have my assistant reschedule this meeting as soon as possible. I'm sorry for the short notice, but I have to go."

Without waiting for a response, Ethan hurried out of the room, his heart pounding and his mind racing. He knew his abrupt departure would raise questions, but he couldn't bring himself to care. All that mattered was getting to Liam, being by his side and offering whatever support and comfort he could.

As he raced out of the building and towards his car, Ethan could feel the weight of his fear and anxiety pressing down on him like a physical thing. But he pushed it aside, forced himself to focus on the task at hand.

Liam needed him, and he would be there. No matter what.

As he wove through the crowded city streets, Ethan's mind was a whirlwind of fear and desperation. He couldn't lose Liam, couldn't bear the thought of living in a world without his crooked smile and his warm, steadfast presence. Liam was more than just a partner, more than just a friend. He was the other half of Ethan's soul, the missing piece that made him whole.

He barely registered the blaring of horns and the screeching of tires as he sped through red lights and wove between lanes of traffic. All he could focus on was the hospital, looming in the distance like a beacon of hope and despair.

When he finally reached the parking lot, Ethan didn't even bother to lock his car. He just leaped out and sprinted towards the entrance, his heart in his throat and his lungs burning with exertion. He burst through the doors, his eyes wild and searching as he scanned the crowded waiting room for any sign of Liam or his team.

And then he saw them - a group of firefighters huddled in the corner, their faces drawn and tired and full of worry. Ethan felt a surge of relief and fear wash over him, his steps faltering as he approached them on shaky legs.

"Where is he?" he demanded, his voice hoarse and raw. "Where's Liam? Is he okay?"

The firefighters looked up at him, their expressions wary and confused. Ethan realized with a start that they had no idea who he was, no clue about his connection to Liam or the desperate, all-consuming love that burned in his heart.

"Who are you?" one of them asked, his voice gruff and suspicious. "What do you want with Liam?"

Ethan opened his mouth to respond, but the words stuck in his throat. He couldn't tell them the truth, couldn't reveal the depth of his feelings for Liam in front of these strangers. But he also couldn't walk away, couldn't leave Liam's side when he needed him most.

And so, in a moment of desperate, reckless inspiration, Ethan blurted out the first thing that came to his mind.

"I'm his boyfriend," he said, his voice shaking slightly. "Liam's my boyfriend."

There was a moment of stunned silence, and then the firefighters erupted into a chorus of murmurs and whispers. Ethan could see the skepticism in their eyes, the doubt and confusion that played across their faces.

"Boyfriend?" one of them repeated, his eyebrows raised in disbelief. "Liam's never mentioned a boyfriend before. How long have you two been together?"

Ethan swallowed hard, his mind racing as he tried to come up with a believable story. "A few months," he said finally, his voice steadier than he felt. "We've been keeping it quiet, you know, because of work and everything."

He didn't care if the firefighters believed him or not, didn't care if they thought he was crazy or delusional.

The firefighters exchanged glances, their expressions softening slightly. Finally, one of them - a tall, broad-shouldered man with kind eyes - stepped forward and placed a hand on Ethan's shoulder.

"Okay," he said gently, his voice warm and reassuring. "Okay, we believe you. And we're glad you're here. Liam's going to need all the support he can get right now."

Ethan felt a wave of gratitude wash over him, his shoulders sagging with relief. He nodded, and allowed the firefighter to guide him to a chair.

The hours ticked by with agonizing slowness, Ethan found himself pacing the waiting room, his mind racing with thoughts of Liam and the uncertainty of his condition. The firefighters sat nearby, their expressions grim and their voices low as they spoke in hushed tones.

"I can't just sit here," Ethan muttered, his fists clenching at his sides. "I need to see him, need to know that he's okay."

Jack, the firefighter who had been eyeing him with skepticism earlier, looked up at him with a furrowed brow. "And what exactly is your relationship with Liam?" he asked, his voice gruff but not unkind. "You said you were his boyfriend, but he's never mentioned you before."

Ethan felt a flicker of panic rising in his chest, but he forced it down with a cocky grin. "Well, you know Liam," he said, his voice dripping with false bravado. "He's never been one to kiss and tell. But trust me, we're close. Very close."

He waggled his eyebrows suggestively, trying to hide the way his heart was racing with fear and uncertainty. Jack just shook his head, a small, reluctant smile tugging at the corners of his mouth.

"Fine, don't tell us," he said, his voice softening with understanding. "But just know that we're here for Liam, and for you too. Whatever you need, we've got your back."

Ethan felt a lump rising in his throat, a wave of gratitude washing over him. He knew that he didn't deserve their kindness, their acceptance, but he couldn't help but be touched by it all the same.

"Thank you," he said, his voice rough with emotion. "That means a lot, really."

Just then, a doctor emerged from the ICU, her face tired but hopeful. "Mr. Quinn is stable for now," she said, her voice calm and reassuring. "We're going to keep him in the ICU overnight for observation, but his vitals are looking good. One of you can stay with him, if you'd like."

The firefighters exchanged glances, their expressions torn. Ethan knew that they all wanted to be there for Liam, to offer their support and comfort in his time of need.

But to his surprise, Jack turned to him with a small, knowing smile. "You should go," he said, his voice soft but firm. "Liam needs you right now, more than anyone else."

Ethan felt his heart skip a beat, a rush of emotions washing over him. He wanted to argue, to insist that the firefighters should be the ones to stay with Liam. But deep down, he knew that Jack was right. He needed to be there for Liam, needed to see with his own eyes that he was alive and breathing.

"Okay," he said, his voice barely above a whisper. "Okay, I'll go."

The firefighters nodded, their expressions solemn but understanding. Ethan took a deep breath, steeling himself for whatever lay ahead. And then, with a final nod of thanks, he turned and followed the doctor into the ICU.

The sight of Liam lying there, his face pale and still beneath the tangle of wires and tubes, made Ethan's heart clench with a pain that was almost physical. He approached the bed slowly, his hand hovering just above Liam's as if afraid to touch him.

"Hey there, Quinn," he said, his voice soft and teasing. "I always knew you were a fan of dramatic entrances, but this is taking it a bit far, don't you think?"

He forced a laugh, but it sounded hollow and strained even to his own ears. He sank into the chair beside the bed, his shoulders slumping with exhaustion and worry.

"You really scared the shit out of me, you know that?" he said, his voice growing serious. "I thought... I thought I might lose you. And I realized that I..."

He trailed off, the words sticking in his throat. He wanted to tell

Liam how he felt, wanted to pour out his heart and confess the depth of his feelings for him. But something held him back, some last stubborn shred of fear and self-preservation.

So instead, he just reached out and took Liam's hand in his own, his fingers trembling slightly as they brushed against his skin. "I need you to be okay, Liam," he said, his voice barely above a whisper. "I need you to wake up and come back to me. Because I... I don't know what I would do without you."

He fell silent then, his eyes fixed on Liam's face as if searching for some sign of life, some flicker of consciousness. And as the minutes ticked by and the machines beeped and hummed around them, Ethan felt a sense of helplessness washing over him, a feeling of powerlessness that he had never known before.

But he refused to give up hope, refused to let the darkness and the fear consume him. Because Liam was strong, stronger than anyone he had ever known. And if anyone could come back from this, if anyone could defy the odds and emerge victorious, it was him.

So Ethan just sat there, his hand clasped tightly in Liam's, his mind spinning with thoughts and emotions that he couldn't quite put into words. And he waited, waited for some sign, some miracle that would bring Liam back to him.

Minutes turned into hours, and still Ethan refused to leave Liam's side. He talked to him, joked with him, even made silly promises about all the things they would do when Liam woke up, anything to fill the silence and keep the darkness at bay.

"You know, if you wanted my undivided attention, you could have just asked," Ethan teased, his voice light despite the heaviness in his heart. "No need for such dramatic measures, handsome."

Just when he thought he couldn't take another moment of the waiting, another second of the uncertainty, Liam began to stir. It was subtle at first, just a flicker of movement beneath his eyelids, a twitch of his fingers against Ethan's palm.

But then, slowly, miraculously, those eyes fluttered open, blinking against the harsh fluorescent lights of the hospital room. And when they finally focused on Ethan's face, when they widened with recognition and relief, it was like the sun breaking through the clouds after an endless, stormy night.

"Hey there, sleeping beauty," Ethan said, his voice rough with emotion. "About time you decided to join the party."

Liam's lips curved into a weak smile, his hand tightening around Ethan's. "What happened?" he rasped, his voice hoarse from disuse.

Ethan's brow furrowed, concern etched in his features. "You don't remember? There was a fire at Time Square, and you… you got hurt pretty badly."

Liam's eyes widened, a flicker of panic crossing his face. "The child… the kidnapper… did they…?"

Ethan shook his head, his expression grim. "I don't know, Liam. But don't worry about that now. The important thing is that you're safe, and you're going to be okay."

Just then, a team of doctors and nurses entered the room, their faces serious as they began to check Liam's vitals and assess his condition. Ethan stepped back, giving them space to work, but he never let go of Liam's hand, never broke the connection between them.

As the medical team bustled around them, Ethan leaned in close, his voice low and urgent. "Liam, what actually happened in there?"

Liam's face clouded, his eyes distant as he struggled to remember. "It was strange," he said, his voice hesitant. "The kidnapper, he… he just vanished. Into thin air. Like he was never there at all."

Ethan's eyes widened, his mind racing with the implications. "Vanished? Like, with powers? Like a mutant?"

Liam nodded, his expression troubled. "I think so. But I've never seen anything like it before. It was like he was there one second, and gone the next."

Ethan's jaw clenched, a flicker of anger and determination crossing his face. "We'll figure it out," he said, his voice low and fierce. "We'll find out who's behind this, and we'll make them pay. I promise you that, Liam."

Liam smiled, a real smile this time, his eyes warm and grateful. "I know we will. Together, there's nothing we can't do." Liam closed his eyes and fell asleep.

And as the doctors finished their examination and declared Liam stable and on the road to recovery, Ethan felt a weight lifting from his shoulders, a sense of relief and hope that he hadn't felt in what seemed like forever.

16

Forced Proximity

Liam

Liam grumbled as the nurse insisted on wheeling him out of the hospital, feeling like a helpless invalid. He knew it was standard procedure, but it still stung his pride to be treated like he couldn't walk on his own two feet.

"This is ridiculous," he muttered, shooting a glare at Ethan who was walking alongside him with a smirk on his face. "I can walk just fine, you know."

Ethan chuckled, his eyes sparkling with amusement. "Oh, I know you can, tough guy. But let's just humor the nice nurse, okay? Besides, I've got a surprise for you."

Liam's brow furrowed, his curiosity piqued. "A surprise? What kind of surprise?"

Ethan just grinned, his expression mischievous. "You'll see. Now stop complaining and let me take care of you for once, okay?"

Liam sighed, settling back into the wheelchair with a huff. He didn't like being kept in the dark, but he knew that arguing with Ethan was a losing battle.

As they made their way out of the hospital and towards Ethan's waiting car, Liam couldn't help but feel a sense of unease wash over him. He had no idea where Ethan was taking him, and the thought of being alone with the other man in an unfamiliar place made his stomach twist with nerves.

"Okay, seriously, Hawke," he said, his voice tight with tension. "Where the hell are we going? I thought you were just giving me a ride home."

Ethan's grin widened, his eyes sparkling with excitement. "Change of plans, Quinn. You're coming home with me."

Liam's eyes widened, his mouth falling open in shock. "What? No, Ethan, I can't impose on you like that. I'll be fine on my own."

But Ethan was already shaking his head, his jaw set with determination. "Not a chance, Quinn. You're still recovering, and you need someone to keep an eye on you. Besides, my place is a lot more comfortable than that shitty apartment of yours."

Liam bristled, his pride stung by Ethan's words. "Hey, my apartment may not be a fucking palace, but it's home. And I don't need a babysitter, Hawke."

Ethan sighed, his expression softening. "I know you don't, Liam. But I need to do this, okay? I need to know that you're safe, that you're being taken care of. Please, just let me do this for you."

There was something in Ethan's voice, a raw vulnerability that Liam had never heard before. It made his heart ache, made him want to reach out and pull the other man into his arms.

But he didn't. Instead, he just nodded, his throat tight with emotion. "Okay, Ethan. Okay. I'll come stay with you. But just until I'm back on my feet, alright?"

Ethan's grin returned, his eyes sparkling with triumph. "Whatever you say, Quinn. Now come on, let's get you home."

As they drove through the city streets, Liam couldn't help but feel a sense of anticipation building in his gut. He had no idea what to expect from Ethan's place, no idea what kind of world he was about to step into.

But when they finally arrived at Ethan's building, Liam felt his jaw drop in awe. The place was a fucking palace, all gleaming glass and sleek metal and opulent marble. It was like something out of a movie, a world so far removed from Liam's own that it might as well have been on another planet.

"Holy shit," he breathed, his eyes wide as he took in the grandeur of the lobby. "You actually live here?"

Ethan chuckled, his hand resting warmly on the small of Liam's back as he guided him towards the elevators. "What can I say? I like my creature comforts."

As they rode up to the top floor, Liam couldn't help but feel a sense of unease wash over him. He had never been to Ethan's place before, had never seen the world that the billionaire vigilante inhabited when he wasn't wearing his mask.

But when the doors finally slid open and he got his first glimpse of the penthouse, Liam felt his breath catch in his throat. It was stunning, all sleek lines and modern furnishings and floor-to-ceiling windows that offered a breathtaking view of the city skyline.

"Wow," he said softly, his eyes wide with wonder. "This is… this is incredible."

Ethan grinned, his chest puffing up with pride. "It's not bad, is it? Come on, let me give you the grand tour."

He led Liam through the penthouse, pointing out the various features and amenities with a casual wave of his hand. There was a state-of-the-art kitchen, a fully-stocked bar, a home theater system that would make even the most die-hard cinephile weep with envy.

But it was the bedroom that made Liam stop short, his heart hammering in his chest. There was only one, a massive king-sized bed that dominated the space like a throne.

"Uh, Ethan?" he said, his voice cracking slightly. "Where am I supposed to sleep?"

Ethan frowned, his brow furrowing in confusion. "What do you mean? You'll sleep in the bed, of course."

Liam felt his cheeks flush, his stomach twisting with a strange mixture of excitement and trepidation. "But… but there's only one bed."

Ethan's eyes widened, a flicker of realization crossing his face. "Oh. Oh, shit. I didn't even think about that." He ran a hand through his hair, his expression sheepish. "Look, Liam, it's not a big deal. The bed is huge, there's plenty of room for both of us."

Liam's blush deepened, his mind racing with the implications of what Ethan was suggesting. He had never shared a bed with another man before, had never even entertained the thought of it.

But there was something about Ethan, something that made Liam's heart race and his palms sweat. He couldn't deny the attraction he felt towards the other man, the way his skin seemed to tingle every time they touched.

"I don't know, Ethan," he said, his voice hesitant. "Maybe I should just sleep on the couch."

But Ethan was already shaking his head, his expression stubborn. "No way, Quinn. You're still recovering, you need a proper bed to rest in. And trust me, that couch may look fancy, but it's about as comfortable as a fucking rock."

Liam sighed, his shoulders slumping in defeat. He knew that there was no arguing with Ethan when he got like this, knew that the other man would just keep pushing until he got his way.

"Fine," he said, his voice resigned. "But if you try any funny business, Hawke, I swear I'll kick your ass right out of this fancy penthouse of yours."

Ethan grinned, his eyes sparkling with mirth. "Wouldn't dream of it, Quinn. I'm a perfect gentleman, remember?"

Liam snorted, his lips twitching with amusement. "Right. And I'm the fucking Queen of England."

But even as they bantered and joked, Liam couldn't shake the feeling that something had shifted between them, that the easy camaraderie they had always shared was starting to give way to something deeper, something more intense.

As Liam settled into Ethan's lavish penthouse, trying to wrap his mind around the fact that he was actually staying here, with Ethan, the man who had somehow wormed his way into his heart, he couldn't help but feel a sense of unease. It was all so new, so unfamiliar, and Liam wasn't sure how to navigate this strange new territory.

Just as he was about to voice his concerns, to try and put into words the jumble of emotions that were swirling around in his head, Ethan's phone rang, shattering the moment.

"It's Zoe and Marcus," Ethan said, glancing down at the screen with a furrowed brow. "They must have an update on the investigation."

Liam felt a flicker of excitement at the prospect of new information, of finally getting some answers to the questions that had been plaguing them for so long. But he also felt a sense of trepidation, a fear of what they might uncover and what it could mean for their already complicated relationship.

Ethan answered the call, putting it on speaker so that Liam could hear as well. "What's up, guys? Please tell me you've got some good news for us."

Zoe's voice crackled through the phone, her tone serious but hopeful. "Actually, we do. We've managed to secure an appointment with Dr. Novak. She's agreed to meet with us and tell her side of the story."

Liam felt his heart skip a beat at the mention of Dr. Novak's name. The thought of finally coming face to face with her, of hearing her perspective and trying to understand her motivations, was both thrilling and terrifying.

"That's great news," Ethan said, his voice tinged with excitement. "When's the meeting?"

"Tomorrow afternoon," Marcus chimed in, his gruff voice filling the room. "But there's something else you should know. From what we've been able to gather, it seems like Dr. Novak might be more of a victim in all of this than we originally thought."

Liam frowned, his mind racing with the implications of Marcus's words. "What do you mean? How could she be a victim if she's been experimenting on mutants and working with Genexis?"

Zoe sighed, her voice heavy with empathy. "It's complicated, Liam. From what we've been able to piece together, it seems like Dr. Novak might have been coerced or manipulated into working with Genexis."

Liam felt a pang of sympathy for Dr. Novak, a sense of kinship with her struggles as a mutant in a world that feared and misunderstood them. He knew all too well what it was like to be judged and persecuted for something he couldn't control, to be seen as less than human simply because of his abilities.

"So what you're saying is, we need to approach this meeting with an open mind," Ethan said, his voice thoughtful. "We need to hear Dr. Novak out and try to understand her perspective, even if it goes against everything we thought we knew."

"Exactly," Zoe agreed, her tone emphatic. "We can't just write her off as a villain or a monster."

Liam nodded, his mind whirling with the possibilities of what they might uncover. He knew that it wouldn't be easy, that they would have to confront some uncomfortable truths and grapple with the moral ambiguity of the situation. But he also knew that it was the only way forward, the only way to get to the bottom of this mystery and bring those responsible to justice.

"Alright," Ethan said, his voice firm with determination. "I'll go to the meeting with Dr. Novak alone. I don't want to put Liam in any more danger than he's already been in."

Liam's head snapped up, his eyes flashing with indignation. "Like hell you will," he growled, his voice low and fierce. "I'm not some damsel in distress that needs to be protected, Ethan. I'm a part of this investigation, and I'm going to see it through to the end, no matter what."

Ethan's eyes widened, a flicker of surprise and something else, something warmer and softer, crossing his face. "Liam, I know you're tough, but you're still recovering. I don't want to risk your safety any more than I already have."

Liam shook his head, his jaw clenched with stubborn determination. "I'm not asking for your permission, Ethan. I'm telling you. We're in this together, whether you like it or not."

For a long moment, Ethan just stared at him, his green eyes searching Liam's face for some sign of hesitation or doubt. But Liam held his gaze, his own eyes blazing with conviction and resolve.

Finally, Ethan sighed, a small, rueful smile tugging at the corners of his mouth. "Alright, fine. We'll go together. But you have to promise me that you'll be careful, Liam. I can't lose you, not now, not when I've just found you."

Liam felt his heart skip a beat at Ethan's words, at the raw vulnerability and emotion that he saw in the other man's eyes. He knew that Ethan was struggling with his own feelings, that he was just as confused and uncertain about this thing between them as Liam was.

But he also knew that there was something there, something real and powerful and undeniable. And he wasn't going to let it slip away, not without a fight.

"I promise," he said softly, his voice thick with emotion. "I'll be careful. But I'm not going to let you face this alone, Ethan. We're partners, in every sense of the word. And partners have each other's backs, no matter what."

Ethan's smile widened, his eyes sparkling with a mixture of affection and exasperation. "You're a stubborn son of a bitch, you know that?"

Liam grinned, his own eyes twinkling with mischief. "Yeah, well, you knew that when you signed up for this. You're stuck with me now, Hawke."

Ethan laughed, the sound rich and warm in the stillness of the penthouse. "I wouldn't have it any other way, Quinn."

As the call ended and the room fell silent once more, Liam felt a sudden weight settle on his shoulders, a reminder of the warning he had received from his captain before leaving the hospital. He knew he needed to tell Ethan, to be honest about the risks they were facing, but a part of him hesitated, not wanting to shatter the fragile peace they had found.

"Ethan," he said softly, his voice heavy with reluctance. "There's something else I need to tell you."

Ethan's brow furrowed, concern etched in the lines of his face. "What is it, Liam? What's wrong?"

Liam sighed, running a hand through his hair as he tried to find the right words. "The chief pulled me aside. He warned me about the consequences of pursuing this investigation, about the danger it could put me in, both personally and professionally."

Ethan's eyes widened, a flicker of anger sparking in their depths. "What the fuck? He's trying to scare you off the case?"

Liam shook his head, a wry smile tugging at his lips. "No, it's not like that. He's just worried about me, about the risks I'm taking. And to be honest, I can't blame him. This whole thing is a fucking mess, Ethan. We're in way over our heads here."

Ethan's jaw clenched, his expression hardening with determination. "I know it's dangerous, Liam. But we can't just walk away, not now, not when we're so close to the truth. We have to see this through, no matter the cost."

Liam felt a surge of frustration rising in his chest, his own temper flaring to match Ethan's. "Damn it, Ethan, this isn't just about the case anymore. This is about our lives, our futures. If we keep pushing, if we keep digging into this conspiracy, there's no telling what kind of backlash we could face."

Ethan's eyes softened, a flicker of understanding passing between them. "I know, Liam. I know the risks. But I also know that we can't let fear control us, can't let it stop us from doing what's right. We have to trust in each other, in the strength of our partnership. Together, we can face anything."

Liam felt his resolve wavering, his heart torn between his sense of duty and his growing feelings for the man in front of him. He knew that Ethan was right, that they had to keep fighting, no matter the odds. But he also knew that the thought of losing Ethan, of watching him get hurt or worse, was more than he could bear.

As the day wore on and the tension between them grew, Liam found himself struggling to keep his emotions in check. The forced proximity of the penthouse, the knowledge that they were alone together, with no one to interrupt or distract them, was like a constant buzz under his skin, a reminder of the growing attraction that simmered between them.

He caught himself staring at Ethan more than once, his eyes lingering on the strong lines of his jaw, the curve of his lips, the way his muscles flexed beneath his shirt as he moved. And each time, he felt a flush of heat rising in his cheeks, a flutter of desire stirring in his belly.

It was maddening, this constant push and pull of wanting and not wanting, of needing and denying. Liam knew that he was falling for Ethan, that his feelings for the other man were growing deeper and more intense with each passing moment. But he also knew that he couldn't act on them, couldn't risk jeopardizing their partnership or their mission.

And so he kept his distance, kept his walls up and his heart guarded. Even as every fiber of his being screamed at him to reach out, to pull Ethan close and never let go.

It was torture, pure and simple. And as the hours ticked by and the tension between them grew thicker and more palpable, Liam found himself wondering how much longer he could hold out, how much longer he could resist the siren call of Ethan's touch and Ethan's smile.

And as he watched Ethan move around the penthouse, as he listened to the sound of his laughter and the cadence of his voice, Liam knew that he was in trouble, knew that he was falling harder and faster than he ever had before.

And he didn't know how to stop it, didn't know how to put the brakes on this runaway train of emotion and desire. All he could do was hold on tight and pray that he wouldn't crash and burn, that he wouldn't take Ethan down with him.

But even as he tried to keep his distance, even as he tried to maintain some semblance of professionalism and control, Liam could feel the walls between them crumbling, could feel the heat and the hunger building in the air like a gathering storm.

The day was almost over and Liam hesitantly followed Ethan into the bedroom, the tension between them thick and palpable. All day, the charged looks and accidental brushes of skin had been building, stoking the ever-present attraction that simmered under the surface of their partnership.

Now, alone in the intimacy of Ethan's bedroom, that tension was reaching a boiling point. Liam's heart raced as his eyes roamed over Ethan appreciatively. The vigilante was devastatingly handsome, his chiseled features and muscular physique enough to make Liam's mouth go dry with want.

Ethan turned to face him, green eyes dark and smoldering with barely restrained desire. "Liam…" he murmured, voice low and rough.

Suddenly, Ethan closed the distance between them in two swift strides. One hand cupped Liam's face as the other snaked around his waist, pulling their bodies flush.

Then Ethan's mouth was on his in a searing, desperate kiss. Liam gasped in surprise before melting into it, lips parting automatically. Ethan took the invitation to plunder Liam's mouth with his clever tongue, kissing him breathless.

They stumbled backwards until Liam's knees hit the bed. Ethan lowered him down gently, mindful of Liam's healing injuries even in the heat of passion. He covered Liam's body with his own, never breaking the intimate press of their lips.

Large, calloused hands slid under Liam's shirt, exploring the hard planes of his chest and abs. Liam arched into the touch with a low moan, his own fingers tangling in Ethan's dark hair.

"Fuck, you feel so good," Ethan growled against his lips. "I've wanted to touch you like this for so long."

"Then touch me," Liam demanded breathlessly. "I want your hands all over me."

Ethan made quick work of removing their clothes, baring heated skin to wandering hands and hungry mouths. He trailed worshipful kisses down the column of Liam's throat, tongue flicking out to taste the salt of his skin.

"You're so fucking beautiful," Ethan praised, voice awed. "I can't believe I get to have you like this."

Liam pulled him up for another searing kiss. "You have me," he promised raggedly. "Now quit teasing and fuck me already."

Ethan chuckled, a wicked smirk curling his kiss-swollen lips. "So impatient. But I'm going to take my time with you. I want to make this so good for you, baby."

He proceeded to do just that, mapping every inch of Liam's skin with reverent kisses and teasing licks. He took Liam apart with his hands and mouth until he was a writhing, begging mess, pain and injuries forgotten in the haze of blinding pleasure.

When Ethan finally pressed inside him, their bodies joining as one, Liam saw stars. "Oh God, Ethan!" he cried out, fingernails digging into the vigilante's muscular back.

"That's it, sweetheart. Take my cock so well," Ethan panted, setting a deep, rolling rhythm that had Liam's toes curling.

Their lovemaking was passionate and intense, weeks' worth of pent-up tension and longing pouring out. The room filled with the erotic sounds of skin slapping against skin and breathy moans and whispered praise.

"I'm close," Liam warned, feeling the telltale tingle at the base of his spine.

"Come for me, Liam," Ethan urged, increasing his pace. "I want to feel you come on my cock."

One, two, three more thrusts and Liam was gone, spilling between their sweat-slicked bodies with a choked off cry. Ethan followed right after, Liam's fluttering muscles milking his climax from him.

They collapsed together in a panting heap of tangled limbs. Ethan pulled out carefully and rolled to the side, gathering Liam close. He pressed tender kisses to Liam's face, tasting the salt of joyful tears on his skin.

"That was..." Liam trailed off, struggling to find words.

"Incredible," Ethan finished, grinning lazily. "Mind-blowing. The best sex of my life."

Liam huffed a laugh and lightly smacked Ethan's chest. "Way to ruin the moment, dork."

They laid together quietly for a long moment, basking in the afterglow. Liam's head rested on Ethan's shoulder, the steady thump of his heartbeat a soothing lullaby.

"Hey, Ethan?" Liam asked softly, tracing idle patterns on Ethan's skin. "What does this mean? For us?"

"It means we have something special here," Ethan replied, serious despite the roguish glint in his eyes. "Whatever this is between us, I don't want it to be just physical. I care about you, Liam, more than I ever thought possible.

He tipped Liam's chin up to meet his eyes. "You're not just a casual hookup to me. You're my partner, in every sense of the word. I want to see where this goes."

Liam's heart soared at the sincerity in Ethan's eyes. "I want that too," he admitted shyly. "I don't know what the future holds, but I know I want you by my side through it all."

"Partners in justice and in pleasure?" Ethan waggled his eyebrows playfully, lightening the heavy moment.

Liam snorted and swatted him with a pillow. "You're ridiculous," he complained, but couldn't fight the fond smile tugging at his lips.

They traded lazy kisses and teasing touches, stoking the embers of desire into a roaring flame once more. Ethan gently rolled Liam beneath him, settling into the welcoming cradle of his thighs.

"Ready for round two already?" Ethan purred, nipping at Liam's kiss-swollen lips. "My, my, someone's eager."

"Less talking, more fucking," Liam demanded, hooking a leg around Ethan's waist to pull him closer.

"So bossy," Ethan tutted, reaching between them to grip Liam's hardening cock. "I love it."

He took his time opening Liam up, claiming his mouth in deep, filthy kisses as he worked him loose. By the time he finally pushed inside, Liam was a trembling mess, utterly lost to pleasure.

"Fuck, you take me so well," Ethan groaned, bottoming out in one smooth thrust. "Like you were made for my cock."

"Maybe I was," Liam panted, rolling his hips to take Ethan even deeper. "Now shut up and fuck me like you mean it."

Ethan set a punishing pace, driving into Liam with deep, powerful thrusts. The headboard slammed against the wall with the force of it, the obscene slap of skin on skin echoing through the room.

Lost in the throes of passion, neither man noticed the slight pull of stitches or throb of bruises. The outside world fell away until there was nothing but the slide of their bodies and the symphony of their mingled moans.

"Touch yourself," Ethan ordered roughly, feeling his orgasm rapidly approaching. "I want to see you come on my cock again."

Liam obeyed instantly, fisting his dripping erection and stroking in time with Ethan's thrusts. A litany of "yes" and "more" and "harder" fell from his lips as he chased his pleasure. He felt it building at the base of his spine, coiling tighter and tighter until it finally snapped.

"Oh fuck, I'm coming!" Liam shouted, cock pulsing as he spilled over his fist. His ass clenched down hard around Ethan, ripping the vigilante's orgasm from him with a strangled groan.

They shuddered through the aftershocks together, trading messy kisses interspersed with gasps and whimpers. Finally spent, Ethan carefully withdrew and flopped over onto his back, chest heaving.

"That was..." he panted, at a rare loss for words.

"Yeah," Liam agreed breathlessly. "It was."

Smiling softly, Ethan drew Liam into his arms and pressed a tender kiss to his sweaty temple. "We should get cleaned up," he murmured, lips brushing Liam's skin.

"Later," Liam replied through a yawn, limbs feeling pleasantly heavy. "M'comfy."

Ethan chuckled fondly and reached down to pull the blankets over their cooling bodies. "Whatever you want, sweetheart. I've got you."

And there, wrapped up in Ethan's embrace, Liam let himself drift off. Tomorrow would bring new challenges, and this thing between them was still so new and fragile. But for tonight, Liam was content, safe and sated in Ethan's arms.

Everything else could wait.

17

A Twist of Perspective

Ethan

Ethan woke slowly, awareness seeping in like honey. He luxuriated in the feel of Liam's warm, solid body pressed against his, the firefighter's head pillowed on his chest. A smile tugged at Ethan's lips as memories of the previous night washed over him - passionate kisses, wandering hands, the exquisite slide of skin on skin. Making love with Liam had been everything Ethan had fantasized about and more.

As if sensing Ethan's gaze, Liam stirred. Sleepy blue eyes blinked open, crinkling at the corners as a matching smile spread across Liam's face.

"Morning," Ethan murmured, voice husky with satisfaction. He dropped a kiss to the top of Liam's head. "Sleep well?"

Liam hummed contentedly, nuzzling into Ethan's neck. "Best sleep of my life. I could get used to waking up like this."

"That's the plan, sweetheart," Ethan replied, heart swelling with affection. He tightened his arms around Liam, marveling at how perfectly they fit together, like two puzzle pieces finally snapping into place.

They dozed for a little while longer, trading lazy kisses and gentle caresses. But eventually, the demands of the day could no longer be ignored. With great reluctance, Ethan extracted himself from Liam's embrace and climbed out of bed.

"How about some breakfast?" he suggested, pulling on a pair of low-slung sweatpants. "I make a mean omelet."

Liam stretched languidly, the sheet slipping down to reveal a tantalizing expanse of toned chest. Ethan's mouth went dry at the sight, desire punching low in his gut.

"Sounds perfect," Liam replied with a grin, as if he knew exactly what effect he was having on Ethan. The little minx.

They moved around each other easily in Ethan's spacious kitchen, shoulders brushing and fingers grazing as they prepared breakfast together. It felt so natural, so domestic, like they'd been doing this for years instead of hours.

As Ethan plated up the omelets, Liam poured them each a cup of coffee. He took a sip and let out an appreciative moan that went straight to Ethan's cock.

"Damn, that's good coffee," Liam praised, leaning against the counter. "Is this another one of your secret talents, along with crime fighting and cooking?"

"I'm a man of many talents," Ethan replied with a cocky grin. Then, because he couldn't resist, he leaned in and stole a coffee-flavored kiss.

They ate breakfast on the balcony, enjoying the view of the city skyline and the closeness of each other's company. A comfortable silence stretched between them, broken only by the clink of cutlery and the occasional contented sigh.

As Ethan watched Liam, the firefighter's face limned in the golden morning light, he knew he had never been happier. Whatever this was between them, it was special. Precious. Something to be cherished and protected at all costs.

"Hey, Ethan?" Liam asked suddenly, setting down his fork. "Can I ask you something?"

"Of course," Ethan replied easily. "Anything."

Liam hesitated, worrying his bottom lip between his teeth. It was fucking adorable, and Ethan was so gone for this man it wasn't even funny.

"Why tarot?" Liam finally asked, curiosity bright in his eyes. "I mean, I know our mutant abilities aren't always specific, but it seems like an odd choice for a vigilante."

Ethan huffed a fond laugh. He should have known Liam's inquisitive mind wouldn't let that detail slide.

"Well, my power is psychic projection," he explained, leaning back in his chair. "Basically, I can manifest constructs with my mind - weapons, shields, illusions, you name it."

Liam's eyes widened in understanding. "So the tarot is just a focus for your abilities, a way to give them structure."

"Exactly," Ethan confirmed with an approving nod. "I could project anything, but the tarot has always resonated with me. My mother was a reader, you see. Some of my earliest memories are of sitting on her lap while she told fortunes for the neighbors."

A wistful smile tugged at Ethan's lips as he lost himself in the memory. He could almost smell the incense, almost feel the worn velvet of his mother's skirt beneath his fingers.

"Anyway," he continued, shaking off the melancholy, "when my powers manifested, it just felt right to incorporate the tarot. It gives me a framework to work within, and honestly? It looks pretty fucking badass."

Liam snorted, rolling his eyes fondly. "Of course you'd say that, you dramatic bastard."

Ethan flashed him a roguish wink. "You love it, admit it."

"I admit nothing," Liam retorted primly. But the twinkle in his eyes and the quirk of his lips gave him away.

They fell quiet for a moment, content to simply bask in each other's presence. But eventually, the specter of the upcoming meeting with Dr. Novak intruded on their peaceful little bubble.

"So," Ethan said, taking a fortifying sip of coffee. "About this meeting today. I know we need to keep an open mind, but I can't help feeling a little uneasy."

Liam sighed, running a hand through his sleep-mussed hair. "I know what you mean. It's hard to trust anyone in this whole fucked up situation. But I think Zoe and Marcus are right. We need to at least hear Dr. Novak out, see what she has to say."

Ethan nodded, conceding the point. "You're right. We can't judge her until we have all the facts. And if she really is a victim in all this, then she deserves our help and compassion."

"Look at you, being all mature and shit," Liam teased, eyes sparkling with mirth. "I think I'm a good influence on you."

"Oh, is that so?" Ethan challenged, arching a brow. "Well then, by all means, feel free to keep influencing me. Thoroughly and repeatedly."

He punctuated the innuendo with a salacious once-over, gaze dragging over Liam's body like a physical caress. Liam shivered, pupils dilating with unmistakable desire.

"Don't tempt me," the fireman warned, voice dropping to a honeyed purr. "Or we'll never make it to that meeting."

"And that would be terrible, because…?" Ethan countered, only half joking. Faced with the prospect of spending the day in bed with Liam, unraveling the mystery of Dr. Novak didn't seem nearly so pressing.

Liam, ever the responsible one, just shook his head with a rueful smile. "Come on, horn dog. Time to put your game face on. We've got a conspiracy to unravel and a doctor to interrogate."

Ethan heaved a put-upon sigh, but obediently stood and began clearing the breakfast dishes. "Fine, but I expect a reward for my good behavior later. Something involving you, me, and a distinct lack of clothing."

"Play your cards right, and I think that can be arranged," Liam replied with a smirk, laying a smacking kiss on Ethan's cheek as he passed by with the empty coffee mugs.

It was a struggle for Ethan to keep his mind on track after that, but he managed. Barely. They got ready quickly, the banter flowing easily between them even as the gravity of the situation pressed close.

* * *

They pulled up to the nondescript office building where the meeting was set to take place, Ethan felt a flicker of unease skitter down his spine. He glanced over at Liam, saw the same mix of anticipation and apprehension reflected in the firefighter's blue eyes.

"Well, this is it," Ethan said, aiming for levity and falling just short. "Time to see if the good doctor is on the level, or if we're walking into a trap."

Liam reached over and squeezed Ethan's hand, the simple gesture grounding and reassuring. "Hey, whatever happens in there, we've got each other's backs. Right?"

Ethan brought their joined hands to his lips, brushing a kiss across Liam's knuckles. "Damn right we do. You and me against the world, sweetheart."

They allowed themselves one more moment of connection, foreheads pressed together and breaths mingling, before straightening up and slipping into their respective roles. Ethan donned his trademark cocky smirk, while Liam's face settled into a mask of cool professionalism.

Game faces firmly in place, they exited the car and made their way into the building. The receptionist directed them to a small conference room on the third floor, where Dr. Novak was already waiting.

She rose to greet them as they entered, a polite smile on her face. Ethan noted that she was younger than he'd expected, with sharp, intelligent eyes and an air of quiet authority.

"Mr. Hawke, Mr. Roy," she said warmly, shaking each of their hands in turn. "Thank you for agreeing to meet with me. I know this situation is…delicate, to say the least."

"That's putting it mildly," Liam replied, a hint of skepticism coloring his tone. "But we're here to listen, Dr. Novak. So why don't you start by telling us your side of the story?"

Dr. Novak nodded, gesturing for them to take a seat at the table. As they settled in, Ethan couldn't shake the feeling that something was off about her. It wasn't anything overt, just a subtle undercurrent of wrongness that set his teeth on edge.

"First, let me clarify one thing," Dr. Novak began, folding her hands primly on the table. "Contrary to what you may have heard, I am not a mutant myself. My interest in mutant genetics is purely scientific."

Ethan and Liam exchanged a surprised glance. That little tidbit went against everything they'd assumed about the doctor's motivations.

"Well, fuck me sideways," Ethan drawled, leaning back in his chair with affected nonchalance. "And here I thought you were one of us, fighting the good fight from the inside."

Dr. Novak's smile turned brittle at the edges. "I assure you, Mr. Hawke, my commitment to mutant rights is no less strong for my lack of an M-gene. But I understand your skepticism. Lord knows I've given you little reason to trust me, given my association with Genexis."

"About that," Liam interjected, leaning forward intently. "How exactly did you get involved with a company like Genexis in the first place? And what was your role in the experimentation on mutants?"

Dr. Novak sighed, a heavy, weary sound. "It's a long and complicated story, but I'll do my best to explain. When I first joined Genexis, it was as a research scientist working on gene therapies for chronic illnesses. The work was challenging but rewarding, and I truly believed we were making a difference."

She paused, taking a sip of water from the glass in front of her. Ethan watched her closely, trying to gauge her sincerity.

"Over time, however, I began to notice irregularities in some of the projects I was assigned to. Discrepancies in the data, unexplained gaps in the records. I started asking questions, and that's when I stumbled upon the truth about Genexis's real agenda."

"Which was?" Ethan prompted, impatient to get to the point.

Dr. Novak met his gaze unflinchingly. "The study and exploitation of mutant abilities. Genexis had been secretly experimenting on mutants for years, trying to isolate the genetic factors that gave rise to their powers. They believed that by understanding the mutant genome, they could unlock the key to human potential."

Liam made a disgusted noise in the back of his throat. "And let me guess, they didn't give a damn about the mutants they were using as guinea pigs in the process."

"No, they didn't," Dr. Novak agreed grimly. "The test subjects were seen as expendable, their lives and well-being secondary to the pursuit of scientific knowledge. When I found out what was really going on, I was horrified. I wanted to blow the whistle right then and there."

Ethan cocked his head, sensing a 'but' coming. "So why didn't you? What made you decide to stay and become complicit in their sick little science fair?"

Dr. Novak's expression turned haunted, her eyes distant. "Because I thought I could do more good from the inside. I convinced myself that by staying, I could mitigate the worst of the abuses, maybe even steer the research in a more ethical direction. I thought I was strong enough to play double agent, to work within the system to change it for the better."

She laughed then, a harsh, bitter sound. "I was naive, and arrogant. I see that now. All I did was provide a veneer of legitimacy to their atrocities, a smokescreen for them to hide behind. And in the process, I became just as guilty as the rest of them."

Ethan studied her closely, trying to reconcile the genuine remorse he saw in her eyes with the nagging sense of wrongness that still prickled at his senses. Beside him, Liam shifted in his seat, clearly struggling with the same conflicting feelings.

"Alright, Dr. Novak," Ethan said, leaning forward with his elbows on the table. "Let's say we buy your little sob story about being an unwitting pawn in Genexis's game. That still doesn't explain why you stayed with the company for so long, even after you discovered what they were really up to."

He fixed her with a penetrating stare, watching for any flicker of deception or evasion. "You're a smart woman, a gifted scientist. You must have known that the work you were doing, however well-intentioned, was causing real harm to real people. Mutants who trusted you, who put their lives in your hands."

Dr. Novak flinched as if struck, her composure cracking for just a moment. "You're right, Mr. Hawke. I did know, on some level, that what we were doing was wrong. But I convinced myself that the ends justified the means, that the potential benefits of our research outweighed the individual costs."

She looked down at her hands, twisting them together in a nervous gesture. "I was arrogant, and blind. I believed that I could control the direction of the experiments, that I could steer us towards a greater understanding of mutant abilities without crossing ethical lines. But the truth is, those lines were blurred from the very beginning."

Ethan sat back, a grim sense of satisfaction warring with a grudging spark of empathy. He knew all too well the seductive allure of power, the way it could make you believe you were untouchable, invincible. But he also knew the bitter taste of regret, the weight of choices that could never be unmade.

"I understand the desire to push the boundaries of science," he said at last, his voice carefully neutral. "To unlock the secrets of the mutant genome and find ways to harness our abilities for the greater good. But at what cost, Dr. Novak? How many lives are you willing to sacrifice on the altar of progress?"

Liam, who had been listening intently, chose that moment to interject. "I don't think it's quite that simple, Ethan," he said, shooting his partner a meaningful look. "As a mutant myself, I know how desperate we can be for answers, for solutions to the challenges we face every day."

He turned to Dr. Novak, his expression open and compassionate. "I'm not excusing what you did, or the part you played in Genexis's crimes. But I do understand the impulse, the desire to use your skills and knowledge to help our people. Even if your methods were misguided, I believe your intentions were good."

Dr. Novak looked up at Liam with gratitude shining in her eyes, even as Ethan scoffed in disbelief. "Intentions don't mean shit, Liam," he argued, his temper starting to fray. "You know what they say about the road to hell, right? Paved with good fucking intentions."

Liam shot him a quelling look, a silent plea for patience and understanding. "I know that, Ethan. But I also know that the world isn't as black and white as you like to pretend it is. There are shades of gray, nuances and complexities that we can't just ignore because they're inconvenient."

Ethan opened his mouth to retort, but Dr. Novak cut him off with a raised hand. "Please, gentlemen. I appreciate your perspectives, but arguing semantics won't change what's already been done. All I can do now is try to make amends, to use what I know to help you bring Genexis to justice."

She took a deep breath, seeming to steel herself for what came next. "The truth is, I wasn't just a passive observer in their experiments. I was an active participant, a lead researcher on some of their most sensitive projects."

Ethan felt his blood run cold, his worst suspicions confirmed. "What kind of projects?" he asked, his voice deceptively soft.

Dr. Novak closed her eyes, as if blocking out a painful memory. "Gene-splicing, DNA manipulation, attempts to artificially induce mutations in baseline human subjects. We were trying to isolate the M-gene, to find a way to activate it on demand."

She opened her eyes, meeting Ethan's gaze with a haunted expression. "Some of the test subjects didn't survive the process. Others were left permanently disfigured, or driven mad by the strain on their minds and bodies. And those were the lucky ones."

Ethan felt bile rise in the back of his throat, horror and disgust churning in his gut. "Jesus fucking Christ," he breathed, running a hand over his face. "You were playing God, tampering with the very building blocks of life. How could you justify that, even to yourself?"

Dr. Novak flinched again, tears welling in her eyes. "I can't," she whispered, her voice cracking. "Not anymore. I've seen the error of my ways, the arrogance and hubris that led me down this path. And I will spend the rest of my life trying to atone for what I've done, even if it means sacrificing my own freedom, my own future."

Liam reached out and laid a hand on her arm, a small gesture of comfort and solidarity. "We appreciate your candor, Dr. Novak," he said gently. "And we'll do everything we can to make sure your information is used to bring Genexis down, once and for all."

He glanced over at Ethan, a silent question in his eyes. Ethan sighed, feeling the weight of responsibility settle heavy on his shoulders. As much as he wanted to condemn Dr. Novak, to write her off as just another monster in a lab coat, he knew it wasn't that simple.

She was a victim too, in her own way. A victim of her own ambition, her own misguided ideals. And if they were going to have any hope of unraveling this conspiracy, they needed her on their side.

"Alright, Dr. Novak," he said at last, his voice gruff but not unkind. "You've given us a lot to think about, and even more to investigate. But if you're serious about helping us take down Genexis, then we're willing to work with you."

He leaned forward, fixing her with an intense stare. "But let me be clear. If I get even a hint that you're double-crossing us, or holding back information that could save lives? All bets are off, and I'll personally make sure you rot in a cell for the rest of your miserable existence. Understand?"

Dr. Novak nodded frantically, fear and relief warring in her expression. "I understand, Mr. Hawke. You have my word, and my full cooperation. I only want to make things right, however I can."

The ride back to Ethan's penthouse was filled with a heavy, contemplative silence. Ethan could practically hear the gears turning in Liam's head as the firefighter stared out the window, his brow furrowed in thought.

"Penny for your thoughts, sweetheart," Ethan said at last, breaking the stillness with his trademark drawl. "You look like you're trying to solve the mysteries of the universe over there."

Liam glanced over at him, a wry smile tugging at the corners of his mouth. "Just trying to wrap my head around everything we learned today," he admitted, running a hand through his hair. "I can't decide if Dr. Novak is a victim or a villain in all this. Maybe a little of both."

Ethan hummed thoughtfully, tapping his fingers against the steering wheel. "I know what you mean. On the one hand, she seems genuinely remorseful for her part in Genexis's fuckery. But on the other hand, she still made the choice to stay with them, even after she knew what they were doing. That's not exactly the mark of an innocent bystander."

Liam sighed, his expression conflicted. "I get that, Ethan. But I also know how easy it is to get caught up in something bigger than yourself, to convince yourself that you're doing the right thing even when all the evidence points to the contrary. Especially when you're a mutant, desperate for answers and acceptance."

Ethan glanced over at his partner, feeling a swell of affection and understanding. Liam's empathy, his ability to see the shades of gray in even the most black-and-white situations, was one of the things Ethan loved most about him.

"You're right, babe," he said softly, reaching over to give Liam's knee a reassuring squeeze. "And that's why we make such a good team. You keep me from going off the rails with my righteous fury, and I keep you from getting too lost in the weeds of moral ambiguity."

Liam chuckled, covering Ethan's hand with his own. "A regular dynamic duo, huh? The cynic and the idealist, fighting crime and making the world a better place, one morally gray scientist at a time."

Ethan grinned, feeling some of the tension drain from his shoulders. Leave it to Liam to find the humor in even the most dire of situations.

"Speaking of our good doctor," he said, sobering slightly, "did you notice anything off about her story? Any inconsistencies or red flags that set your spidey senses tingling?"

Liam frowned, considering. "Not anything specific, no. But there were a few moments where her body language seemed…I don't know, evasive? Like she was holding something back, or not telling us the whole truth."

Ethan nodded grimly, his own suspicions confirmed. "I noticed that too. And call me paranoid, but I don't think it's just garden-variety guilt or shame. I think there's more to her involvement with Genexis than she's letting on, something deeper and darker than just a misguided attempt at playing both sides."

"You think she's dangerous?" Liam asked, his voice low and serious.

Ethan shrugged, a humorless smile twisting his lips. "I think anyone who's willing to experiment on innocent people, to play God with the very building blocks of life, has the potential to be dangerous. And I think we'd be idiots to take Dr. Novak at face value, no matter how convincing her sob story might be."

Liam blew out a breath, leaning his head back against the seat. "Fuck. Just when I thought this case couldn't get any more complicated, we get thrown another curveball. Remind me again why we signed up for this hero gig?"

Ethan chuckled, bringing Liam's hand to his lips for a quick, affectionate kiss. "Because we're gluttons for punishment, sweetheart. And because someone's gotta stand up for the little guy, even when the little guy is a genetically-enhanced super-being with the power to level a city block."

Liam snorted, shaking his head fondly. "You're ridiculous, you know that? But you're also not wrong. As much as I hate to admit it, we're in this for the long haul, aren't we?"

"Afraid so, babe," Ethan confirmed, pulling into the underground garage of his building. "But hey, there's nobody I'd rather have by my side as we wade through this clusterfuck of a conspiracy. You're my rock, Liam. My anchor in the storm."

Liam's eyes softened, a tender smile spreading across his face. "And you're mine, Ethan. My partner, in every sense of the word. I couldn't do this without you, any of it."

Ethan felt his heart skip a beat, a rush of emotion clogging his throat. He still wasn't used to this, to the raw, unguarded moments of vulnerability that Liam seemed to draw out of him without even trying.

But he was learning to embrace it, to let himself feel the depth and breadth of his love for this incredible, infuriating, utterly irreplaceable man.

They made their way up to the penthouse in comfortable silence, the events of the day settling over them like a heavy, contemplative shroud. As they stepped inside, shedding jackets and kicking off shoes, Ethan couldn't help but marvel at how much had changed in such a short time.

It was terrifying and exhilarating all at once, the knowledge that he was no longer alone in this fight. That he had someone to lean on, to trust with his deepest fears and his wildest dreams.

18

Duty and Desire

Liam

He sighed contentedly, nuzzling into the crook of his Ethan's neck and breathing in the intoxicating scent of sleep-warmed skin and lingering cologne.

This was heaven, pure and simple. Lying here in Ethan's arms, their bodies entwined and their hearts beating in sync, Liam felt a sense of peace and belonging that he had never known before.

It was like coming home after a long, weary journey, like finding a missing piece of himself that he hadn't even known was lost.

But even as he reveled in the perfection of the moment, Liam felt a nagging sense of responsibility tugging at the edges of his consciousness. He had a job to do, a duty to fulfill, and as much as he wanted to stay here forever, wrapped up in Ethan and shutting out the rest of the world, he knew he couldn't.

With a heavy sigh, Liam began to disentangle himself from Ethan's embrace, pressing a soft, regretful kiss to his lover's sleep-slackened mouth.

Ethan stirred, his eyes fluttering open and a lazy smile spreading across his face. "Mornin', sweetheart," he murmured, his voice rough with sleep. "Where do you think you're going?"

Liam's heart clenched at the endearment, at the open affection and vulnerability in Ethan's gaze. God, how had he gotten so lucky, to have this incredible, infuriating, utterly irreplaceable man in his life?

"I have to get back to the firehouse," he said softly, brushing a stray lock of hair from Ethan's forehead. "I've already been away too long, and I don't want to raise any more suspicions than I already have."

Ethan's expression sobered, a flicker of concern darkening his eyes. "Are you sure you're ready for that, Liam? You've been through hell these past few days, and I don't want you pushing yourself too hard."

Liam smiled, touched by Ethan's care and consideration. "I'll be fine, Ethan. I'm a big boy, remember? I can handle a little hard work and a few nosy questions from my colleagues."

But even as he said the words, Liam felt a twist of unease in his gut. He knew that going back to the firehouse meant facing the scrutiny and suspicion of his captain and his fellow firefighters, meant putting on a brave face and pretending that everything was business as usual.

And he wasn't sure he was ready for that, wasn't sure he had the strength to keep up the charade when all he wanted was to stay here, safe and loved in Ethan's arms.

Ethan must have sensed his hesitation, because he sat up and pulled Liam into a fierce, protective embrace. "Hey," he said softly, his breath warm against Liam's ear. "You've got this, Liam. You're the strongest, bravest, most stubborn son of a bitch I know. And if anyone gives you any shit, just remember that you've got me in your corner, always."

Liam felt his throat tighten with emotion, his eyes stinging with unshed tears. "I know," he whispered, hugging Ethan back just as tightly. "And I can't tell you how much that means to me, Ethan. Knowing that you've got my back, that you believe in me...it's everything."

They stayed like that for a long moment, just holding each other and breathing in the quiet intimacy of the morning. But eventually, Liam knew he had to let go, had to face the day and all the challenges it would bring.

With a final, lingering kiss, he pulled away from Ethan and climbed out of bed, his body already aching with the loss of his lover's warmth and strength.

"I'll call you later," he promised, his voice rough with suppressed emotion. "And remember, as far as anyone knows, we're still enemies. We have to keep up appearances, at least for now."

Ethan nodded, his expression grim but understanding. "I know, sweetheart. Now go on, get out of here before I drag you back to bed and never let you leave."

Liam laughed, shaking his head fondly as he grabbed his clothes and headed for the bathroom. "Promises, promises," he called over his shoulder, reveling in the rich, warm sound of Ethan's answering chuckle.

But even as he went through the motions of getting ready, of donning his uniform and his professional mask, Liam couldn't shake the sense of unease that coiled in his gut, the nagging fear that something was about to go terribly, terribly wrong.

He tried to push it aside, tried to focus on the task at hand and the knowledge that he had Ethan's love and support to bolster him. But as he made his way out of the penthouse and into the cold, gray light of dawn, Liam couldn't help but feel like he was walking into a storm, one that could very well tear his world apart.

The firehouse was already bustling with activity when Liam arrived, the familiar sounds and smells of the station washing over him like a bittersweet homecoming. He took a deep breath, steeling himself for the barrage of questions and concerned looks he knew were coming.

Sure enough, as soon as he stepped into the locker room, he was surrounded by his colleagues, their faces a mix of relief and worry.

"Liam!" Jack exclaimed, pulling him into a rough, one-armed hug. "Thank God you're okay, man. We were all so fucking worried about you."

Liam returned the hug, feeling a swell of affection for his friend and teammate. "I'm sorry, Jack," he said sincerely, pulling back to look the other man in the eye. "I didn't mean to scare you guys. I just…I had some personal stuff to deal with, and I needed some time to sort it out."

Jack's expression softened, his eyes filled with understanding. "Hey, no need to apologize, Liam. We all have our shit to deal with, and we've got your back, no matter what. Just don't forget that we're here for you, okay?"

Liam nodded, swallowing past the lump in his throat. "I know, Jack. And I appreciate it, more than you could ever know."

He turned to the rest of his team, his expression serious but determined. "I'm ready to get back to work, guys. The city needs us, and I'm not going to let it down."

There were nods and murmurs of agreement, a sense of camaraderie and purpose filling the room. But before Liam could say anything else, a gruff voice cut through the chatter, making him stiffen with apprehension.

"Quinn, my office. Now."

Liam turned to see his captain standing in the doorway, his expression stern and unreadable. He felt a flicker of dread in his stomach, but he forced himself to nod and follow the older man down the hall, ignoring the worried looks his teammates shot him as he went.

As soon as the door closed behind them, the captain turned to Liam with a frown, his arms crossed over his broad chest.

The captain leaned forward in his chair, his brow furrowed with concern. "Liam, I know you've been through a lot recently, with the accident and your recovery. I just want to make sure you're really ready to come back to work."

Liam met his captain's gaze steadily, his voice calm and assured. "I appreciate your concern, sir, but I'm fine. The doctors cleared me for duty, and I've been following all of their recommendations for physical therapy and rest."

The captain sighed, rubbing a hand over his face. "It's not just your physical health I'm worried about, Liam. Being in the hospital, going through recovery…that kind of thing can take a toll on your mental and emotional well-being too."

Liam's jaw tightened, a flicker of defensiveness rising in his chest. "With all due respect, sir, I know my own limits. If I wasn't ready to come back, I wouldn't be here."

The captain studied him for a long moment, his expression unreadable. "I know you're a dedicated firefighter, Liam. One of the best I've ever worked with. But even the strongest people need support sometimes. I just want you to know that if you ever need to talk, or if you start feeling overwhelmed, my door is always open."

Liam felt a sudden rush of gratitude, his anger and defensiveness fading away. He knew the captain was just looking out for him, in his own gruff, no-nonsense way. "Thank you, sir. I appreciate that, truly. But I promise you, I'm ready to be back. This job, this team…it's where I belong."

The captain nodded slowly, a small smile tugging at the corner of his mouth. "Alright, Quinn. I trust your judgment. But remember what I said…if you need anything, don't hesitate to ask. We're all here for you."

Liam stood up, feeling a renewed sense of purpose and determination. "I won't forget, sir. Thank you again. Will that be all?"

The captain fixed him with a long, measuring look, as if trying to peer into Liam's very soul. Then, with a heavy sigh, he leaned back in his chair and rubbed a hand over his face.

"No, Quinn, that's not all. I have a new assignment for you, one that I think you're uniquely qualified for."

Liam frowned, a sense of unease prickling at the back of his neck. "What kind of assignment, sir?"

The captain reached into his desk drawer and pulled out a file, tossing it onto the desk in front of Liam. "We have a new recruit joining the department today. His name is Alex Chen, and he's a mutant with the ability to manipulate water."

Liam's eyes widened, his heart skipping a beat in his chest. A mutant firefighter? That was rare, even in a city as diverse as this one. Most mutants stuck to their own communities, too afraid of the prejudice and hostility they faced in the human world.

"I want you to take him under your wing, Quinn," the captain said, his voice brooking no argument. "Train him, mentor him, show him the ropes. With your unique perspective as a mutant yourself, I think you're the perfect person to guide him through this transition."

Liam felt a weight settle on his shoulders, a sense of responsibility that he wasn't sure he was ready for. With everything else going on in his life right now - the investigation, his relationship with Ethan, the constant fear of discovery - the last thing he needed was a rookie to babysit.

But he also knew that he couldn't refuse, not without raising even more suspicions about his loyalties and his priorities. So he simply nodded, picking up the file and flipping it open to scan the contents.

"I'll do my best, sir," he said, his voice carefully neutral. "When does he start?"

"Today," the captain replied, standing up and buttoning his jacket. "He should be here any minute, actually. I'll introduce you, and then I expect you to take it from there. Understood?"

Liam stood as well, tucking the file under his arm and giving the captain a curt nod. "Yes, sir. I won't let you down."

The captain grunted, his expression unreadable. "See that you don't, Quinn. I'm taking a big risk here, putting my faith in you. Don't make me regret it."

With that, he strode out of the office, leaving Liam alone with his thoughts and his growing sense of trepidation. He took a deep breath, trying to center himself and push down the anxiety that threatened to overwhelm him.

He could do this. He had to do this. For his own sake, for Ethan's sake, for the sake of every mutant who had ever been marginalized or oppressed by a world that feared and misunderstood them.

He would train Alex, and he would do it well. He would prove to the captain, to the department, to the whole fucking world that mutants were just as capable, just as brave and dedicated as any human firefighter.

And maybe, just maybe, he would find a way to balance his duties and his desires, to be the hero that the city needed while still holding onto the love and the passion that made his life worth living.

With a final, steadying breath, Liam squared his shoulders and stepped out of the office, ready to face whatever challenges lay ahead.

Alex Chen was young, maybe early twenties, with a lean, wiry build and a mop of unruly black hair. He had the look of someone who had grown up hard and fast, with a wariness in his eyes that belied his youthful appearance.

But there was also a spark of determination there, a fire that Liam recognized all too well. It was the same fire that had driven him to become a firefighter, to use his powers for good and to make a difference in the world.

"Alex, this is Liam Quinn," the captain said, nodding towards Liam as he made the introductions. "He'll be your training officer and your mentor as you get settled into the department. Listen to him, learn from him, and do whatever he tells you to do. Understood?"

Alex nodded, his gaze flicking over to Liam with a mix of curiosity and apprehension. "Yes, sir. I'm ready to learn."

The captain clapped him on the shoulder, a rare smile tugging at the corners of his mouth. "Good man. I'll leave you two to get acquainted, then. Quinn, I expect regular progress reports on his training. Don't let me down."

With that, he turned and strode away, leaving Liam and Alex alone in the locker room. For a moment, they just stared at each other, sizing each other up and trying to get a read on the other's intentions.

Finally, Liam broke the silence, sticking out his hand and giving Alex a firm shake. "Welcome to the department, Chen. I'm not going to lie to you, this job is tough as hell and it takes a special kind of person to do it well. But if you're willing to work hard and follow my lead, I think you've got what it takes to be a damn good firefighter."

Alex's grip was strong, his palm callused and rough against Liam's own. "I'm ready, sir. I'll do whatever it takes to prove myself and earn my place here."

Liam nodded, a flicker of approval warming his chest. The kid had spirit, that was for sure. And spirit was something that couldn't be taught, only nurtured and honed through experience and guidance.

"Alright then, let's get started. But first, let me introduce you to the rest of the team."

Liam led Alex out into the common area, where the other firefighters were milling about, chatting and checking their gear. They looked up as Liam and Alex approached, curiosity and a hint of wariness in their eyes.

"Listen up, everyone," Liam called out, his voice commanding attention. "This is Alex Chen, our new recruit. He's a mutant with the ability to manipulate water, and he's going to be training with us from now on."

There was a moment of silence, a palpable tension in the air as the others digested this information. Liam could see the flicker of doubt, of unease in some of their faces, and he felt a surge of protective anger on Alex's behalf.

But before he could say anything, Jack stepped forward, a broad grin on his face as he clapped Alex on the back. "Welcome to the team, Chen," he said, his voice warm and genuine. "We're glad to have you aboard. And don't worry about the whole mutant thing - as far as we're concerned, you're one of us now."

Liam felt a swell of gratitude and pride towards his friend, a reminder of why he loved this job and these people so damn much. The other firefighters murmured their agreement, stepping forward to shake Alex's hand and offer their own words of welcome.

Alex looked a little overwhelmed, but there was a glimmer of relief and happiness in his eyes as he returned their greetings. Liam could see the tension draining from his shoulders, the wariness in his posture giving way to a tentative openness.

"Thank you," Alex said, his voice soft but sincere. "I'm honored to be here, and I promise I won't let you down."

Liam smiled, feeling a sense of rightness settle over him. This was how it should be, how it could be if people just took the time to look past their differences and see the humanity in each other.

"Alright, enough chit-chat," he said, clapping his hands together. "Let's get to work. Alex, you're with me. We're going to start with some basic drills, get you familiar with the equipment and the protocols."

Alex nodded eagerly, falling into step beside Liam as they headed towards the training yard. As they walked, Liam glanced over at his new charge, taking in the determined set of his jaw and the fire in his eyes.

"So, Chen," he said, his voice casual but probing. "What made you decide to become a firefighter? It's not exactly the most common career choice for a mutant."

Alex was quiet for a moment, his gaze distant and thoughtful. "I guess I just wanted to make a difference," he said at last, his voice soft but intense. "Growing up on the streets, I saw a lot of bad shit happen to good people. And I always wished I could do something about it, you know? Use my powers to help instead of just survive."

Liam nodded, a pang of empathy and understanding twisting in his chest. He knew all too well what it was like to feel powerless in the face of injustice, to want desperately to make things better but not know how.

"I get that," he said, his voice rough with emotion. "Believe me, I do. And I think you're in the right place, Chen. This job… it's not easy, and it's not always pretty. But at the end of the day, we get to go home knowing that we made a difference. That we saved lives and protected the innocent. And that's worth all the blood, sweat, and tears we put into it."

Alex looked over at him, a flicker of understanding and respect in his eyes. "I want that," he said, his voice fierce with conviction. "I want to earn that feeling, that knowledge that I did something good with my life. Something that matters."

Liam felt a swell of pride and protectiveness wash over him, a bone-deep certainty that he would do whatever it took to help Alex achieve that goal. To guide him and mold him into the best damn firefighter he could be, and to show the world that mutants were just as capable of heroism and sacrifice as anyone else.

"Then let's get to work," he said, a grin spreading across his face as they reached the training yard. "We've got a lot of ground to cover, and not a lot of time to do it in."

* * *

Liam put Alex through his paces, running him through drill after drill and scenario after scenario. He pushed the young mutant to his limits, testing his strength, his endurance, and his control over his powers.

"Keep that water pressure steady, Chen!" Liam barked, watching as Alex directed a stream of water at a flaming target. "You lose control for even a second, and you could end up doing more harm than good."

Alex gritted his teeth, sweat beading on his brow as he struggled to maintain his focus. "Yes, sir," he panted, his hands shaking with the effort of manipulating the water.

Liam watched him closely, ready to step in if needed. But Alex held firm, his power flowing through him like a conduit as he extinguished the flames with a final, triumphant burst of water.

"Nicely done," Liam said, clapping him on the shoulder. "You're getting better every minute, Chen. Keep this up, and you'll be ready for the real thing in no time."

Alex beamed at the praise, his eyes shining with pride and excitement. "Thank you, sir. I won't let you down."

But even as they trained, Liam couldn't shake the feeling of unease that had been growing in the pit of his stomach all day. There was something in the air, a tension and a sense of impending danger that he couldn't quite put his finger on.

And then, just as they were about to break for lunch, the alarm suddenly blared to life, the sound echoing through the station like a klaxon.

Liam frowned, reaching for his radio. "Dispatch, what's the situation? Over."

The dispatcher's voice crackled through the speaker, tense and urgent. "All units, we have a report of a mutant with explosive powers causing a disturbance in the city center. Multiple injuries reported, and the suspect is still at large. Proceed with caution, over."

Liam's heart sank, a cold sense of dread settling in his stomach. This was the moment he had been dreading, the crisis that he had known was coming but had hoped to avoid.

He turned to Alex, his expression grim. "Suit up, Chen. It looks like you're getting your first taste of action sooner than we thought."

Alex swallowed hard, but there was a determined glint in his eyes. "I'm ready, sir. Let's do this."

As they raced to the scene, sirens blaring and adrenaline pumping, Liam's mind was a whirlwind of thoughts and emotions. He knew that this was no ordinary call, no routine disturbance that could be handled with a few well-placed words and a show of force.

This was a mutant with deadly powers, a threat to the entire city. And it was up to Liam and his team to stop them before it was too late.

As they arrived at the scene, Liam felt his heart sink even further. The city center was in chaos, with terrified civilians running for cover and the rogue mutant - the M-Force, he heard someone call them - ranting and raving in the middle of the square, his hands glowing with deadly energy.

"I'll make you all pay!" the mutant shouted, his voice echoing off the buildings like a thunderclap. "You think you can control us, keep us in check with your laws and your prisons? Well, think again! Today, the mutants rise up and take back what's ours!"

Liam exchanged a grim look with Alex, both of them knowing that they were in for the fight of their lives. This wasn't just about stopping a dangerous criminal anymore, it was about preventing a catastrophe that could tear the city apart and reignite the simmering tensions between humans and mutants.

"Alright, listen up!" Liam barked, gathering his team around him. "Our top priority is evacuating any civilians still in the area and containing the threat. Chen and I will take point, using our powers to create a distraction and draw the fire. The rest of you, focus on crowd control and setting up a perimeter. We have to move fast and stay sharp, understood?"

A chorus of "Yes, sir!" rang out, and Liam felt a surge of pride and determination. These were his people, his family, and he knew that they would give everything they had to see this through.

With a final nod, he turned to Alex, his expression serious. "Stay close to me, kid. You've got this."

Alex swallowed hard, but there was a fierce determination in his eyes. Let's take this bastard down."

Together, they moved forward, their powers at the ready and their hearts pounding in their chests. Liam could feel the heat of his fire coursing through his veins, could taste the smoke and ash on his tongue as he prepared to unleash hell.

"Hey, asshole!" he shouted, his voice cutting through the chaos like a knife. "Why don't you pick on someone your own size?"

The mutant whirled around, his eyes widening as he caught sight of Liam and Alex. He sneered, a manic grin spreading across his face. "If it isn't the famous Liam Quinn, the mutant firefighter. I've heard all about you, how you use your powers to save the humans who hate and fear us. You're a traitor to your own kind!"

Liam gritted his teeth, his fists clenching at his sides. "I'm no traitor," he growled, his voice low and dangerous. "I'm a protector, a guardian of the innocent. And right now, the only one I see threatening innocent lives is you."

The mutant laughed, a harsh, grating sound that set Liam's teeth on edge. "Innocent? There's no such thing, not in this world. The humans will never accept us, never see us as equals. The only way we'll ever be free is to make them fear us, to show them that we are the superior species!"

"You're wrong," Alex said, stepping forward to stand beside Liam. "Violence and fear will only breed more violence and fear. The only way to change things is through understanding, through building bridges instead of burning them."

The mutant's eyes narrowed, his gaze flicking to Alex with a mix of contempt and curiosity. "And who the hell are you, kid? Another mutant lapdog, come to do the humans' bidding?"

Alex straightened his spine, his chin lifting in defiance. "My name is Alex Chen, and I'm a firefighter. Just like Liam. And just like him, I'm here to stop you before you hurt anyone else."

The bastard grinned, a feral, predatory thing. "Is that so? Well, let's see what you've got then, little water boy."

And with that, the M-Force unleashed a blast of explosive energy, the force of it slamming into Liam and Alex like a physical blow. They were thrown backwards, their bodies smashing into the hard concrete with bone-jarring impact.

Liam groaned, his head ringing and his vision blurring as he struggled to push himself upright. Beside him, Alex was already climbing to his feet, his face set with grim determination.

"Is that all you've got?" the young mutant taunted, his hands curling into fists at his sides. "I've taken harder hits from my grandma!"

The rogue snarled, his eyes flashing with rage as he launched another blast of energy towards them. But this time, Alex was ready. He threw up his hands, a wall of water surging up from the ground to meet the incoming attack.

The two forces collided with a deafening boom, the shockwave rippling outwards and shattering windows for blocks in every direction. But Alex's water wall held firm, absorbing the brunt of the blast and shielding him and Liam from harm.

Liam staggered to his feet, his heart pounding with a mix of fear and exhilaration. He had never seen a display of power like that before, not even from Ethan. Alex was stronger than he had ever imagined.

"Good job, kid," Liam said, clapping Alex on the shoulder. "Now it's my turn."

He stepped forward, his eyes locked on the mutant as he summoned the fire that burned within him. It started as a spark, a tiny ember that grew and swelled until it consumed him, until he was wreathed in flames from head to toe.

The mutant's eyes widened, a flicker of fear passing across his face as he realized the true extent of Liam's power. He threw up his hands, another blast of energy surging towards the firefighter in a desperate attempt to stop him.

But Liam was too fast, too strong. He met the attack head-on, the flames of his power consuming the energy and turning it to ash in an instant. And then he was moving, his body a blur of heat and light as he closed the distance between them.

The bastard tried to run, tried to summon another blast to defend himself. But it was too late. Liam was on him in a heartbeat, his hands closing around the mutant's throat as he slammed him into the ground.

"It's over," Liam growled, his voice low and dangerous. "You're done hurting people, done spreading fear and hate. You're going to pay for what you've done."

The fucker laughed, a harsh, bitter sound that was cut off abruptly as Liam tightened his grip. "You think this is over?" he gasped, his eyes wide and manic. "You think you've won? This is just the beginning. There are more like me out there, more mutants who are tired of being oppressed and afraid. And they will rise up, they will fight back against the humans who seek to control us. You can't stop the revolution!"

Liam's jaw clenched, his eyes hardening with resolve. "Watch me," he said, his voice cold and implacable. "I will stop you, and anyone else who tries to hurt innocent people. I will fight for peace, for understanding, for a world where mutants and humans can live together in harmony. And I will never, ever give up."

With those words, he hauled the rogue mutant to his feet, his grip never loosening as he dragged him towards the waiting police officers. He could hear the cheers and applause of the gathered crowd, could see the relief and gratitude in their faces as they realized that the threat had been neutralized.

But Liam didn't let it go to his head. He knew that this was just one battle, one small victory in a much larger war. There would be other threats, other challenges to face in the days and weeks and months to come.

And he would be ready for them.

19

The Price of Justice

Ethan

A figure stepped out of the shadows, blocking Ethan's path. He was tall and lean, with angular features and piercing blue eyes that seemed to bore into Ethan's soul.

"Ethan Hawke," the man said, his voice smooth and cultured. "Or should I say, The Arcana?"

Ethan felt a jolt of surprise and unease at the use of his alias. How did this man know who he was? And more importantly, what did he want?

He summoned a cocky grin, masking his inner turmoil with bravado. "I'm sorry, have we met? Because I'm pretty sure I would remember a face like yours."

The man chuckled, a low, rich sound that sent a chill down Ethan's spine. "We haven't met, not officially. But I've been following your work, Mr. Hawke. And I must say, I'm impressed."

Ethan's eyes narrowed, his senses on high alert. There was something off about this man, something that set his teeth on edge. He could feel it in his gut, a prickling sense of wrongness that he couldn't quite put his finger on.

"Is that so? And just who exactly are you, my mysterious admirer?"

The man smiled, a sharp, predatory thing that didn't quite reach his eyes. "Oh, how rude of me. Allow me to introduce myself. My name is Sebastian Caine, and like you, I have a vested interest in the fate of our mutant brethren."

Ethan's brow furrowed, a flicker of recognition sparking in his mind. Sebastian Caine… the name sounded familiar, but he couldn't quite place it. And yet, there was something about the man's face, his bearing, that seemed almost uncannily familiar.

"Is that right?" Ethan said, his tone casual but his body tensed for action. "And just what exactly is your interest in the mutant disappearances, Mr. Caine?"

Sebastian's smile widened, his eyes glinting with a dark amusement. "Let's just say that I have a personal stake in the matter. And that I believe you and I could be of great help to each other, if you're willing to listen to what I have to say."

Ethan's jaw clenched, his mind racing with possibilities. This man knew something, that much was clear. But what was his angle? What did he stand to gain from inserting himself into Ethan's investigation?

He reached out with his mind, summoning the power of The High Priestess card. The ethereal image shimmered into existence, granting him a flash of insight and intuition.

And what he saw made his blood run cold.

Sebastian Caine was not what he appeared to be. There was a darkness in him, a twisted, malevolent energy that coiled beneath the surface of his polished exterior. He had secrets, hidden agendas that went far beyond a simple interest in the mutant cause.

Ethan's power receded, the tarot card fading back into the ether. He fixed Sebastian with a hard, assessing stare, his expression carefully neutral.

"I'm listening," he said, his voice low and controlled. "But let's get one thing straight, Caine. I don't play well with others, especially when I don't know their game. So if you've got something to say, you'd better spit it out before I lose my patience."

Sebastian chuckled again, the sound grating on Ethan's nerves like nails on a chalkboard. "Oh, I like you, Mr. Hawke. You've got spirit, and a refreshing lack of bullshit. Very well, I'll cut to the chase."

He leaned in closer, his voice dropping to a conspiratorial whisper. "I have information, Mr. Hawke. Information that could blow the lid off this whole sordid affair and bring the true culprits to justice. But I can't do it alone. I need someone with your particular set of skills, your resources and your connections."

Ethan's eyes narrowed, his senses screaming at him that this was a trap, a setup designed to lure him into a false sense of security. But he couldn't afford to let the opportunity slip through his fingers, not if there was even a chance that Sebastian was telling the truth.

"And what's in it for you?" he asked, his tone sharp and probing. "Why come to me, why not go to the authorities or the media with what you know?"

Sebastian's smile turned razor-thin, his eyes glinting with a malicious humor. "Let's just say that I have my reasons, Mr. Hawke. Reasons that are best kept between us, for now. Suffice it to say that we both stand to benefit from a mutual partnership, one that could change the course of mutant history forever."

Ethan's mind raced, trying to piece together the fragments of information and intuition that swirled in his head. He didn't trust Sebastian, not for a second. But he also couldn't ignore the tantalizing promise of answers, of a breakthrough that could finally unravel the mystery that had consumed him for so long.

"Alright, Caine," he said at last, his voice hard and unyielding. "I'll play your little game, for now. But let me make one thing crystal fucking clear. If I get even a hint that you're double-crossing me, or holding back information that could save lives? All bets are off, and I'll personally make sure you regret the day you ever heard my name."

Sebastian's grin widened, his eyes sparkling with a dark, twisted glee. "Oh, I have no doubt of that, Mr. Hawke. No doubt at all. But trust me when I say that we're on the same side, you and I. We both want the same thing - justice for our people, and the truth brought to light."

He reached into his pocket and pulled out a small, black card, pressing it into Ethan's hand with a flourish. "My contact information, should you change your mind or require my assistance. Until then, I bid you good day and happy hunting, Mr. Hawke. I have a feeling we'll be seeing each other again very soon."

And with that, he turned and melted back into the shadows, leaving Ethan alone on the street with a head full of questions and a heart heavy with foreboding. He stared down at the card in his hand, the embossed letters seeming to mock him with their air of mystery and menace.

Just who the hell was this man, and what did he really want? Ethan had a sinking feeling that he was about to find out, whether he wanted to or not.

But before he could dwell on the unsettling encounter any longer, his phone buzzed with an incoming message. Ethan fished it out of his pocket, his brow furrowing as he read the text from Marcus.

"Got a lead on the disappearances. Might be connected to that fire your boy toy responded to."

Ethan's heart skipped a beat, a surge of adrenaline and anticipation coursing through his veins. Finally, a concrete lead, something tangible to sink his teeth into. And if it was connected to Liam's case...

He shook his head, pushing aside the pang of worry that flared in his chest. Liam could take care of himself, he knew that. The man was a fucking force of nature, all rippling muscles and smoldering intensity. Just the thought of him made Ethan's blood run hot, his mind conjuring up vivid memories of stolen kisses and heated glances.

But now was not the time for distractions, no matter how tempting they might be. He had a job to do, a mystery to unravel. And he'd be damned if he let anything stand in his way, not even his own raging libido.

With a final, furtive glance around to make sure he wasn't being followed, Ethan set off towards the rendezvous point, his mind already racing with the possibilities of what he might uncover.

An hour later, he was striding into the headquarters, his coat billowing behind him like a cape. Zoe and Marcus looked up from their respective workstations, their expressions a mix of curiosity and concern.

"What's the word, boss?" Zoe asked, her fingers never pausing in their dance across the keyboard. "You look like you just saw a ghost, or got laid. Maybe both."

Ethan rolled his eyes, but he couldn't quite suppress the grin that tugged at the corner of his mouth. "Very funny, Z. No, Marcus just sent me some intel on the disappearances. And it might be connected to Liam's fire incident."

That got their attention. Zoe leaned forward, her brow furrowed in concentration. "Connected how? What's the source?"

Marcus cleared his throat, his expression serious. "I've been digging into the backgrounds of the missing people, trying to find any commonalities or patterns. And I stumbled across something interesting. Turns out, several of them had ties to a group that's been known to frequent the area where the fire took place. It's possible that someone from that group was there that night, using the chaos as cover for their activities."

Ethan nodded, his mind already racing with the implications. "Good work, Marcus. That's a solid lead. But how do we follow up on it without tipping our hand or putting Liam in danger?"

Zoe let out a low whistle, her eyes widening. "Well, shit. That's a hell of a puzzle, E. But I might have an idea. Can you pull up the security cam footage from the fire? If we can spot anyone suspicious lurking around the edges, we might be able to ID them and track their movements."

Ethan grinned, his chest swelling with pride and affection for his team. "Brilliant, Z. Let's do it. Marcus, can you queue up those tapes?"

Marcus nodded, his fingers already flying over the keys. "On it, boss. Give me just a sec and I'll have that footage ready to go."

But it was what happened next that made his blood run cold.

There, in the background of the shot, was a figure lurking in the shadows. A figure that seemed to be taking advantage of the chaos and confusion to slip unnoticed into the crowd, a small, struggling bundle clutched in their arms.

Ethan's eyes narrowed, his mind racing as he tried to make out the details of the figure's face. And then, with a jolt of recognition, it clicked.

"Son of a bitch," he breathed, his fists clenching at his sides. "That's Damon fucking Reeves. I'd know that ugly mug anywhere."

Marcus frowned, his expression grim. "Reeves? As in the second-in-command of the Purifiers, the anti-mutant hate group?"

Ethan nodded, his jaw tight with anger. "The very same. Looks like he was using the fire as a distraction to snatch a mutant kid right out from under everyone's noses."

Zoe's face paled, her eyes wide with horror. "Jesus, E. We have to do something. We can't just let that sick fuck get away with kidnapping a child."

Ethan's mind was already racing ahead, formulating a plan. He reached out with his powers, summoning the ethereal image of The Magician card. It shimmered into existence before him, pulsing with arcane energy.

"We won't, Z. I promise you that. But we have to be smart about this. We can't just go charging in guns blazing, not without more information." He turned to Marcus, his expression serious. "I need you to tap your contacts in the mutant community, see if anyone's heard anything about Reeves or the Purifiers' recent activities. And keep an ear out for any chatter about the missing kid. We need to find them before it's too late."

Marcus nodded, already reaching for his phone. "On it, boss. I'll shake every tree and rattle every cage until something shakes loose."

Ethan turned back to the screen, his eyes hardening with determination. "In the meantime, I'm going to track down Reeves myself. See if I can't persuade him to spill his guts about what the Purifiers are up to."

Zoe's brow furrowed, concern etched in the lines of her face. "Are you sure that's a good idea, E? Reeves is a dangerous motherfucker, and he's got a serious hate-on for mutants. Especially ones that get in his way."

Ethan grinned, a sharp, feral thing that was all teeth and promise. "Oh, I'm counting on it, Z. In fact, I'm looking forward to it. It's been too long since I've had a good old-fashioned throw-down with a bigoted piece of shit."

He stood up, his coat swirling around him like a living thing as he summoned his powers once more. The Magician card pulsed brighter, its energy thrumming through his veins like liquid fire.

"Keep digging on your end, and let me know if you find anything. In the meantime, I've got a date with a hate-monger. And I plan on showing him just how much I appreciate his kind's hospitality."

With that, he turned and strode out of the headquarters, his steps purposeful and his heart pounding with the thrill of the hunt. He knew he was taking a risk, going after Reeves alone. But risks be damned.

***

He found the abandoned house that he knew the purifiers were hiding, he could feel the weight of his tarot deck thrumming with energy at his side. He reached out with his mind, summoning the ethereal image of The Moon card. It shimmered into existence before him, casting an eerie, silver glow over the decrepit building.

"Alright, you bastards," Ethan muttered under his breath, a feral grin spreading across his face. "Let's see what secrets you're hiding in the dark."

He moved forward, his steps silent and sure as he slipped through the shadows. The Moon's light guided him, revealing hidden paths and secret doorways that would have remained invisible to the naked eye.

As he delved deeper into the house, Ethan could feel the presence of something malevolent, a darkness that seemed to seep from the very walls themselves. It set his teeth on edge, his instincts screaming at him to be on his guard.

And then, he saw it. A room at the end of a long, narrow hallway, its door slightly ajar. Through the crack, Ethan could see the flicker of candlelight, the gleam of metal and glass.

He approached cautiously, his senses straining for any sign of movement or sound. But the house was deathly still, the only noise the pounding of his own heart in his ears.

With a deep breath, Ethan pushed open the door and stepped inside. And what he saw made his blood run cold.

The room was a shrine to madness and cruelty, its walls lined with photographs and documents detailing the abduction and torture of countless mutants. There were maps and diagrams, lists of names and locations that made Ethan's stomach turn.

And there, in the center of it all, was Reeves himself. The man was hunched over a table, his back to the door, muttering to himself as he pored over a sheaf of papers.

Ethan felt a surge of rage boil up inside him, a white-hot fury that threatened to consume him entirely. This was the face of evil, the embodiment of everything he had sworn to fight against. And he would be damned if he let this sick fuck walk away unscathed.

"Hello, Reeves," Ethan said, his voice low and dangerous as he stepped fully into the room. "Fancy meeting you here. I don't suppose you'd care to explain what the fuck all of this is?"

Reeves spun around, his eyes widening in surprise and fear as he took in the sight of Ethan standing before him. But the fear quickly gave way to a sneer of contempt, a look of pure hatred that twisted his features into an ugly mask.

"Well, well, if it isn't the famous Arcana," Reeves spat, his hand inching towards the gun at his hip. "Come to stick your nose where it doesn't belong, have you? You freaks never learn."

Ethan just smiled, a cold, predatory thing that held no warmth or mercy. "Oh, I think I'm exactly where I belong, Reeves. In fact, I'd say I'm the only one here with a fucking moral compass. Now, why don't you be a good little bigot and tell me where you're keeping the mutants you've taken?"

Reeves barked out a harsh, mocking laugh. "You think I'm going to tell you anything, mutie? You're even dumber than you look. The only thing you're going to get from me is a bullet between the eyes."

Ethan's grin widened, his eyes flashing with a dangerous light. "I was hoping you'd say that."

And with that, he lunged forward, his body moving with a speed and grace that was almost inhuman. But before he could reach Reeves, the man vanished into thin air, only to reappear behind Ethan, a wicked grin on his face.

It was like fighting a mirror image of himself, a dark reflection of his own abilities.

"Surprised, mutie?" Reeves taunted, his voice filled with a sneering triumph. "You're not the only one with tricks up your sleeve. The boss has been cooking up something special, just for freaks like you."

Ethan's eyes narrowed, his mind racing as he tried to make sense of what he was seeing. Non-mutants with powers, abilities that matched his own... it was impossible. Or was it?

He thought of the missing mutants, the experiments and torture that Reeves and his ilk had been carrying out in secret. And with a sickening lurch, he realized the truth.

They were trying to replicate mutant powers, to create their own twisted army of enhanced humans. And they were using the captured mutants as their guinea pigs, their living test subjects.

The thought filled Ethan with a rage that bordered on madness, a fury that burned like a supernova in his chest. He redoubled his efforts, his powers flaring to life as he summoned every ounce of strength and skill he possessed.

But he was nothing if not adaptable, his powers and his wits more than a match for any challenge. He reached out with his mind, summoning The Magician card to his aid.

It shimmered into existence before him, a glowing figure wreathed in arcane energy. With a flick of his wrist, Ethan sent a blast of force hurtling towards Reeves, hoping to catch him off guard.

But Reeves was too quick, his body blinking out of existence just before the blast could connect. He reappeared behind Ethan once more, his fist slamming into the vigilante's kidney with brutal force.

Ethan grunted in pain, his body spinning around to face his

opponent. But Reeves was already gone, his mocking laughter echoing through the room as he flickered in and out of view.

It was like fighting a ghost, a phantom that could strike from any angle without warning. Ethan's powers were formidable, but even he couldn't hit what he couldn't see.

He needed to change his strategy, to find a way to level the playing field. With a growl of frustration, he summoned The Tower card, its destructive energy surging through his veins like liquid fire.

With a roar of effort, he slammed his fist into the ground, sending a shockwave of force rippling outwards in all directions. The room shook with the impact, the walls and ceiling cracking and crumbling under the onslaught.

And there, caught in the blast, was Reeves. His body flickered into view, his eyes wide with shock and pain as he was thrown backwards against the far wall.

Ethan was on him in an instant, his hands closing around the man's throat as he slammed him into the ground. "It's over, Reeves," he snarled, his voice low and dangerous. "Now, tell me what the fuck is going on here. Who's behind all this? What do they want with the mutants they've taken?"

Reeves laughed, a harsh, gurgling sound that was half-choked by Ethan's grip. "You really think I'm going to tell you anything, mutie? You're even dumber than I thought."

Ethan's grip tightened, his eyes blazing with fury. "I'm not playing around here, Reeves. You've got three seconds to start talking before I start breaking bones."

But Reeves just grinned, his teeth stained with blood. "You want answers, Arcana? Fine, I'll give you a little taste. But it won't do you any good in the end."

He leaned forward, his voice dropping to a conspiratorial whisper. "There's a storm coming, mutie. A reckoning that's been a long time in the making. And when it hits, everything you know, everything you love… it'll all come crumbling down."

Ethan's heart pounded in his chest, a sickening sense of dread washing over him. "What the fuck are you talking about, Reeves? Stop speaking in riddles and give me a straight answer!"

But Reeves just laughed again, his eyes gleaming with a mad, fanatical light. "You'll see soon enough, Arcana. The mutant problem, the disappearances, the experiments… it's all connected. And it's just the beginning."

Ethan's grip tightened, his fingers digging into the soft flesh of Reeves' neck. "The beginning of what? What the fuck are you planning?"

But Reeves just grinned, his teeth bared in a final, defiant snarl. "Hail…Prometheus."

With those ominous words ringing in his ears, Ethan watched as the life drained from Reeves' eyes, his body going limp in the vigilante's grasp. For a long moment, he just stared down at the man's face, his mind whirling with the implications of what had just transpired.

He had killed a man, had taken a life with his own two hands. It wasn't the first time, but it never got any easier, never felt any less like a stain on his soul.

As he made his way back to his base, Ethan couldn't shake the feeling of unease that settled in the pit of his stomach. He was a vigilante, a man who operated outside the law in pursuit of his own brand of justice. But at what point did the ends stop justifying the means? At what point did he cross the line from hero to villain?

Ethan shook his head, trying to banish the doubts that clouded his mind. He couldn't afford to second-guess himself, not now. Not when there were still so many questions left unanswered, so many lives hanging in the balance.

As he stepped into the base, he was greeted by the sight of Zoe and

Marcus huddled around a computer screen, their faces grim and their eyes tired.

"Tell me you've got some good news," Ethan said, his voice rough with exhaustion and pent-up frustration.

Zoe looked up at him, her expression unreadable. "That depends on your definition of good, boss. We've been monitoring the chatter on the dark web, and it looks like the Purifiers are getting bolder. There are rumors of more abductions in the works, and some of the language is getting pretty fucking scary."

Ethan frowned, his heart sinking in his chest. "What kind of language?"

Marcus spoke up, his voice low and serious. "Talk of a final solution, of wiping the mutant scourge from the face of the earth. It's like they're gearing up for war, Ethan. And we're the enemy."

Ethan felt a chill run down his spine, a sickening sense of dread that made his stomach churn. This was worse than he had feared, a threat that went beyond a few hate-fueled attacks and abductions.

"Fuck," he breathed, running a hand through his hair. "This is bad, guys. Really fucking bad."

Zoe nodded, her expression grim. "No shit, Sherlock. But that's not all. We did some digging into Reeves' background, and it looks like he was just a small fish in a much bigger pond. There are other cells out there, other groups with the same fucked-up agenda. And they're all connected, all part of something bigger."

"We need to act fast," he said, his voice hard with determination. "We can't let these bastards get away with this, can't let them hurt any more of our people. We have to find them, have to stop them before it's too late."

Marcus nodded, his expression serious. "I agree. But Ethan, what you did tonight... it's going to have consequences. Killing Reeves, it's not going to just go away. There will be fallout, and we need to be prepared for it."

Ethan's jaw clenched, his eyes flashing with a mix of anger and guilt. "I know that, Marcus. And I'll take full responsibility for my actions. But right now, we need to focus on the mission. We need to find these fuckers and shut them down, no matter what it takes."

Zoe and Marcus exchanged a glance, their expressions torn. They knew the stakes, knew the risks that came with the life they had chosen. But they also knew that they would follow Ethan to the ends of the earth, would stand by his side no matter what challenges lay ahead.

"Alright, boss," Zoe said, her voice firm with resolve. "We're with you, all the way. So what's the plan?"

Ethan's mind raced, his thoughts spinning with possibilities and strategies. They needed to be smart about this, needed to use every resource and every advantage at their disposal.

"We start with the intel we've gathered so far," he said, his voice low and intense. "We cross-reference Reeves' known associates with the data from the dark web, see if we can find any patterns or connections. And we keep our ears to the ground, keep monitoring the chatter for any hint of where they might strike next."

Marcus nodded, his expression thoughtful. "I've got some contacts in the mutant underground, people who might have heard things that haven't made it onto the web. I'll reach out, see what I can dig up."

"Good," Ethan said, his mind already racing ahead. "In the meantime, we need to shore up our defenses, make sure we're ready for whatever these fuckers might throw at us. Zoe, I want you to double-check our security systems, make sure there aren't any gaps or vulnerabilities that they could exploit."

Zoe grinned, her fingers already flying over the keyboard. "On it, boss. I'll make this place so tight, even a fucking gnat couldn't get in without us knowing about it."

Ethan felt a flicker of pride and affection for his team, for their dedication and their unwavering loyalty. They were more than just his colleagues, more than just his friends. They were his family, the ones who stood by him through thick and thin, no matter the cost.

As the night wore on and the base fell silent, Ethan found himself alone in his penthouse, his mind haunted by the ghosts of the choices he had made. He stared out at the city skyline, at the twinkling lights and the endless sea of humanity that stretched out before him.

And then, in a moment of weakness, he reached for his phone. His fingers hovered over Liam's number, his heart pounding in his chest as he wrestled with the urge to hear his voice, to feel the comfort of his presence.

Before he could talk himself out of it, he hit the call button. The phone rang once, twice, three times, each one feeling like an eternity.

And then, just when he thought it would go to voicemail, he heard the click of the line connecting, and Liam's voice, warm and familiar, filled his ear.

"Ethan? Is everything okay?"

Ethan closed his eyes, letting the sound of Liam's voice wash over him like a balm. "Yeah," he said, his own voice rough with emotion. "Yeah, everything's fine. I just… I needed to hear your voice."

There was a pause, a moment of silence that stretched out between them like a chasm. And then Liam spoke again, his voice soft and full of understanding.

"I'm here, Ethan. Whatever you need, I'm here."

Ethan felt a lump form in his throat, a wave of emotion that threatened to overwhelm him. He knew he didn't deserve this man, didn't deserve the love and the loyalty that Liam offered so freely.

But in that moment, he couldn't bring himself to care. He needed Liam, needed his strength and his warmth and his unwavering faith in the goodness of the world.

"Can you come over?" he asked, his voice barely above a whisper. "I know it's late, but… I need to see you."

And Liam, bless him, didn't hesitate for even a second. "I'll be there in twenty minutes," he said, his voice firm with resolve. "Just hold on, Ethan. I'm on my way."

20

Connecting the Dots

Liam

Ethan's voice on the phone had sounded so raw, so vulnerable, like he was teetering on the edge of some dark abyss.

And Liam knew, with a bone-deep certainty, that he would do anything to pull him back from that edge. To be the light in Ethan's darkness, the anchor that tethered him to the world of the living.

He reached the door and knocked, his breath coming in short, sharp gasps. For a moment, there was only silence, a heavy, oppressive weight that seemed to press down on him from all sides.

And then the door swung open, and there was Ethan. His green eyes were haunted, his face pale and drawn with exhaustion. But when he saw Liam, something in his expression cracked, a flicker of desperate, aching need that made Liam's heart clench in his chest.

"Liam," Ethan breathed, his voice rough and raw. "You came."

Liam didn't hesitate. He surged forward, his arms wrapping around Ethan's waist as he pulled him close. Their lips met in a bruising, desperate kiss, all tongue and teeth and pent-up hunger.

Ethan groaned into Liam's mouth, his hands fisting in the fabric of

Liam's shirt. "Fuck, Liam. I need you. I need you so fucking much."

Liam growled in response, his own desire rising to meet Ethan's. He walked them backwards into the penthouse, kicking the door shut behind him. They stumbled towards the bedroom, shedding clothes as they went, their hands roaming over each other's bodies with a frantic, almost feverish intensity.

By the time they reached the bed, they were both naked, their skin slick with sweat and their cocks hard and aching. Liam pushed Ethan down onto the mattress, crawling on top of him and pinning his wrists above his head.

"You're mine, Ethan," he rasped, his voice low and rough with want. "Mine to touch, mine to taste, mine to fuck. Say it."

Ethan's eyes blazed with a mix of defiance and desire, his hips bucking up against Liam's. "Yours," he panted, his voice breaking on the word. "I'm yours, Liam. Always."

Liam's heart soared at the admission, a fierce, possessive joy that burned through him like wildfire. He claimed Ethan's mouth in another searing kiss, his tongue delving deep as he ground their hips together.

Ethan moaned, his body arching up into Liam's touch. "Please, Liam. I need you inside me. Need to feel you, need to know you're real."

Liam's breath caught in his throat, a wave of tenderness and understanding washing over him. Ethan was hurting, was lost and adrift in a sea of darkness and doubt. And Liam knew, with a bone-deep certainty, that he would do anything to bring him back to shore.

He reached for the lube on the nightstand, coating his fingers and pressing them against Ethan's entrance. Ethan hissed at the coldness, but soon he was pushing back against Liam's hand, his body opening up to the intrusion.

"That's it, baby," Liam murmured, his voice low and soothing. "Let me in, let me take care of you."

He worked Ethan open slowly, gently, taking his time to stretch him out and get him ready. And when he finally sank into that tight, perfect heat, it was like coming home, like finding a piece of himself that he hadn't even known was missing.

"Fuck, Ethan," he groaned, his hips snapping forward in a deep, powerful thrust. "You feel so fucking good. So tight, so hot. Like you were made for me."

Ethan cried out, his legs wrapping around Liam's waist as he urged him deeper. "Harder, Liam. Fuck me harder. I want to feel you, want to forget everything but you."

Liam growled, his control snapping like a twig. He pistoned his hips, fucking into Ethan with a primal, animalistic fury. The bed shook beneath them, the headboard slamming against the wall with each brutal thrust.

"You're mine," Liam snarled, his teeth sinking into the curve of Ethan's neck. "Mine to fuck, mine to claim, mine to cherish. Say it, Ethan. Say you're mine."

"Yours," Ethan gasped, his voice wrecked and broken. "I'm yours, Liam. Always and forever. Yours."

Liam felt a wave of emotion crash over him, a love and a devotion so fierce it stole the breath from his lungs. He reached between them, wrapping his hand around Ethan's cock and stroking him in time with his thrusts.

"Come for me, baby," he commanded, his voice low and rough with need. "Come on my cock, let me feel you."

Ethan's back arched, his mouth falling open in a silent scream as his orgasm tore through him. Liam followed a moment later, his own release pulsing hot and deep inside Ethan's body.

They collapsed onto the bed, their chests heaving and their bodies slick with sweat. For a long moment, they just held each other, their hearts beating in sync as they rode out the aftershocks of their lovemaking.

And then Ethan spoke, his voice small and hesitant in the stillness of the room.

"Liam, there's something I need to tell you. Something about the Purifiers, about what I found out tonight."

Liam's heart clenched, a flicker of fear and uncertainty washing over him. But he pushed it aside, focusing instead on the man in his arms, the man who needed him now more than ever.

"Tell me," he said softly, his fingers carding through Ethan's hair.

Ethan took a deep breath, his eyes squeezing shut as if he were steeling himself for a blow. "Reeves, the Purifier I confronted tonight… he had abilities, Liam. Powers that no human should have. It was like fighting a mutant, but one with a sick, twisted agenda."

Liam frowned, his mind racing with the implications of Ethan's words. "What are you saying, Ethan? That the Purifiers are somehow giving themselves mutant abilities? How is that even possible?"

Ethan shook his head, his expression grim. "I don't know, Liam. But whatever they're doing, it's big. Bigger than anything we've faced before. Reeves mentioned something called Prometheus, said that it was just the beginning of their plan to wipe out mutants for good."

Liam felt a chill run down his spine, a sickening sense of dread that made his stomach churn. The Purifiers had always been a threat, a constant shadow lurking at the edges of the mutant community. But this… this was something else entirely.

"Fuck," he breathed, his arms tightening around Ethan's waist. "We have to stop them, Ethan. We can't let them get away with this."

Ethan nodded, his eyes hard with determination. "I know, Liam. And we will. We'll find out what they're up to, and we'll put an end to it once and for all. Even if it means taking them down one by one, we'll make sure they never hurt another mutant again."

Liam felt a surge of pride and love wash over him, a fierce, unshakable faith in the man he held in his arms. But even as he reveled in the strength of their bond, he couldn't shake the feeling of urgency that gnawed at his gut.

"Ethan," he said softly, his fingers tracing idle patterns on Ethan's sweat-slicked skin. "We need to move fast on this. Every day we wait, every moment we hesitate… it's another chance for the Purifiers to strike, to hurt more of our people."

Ethan sighed, his breath warm against Liam's neck. "I know, Liam. Believe me, I know. But we can't just go charging in blind."

Liam's jaw clenched, his stubborn streak rearing its head. "And how many more mutants will disappear while we're busy making plans? How many more lives will be ruined, families torn apart? We can't just sit on our asses and wait for the perfect moment, Ethan. We have to act, and we have to act now."

Ethan pushed himself up on one elbow, his green eyes boring into Liam's with an intensity that made the firefighter's heart skip a beat. "You think I don't know that? You think I don't feel that same fucking urgency, that same drive to protect our people at any cost? I'm the one who put a bullet in Reeves' head tonight, Liam. I'm the one with his blood on my hands."

Liam flinched at the reminder, a pang of sympathy and understanding twisting in his chest. He knew the toll that taking a life could take, the weight of guilt and regret that could crush even the strongest of souls.

"I'm sorry, Ethan," he said softly, his hand coming up to cup his lover's cheek. "I didn't mean to imply that you don't care, that you're not just as invested in this fight as I am. I just… I hate feeling helpless, hate knowing that there are people out there suffering while we sit here in this fancy fucking penthouse."

Ethan's expression softened, a glimmer of affection and understanding shining in his eyes. "I know, Liam. And trust me, there's nothing

I want more than to storm the gates and take these fuckers down. But we have to be smart about this, have to make sure we're not just painting a target on our own backs."

Liam nodded, a rueful smile tugging at the corners of his mouth. "You're right, of course. As much as it pains me to admit it, that strategic mind of yours is one of the things I admire about you. Well, that and your absolutely magnificent cock."

Ethan barked out a laugh, the sound warm and rich in the stillness of the bedroom. "And here I thought you were only with me for my dashing good looks and sparkling wit."

Liam grinned, leaning in to steal a quick, playful kiss. "Oh, those are just icing on the cake, baby. The real draw is that big, beautiful brain of yours. And speaking of which… any brilliant insights on how we're going to take down a bunch of juiced-up, mutant-hating assholes?"

Ethan's brow furrowed, his mind clearly racing with possibilities and plans. And then, all at once, his eyes widened, a flicker of realization and excitement sparking to life in their emerald depths.

"Holy shit," he breathed, his voice low and urgent. "Liam, I think I might have just figured out the connection we've been missing."

Liam sat up straighter, his heart pounding with anticipation. "What is it, Ethan? What did you see?"

Ethan swung his legs over the side of the bed, his body practically vibrating with adrenaline. "When I was fighting Reeves, I remember seeing something in his hideout, something that didn't quite fit with the whole Purifier aesthetic. It was a piece of equipment, sleek and high-tech, with a logo stamped on the side. A logo I've seen before, in a very different context."

Liam's eyes narrowed, his mind racing to put the pieces together. "What logo, Ethan? What are you saying?"

Ethan turned to face him, his expression grim and determined. "Genexis, Liam. The same fucking company that we've been investigating for their shady-ass mutant experimentation. I saw their logo on Reeves' equipment, clear as day."

Liam felt a chill run down his spine, a sickening sense of dread that made his stomach churn. "Fuck," he breathed, his voice low and hoarse. "Ethan, if Genexis is involved with the Purifiers, if they're the ones supplying them with the means to gain mutant abilities…"

"Then we're dealing with a threat far greater than we ever imagined," Ethan finished, his jaw clenching with resolve. "A threat that goes beyond just a bunch of hate-fueled radicals with delusions of grandeur. This is a fucking corporate conspiracy, Liam. And we need to get to the bottom of it, fast."

Liam's mind raced, trying to piece together the fragments of information and theory into a coherent picture. If Genexis was involved, if they were the ones behind the Purifiers' newfound abilities, then that meant…

"The missing mutants," he said slowly, his eyes widening with horrified realization. "Ethan, what if Genexis is using them as test subjects, as guinea pigs for whatever fucked-up process they've cooked up to give humans mutant powers? What if that's been their endgame all along, to create an army of enhanced radicals to wipe us out?"

Ethan's hands clenching into fists at his sides. "That's what I thought as well. I knew those Genexis fuckers were up to no good, but this… this is beyond anything I could have imagined."

"We need to move fast," he said, his voice urgent and intense. "Every second we wait is another chance for Genexis and the Purifiers to hurt more of our people, to push their sick, twisted agenda even further."

Ethan nodded, his eyes hard with determination. "You're right. We need to gather the team, pool our resources and figure out our next move."

He reached for his phone, his fingers flying over the screen as he typed out a message. "I'm calling an emergency meeting at headquarters. We need Zoe and Marcus on this, need their skills and their intel if we're going to crack this fucking thing wide open."

Liam felt a flicker of anticipation and dread, a sense that they were standing on the brink of something huge, something that could change the course of their lives and the fate of the mutant community forever. But he pushed down his fear, focusing instead on the task at hand and the man by his side.

"Let's do this," he said, his voice rough with emotion. "Let's take these bastards down and show them what happens when you fuck with the wrong people."

Ethan grinned, a fierce, feral thing that sent shivers down Liam's spine. "Damn straight, baby. They picked the wrong mutants to mess with, and now they're going to pay the price."

* * *

They arrived at headquarters to find Zoe and Marcus already waiting for them, their faces grim and their eyes tired but determined. Liam could see the weight of the past few days etched into every line of their faces, the toll that this fight was taking on all of them.

But he also saw the fire in their eyes, the unshakable resolve that burned bright and hot and fierce. They were warriors, all of them, fighters for a cause that was bigger than any one person or any one battle.

"Alright, team," Ethan said, his voice ringing out clear and strong in the stillness of the room. "We've got a new lead, a connection between Genexis and the Purifiers." He turned to Zoe, his expression serious. "Z, I need you to dig into Genexis' financials, see if you can find any evidence of them funneling money to known Purifier fronts or shell companies. If they're bankrolling these fuckers, we need to know about it."

Zoe nodded, her fingers already flying over the keys of her laptop. "On it, boss. If there's a money trail, I'll find it. These corporate scumbags always leave a trace, no matter how hard they try to cover their tracks."

Liam felt a surge of gratitude and affection for the young hacker, for her skills and her dedication and her unwavering loyalty to the cause. She was a vital part of their team, a key player in the fight against the forces that sought to destroy them.

As Zoe worked her magic, the rest of the team huddled around the table, their minds racing with possibilities and plans. Ethan filled them in on what he had learned from Reeves, the Genexis logo he had seen on the Purifier's equipment and the implications of a connection between the two groups.

"If Genexis is involved," Marcus said, his voice low and serious, "then this is bigger than we ever imagined. A conspiracy of that scale, with that kind of money and resources behind it… it's like nothing we've ever faced before."

Liam nodded, his jaw clenching with anger and determination. "And that's exactly why we have to stop them, why we have to put an end to their sick, fucked-up plans before they can hurt anyone else."

Zoe's voice cut through the tension like a knife, her tone urgent and excited. "Guys, I think I found something. There are dozens of transactions between Genexis and these shell companies, all linked to known Purifier members and fronts. It's like a fucking money laundering scheme, but instead of drugs or guns, they're financing hate and bigotry."

Ethan's eyes narrowed, his mind already racing ahead to the next step. "Okay, so we know they're connected financially. But what about the Purifiers' new abilities, the mutant powers they've somehow managed to gain? There has to be more to it than just money."

Zoe's brow furrowed, her fingers flying over the keys once more. "Hold on, let me see if I can dig a little deeper, see if there's any mention of... oh shit."

Liam's heart clenched, a sickening sense of dread washing over him. "What is it, Zoe? What did you find?"

The hacker looked up, her face pale and her eyes wide with horror. "Project Prometheus. It's some kind of experimental program, aimed at transferring mutant abilities to baseline humans. And from the looks of these files... they're using the missing mutants as test subjects, as fucking guinea pigs for their sick, twisted science fair project."

The room fell silent, a heavy, oppressive weight settling over them like a shroud. Liam felt bile rise in the back of his throat, a wave of nausea and fury that threatened to consume him entirely.

"Those fucking monsters," he snarled, his fists clenching at his sides. "They're not just supporting the Purifiers, they're turning them into mutants, into living weapons to use against us. It's fucking genocide, plain and simple."

Ethan's face was a mask of cold, implacable rage, his eyes burning with a fire that Liam had never seen before. "And we're going to stop them," he said, his voice low and dangerous. "We're going to burn their whole fucking operation to the ground, and make sure they never hurt another mutant again."

Marcus nodded, his expression grim. "But why would Genexis do this? What's their endgame, their motive for empowering a bunch of mutant-hating terrorists?"

Liam's mind raced, trying to piece together the fragments of information and theory into a coherent picture. And then, with a sickening lurch, it clicked.

"Control," he said, his voice barely above a whisper. "They want to control us, to blur the lines between mutant and human until there's no difference, no distinction. If they can create their own mutants, their own enhanced humans… then they hold all the power. They can justify their experiments, their hate, their fucking genocide. Because in their eyes… we're all just subjects, just lab rats to be poked and prodded and disposed of when we're no longer useful."

The room fell silent once more, the weight of Liam's words hanging heavy in the air. And then Ethan spoke, his voice rough with emotion and fierce with determination.

"Fuck that," he growled, his eyes flashing with a wild, reckless light. "Fuck them and their bullshit justifications, their sick, twisted science projects. We're not going to let them win, not going to let them turn us into something we're not. We're going to fight back, going to show them what it means to be a mutant, to be proud and strong and unafraid in the face of their hate."

They were walking into the lion's den, into the heart of a conspiracy that sought to destroy everything they held dear.

But they were ready for it.

21

The Offer

Ethan

They were so close, so fucking close to putting an end to the nightmare that had haunted the mutant community for far too long.

But even as he reveled in the thrill of the hunt, in the adrenaline that pumped through his veins like liquid fire, he couldn't shake the feeling of unease that prickled at the back of his neck. Something was off, something that he couldn't quite put his finger on.

He glanced over at Liam, he was deep in conversation with Zoe and Marcus, his brow furrowed with concentration as they pored over the files and data they had gathered.

But even as he basked in the warmth of Liam's presence, Ethan couldn't shake the feeling that something was about to go terribly, horribly wrong. It was like a sixth sense, a tingling at the base of his spine that warned him of impending danger.

Suddenly, a loud crash echoed through the building, the sound of splintering wood and shattering glass filling the air. Ethan whirled around, his heart pounding in his chest as he saw a group of heavily armed figures storming into the room, their weapons drawn and their faces obscured by dark, featureless masks.

"DMA!" he shouted, his mind already racing with the implications of the agency's presence. "Everybody, get down!"

Chaos erupted as the team scrambled for cover, Zoe and Marcus diving behind a bank of computers while Liam and Ethan took up defensive positions on either side of the room. The DMA agents fanned out, their movements precise and coordinated as they advanced on the team's position.

"Well, well, well," Ethan drawled, his voice dripping with sarcasm as he summoned The Magician card to his hand. "If it isn't my favorite group of government lapdogs. To what do we owe the pleasure of your company?"

The lead agent, a tall, broad-shouldered man with cold, calculating eyes, stepped forward, his weapon trained on Ethan's chest. "Ethan Hawke, aka The Arcana," he said, his voice flat and emotionless. "You and your team are under arrest for conspiracy, terrorism, and crimes against the state. Surrender now, or we will use deadly force."

Ethan barked out a laugh, the sound harsh and mocking in the tense silence of the room. "Conspiracy? Terrorism? Fuck, you guys really need to update your playbook. We're the ones trying to stop the real criminals here, the ones who are kidnapping and experimenting on innocent mutants."

The agent's eyes narrowed, his finger tightening on the trigger of his weapon. "Last chance, Hawke. Surrender peacefully, or face the consequences."

Ethan's grin widened, his eyes sparking with a wild, reckless light. "Consequences? Oh, you mean like this?"

With a flick of his wrist, he sent The Tower card hurtling towards the agent, the ethereal construct exploding in a burst of blinding light and concussive force. The agent staggered back, his weapon flying from his hand as he was thrown off balance.

And then all hell broke loose.

The DMA agents opened fire, their weapons spitting out bursts of searing energy that cut through the air like lightning. But Ethan was ready for them, his powers surging to life as he summoned The Tower card to his aid.

A wall of shimmering force erupted from the floor, the barrier absorbing the brunt of the agents' attack and giving the team a moment's respite. Ethan glanced over at Liam, his heart clenching at the sight of the firefighter's face, set with grim determination as he fought by Ethan's side.

"We need to take these fuckers down fast," Ethan growled, his mind already racing with possibilities and plans. "Zoe, Marcus, see if you can flank them from the sides. Liam and I will keep them busy from the front."

The team nodded, their expressions fierce with resolve as they moved into position. Ethan summoned The Chariot card, feeling the rush of speed and agility that flooded through his veins like a drug.

He charged forward, his body moving with inhuman grace and precision as he closed the distance between himself and the nearest agent. The man raised his weapon, a strange, pulsing device that Ethan had never seen before, but he was too slow, too clumsy to match The Arcana's speed.

Ethan slammed into him with the force of a freight train, his fists and feet flying in a blur of motion as he rained down blow after punishing blow. The agent crumpled to the ground, his weapon clattering to the floor at Ethan's feet.

But even as Ethan reveled in his victory, he heard Liam cry out in pain, the sound cutting through the chaos of the battle like a knife. He whirled around, his heart in his throat as he saw the love of his life crumple to the ground, clutching at his chest in agony.

"Liam!" Ethan screamed, his voice raw with fear and desperation. He charged towards the fallen firefighter, his mind a whirlwind of panic and fury.

But the DMA agents were faster, their weapons trained on Ethan's back as they advanced on his position. Ethan summoned The World card, feeling the rush of power that surged through his body like a tidal wave.

With a roar of effort, he unleashed the full force of the arcana, the very fabric of reality warping and twisting around him like a living thing. The agents were thrown back, their weapons shattering into a thousand glittering shards as they were caught in the maelstrom of Ethan's power.

And then Ethan was at Liam's side, his hands shaking as he gathered the fallen man into his arms. "Liam," he whispered, his voice choked with emotion. "Liam, baby, talk to me. What happened? What did they do to you?"

Liam's face was pale, his eyes glazed with pain as he struggled to focus on Ethan's face. "The weapon," he rasped, his voice weak and thready. "It did something to my powers, Ethan. I can't... I can't feel them anymore."

Ethan felt a surge of cold, sickening dread wash over him, a fear that threatened to consume him entirely. He had seen the strange weapons the DMA agents had wielded, had felt the wrongness that emanated from them like a physical thing.

If they could neutralize a mutant's powers, render them helpless and vulnerable... then the entire community was at risk, their very way of life threatened by a force that sought to destroy them.

Ethan's mind raced as he cradled Liam's weakened form, his heart pounding with a sickening mix of fear and fury. This couldn't be happening, not now, not when they were so close to unraveling the truth behind Genexis and the Purifiers.

But even as despair threatened to overwhelm him, Ethan's stubborn streak reared its head, a defiant fire sparking to life in his chest. Like hell was he going to let some government goons with fancy toys take down The Arcana and his team. They'd fought too hard, come too far to quit now.

Just as he was about to summon another tarot construct, ready to blast his way out of this clusterfuck with Liam in tow, a commanding voice rang out across the chaos.

"Stand down! I said stand the fuck down, all of you!"

Ethan's head snapped up, his eyes widening as he took in the newcomer striding into the fray. It was a woman, tall and imposing, with steel-gray hair and a bearing that screamed authority. And unless Ethan was very much mistaken, the insignia on her jacket marked her as the head of the fucking DMA.

"Well, who do we have here?" he drawled, his signature smirk sliding into place even as his mind whirred with the implications of her presence. "If it isn't the grand high bitch herself, deigning to grace us with her presence. To what do we owe the honor, Director…?"

"Thorne," she supplied, her voice clipped and cool. "Director Evelyn Thorne. And you'd do well to watch your tongue, Mr. Hawke. I'm not here to bandy words with a reckless vigilante."

Ethan bristled, his grip on Liam tightening protectively. "Oh, I'm sorry, am I supposed to be impressed? Grateful, even, that you called off your attack dogs before they could put any more of my people in the fucking ground?"

Thorne's eyes narrowed, a flicker of irritation passing over her severe features. "Believe it or not, Hawke, I'm not your enemy. If I wanted you dead or captured, we wouldn't be having this conversation."

Ethan barked out a harsh, disbelieving laugh. "Could've fooled me, what with the shock and awe routine your goons just pulled. Speaking of, what the hell kind of weapons are you packing these days? Because last I checked, the DMA was supposed to protect and serve mutants, not strip them of their powers and leave them defenseless."

Thorne sighed, a hint of weariness creeping into her voice. "It's a long story, and one better told in private. I came here to talk, Hawke. To you and your partner both. I have a proposition for you, one that I think you'll want to hear."

Ethan's eyebrows shot up, a bark of incredulous laughter escaping his lips. "A proposition? What, like a deal with the devil? Thanks but no thanks, Director. We're not interested in being your lapdogs or your science experiments."

But Liam, who had been silent throughout the exchange, struggling to catch his breath, suddenly spoke up. "Wait," he rasped, his voice thin and pained. "Let's... let's hear her out, Ethan. We can't afford to burn any bridges, not now."

Ethan looked down at Liam his heart clenching at the exhaustion and vulnerability he saw in those blue eyes. Liam was right, damn him. They were in no position to be turning away potential allies, even ones as slippery and untrustworthy as the DMA.

"Fine," he bit out, his jaw tight with reluctance. "But we do this on our terms, Thorne. And if I get even a whiff of betrayal or double-cross, all bets are off."

Thorne inclined her head, a tiny, grim smile playing about her lips. "I'd expect nothing less from you, Hawke. Now, shall we adjourn to somewhere more comfortable? I believe we have much to discuss."

Minutes later, they were ensconced in a small, nondescript room deep within the DMA headquarters. Ethan paced like a caged tiger, his body thrumming with pent-up energy and barely-leashed aggression. Liam sat slumped in a chair, his face pale and drawn, but his eyes sharp and attentive.

Thorne stood before them, her arms crossed and her expression inscrutable. "First things first," she said, her voice crisp and businesslike. "Your friend's condition is temporary. The weapon used on him is a prototype, designed to dampen mutant abilities for a short period of time. He'll be back to full strength within a few hours."

Ethan's eyes flashed, a low growl building in his throat. "And that's supposed to make me feel better? You're developing weapons specifically targeted at mutants, and you expect us to trust you?"

Thorne's gaze was level, unflinching. "The weapons are a necessary evil, Hawke. A last resort, to be used only in the most dire of circumstances. There are threats out there, dangers that even you and your little band of misfits are unaware of. The DMA must be prepared to face them, by any means necessary."

Liam leaned forward, his brow furrowed with tension. "What kind of threats are we talking about, Director? Because from where I'm sitting, the biggest danger to mutants right now is your agency and its 'necessary evils.'"

Thorne sighed, a flicker of something like regret passing over her face. "There's a lot of evil in this world these days but you may know one of them. Genexis," she said simply, the word hanging heavy in the air. "And the Purifiers. We've been watching them for months, tracking their movements and trying to piece together their endgame. But they're always one step ahead, always just out of reach."

Ethan's eyes narrowed, suspicion and surprise warring in his gut. "And just how do you know about our investigation into Genexis? Have you been spying on us, Thorne?"

The Director shook her head, a wry smile tugging at her lips. "Please, Hawke. Give me some credit. Your exploits may have escaped the notice of the general public, but the DMA has had its eye on you for quite some time. You've been making waves, stirring up trouble in all the right places. It was only a matter of time before our paths crossed."

Liam shifted in his seat, wincing as the movement pulled at his injured muscles. "So what is it that you want from us, Director? You said you had a proposition, a reason for coming here tonight. So let's hear it."

Thorne nodded, her expression turning serious once more. "I want you to work with us, Hawke. You and your team. The DMA could use operatives like you, mutants with the skills and the drive to take the fight to Genexis and the Purifiers."

Ethan scoffed, a bark of harsh laughter escaping his lips. "You want us to be your pet mutants, your secret weapons in this little shadow war of yours? I think I'll pass, thanks. We're not exactly the 'take orders and trust the system' type."

But Thorne was undeterred, her gaze boring into Ethan's with a fierce intensity. "You misunderstand me, Hawke. I'm not asking you to be mindless drones or unquestioning soldiers. I'm offering you a chance to make a real difference, to strike at the heart of the conspiracy that threatens your people."

She leaned forward, her voice dropping to a low, urgent murmur. "The DMA has resources, Hawke. Intel, technology, manpower. Things that could take your little operation to the next level, give you a fighting chance against the forces arrayed against you. And in return, all we ask is that you share what you learn, that you work with us to bring Genexis and the Purifiers to justice."

Ethan's mind raced, torn between his instinctive mistrust of author-ity and the tantalizing promise of Thorne's offer. He glanced at Liam, saw the same conflicted emotions playing out across his lover's face.

"And what about our normal lives?" Liam asked, his voice hoarse but determined. "Our jobs, our identities outside of this mutant vigilante bullshit? Are you asking us to give that up, to become full-time DMA lackeys?"

Thorne shook her head, a tiny smile playing about her lips. "On the contrary, Mr. Quinn. We want you to keep your cover, to maintain the illusion of normalcy. It's what makes you so valuable, so effective. You're not just nameless, faceless agents - you're embedded in the community, in the very heart of the mutant world. That's a perspective, an insight that the DMA sorely needs."

She paused, letting her words sink in before continuing. "Of course, we would expect you to make yourself available when called upon, to share any pertinent information you uncover in the course of your... extracurricular activities. But your day-to-day lives would remain your own, as long as you operate within certain parameters."

Ethan's lip curled, a spark of defiance flaring in his chest. "Parameters? You mean like not exposing your dirty little secrets, not blowing the whistle on the DMA's less-than-legal tactics? Yeah, I think I'll pass on the leash and collar, thanks."

But even as the words left his mouth, Ethan could feel the gravity of the situation pressing down on him like a physical weight. As much as he hated to admit it, Thorne's offer was tempting - the promise of access, of resources and intel that could finally give them a fighting chance against Genexis and the Purifiers.

And yet, he couldn't shake the feeling of unease that coiled in his gut, the nagging suspicion that the DMA's intentions were far from pure. He glanced at Liam, saw the same conflicted emotions playing out across his lover's face.

"I don't know, Ethan," Liam said slowly, his brow furrowed with tension. "I mean, I get the appeal of having the DMA's backing, but at what cost? We'd be putting ourselves under their thumb, letting them call the shots and pull our strings. Is that really a trade-off we're willing to make?"

Ethan ran a hand through his hair, frustration and indecision warring in his chest. "I hear you, Liam. Believe me, the thought of being the DMA's bitch makes my skin crawl. But we have to think about the bigger picture here. If they really do have the kind of intel and resources they're claiming, it could be a game-changer. We can't just dismiss that out of hand."

Liam's jaw clenched, a flicker of anger sparking in his eyes. "And what about the risks, Ethan? The danger of getting too close to an agency that's been developing weapons specifically designed to neutralize mutants? How do we know they won't turn those same weapons on us the second we step out of line or become inconvenient?"

Thorne cleared her throat, drawing their attention back to her. "Gentlemen, I understand your reservations. But I urge you to consider the alternative. The DMA has been monitoring your activities for some time now, and while we've chosen to take a hands-off approach thus far, that could change at any moment. Accepting our offer would grant you a measure of protection, a certain... leeway in your operations. Refusing it, on the other hand..."

She trailed off, letting the implication hang heavy in the air.

Ethan's eyes narrowed, a cold, sinking feeling settling in his stomach. "So that's how it is, huh? Play ball or get crushed under the DMA's boot heel? Gotta say, Director, you sure know how to make a compelling argument."

Thorne's lips thinned, a flicker of impatience passing over her face. "Spare me the sarcasm, Hawke. I'm not here to coerce or threaten you. I'm simply laying out the facts, the reality of the situation you find yourselves in. The DMA has a vested interest in bringing Genexis and the Purifiers to justice, and we believe that working with you is the best way to achieve that goal. But make no mistake - we will pursue that goal with or without your cooperation. The choice is yours."

Ethan exchanged a long, weighted look with Liam, a silent conversation passing between them in the space of a heartbeat. He could see the reluctance in Liam's eyes, the lingering distrust and suspicion. But he could also see the glimmer of hope, the desperate, aching need to find a way forward in this impossible situation.

"Alright, Thorne," he said at last, his voice rough with resignation. "We'll consider your offer. But we need time to discuss it as a team, to weigh the pros and cons and come to a decision. This isn't the kind of thing we can just jump into blindly."

Thorne inclined her head, a tiny, grim smile playing about her lips. "Of course. Take all the time you need. But don't take too long - the clock is ticking, and every moment we waste is another chance for Genexis and the Purifiers to slip through our fingers."

With that, she turned and strode from the room, leaving Ethan and Liam alone with their thoughts and the weight of the choice before them. For a long moment, neither of them spoke, the silence stretching out between them like a physical thing.

And then Liam let out a shaky breath, his shoulders slumping with exhaustion and defeat. "Fuck, Ethan. What the hell are we supposed to do here? I don't trust the DMA as far as I can throw them, but I can't deny that their offer is tempting. The kind of access and resources they're promising… it could be a real game-changer."

Ethan reached out, taking Liam's hand in his own and giving it a gentle, reassuring squeeze. "I know, babe. Believe me, I'm just as torn as you are. But we can't make this decision alone. We need to talk to Zoe and Marcus, get their take on the situation. They're just as invested in this fight as we are, and they deserve a say in how we move forward."

Liam nodded, a flicker of determination sparking to life in his eyes. "You're right. Let's head back to the safehouse, regroup with the others. We'll figure this out together, as a team. Just like we always do."

Ethan's heart swelled with love and pride, a fierce, unshakable faith in the man by his side and the team they had built together. "Damn straight, we will. The Arcana, the firefighter, the zappy hacker chick, and the beefcake with a heart of gold. Saving the world, one impossible choice at a time."

Liam cracked a smile at that, a tiny, fleeting thing that nevertheless made Ethan's pulse skip a beat. "Careful, Hawke. Keep talking like that and you might just end up leading us into a cheesy eighties montage."

Ethan clutched his heart in mock offense. "Bite your tongue, Quinn. We are far too cool and edgy for cheesy montages. We do gritty, aesthetically pleasing montages set to moody indie rock only."

They were joking, falling back on the playful banter and easy camaraderie that had become the bedrock of their relationship. But Ethan could see the fear lurking behind Liam's eyes, the cold, clammy dread of a future that felt more uncertain than ever before.

He knew that his lover was scared, that they were all scared. The world they had known, the fight they had been waging for so long… it was all changing, all shifting beneath their feet like quicksand.

But he also knew that they couldn't let that fear consume them, couldn't let it paralyze them into inaction. They had to keep moving forward, keep fighting for the people they loved and the world they believed in.

Even if that meant making impossible choices and dancing with the devil in the pale moonlight.

Back at the safehouse, Ethan paced the length of the room like a caged tiger, his mind whirring with the implications of Thorne's offer. Zoe and Marcus watched him with wary, expectant eyes, their faces tight with tension and uncertainty.

"Alright, team," he said at last, his voice rough with exhaustion and pent-up emotion. "We've got a decision to make, and it's not going to be an easy one. The DMA has offered us a deal, a chance to work with them to take down Genexis and the Purifiers. But it comes with strings attached, risks and compromises that we need to weigh carefully."

He took a deep breath, running a hand through his hair as he gathered his thoughts. "On the one hand, having access to the DMA's resources and intel could be a real game-changer. We've been flying blind for so long, piecing together scraps of information and half-formed theories. This could be our chance to finally get ahead of Genexis, to strike at the heart of their operation."

Zoe leaned forward, her brow furrowed with concern. "But at what cost, Ethan? The DMA has never been a friend to mutants. They've been developing weapons specifically designed to neutralize our powers, stripping us of the very things that make us who we are. How can we trust them not to turn those same weapons on us the second we step out of line?"

Ethan nodded, a grim smile tugging at the corner of his mouth. "Believe me, Zo, I'm under no illusions about the DMA's intentions. They're not offering us this deal out of the goodness of their hearts. They want something from us, and they're not afraid to play hardball to get it."

Marcus shifted in his seat, his expression thoughtful. "But maybe that's not such a bad thing," he said slowly, his deep voice rumbling through the room. "The DMA's involvement could lend legitimacy to our cause, could help sway public opinion in our favor. If we're seen as working with the government, as part of an official investigation… it could change the whole narrative around mutants and our place in society."

Ethan's eyebrows shot up, surprise and skepticism warring in his gut. "You really think the public is going to buy that, Marcus? That they're going to see us as anything other than freaks and dangerous vigilantes, even with the DMA's stamp of approval?"

Marcus shrugged, a wry smile playing about his lips. "I think it's worth considering, at least. The court of public opinion is a fickle thing, Ethan. One day you're a hero, the next you're a villain. If we can use the DMA's involvement to shift that balance in our favor… it could be a powerful tool in our arsenal."

Zoe shook her head, her expression darkening with worry. "Or it could backfire spectacularly. The public is already wary of mutants, already sees us as a threat to their way of life. If they find out that we're working with the government, that we have access to all this classified intel and advanced tech… it could just confirm their worst fears about us. We could end up facing even more scrutiny and regulation than before."

Ethan sighed, rubbing a hand over his face as he tried to reconcile the conflicting viewpoints. He could see the merit in both arguments, could understand the appeal of having the DMA's backing and the risk of losing control over their own narrative.

But in the end, he knew that it all came down to one simple question: what was best for the mission? What course of action would give them the best chance of stopping Genexis and the Purifiers, of protecting the innocent lives that hung in the balance?

He turned to Liam, his eyes searching his lover's face for guidance, for the wisdom and clarity that he so often found there. "What do you think, Liam? You've been quiet so far. Where do you stand on all of this?"

Liam was silent for a long moment, his brow furrowed with thought and his jaw tight with tension. And then he let out a long, slow breath, his shoulders slumping with the weight of the decision before them.

"I don't know, Ethan," he said softly, his voice rough with emotion. "I wish I had an easy answer, a clear path forward. But the truth is, I'm just as torn as the rest of you. I see the potential benefits of working with the DMA, but I also see the risks, the dangers of getting too close to an agency that has never had our best interests at heart."

He paused, his eyes finding Ethan's and holding them with a fierce, unwavering intensity. "But I do know one thing. Whatever we decide, whatever path we choose… we do it together. As a team, as a family. We watch each other's backs, we support each other through the hard times and the impossible choices. Because that's what we do, Ethan.

That's who we are."

Ethan felt a lump form in his throat, a wave of emotion crashing over him like a tidal wave. He reached out, taking Liam's hand in his own and squeezing it tight, a silent promise passing between them in the space of a heartbeat.

"Together," he echoed, his voice rough with feeling. "Always and forever, no matter what."

He turned back to Zoe and Marcus, his expression hardening with resolve. "Alright, team. Let's put it to a vote. All in favor of accepting the DMA's offer and seeing where this rabbit hole takes us?"

For a long, tense moment, no one moved. And then, slowly, reluctantly, three hands raised into the air.

Ethan nodded, a grim smile tugging at the corner of his mouth. "Looks like the ayes have it. We're in this now, for better or worse. Let's just hope we don't end up regretting it."

22

Dancing with the Devil

Liam

Stepping into the firehouse, his mind was still reeling from the weight of the decision he and Ethan had made. The DMA partnership loomed over him like a dark cloud, a constant reminder of the dangers that lay ahead.

"Hey, Quinn!" Jack called out, his voice cutting through the haze of Liam's thoughts. "You okay, man? You look like you've seen a ghost."

Liam forced a smile, trying to shake off the unease that had settled in his gut. "I'm fine, Jack. Just didn't get much sleep last night."

Jack raised an eyebrow, a knowing smirk playing at the corners of his mouth. "Oh, I bet. Late night with that mysterious boyfriend of yours?"

Liam rolled his eyes, punching Jack playfully on the arm. "Fuck off, man. It's not like that."

But even as the words left his mouth, Liam couldn't help but think of Ethan, of the way his touch made Liam's skin tingle and his heart race. He pushed the thought aside, focusing instead on the day's tasks.

As he went about his duties, checking equipment and running drills,

Liam couldn't shake the feeling that everything was about to change. The DMA partnership was a gamble, a leap of faith into the unknown. And Liam wasn't sure if he was ready for what lay on the other side.

"Hey, Quinn!" Martinez called out, his voice tinged with concern. "You sure you're okay? You've been quiet all day."

Liam sighed, running a hand through his hair. He knew he could trust Martinez, knew that the man had his back no matter what. But he also knew that he couldn't reveal the true nature of his involvement with the DMA, not without putting everyone at risk.

"I've just got a lot on my mind," he said finally, his voice low and rough. "Personal stuff, you know?"

Martinez nodded, his expression softening with understanding. "I get it, man. This job, it takes a toll on all of us. But you're one of the strongest, most resilient people I know. Whatever you're going through, I know you'll come out the other side."

Liam felt a lump form in his throat, a wave of gratitude washing over him. "Thanks, Martinez. That means a lot."

He clapped the other man on the shoulder, a silent acknowledgment of the bond they shared. And for a moment, Liam felt a flicker of hope, a sense that maybe, just maybe, everything would be okay.

After his shift, Liam found himself standing outside Ethan's penthouse, his heart pounding with a mix of anticipation and dread. He knew that they needed to talk, needed to prepare for the meeting with Director Thorne and the DMA. But a part of him just wanted to lose himself in Ethan's arms, to forget about the world outside and all the dangers that lurked in the shadows.

Liam took a deep breath and knocked on the door, his palms sweating and his mouth dry. When Ethan answered, his green eyes sparkling with warmth and affection, Liam felt a rush of emotion that threatened to overwhelm him.

"Hey, you," Ethan murmured, pulling Liam into a tight embrace. "I missed you today."

Liam buried his face in the crook of Ethan's neck, breathing in the scent of his skin and letting the warmth of his body soothe the ache in his chest. "I missed you too," he whispered, his voice muffled against Ethan's throat.

They held each other for a long moment, neither of them wanting to let go. But eventually, Ethan pulled back, his expression turning serious.

"We need to talk about tomorrow," he said softly, his fingers tracing the line of Liam's jaw. "The meeting with Thorne, the DMA… it's not going to be easy."

Liam sighed, leaning into Ethan's touch. "I know. But we'll face it together, just like we always do."

Ethan smiled, a soft, tender thing that made Liam's heart skip a beat. "Together," he echoed, his voice rough with emotion. "No matter what happens, I'll always have your back."

Liam nodded, a fierce, unshakable determination settling over him. "And I'll have yours. Always."

They spent the rest of the night wrapped in each other's arms, trading soft kisses and whispered promises. And as Liam drifted off to sleep, his head pillowed on Ethan's chest, he knew that whatever challenges lay ahead, they would face them as one.

* * *

Liam, Ethan, Zoe, and Marcus arrived at the DMA headquarters, their hearts pounding with a mix of anticipation and dread. They were escorted through layers of security, the tension and anticipation building with each step.

"Fucking hell," Liam muttered under his breath, his eyes darting around the sterile, high-tech facility. "I feel like we're walking into the belly of the beast."

Ethan chuckled, his hand finding Liam's and giving it a reassuring squeeze. "Relax, babe. We've got this. And if things go sideways, we'll just blast our way out with some good old-fashioned mutant powers and witty one-liners."

Liam rolled his eyes, but he couldn't help the smile that tugged at the corners of his mouth. Leave it to Ethan to find humor in even the most dire of situations.

As they entered the briefing room, Director Thorne greeted them with a nod, her expression grim and her eyes hard. "Welcome, team," she said, her voice clipped and businesslike. "Let's get started."

She launched into a detailed explanation of Project Prometheus, revealing that it was not just a project, but a person – the mastermind behind the mutant experiments. Liam felt a chill run down his spine, a sickening sense of dread that made his stomach churn.

"Hold on," he said, his voice tight with barely contained anger. "You're telling us that this Prometheus asshole has been experimenting on mutants, turning them into fucking lab rats? And the DMA is just now getting around to doing something about it?"

Thorne's eyes narrowed, her lips thinning with displeasure. "Mr. Quinn, I understand your frustration. But the reality is that Prometheus has been operating in the shadows for years, always staying one step ahead of us. It's only recently that we've been able to gather enough intel to even begin to piece together the scope of their operation."

Liam scoffed, his fists clenching at his sides. "Right. And I'm sure the fact that mutants are the ones being targeted has nothing to do with the DMA's lack of urgency."

"Liam," Ethan murmured, his hand coming to rest on the small of Liam's back. "I know you're pissed, and you have every right to be.

But we need to hear Thorne out, need to get all the information before we start throwing accusations around."

Liam took a deep breath, forcing himself to push down the anger that simmered in his gut. He knew Ethan was right, knew that flying off the handle wouldn't do anyone any good. But it was hard, so fucking hard, to keep his cool in the face of such blatant injustice.

"Fine," he said through gritted teeth, his eyes never leaving Thorne's face. "But I want it on record that I think this whole situation is fucked up beyond belief."

Thorne nodded, her expression unreadable. "Noted, Mr. Quinn. Now, if we could move on?"

She gestured to the large screen behind her, where a map of the city was displayed. Red dots peppered the landscape, each one marking the location of a mutant disappearance.

"As you can see, the disappearances have been concentrated in specific areas of the city. Hell's Kitchen, Harlem, the Bronx. All neighborhoods with high populations of mutants."

Liam's heart clenched as he scanned the map, his eyes catching on a familiar location. "Wait," he said, his voice hoarse with emotion. "I know that kid. The one who disappeared from Hell's Kitchen. I rescued him from a fire a few months back. He was just a child, couldn't have been more than ten years old."

The room fell silent, the weight of Liam's words hanging heavy in the air. And in that moment, Liam knew that he would do whatever it took to bring that child home, to stop Prometheus and the twisted experiments that threatened to tear the city apart.

"There's more," Thorne said, her voice cutting through the stillness like a knife. "We've intercepted intelligence suggesting that Prometheus is planning a major operation in the near future. One that could have catastrophic consequences for the city and the mutant community as a whole."

Zoe's eyes widened, her fingers flying over the keys of her ever-present laptop. "What kind of operation are we talking about here? Some sort of mass abduction? A terrorist attack?"

Thorne shook her head, her expression grim. "We don't know the specifics yet. But our sources indicate that it's something big, something that Prometheus has been working towards for years. And if we don't stop them…"

She trailed off, letting the implication hang heavy in the air. Liam felt a shiver run down his spine, a cold, creeping dread that seemed to seep into his very bones.

"So what's the plan?" Marcus asked, his deep voice rumbling through the room. "How do we stop these bastards before they can put their plan into action?"

Thorne leaned forward, her eyes flashing with a fierce, determined light. "That's where you come in. We need you to use your unique skills and resources to infiltrate Prometheus' organization, to gather intel and evidence that we can use to bring them down once and for all."

Ethan raised an eyebrow, a wry smile tugging at the corner of his mouth. "And what's in it for us? Besides the warm and fuzzy feeling of doing the right thing, of course."

Thorne's lips twitched, a hint of amusement passing over her face. "Full access to DMA resources and support. State-of-the-art equipment, classified intel, a get-out-of-jail-free card for any… extralegal activities that may be necessary in the course of your investigation."

Liam frowned, his stubborn streak rearing its head. He didn't like the idea of being beholden to the DMA, of dancing to their tune like a bunch of well-trained monkeys.

But he also knew that they were out of options, that the fate of countless innocent lives hung in the balance. And if working with the DMA was the only way to stop Prometheus and their twisted machinations?

Then he would grit his teeth and bear it, would swallow his pride and do whatever it took to see this through to the end.

"Alright," he said finally, his voice rough with resignation. "We're in. But let's get one thing straight, Thorne. This is just our first run and if you fuck us over then we're done. We're not your fucking lapdogs. We do things our way, and if we find out you're holding out on us or playing us for fools? All bets are off."

Thorne inclined her head, a tiny, grim smile playing about her lips. "I wouldn't have it any other way, Mr. Quinn. Now, let's get to work."

As the team filed out of the briefing room, their minds whirling with the weight of the task before them, Liam couldn't shake the feeling that they were walking into the lion's den. That they were about to face horrors and challenges beyond anything they had ever encountered before.

But before they could disperse, Thorne called them back, a grim expression etched on her face. "There's one more thing you need to see," she said, her voice heavy with foreboding.

She tapped a few keys on her computer, and the screen behind her flickered to life, revealing a map of the city. Red dots peppered the landscape, each one marking the location of a mutant disappearance.

"As you can see," Thorne said, gesturing to the screen, "the disappearances have been concentrated in specific areas of the city. But what's more interesting is the pattern they seem to form."

Liam squinted at the map, his brow furrowing in concentration. At first glance, the dots seemed random, scattered across the city like a handful of spilled marbles. But as he looked closer, he began to see what Thorne was talking about.

The dots seemed to cluster around a central point, forming a rough triangle that spanned the length and breadth of the city. And at the very center of that triangle, a single, pulsing red light.

"What the hell is that?" Liam asked, his voice rough with a mix of curiosity and dread.

Thorne's lips thinned, her expression grim. "That, Mr. Quinn, is the location of a massive, intermittent power surge that our sensors have been detecting for the past few weeks. We believe it may be connected to the disappearances, and to Prometheus themselves."

Zoe leaned forward, her keen eyes scanning the map with laser-like focus. "Hold on," she said, her voice tight with excitement. "I think I see something. The disappearances, they're not just clustered around that central point. They're triangulating to it."

Thorne nodded, a tiny, approving smile tugging at the corner of her mouth. "Very good, Ms. Tanaka. You're correct. The disappearances seem to be converging on that location, like spokes on a wheel."

Ethan frowned, his green eyes flashing with a mix of curiosity and concern. "But why? What's so special about that spot? And what do the power surges have to do with it?"

Thorne shook her head, her expression troubled. "We don't know for sure. But our analysts have been working around the clock to try and make sense of the data, and they've come up with a few theories."

She tapped a few more keys, and the map zoomed in on the central location, revealing a dense tangle of streets and buildings. "This area of the city is old, one of the oldest in New York. It's riddled with abandoned warehouses, forgotten tunnels, and hidden spaces that have been lost to time. The perfect place for a secret lab or base of operations."

Marcus leaned forward, his deep voice rumbling through the room. "So you think that's where Prometheus is hiding out? Where they're conducting their experiments on the missing mutants?"

Thorne nodded, her expression grim. "It's a possibility. But there's more. The power surges we've been detecting are like nothing we've ever seen before. They're massive, almost off the scale. And they seem to be coming from a single, concentrated source."

Liam's heart skipped a beat, a sudden, terrible thought occurring to him. "A mutant," he said, his voice hoarse with dread. "You think Prometheus has a mutant working for them. Someone with an ability that requires massive amounts of energy to operate."

Ethan nodded, his expression thoughtful. "It would make sense. I've seen some powerful mutations in my time, but nothing on the scale of what you're describing. If Prometheus has managed to harness that kind of power…"

He trailed off, letting the implication hang heavy in the air. Liam felt a shiver run down his spine, a cold, creeping dread that seemed to seep into his very bones.

"Fuck," he muttered, running a hand through his hair. "This is bad. Like, end of the fucking world bad. If Prometheus has that kind of firepower on their side, who knows what they're capable of?"

Thorne nodded, her expression grave. "Exactly. Which is why it's so crucial that we act now, before they have a chance to put their plan into motion. If we don't stop them…"

She trailed off, her eyes distant and haunted. "The consequences could be catastrophic. Not just for the mutant community, but for the entire city. Millions of lives could be at risk."

Liam felt a wave of nausea wash over him, a sickening sense of dread that made his stomach churn. He thought of the missing mutants, the experiments and torture they must have endured. He thought of the innocent civilians, going about their lives, unaware of the danger that lurked in the shadows.

And he knew, with a bone-deep certainty, that he would do whatever it took to stop Prometheus. To bring them to justice and make them pay for their crimes.

"Alright," he said, his voice rough with determination. "So we know where they are, and we know what they're capable of. The question is, what the hell are we going to do about it?"

Ethan grinned, a fierce, feral thing that sent shivers down Liam's spine. "Oh, I've got a few ideas. And they all involve a lot of property damage and a heaping helping of good old-fashioned ass-kicking."

Zoe snorted, rolling her eyes. "Of course they do. Because why solve a problem with subtlety and finesse when you can just blow shit up instead?"

Marcus chuckled, a deep, rumbling sound that seemed to fill the room. "Hey, sometimes the direct approach is the best approach. Especially when you're dealing with a bunch of evil, mutant-experimenting fuckwads."

Liam couldn't help but smile, a fierce, determined grin that stretched across his face. He loved this team, loved their bravery and their humor and their unwavering loyalty to each other and to the cause.

But he also knew that they were facing an enemy unlike any they had ever encountered before. An enemy with vast resources and terrifying power, and a complete disregard for the sanctity of human life.

They would need to be smart. They would need to be careful. And above all, they would need to stick together, to have each other's backs no matter what challenges lay ahead.

"Alright," he said, his voice ringing out clear and strong. "Let's do this. Let's take these fuckers down and make them regret the day they ever decided to fuck with the mutant community."

The others nodded, their expressions grim but determined. Thorne stepped forward, her eyes flashing with a fierce, unwavering light.

"I'll mobilize our resources and start gathering intel on the location. With any luck, we can have a strike team ready to go within the next forty-eight hours."

She fixed them with a hard, steely gaze, her voice low and urgent. "In the meantime, I need you to prepare yourselves. Gather your gear, shore up your powers, do whatever you need to do to be at the top of your game. Because when the time comes, there will be no room for error. The fate of the city, and the fate of every mutant within it, will be resting on your shoulders."

Liam felt a weight settle on his chest, a heavy, suffocating pressure that threatened to steal the breath from his lungs. But he pushed it down, forced himself to stand tall and meet Thorne's gaze with a fierce, unwavering determination.

"We'll be ready," he said, his voice rough with emotion. "We'll face whatever comes, and we'll come out the other side victorious. Because that's what we do. That's who we are."

23

The Betrayal

Ethan

They stood in the DMA's briefing room, his heart pounding with a heady mix of anticipation and dread. All around him, a team of agents and specialists were gearing up, checking their weapons and running through the plan one last time.

But Ethan's eyes were fixed on Liam, on the man who had become his partner in every sense of the word. The firefighter looked tense, his jaw clenched and his brow furrowed with worry.

"Hey," Ethan murmured, sliding up beside him and bumping their shoulders together. "You doing okay, hot stuff?"

Liam glanced over at him, a wry smile tugging at the corner of his mouth. "Oh, you know. Just getting ready to infiltrate a secret underground lab full of mutated horrors and evil scientists. Typical Tuesday, really."

Ethan grinned, his heart swelling with affection and pride. "That's the spirit. And just think, when this is all over, we can celebrate with a nice, romantic dinner. Candlelight, wine, the whole shebang."

Liam snorted, shaking his head. "Only you would be thinking about romance at a time like this. Fucking incorrigible, that's what you are."

But Ethan could see the warmth in his eyes, the devotion that lay beneath the surface of his gruff exterior. It made his heart skip a beat, made him want to pull Liam close and never let go.

"Alright, listen up!" Director Thorne called out, her voice cutting through the chatter like a knife. "We're about to embark on one of the most dangerous and critical missions in the history of the DMA. The fate of countless lives hangs in the balance, and failure is not an option."

She gestured to the large screen behind her, where a map of the underground facility was displayed. "Our target is the heart of the Prometheus conspiracy. A secret lab where they've been conducting their twisted experiments on mutants. We believe that the mastermind behind this operation, the individual known as Prometheus, may be on site, overseeing the experiments."

Ethan's eyes narrowed, a flicker of anger sparking to life in his chest. Prometheus, the shadowy figure pulling the strings behind the scenes. The monster responsible for the disappearances and the suffering of so many mutants.

Oh, he was going to enjoy taking them down. Enjoy making them pay for every life they had ruined, every mutant they had tortured and experimented on.

"The plan is simple," Thorne continued, her voice grim. "We infiltrate the facility through the main entrance, using Zoe's tech to bypass their security systems. From there, we split into two teams. Team A will focus on securing the lab and gathering evidence, while Team B will seek out Prometheus and any other high-value targets."

Ethan glanced over at Liam, a silent question passing between them. They both knew which team they would be on, which role they would play in this deadly game of cat and mouse.

"I'm going after Prometheus," Ethan said, his voice low and fierce.

"That bastard has a lot to answer for, and I intend to make sure they pay for their crimes."

Liam nodded, his expression grim. "I'll be right by your side, Ethan. Where you go, I follow."

Thorne studied them for a long moment, her eyes sharp and assessing. "Very well. Quinn, Benton, you'll be leading Team B. But remember, your priority is to secure Prometheus alive. We need them to take down the rest of the operation."

Ethan's jaw clenched, a flicker of frustration passing through him. He wanted nothing more than to put a bullet between Prometheus' eyes, to watch the life drain from their face as they paid for their sins.

But he knew that Thorne was right. Prometheus was the key to unraveling this whole fucked-up conspiracy. If they wanted to take down the operation once and for all, they needed them alive and talking.

"Fine," he bit out, his voice tight with barely-controlled anger. "But if they so much as twitch in the wrong direction, I'm taking them down."

Liam laid a hand on his shoulder, a gentle, grounding pressure that seemed to anchor him to the earth. "We'll do what needs to be done, Ethan. But we'll do it the right way. The way that brings justice to the victims and closure to the families."

Ethan took a deep breath, forcing himself to push down the rage that simmered in his gut. Liam was right. They had to be smart about this, had to think with their heads instead of their hearts.

Even if every fiber of his being screamed out for vengeance, for blood and fire and the sweet, sweet taste of retribution.

"Alright, team," Thorne said, her voice cutting through the tension like a knife. "Let's move out. And remember, the world is counting on us. We cannot fail."

With those words, the team sprang into action, gathering their gear and checking their weapons one last time. Ethan reached out with his mind, summoning The Magician card to his hand.

As the team filed out of the room, Zoe and Marcus approached Ethan, their expressions grim but determined.

"Hey, boss," Zoe said softly, worry lining her youthful face. "You sure you want to be part of the strike team? Marcus and I can run point on this one if you want to stay back, keep an eye on the big picture."

Ethan smiled at her, grateful for her concern. "I'll be fine, Z," he said, his voice low and reassuring. "It's me who needs to confront Prometheus. This is personal."

Marcus put a strong hand on his shoulder. "Just remember, E. Revenge isn't everything. Don't lose yourself in the darkness."

Ethan's smirk told them he knew the risks, the temptations. "Hey now, the darkness should be worrying about losing itself in me, big guy." His tone softened. "But really, thanks. Both of you. For always having my back."

He gave them each a meaningful nod before turning to join Liam and the DMA agents. It was time.

The ethereal image shimmered in his hand, a glowing figure wreathed in arcane energy. He could feel its power thrumming through his veins, a constant, reassuring presence that reminded him of who he was and what he was capable of.

He was The Arcana, the defender of the innocent and the scourge of the wicked. And he would not rest until every last member of Prometheus' twisted operation was brought to their knees, begging for mercy that would never come.

As they descended into the hidden lab, the tunnels twisting and turning like the guts of some great, slumbering beast. Ethan felt a tingle of anticipation run down his spine, a premonition of the horrors that lay ahead.

He could sense them, the twisted, mutated experiments lurking in the depths of the facility. Each one a testament to Prometheus' cruelty and madness, each one a reminder of just how high the stakes truly were.

But he refused to let fear cloud his senses or dull his powers. He was The Arcana, damn it. If anyone was going to put an end to this nightmare, it was going to be him.

"So, Liam, my dear," Ethan quipped, his voice echoing off the damp concrete. "Is it everything you dreamed of for our first real date? Dark, dank, filled with unspeakable monstrosities…"

Liam huffed a reluctant laugh as he swept his flashlight beam across the corroded pipes and ancient brickwork. "Yeah, you sure know how to woo a guy, Hawke. Next time, maybe try dinner and a movie instead of B-movie horror central?"

"Aw, but where's the fun in that?" Ethan winked and slid a hand over to entwine with Liam's for a brief, electric moment. "I've got to keep you on your toes or you'll get bored of me."

As they rounded another bend in the subterranean labyrinth, Ethan suddenly stiffened, his senses screaming a warning. Just ahead, the signs of Prometheus' grim work were becoming all too clear. Failed experiments and mutated monstrosities lined the hall, each one more horrifying than the last.

"Well, boys and girls," Ethan said, his voice grim as he channeled The Chariot, its spectral energy flowing through him like a shot of pure adrenaline. "Looks like the party's just getting started. Stay sharp and watch each other's backs. Whoever this Prometheus fucker is, they aren't going down without a fight."

Liam nodded grimly, flames sparking to life around his clenched fists. The DMA agents readied their high-tech weaponry, faces set like stone behind sleek tactical gear.

Game on, Prometheus. Game fucking on.

* * *

As they ventured deeper into the nightmarish labyrinth, Ethan couldn't shake the feeling that they were being watched. Every shadow seemed to conceal a hidden threat, every echoing footstep a harbinger of the horrors to come.

And then, as they rounded a corner into a cavernous chamber, they found themselves face to face with their worst fears made flesh.

A squad of heavily armed Purifiers stood before them, their weapons trained on the team with deadly precision. But it was the figures standing beside them that made Ethan's blood run cold.

Mutants, their bodies twisted and warped by Prometheus' experiments, their powers amplified to a level that Ethan had never seen before. They crackled with dark energy, their eyes glowing with an unnatural, malevolent light.

Ethan's jaw clenched, a white-hot rage boiling up inside him. He couldn't believe what he was seeing, couldn't process the fact that these once innocent mutants had been turned into monsters.

But he didn't have time to dwell on it. Because in the next instant, all hell broke loose.

The Purifiers opened fire, their weapons spitting out bursts of searing energy that lit up the chamber like the Fourth of July. At the same time, the mutant hybrids surged forward, their powers flaring to life in a dazzling display of destruction.

Ethan reacted on instinct, calling upon the power of The Tower. A shimmering barrier of arcane energy sprang up around the team, deflecting the incoming fire and buying them a precious few seconds to regroup.

"Liam, take the left flank!" Ethan yelled, his voice barely audible over the din of battle. "Zoe, provide tactical support! I'll handle the mutants."

The team sprang into action, their movements fluid and precise as they fell into the familiar rhythm of combat. Liam unleashed a torrent of flames, driving back a group of Purifiers who had tried to flank them from the side. Zoe, her fingers flying over her tactical pad, fed them real-time intel on their enemies' positions and weaknesses.

And Ethan, his eyes locked on the twisted mutant hybrids, called upon the power of The World. The ethereal card shimmered to life in his hand, its energy pulsing through his veins like liquid fire.

He charged forward, a wordless battle cry tearing from his throat as he closed the distance between himself and the mutants. They grinned, their bodies crackling with dark energy as they met Ethan's charge head-on.

They clashed in a blinding flash of light and sound, their powers colliding with the force of a small supernova. Ethan could feel the strain on his mind and body as he poured every ounce of his strength into the fight, his muscles screaming with the effort of holding back the mutants' enhanced strength.

"It doesn't have to be this way!" Ethan yelled, his voice raw with emotion. "We can help you, we can find a way to reverse what they've done to you!"

But the mutants just laughed, cold, cruel sounds that sent shivers down Ethan's spine. They were too far gone, too consumed by the dark power that coursed through their veins.

With a burst of arcane energy, Ethan sent the mutants flying backwards, their bodies slamming into the far wall of the chamber with bone-jarring force. They slumped to the ground, unconscious or worse, but Ethan had no time to check.

Because in that moment, through the haze of smoke and chaos, he saw her.

Dr. Novak, her pristine lab coat fluttering around her as she stepped out of the shadows. Her face was a mask of cold, clinical detachment, her eyes glittering with a malevolent intelligence that made Ethan's skin crawl.

"Well, well, well," she said, her voice dripping with contempt. "If it isn't the famous Arcana and his little band of misfits. I must say, I'm thoroughly unimpressed."

Ethan snarled, his fists clenching at his sides as he summoned the power of The Devil. "Novak. I should have known you were behind this. You two-faced, backstabbing bitch."

Dr. Novak laughed, a cold, mirthless sound that echoed off the walls of the chamber. "Oh, Ethan. You have no idea how wrong you are. I'm not just behind this. I am this."

She spread her arms wide, a twisted smile stretching across her face. "I am Prometheus, the creator of a new world order. A world where mutants reign supreme, and the pathetic, inferior humans are nothing more than cattle to be experimented on and disposed of at will."

Liam, his face streaked with soot and his eyes blazing with righteous fury, stepped forward to stand beside Ethan. "You're insane, Novak. You're talking about genocide, about wiping out an entire species."

Dr. Novak shook her head, a patronizing smile playing at the corners of her mouth. "No, Liam. I'm talking about evolution. About taking the next step in our development as a species, and leaving the weak and the inferior behind."

She gestured to the twisted mutant hybrids surrounding her, her eyes gleaming with pride and madness. "Look at them, Ethan. Look at what I've created. The next generation of mutants, enhanced and amplified beyond anything the world has ever seen. With an army like this at my command, nothing can stop me. Not the DMA, not the Purifiers, and certainly not you."

Despite her ruthless methods, Dr. Novak genuinely cared for her fellow mutants and saw herself as their savior and protector. She was willing to make hard choices and sacrifices for what she believed was the greater good - creating a haven for mutants where they could live free from persecution and reach their full potential.

Ethan's mind raced, desperately searching for a way out, a way to turn the tables on Novak and her monstrous creations. But everywhere he looked, he saw only death and defeat staring back at him.

They were outnumbered, outgunned, and hopelessly outmatched. Novak had planned this all too well, had lured them into a trap from which there was no escape.

But even as despair threatened to overtake him, Ethan felt a flicker of defiance spark to life in his chest. He was The Arcana, damn it. He had faced impossible odds before, had stared death in the face and spat in its eye.

And he wasn't about to quit now. Not when the fate of the world hung in the balance.

"You know what, Novak?" he said, his voice hard with determination. "You're fucking delusional. You think you can scare me with your mutant henchmen and your fucking super soldier bullshit? I can take anything you can dish out and keep on ticking."

He slid his gaze to Liam. His eyes widened, taking in Liam's bloody-knuckled fists, his mud-streaked uniform, his unyielding fire. How was it possible that in the middle of all this horror, Liam had never looked more fucking gorgeous, more heroic?

Liam looked back at him, battered but unbowed. Their gazes locked, unspoken volumes passing between them. With Liam at his side, Ethan was invincible. Together, they could withstand anything.

Ethan turned back to Novak, his smirk razor-sharp. "Alright, bitch, you want a fight? Let's fucking dance. Bring it on. Because the Arcana is here to hand out so many beatdowns, you'll think you wandered into a BDSM club by mistake."

Dr. Novak's cool smile never wavered. "Oh, Ethan. You have no idea what you're up against, do you? You think you understand the true extent of my power, of my vision for the future of mutant kind?"

She began to pace, her heels clicking against the cold metal floor. "With my army of enhanced mutants at my side, I will usher in a new era of mutant supremacy. We will take our rightful place as the dominant species on this planet, and the humans will learn to bow before their new masters."

Liam stepped forward, his fists clenched at his sides and his eyes blazing with righteous fury. "You're a monster, Novak. You think you're fighting for mutant rights, but all you're doing is perpetuating the same cycle of hatred and violence that we've been trying to break free from for generations."

As Ethan and Liam confronted Dr. Novak, they realized they were not only facing a powerful adversary but also the complex moral questions raised by her actions and motivations. The confrontation would determine not only the fate of the city but also challenge each character to examine their own beliefs and the lengths they were willing to go to protect what they held dear.

Ethan's mind raced, desperately searching for a way to reason with Novak, to make her see the insanity of her plan. But even as he opened his mouth to speak, he heard a sound that made his blood run cold.

The click of a dozen safeties being released, the whine of energy weapons powering up. He spun around, his eyes widening in disbelief as he saw the DMA agents who had accompanied them into the facility turning their weapons on Liam, Zoe, and himself.

"What the fuck?" he snarled, his hands curling into fists at his sides. "What are you doing?"

The lead agent, a cold-eyed woman with a scar running down the side of her face, smiled thinly. "Following orders, Mr. Hawke. Dr. Novak's orders."

Ethan's heart sank, a wave of betrayal and fury washing over him. "You traitorous fucks," he spat, his voice shaking with barely-controlled rage. "You were working with her all along, weren't you? Leading us into a trap like lambs to the fucking slaughter."

The agent shrugged, her expression bored and indifferent. "What can I say? Dr. Novak made us a better offer. A chance to be on the winning side of history, to take our place as the rightful rulers of this world."

She leveled her weapon at Ethan's chest, the barrel glowing with the same sickly green energy that had neutralized Liam's powers earlier. "Now, are you going to come quietly, or are we going to have to do this the hard way?"

Ethan gritted his teeth, his mind racing as he tried to calculate his odds of success. With the DMA agents turned against them and Novak's mutant hybrids closing in, they were outnumbered and outgunned. Even with his tarot powers and Liam's pyrokinesis, the odds were not in their favor.

But then, out of the corner of his eye, he saw Zoe's fingers twitching, a small, barely-perceptible movement that he recognized immediately. Their secret signal, the one they used to communicate silently during missions.

He glanced over at her, his eyes widening as he saw the small, metallic disc she had palmed in her hand. An EMP grenade, one of her own design. Capable of short-circuiting any electronic device within a twenty-foot radius.

Including the energy weapons currently pointed at their heads.

Ethan's lips twitched, a ghost of a smile flitting across his face. He looked back at the DMA agent, his voice dripping with contempt. "You know what, sweetheart? I think we're going to have to go with option B."

And then, with a speed born of desperation and adrenaline, he dove to the side, summoning The Chariot to enhance his agility as Zoe hurled the EMP grenade into the center of the room.

The device detonated with a blinding flash of light and a deafening roar, the shockwave slamming into the DMA agents and sending them flying like ragdolls. Their weapons sparked and fizzled, rendered useless by the electromagnetic pulse.

Ethan hit the ground rolling, coming up in a crouch with The Tower shimmering in his hand. He unleashed a blast of concussive force, sending Novak's mutant hybrids tumbling head over heels.

"Liam, now!" he yelled, his voice raw with urgency. "Hit them with everything you've got!"

Liam needed no further prompting. With a roar of fury, he unleashed a torrential inferno, the flames swirling around him like a living thing as he directed them towards the stunned DMA agents and mutant hybrids.

The stench of burning flesh and hair filled the air, the screams of the dying mingling with the crackle of the flames. Ethan's stomach churned, bile rising in the back of his throat as he watched the carnage unfold.

But he pushed down his revulsion, his horror at the necessary brutality of their actions. They had no choice. It was kill or be killed, and he would be damned if he let Novak or her lackeys lay a finger on the people he loved.

The battle raged on, a whirlwind of fire and fury as Ethan and his team fought tooth and nail against the combined forces of the Purifiers, mutant hybrids, and rogue DMA agents. Ethan summoned his tarot powers in a dizzying display of arcane might, The Tower and The Devil striking down foes left and right.

Beside him, Liam was a firestorm incarnate, his flames consuming all in their path. Zoe and Marcus held their own, their weapons and wits a match for any who dared stand against them.

But even as they fought with all their strength, Ethan could feel the tide turning against them. The enemy's numbers seemed endless, their resolve unbreakable. For every foe they struck down, two more rose to take their place.

"There's too many of them!" Liam yelled over the din of battle, his face streaked with sweat and soot. "We can't hold out much longer!"

Ethan gritted his teeth, his mind racing as he tried to formulate a plan. But before he could respond, a searing pain lanced through his skull, bringing him to his knees. He looked up, his vision blurring, to see Dr. Novak standing over him, a cruel smile twisting her features.

"Did you really think you could defeat me, Ethan?" she purred, her voice dripping with malice. "I am the future of mutant kind, the architect of our ascension. And you? You're nothing but a relic of the past, a fossil to be swept aside in the coming revolution."

Ethan tried to summon his powers, to lash out at Novak with all his remaining strength. But his mind was foggy, his thoughts sluggish and unresponsive. He could feel his consciousness slipping away, the world fading to black around him.

The last thing he saw before the darkness claimed him was Liam's face, contorted in anguish as he struggled against the grip of a dozen Purifiers. "Ethan!" he screamed, his voice raw with desperation. "Ethan, no!"

And then there was nothing but the void, a yawning chasm of emptiness that swallowed Ethan whole.

* * *

He awoke to the sensation of cold metal against his skin, the harsh glare of fluorescent lights burning his eyes. He tried to move, to sit up and take stock of his surroundings, but he found himself bound tight, his wrists and ankles secured to a table with thick, unyielding straps.

"Ah, you're awake," a familiar voice purred, sending a chill down Ethan's spine. "Good. I was starting to think I'd broken you already."

Ethan twisted his head, his heart sinking as he saw Dr. Novak looming over him, her eyes alight with a fanatical gleam. She was dressed in a pristine white lab coat, a tray of gleaming surgical instruments laid out before her.

"Novak," Ethan spat, his voice hoarse and ragged. "Where the fuck am I? Where are the others?"

Dr. Novak chuckled, a low, menacing sound that made Ethan's skin crawl. "Oh, don't worry about your little friends, Ethan. They're being well taken care of. As for you? You're exactly where you need to be. Right here, in my lab, ready to become the crowning achievement of my life's work."

She ran a finger along the edge of a scalpel, her touch almost tender. "You see, Ethan, I've been studying you for a long time. Your powers, your abilities… they're quite remarkable. The way you can summon those tarot constructs, the way you can manipulate energy and matter with nothing but your mind? It's a level of mutant power I've never seen before."

Ethan's heart raced, a sinking feeling of dread settling in the pit of his stomach. "What the fuck are you talking about, Novak? What do you want with me?"

Dr. Novak smiled, a twisted, hungry expression that made Ethan's blood run cold. "I want to unlock the secrets of your power, Ethan. I want to splice your abilities with those of my other subjects, to create the ultimate mutant warrior. A being of unparalleled strength and potential, loyal only to me and my cause."

She leaned in close, her breath hot against Ethan's ear. "Imagine it, Ethan. An army of super-powered mutants, each one imbued with a fragment of your might. We would be unstoppable, a force to reshape the world in our image."

Ethan recoiled, his stomach churning with revulsion. "You're insane," he hissed, straining against his bonds with all his strength. "I'll never help you, Novak. I'll die before I let you turn me into one of your twisted abominations."

But even as he spoke the words, Ethan could feel a creeping sense of despair washing over him. His powers were gone, suppressed by the same neutralizing technology that had rendered Liam helpless. He was trapped, at the mercy of a madwoman with delusions of grandeur.

And yet, even in his darkest moment, Ethan refused to give up hope. He thought of his team, of the unbreakable bonds that held them together. Liam, Zoe, Marcus… they would come for him. They would find a way to stop Novak and her insane plans, no matter the cost.

As if sensing his thoughts, Dr. Novak chuckled, a low, mocking sound that made Ethan's skin crawl. "Oh, Ethan. You still think your little band of misfits is going to save you? How touchingly naive."

She turned away, busying herself with her tray of instruments. "They're probably dead by now, you know. Gunned down by my Purifiers, or torn apart by my mutant hybrids. And even if they are still alive? They'll never find you here. This facility is hidden, off the grid. A perfect little slice of hell, just for you and me."

Ethan gritted his teeth, refusing to let Novak's taunts get under his skin. "You underestimate them," he ground out, his voice rough with emotion. "They're the best fucking team in the world. They'll find me. And when they do? They'll burn this place to the ground, with you in it."

Dr. Novak just smiled, a pitying, condescending thing that made Ethan's blood boil. "We'll see, Ethan. We'll see."

She picked up a syringe, the needle glinting in the harsh light. "But enough talk. It's time to begin the procedure. Don't worry, Ethan. This will only hurt… a lot."

Ethan braced himself, his heart pounding and his mind racing as he tried to think of a way out, a way to escape the nightmare that was unfolding around him. But just as Dr. Novak was about to plunge the needle into his skin, he felt a faint vibration against his wrist. At first, he thought it was just his imagination, a trick of his adrenaline-fueled mind.

But then, in a flash of realization, he remembered the tracking device Zoe had slipped him before the mission. A contingency plan, she had called it, in case things went sideways.

"If anything happens to you, boss," she had said, her voice uncharacteristically serious, "this little baby will lead us right to you. We'll always have your back, no matter what."

Ethan's heart leaped, a sudden, desperate hope blossoming in his chest. They were coming for him. His team, his family… they were on their way.

He just had to hold on, to endure whatever horrors Novak had in store for him. And when the time came? He would be ready to fight, to stand alongside his friends and take down this twisted bitch once and for all.

"Do your worst, Novak," he snarled, his eyes blazing with defiance. "But know this: you'll never break me. And when my team gets here? We're going to fucking end you."

Dr. Novak just laughed, her eyes glittering with a mad, fanatical light. "Oh, Ethan. I do so love a challenge."

And with that, she plunged the needle into his arm, and the world dissolved into a haze of pain and terror.

But even as Ethan screamed, his body convulsing against the table, he held onto that tiny spark of hope, that glimmer of light in the darkness.

24

The Final Stand

Liam

They stumbled into the DMA headquarters, his heart pounding and his mind reeling from the horrors he had just witnessed. The image of Ethan being dragged away, his cries of pain echoing in Liam's ears, was seared into his memory like a brand.

He couldn't shake the overwhelming sense of dread that threatened to consume him, the fear that he might never see Ethan again, never hold him in his arms or hear his cocky laughter.

"Fuck," he muttered, slamming his fist against the wall in frustration. "Fuck, fuck, fuck."

Zoe and Marcus were right behind him, their faces grim and their eyes haunted. They looked as shaken as Liam felt, their clothes torn and their skin bruised from the desperate battle they had just fought.

"We have to get him back," Liam said, his voice rough with emotion. "We can't leave Ethan in that psycho bitch's hands. Who knows what she's doing to him right now?"

Zoe nodded, her expression fierce. "We will, Liam. We'll find him, and we'll make Novak pay for what she's done. But first, we need to regroup, come up with a plan."

Marcus grunted in agreement, his massive frame still tense with adrenaline. "Zoe's right. We can't just go charging in blind. We need intel, resources. And we need to figure out who we can trust in this fucking snake pit of an agency."

Liam knew they were right, but it didn't make the waiting any easier. Every fiber of his being screamed at him to act, to do something, anything to bring Ethan back.

But he forced himself to take a deep breath, to push down the panic and the rage that threatened to overwhelm him. He had to be strong, had to keep his head in the game.

For Ethan's sake.

"Alright," he said, his voice hard with determination. "Let's go see Thorne. It's time for her to give us some goddamn answers."

They burst into Thorne's office like a hurricane, Liam's eyes blazing with a fire that had nothing to do with his mutant abilities. Thorne looked up from her desk, her expression startled and wary.

"What the hell is going on?" she demanded, rising to her feet. "Where's Hawke?"

Liam slammed his hands down on her desk, his face inches from hers. "Ethan's gone," he snarled, his voice shaking with barely-controlled fury. "Novak took him. And she had help, Thorne. From your fucking agents."

Thorne's eyes widened, a flicker of shock and confusion passing over her face. "What? That's impossible. My agents are loyal, they would never-"

"Well, they did," Zoe cut in, her voice cold as ice. "They turned on us, Thorne. Sided with Novak and her band of merry mutant freaks. And now Ethan is paying the price."

Thorne shook her head, her expression troubled. "I don't understand. I had no idea, I swear. I've been kept in the dark about so much, ever since this whole Prometheus mess started."

Liam scoffed, his lip curling in disgust. "Bullshit. You expect us to believe that you, the director of the fucking DMA, had no clue what was going on under your own nose?"

He leaned in closer, his voice dropping to a low, menacing growl. "How do we know you're not part of this, Thorne? How do we know you're not working with Novak, helping her create her little mutant army?"

Thorne's eyes flashed with anger, her jaw clenching. "How dare you," she hissed, her voice tight with indignation. "I have dedicated my life to protecting the mutant community, to fighting against the very kind of bigotry and hatred that Novak represents."

She reached into her desk drawer, pulling out a small, black device. "If you don't believe me, then perhaps this will convince you."

Liam eyed the device warily, his muscles tensing. "What the fuck is that?"

Thorne held it up, her expression grim. "A failsafe. A remote kill-switch that can neutralize any DMA agent who turns against us. If my people have truly betrayed us, then I will not hesitate to use it."

Liam's eyes widened, a flicker of hope sparking in his chest. "Wait, so you're saying you can shut them down? Just like that?"

Thorne nodded, her gaze unflinching. "Yes. It's a last resort, one I hoped I would never have to use. But if it means stopping Novak and saving Ethan? I'll do whatever it takes."

"How do I know you won't just use us like you used those rogue agents?" he asked, his voice tight with suspicion. "How do I know you won't just toss us aside when we're no longer useful to you?"

Thorne sighed, running a hand through her hair in frustration. "Liam, listen to me. You and your team are not like those agents. Your skills, your expertise… they're invaluable. I would never discard assets like that."

She stepped closer, her gaze intense and unwavering. "I know I've made mistakes. I know I've kept things from you, things that maybe I shouldn't have. But I swear to you, on everything I hold dear, that I am not your enemy. I want to stop Novak just as much as you do."

Liam stared at her for a long moment, his mind whirling with conflicting emotions. He wanted to believe her, wanted to trust that she was telling the truth. But the memory of Ethan's cries, of the betrayal that had led to his capture…

"Fuck," he muttered, running a hand over his face in frustration. "I don't like this, Thorne. I don't like it one goddamn bit. But you're right. We need to work together, for Ethan's sake."

He fixed her with a hard, unyielding stare. "But let me make one thing crystal fucking clear. If you double-cross us, if you do anything to jeopardize Ethan's life or the lives of my team? I will personally make sure you regret it for the rest of your miserable existence."

Thorne nodded, her expression grim. "Understood, Liam. You have my word."

With that, they set to work, a ragtag alliance forged in the fires of desperation and necessity. Liam, Zoe, Marcus, and a handpicked team of loyal DMA agents pored over every scrap of intelligence they could find, analyzing data and chasing down leads with a frenzied intensity.

Time was running out, and they all knew it. Every second that ticked by was another second that Ethan was in Novak's clutches, another second that he was being subjected to God knows what kind of twisted experiments.

Liam's mind raced as he worked, his thoughts consumed by images of Ethan strapped to a table, his body wracked with pain as Novak's machines tore into him. He couldn't shake the feeling of helplessness, the fear that he might already be too late.

But he pushed those thoughts aside, forcing himself to focus on the task at hand. He couldn't afford to let his emotions cloud his judgment, not now. Not when Ethan's life hung in the balance.

As he sifted through a stack of files, a familiar name caught Liam's eye. His heart clenched, a wave of grief and anger washing over him as he read the details.

It was the boy, the young mutant he had rescued from a fire all those months ago. The one whose face had haunted his dreams, whose innocent smile had reminded him of why he did what he did.

And there, in stark black and white, was the truth of what had happened to him. Novak had taken him, had experimented on him like a fucking lab rat. Had twisted and warped his body and mind until there was nothing left but a shell, a husk of the bright, vibrant child he had once been.

Liam's vision blurred, hot tears of rage and sorrow pricking at the corners of his eyes. He thought of all the other names on that list, all the other mutants who had suffered and died at Novak's hands.

And he knew, with a sudden, fierce certainty, that he would make her pay for every last one of them.

"Liam?" Zoe's voice cut through his thoughts, her tone sharp with concern. "You okay? You look like you've seen a ghost."

Liam shook his head, his jaw clenching with barely-contained fury. "I'm fine," he bit out, his voice rough with emotion. "Just found something that reminded me why we're doing this. Why we have to stop that bitch Novak before she can hurt anyone else."

Zoe's eyes widened, understanding dawning on her face. "The boy," she said softly, her voice heavy with sympathy. "The one you rescued from the fire. He was one of Novak's victims, wasn't he?"

Liam nodded, his throat tight with grief. "He was just a kid, Zoe. A fucking kid. And she… she destroyed him. Like he was nothing, like his life didn't matter."

Zoe placed a hand on his shoulder, her touch warm and comforting.

"We'll make her pay, Liam. For him, and for all the others. I promise you that."

Liam took a deep, shuddering breath, forcing himself to push down the rage and the pain. He couldn't afford to lose focus, not now. Not when they were so close to finding Ethan.

"Guys," Marcus called out, his voice tight with excitement. "I think I might have something."

Liam's head snapped up, his heart pounding with sudden hope. "What is it, Marcus? What did you find?"

Marcus gestured to his screen, where a map of the city was displayed. "I was going through the data from Ethan's tracking device, trying to pinpoint his location. And I noticed something weird."

He zoomed in on a specific area, his finger tracing a pattern of red dots. "See these energy spikes? They're coming from a remote location outside the city, a place that shouldn't have any power signatures at all."

Liam's eyes widened, realization dawning. "Novak's facility. It has to be."

Zoe nodded, her fingers flying over her keyboard as she pulled up more information. "It makes sense. A hidden lab, off the grid, where she can conduct her experiments without anyone knowing."

Liam felt a surge of adrenaline, a fierce, unshakable determination. They had a location. They had a target.

Now all they needed was a plan.

"Thorne," he barked, his voice ringing out with authority. "Gather your best agents. We're going in, and we're going in hard. Ethan's life depends on it."

Thorne nodded, her expression grim. "Understood. We'll be ready to move out in thirty minutes."

As the team scrambled to prepare, Liam took a moment to himself, his eyes closing as he pictured Ethan's face.

And he made a silent promise, a vow that he would not rest until Ethan was safe in his arms once more.

"Hold on, babe," he whispered, his voice hoarse with emotion. "I'm coming for you. Just hold on a little longer."

It was time to bring the fucking thunder, to rain down hell on Novak and her twisted empire.

And heaven help anyone who got in his way.

* * *

The journey to Novak's hidden facility was a blur of tense silence and barely-contained fury. Liam could feel the adrenaline pumping through his veins, his muscles coiled tight with the need to act, to fight, to save the man he loved.

As they approached the nondescript building, tucked away in the heart of an abandoned industrial complex, Liam couldn't shake the sense of unease that prickled at the back of his neck. It was too quiet, too still. Like the calm before the storm.

"I don't like this," he muttered, his eyes scanning the perimeter for any sign of movement. "It's too easy. Where are the guards, the security measures?"

Thorne frowned, her hand tightening on the grip of her weapon. "You're right. Something's off. Everyone, stay alert. This could be a trap."

But even as the words left her mouth, all hell broke loose. The doors of the facility burst open, and a horde of Purifiers and mutant hybrids poured out, their weapons blazing and their eyes filled with mindless rage.

"Fuck!" Liam yelled, diving for cover behind a rusted-out shipping container. "It's an ambush!"

The air erupted with the sound of gunfire and the crackle of energy weapons, the ground shaking with the force of the explosions. Liam could feel the heat of the blasts, could smell the acrid tang of smoke and ozone.

But he didn't have time to dwell on the chaos around him. He had a job to do, and he was going to see it through, no matter the cost.

With a roar of fury, Liam unleashed his pyrokinesis, his eyes blazing with an inner fire as he channeled the flames that burned within him. The air shimmered with heat, the very molecules seeming to bend and warp under the force of his power.

He carved a path through the enemy forces, his flames consuming all in their wake. Purifiers screamed as their flesh blistered and charred, their weapons melting in their hands. Mutant hybrids howled in agony as the fire seared their twisted flesh, their enhancements no match for the sheer, raw power of Liam's rage.

"Holy shit," Marcus breathed, his eyes wide with awe as he watched Liam work. "Remind me never to piss him off."

Zoe grinned, her own powers crackling at her fingertips as she sent bolts of lightning arcing through the air. "You and me both, big guy. Our boy is on a mission, and heaven help anyone who gets in his way."

Together, they fought their way into the facility, the loyal DMA agents providing cover fire as they advanced. The halls were a maze of twisting corridors and sealed doors, each one leading deeper into the heart of Novak's lair.

But Liam didn't falter, didn't hesitate. He could feel Ethan's presence, could sense him like a beacon in the darkness. And he would not rest until he had him safe in his arms once more.

Finally, they reached the inner sanctum, a cavernous chamber filled with the hum of machinery and the sickly-sweet stench of chemicals. And there, in the center of it all, was Ethan.

He was strapped to a table, his body writhing in agony as a tangle of tubes and wires pumped God knows what into his veins. His face was pale, his eyes glazed with pain, but when he saw Liam, a flicker of hope sparked to life in their depths.

"Liam," he rasped, his voice hoarse and broken. "You came for me."

Liam's heart clenched, a wave of love and relief washing over him. "Of course I did, you idiot," he said softly, his hands shaking as he tore at the restraints that held Ethan down. "I'll always come for you."

But before he could free him, a cold, mocking laugh echoed through the chamber. Liam spun around, his eyes widening in horror as he saw Novak stepping out of the shadows.

But it was not the Novak he remembered. Gone was the cool, clinical scientist, the woman who had played them all for fools. In her place was a monster, a twisted abomination of flesh and metal and pulsing, sickly-green energy.

"You fools," she hissed, her voice layered with the echoes of a thousand stolen powers. "You think you can stop me? I am the future, the next step in evolution. And you… you are nothing but relics of a bygone age, fit only to be ground beneath my heel."

Liam snarled, his fists clenching at his sides as he stepped forward to face her. "You're insane, Novak. All this suffering, all this death… and for what? Some twisted fantasy of mutant supremacy?"

Novak laughed, the sound grating and inhuman. "Insane? No, Liam. I am the only one who sees clearly. The only one who understands the true potential of our kind."

She spread her arms wide, her body crackling with stolen power. "Behold the glory of the Prometheus Splice, the true and perfect blend of science and mutation. With the powers of a thousand mutants at my command, I will remake this world in my image. And you… you will be the first to fall before my might."

Liam's jaw clenched, a white-hot rage boiling up inside him. "Like hell," he spat, his eyes blazing with an inner fire. "Bring it on, bitch.

Let's see what you're made of."

And with that, the battle was joined. Novak unleashed a barrage of powers, her body shifting and warping like some nightmarish kaleidoscope. Energy blasts and force fields, telekinetic waves and psionic lances, all of them aimed squarely at Liam and his team.

But Liam was ready for her. He met her powers with his own, his flames roaring to life as he poured every ounce of his strength, every ounce of his love and his rage, into the fight.

It was a battle unlike any he had ever known, a clash of wills and powers that shook the very foundations of the facility. The ground cracked and buckled beneath their feet, the walls crumbling and shattering under the onslaught of their unleashed abilities.

And through it all, Liam never wavered, never faltered. He fought with a fierce, unyielding determination, his mind focused on one thing and one thing only.

Saving Ethan. Stopping Novak. No matter the cost.

"Liam!" Zoe yelled, her voice barely audible over the din of battle. "We can't hold her off much longer! We need to end this, now!"

Liam gritted his teeth, his mind racing as he tried to find a way to turn the tide. And then, with a sudden, blinding clarity, he knew what he had to do.

"Novak!" he shouted, his voice ringing out like a clarion call. "You think you're so powerful, so evolved? Prove it. Face me, one on one. No powers, no tricks. Just you and me, in a test of wills."

Novak paused, her head cocked to the side as she considered his challenge. "And why should I bother with such a pointless exercise?" she sneered, her lips curling in disdain.

Liam grinned, a fierce, feral thing. "Because if you win, I'll surrender. I'll let you do whatever you want with me, no resistance. But if I win… you let Ethan go, and you come quietly. No more fighting, no more bloodshed."

For a long, tense moment, Novak stared at him, her eyes glittering with a mad, calculating light. And then, slowly, she nodded.

"Very well, Liam Quinn. I accept your challenge. Let us see who is truly the stronger, the more evolved. And when I crush you beneath my heel… I will savor the look of despair on your face as I tear your precious Ethan apart, piece by piece."

"Let's do this," he growled, his eyes locked on Novak's in a silent challenge. "Let's finish this, once and for all."

The battle was fierce, a whirlwind of fists and fury as Liam and Novak clashed in the center of the chamber. Novak was strong, her body enhanced by the countless powers she had stolen, but Liam was fueled by something even greater - the love and the rage that burned in his heart, the unbreakable bond that tied him to Ethan.

They traded blows like titans, their limbs a blur of motion as they struck and parried and dodged. Liam could feel the impact of each hit, the jarring force that rattled his bones and set his teeth on edge.

But he didn't falter, didn't waver. He poured every ounce of his strength, every ounce of his will, into the fight. He would not let Novak win, would not let her twisted vision become a reality.

And then, just when it seemed like the battle would go on forever, a cry rang out from across the chamber. Liam's head snapped around, his eyes widening in shock and horror as he saw Ethan struggling to his feet, his body weak and trembling but his eyes blazing with determination.

"Ethan!" Liam yelled, his heart in his throat. "What the fuck are you doing? Get out of here, now!"

But Ethan just shook his head, a grim smile tugging at the corners of his mouth. "Not a chance, babe. You think I'm just going to sit back and watch you have all the fun? You should know me better than that by now."

With a grunt of effort, he summoned The Judgment card, his ultimate and most powerful arcana. The ethereal construct shimmered in the air before him, a being of pure light and energy that seemed to radiate an aura of divine retribution.

Novak's eyes widened, a flicker of fear passing over her face. "No," she hissed, her voice tight with strain as she struggled against Liam's hold. "You can't… you don't have the strength…"

But Ethan just grinned, a fierce, feral thing that sent shivers down Liam's spine. "Watch me, bitch."

And with that, he channeled every last ounce of his power into The Judgment card, pouring his very life force into the construct. The air crackled with energy, the ground shaking beneath their feet as the arcana swelled and grew, its light burning brighter and hotter with each passing second.

Novak screamed, her body convulsing as The Judgment card's power tore through her defenses like tissue paper. Stolen abilities and twisted enhancements alike were stripped away, leaving her naked and powerless before the onslaught of Ethan's will.

And then, with a final, blinding flash of light, it was over. Novak collapsed to the ground, her body broken and her mind shattered. The threat was ended, the world saved from her mad ambitions.

But the cost had been high. Too high.

Liam watched in horror as Ethan slumped to the ground, his body drained and his eyes fluttering closed. He was at his side in an instant, gathering his lover into his arms and cradling him close.

"Ethan," he whispered, his voice hoarse with fear and desperation. "Ethan, baby, please. Open your eyes, look at me."

But Ethan was still, his face pale and his breathing shallow. Liam could feel the life force ebbing from his body, could sense the spark of his spirit growing weaker with each passing moment.

Around them, the loyal DMA agents sprang into action, securing Novak and rounding up the last of her minions. But Liam barely noticed, his entire world narrowed down to the man in his arms, the man he loved more than life itself.

"Don't you fucking dare, Ethan Hawke," he growled, his voice raw with emotion. "Don't you dare leave me, not now. Not after everything we've been through."

Tears streamed down his face, hot and bitter as he pressed his forehead against Ethan's. "I love you," he whispered, his voice breaking. "I love you so goddamn much. Please, baby. Please come back to me."

But Ethan was silent, his body still and his breath fading. And Liam felt a part of himself breaking, shattering into a million jagged pieces.

It couldn't end like this. It couldn't. Not after everything they had endured, everything they had sacrificed. Ethan was a fighter, a survivor. He had to come back, had to open his eyes and flash that cocky, infuriating grin that Liam loved so much.

But the seconds ticked by, and Ethan remained still, his life force flickering like a guttering candle. Liam's heart clenched, a wave of despair washing over him like a tide.

And then, just when all hope seemed lost, a miracle happened.

Ethan's eyes fluttered open, hazy and unfocused but alive. Alive.

"Liam?" he rasped, his voice weak and thready. "What... what happened? Did we... did we win?"

Liam let out a sob of relief, his arms tightening around Ethan as he pressed a fierce, desperate kiss to his lips. "Yeah, baby. We won. You won. You saved us all."

Ethan smiled, a tired, triumphant thing that made Liam's heart ache with love. "I had a little help," he murmured, his hand coming up to cup Liam's cheek. "Couldn't have done it without my knight in shining armor."

Liam laughed, the sound watery and choked with emotion. "You're a fucking idiot, you know that? Don't ever scare me like that again."

Ethan's grin widened, a spark of his old mischief glinting in his eyes.

"No promises, babe. You know me, always looking for new ways to keep you on your toes."

Before Liam could retort, a commotion drew their attention. They looked up to see Novak being dragged away in chains, her face a mask of hatred and defeat.

But even in her lowest moment, she couldn't resist one final barb. "You think this is over?" she spat, her voice dripping with venom. "You think you've won? I'm just the beginning, the first of many who will rise up to claim our rightful place in the world. You can't stop the future, Liam Quinn. Sooner or later, the mutants will rule, and the humans will be nothing but cattle for us to use and discard as we see fit."

Liam's jaw clenched, his eyes hardening with resolve. "We'll see about that, Novak. We'll see."

As the DMA agents dragged her away, Liam turned back to Ethan, his expression softening with love and concern. "Come on, baby. Let's get you out of here, get you checked out by a doctor."

Ethan groaned, his nose wrinkling in distaste. "Do I have to? You know how I feel about hospitals, Liam."

Liam rolled his eyes, a fond smile tugging at his lips. "Tough shit, Hawke. You're going, and that's final. I'm not taking any chances with your stubborn ass."

Ethan sighed, but there was a glimmer of amusement in his eyes. "Fine. But only if you promise to stay with me the whole time, hold my hand and tell me what a brave little soldier I am."

Liam snorted, shaking his head in exasperation. "You're impossible, you know that?"

But even as he said it, he was already gathering Ethan into his arms, his heart swelling with love and gratitude. They had won, against all odds. They had saved the world, and each other.

And as they made their way out of the facility, battered and bruise but alive, Liam knew that he would never take a single moment for granted again. Because life was precious, and love was a gift, and every second that he had with Ethan was a treasure beyond measure.

They had fought the darkness and emerged victorious. And whatever challenges lay ahead, whatever threats might rise to face them in the future, Liam knew that they would face them together.

Always together, until the very end.

25

New Beginnings

Ethan

He leaned back in his chair, his signature smirk firmly in place as he surveyed the bustling activity of the DMA headquarters. It had been a few days since their showdown with Dr. Novak, and the world was still reeling from the aftermath of her twisted machinations.

But for Ethan, the real challenge was just beginning. He knew that the DMA would want answers, would want to debrief him and Liam on every little detail of their mission. And while he was grateful for their help in stopping Novak, he couldn't shake the feeling of unease that coiled in his gut at the thought of being beholden to anyone, even an agency as powerful as the DMA.

Beside him, Liam shifted in his seat, his brow furrowed with the same mixture of anticipation and wariness that Ethan felt. They had been through hell together, had faced down a madwoman with delusions of grandeur and lived to tell the tale. But now, as they sat in the heart of the DMA's power, Ethan couldn't help but wonder what the future held for them, and for their fragile, newfound partnership.

297

The door to Director Thorne's office swung open, and the woman herself strode out, her expression unreadable as she took in the sight of Ethan and Liam. Ethan felt a flicker of amusement at the way her eyes widened slightly, a hint of surprise and perhaps even a touch of awe passing over her face before she schooled her features back into a mask of cool professionalism.

"Gentlemen," she said, her voice crisp and businesslike. "Thank you for coming. Please, step into my office."

Ethan exchanged a glance with Liam, a silent conversation passing between them in the space of a heartbeat. Then, with a shrug and a cocky grin, he pushed himself to his feet and sauntered into Thorne's office, Liam following close behind.

As the door swung shut behind them, Thorne settled herself behind her desk, her hands steepled in front of her as she regarded them with a steady, assessing gaze. "First of all," she said, her voice softening slightly, "I want to express my deepest gratitude for your actions in stopping Dr. Novak. What you did… it was nothing short of heroic. You saved countless lives, and you have the thanks of the entire DMA for your bravery and sacrifice."

Ethan felt a warmth bloom in his chest at her words, a flicker of pride and satisfaction that he couldn't quite suppress. But he kept his expression carefully neutral, his voice light and airy as he replied, "Just doing our job, Director. It's what we do."

Liam snorted, shaking his head in fond exasperation. "What he means is, we were happy to help. Novak needed to be stopped, and we were in a position to do something about it."

Thorne nodded, a tiny smile tugging at the corner of her mouth. "Indeed. And your efforts have not gone unnoticed. The DMA has been working around the clock to secure all of Novak's research materials and shut down any remaining Genexis operations. As far as we can tell, the entire organization was under her control, and with her in custody, the threat has been neutralized."

Ethan felt a flicker of relief at her words, a weight lifting from his shoulders that he hadn't even realized he'd been carrying. But even as he savored the moment of triumph, he couldn't shake the nagging sense of unease that lurked at the back of his mind.

"That's great news, Director," he said, his voice carefully casual. "But I have to ask… what happens now? With Novak out of the picture, where does that leave us? And more importantly, where does that leave the DMA?"

Thorne's expression turned serious, her eyes sharp and assessing as she studied Ethan's face. "That's actually what I wanted to discuss with you both. The DMA is grateful for your assistance, and we would like to continue our partnership moving forward. Your skills, your knowledge… they would be invaluable in helping us to combat future threats to the mutant community."

Ethan's eyes narrowed, his guard immediately going up at her words. He knew that the DMA wasn't offering this out of the goodness of their hearts. They wanted something from him and Liam, wanted to use their abilities for their own ends. And while he was willing to work with them to a certain extent, he wasn't about to become their goddamn lapdog.

"I appreciate the offer, Director," he said, his voice cool and measured. "But I think it's important that we establish some ground rules before we agree to anything. Liam and I… we're not interested in becoming full-time DMA agents. We value our independence, and we're not willing to give that up, even for the greater good."

Thorne's brow furrowed, a hint of frustration passing over her face. "I understand your concerns, Ethan. But surely you can see the benefits of working more closely with us? The resources, the support… it could make a real difference in the fight against those who would do harm to our kind."

Liam leaned forward, his expression serious. "We're not saying we won't work with you, Director. But it has to be on our terms. We're willing to collaborate on specific cases, to share information and lend our expertise when needed. But we need to maintain our autonomy, to be able to operate independently when the situation calls for it."

Ethan nodded, a fierce, stubborn light in his eyes. "Liam's right. We're not going to be at your beck and call, Thorne. We have our own lives, our own missions. And while we're happy to help out when we can, we're not going to drop everything just because the DMA says so."

For a long, tense moment, Thorne stared at them, her expression unreadable. Ethan could practically see the gears turning in her head, the calculations and assessments as she weighed the pros and cons of their proposal.

Finally, she let out a long, slow breath, her shoulders slumping slightly in resignation. "Very well. I can accept those terms, with one condition. If a threat emerges that is beyond the scope of the DMA's capabilities, if we find ourselves in a situation where your unique skills are required… I need your word that you will answer the call. That you will put aside your personal reservations and work with us to protect the innocent and bring those responsible to justice."

Ethan exchanged a glance with Liam, a silent conversation passing between them in the space of a heartbeat. It was a risk, he knew. A gamble that could come back to bite them in the ass if they weren't careful. But he also knew that they couldn't turn their backs on the world, couldn't ignore the responsibility that came with their powers and their abilities.

And so, with a deep breath and a nod of agreement, Ethan turned back to Thorne, his voice low and serious. "Alright, Director. You have our word. If the shit hits the fan and you need us… we'll be there. But only on our terms. Only when we say so."

Thorne's lips thinned, but she nodded, a flicker of respect passing over her face. "I can accept that. Welcome to the team, gentlemen. I look forward to working with you both in the future."

As they shook hands and made their way out of the office, Ethan couldn't help but feel a sense of unease wash over him. He knew that they had made the right choice, that they had navigated the treacherous waters of the DMA's politics as best they could.

But he also knew that this was just the beginning, that there would be challenges and obstacles ahead that they could never anticipate. Novak's cryptic warning still echoed in his mind, the promise of future threats and hidden enemies that lurked in the shadows.

He glanced over at Liam, taking in the determined set of his jaw and the fire that burned in his eyes. And he knew, with a bone-deep certainty, that whatever lay ahead, they would face it together. They were partners, in every sense of the word. And nothing, not the DMA, not the forces of darkness, could ever tear them apart.

As they stepped out into the bright, golden sunlight of the city, Ethan threw his arm around Liam's shoulders, a cocky grin spreading across his face. "Well, that went better than expected. Looks like we're officially in bed with the DMA now. Just promise me one thing, babe?"

Liam raised an eyebrow, a hint of amusement playing at the corners of his mouth. "What's that, Ethan?"

Ethan's grin widened, his eyes sparkling with mischief. "If Thorne ever tries to put a leash on us, you'll let me be the one to tell her to go fuck herself. I've been practicing my dramatic exits, and I think I've got the perfect line ready."

Liam snorted, shaking his head in exasperation. But Ethan could see the love and the laughter shining in his eyes, the unbreakable bond that had been forged in the fires of their trials and triumphs.

"You're a fucking idiot, Ethan Hawke," Liam said, his voice warm and fond. "But you're my idiot. Now come on, let's go home. We've got a lot to do if we're going to be ready for whatever the future throws at us."

And as they walked away, hand in hand, Ethan knew that he had never been happier, never been more at peace. Because with Liam by his side, he could face anything. With Liam by his side, he was invincible.

Bring it on, world. Ethan fucking Hawke was ready for anything.

Later that evening, as they sat on the balcony of Ethan's penthouse, sipping beers and watching the sun set over the city skyline, Ethan couldn't help but feel a sense of contentment wash over him. It had been one hell of a ride, but they had made it through. They had faced down the darkness and emerged victorious, stronger and more united than ever before.

Beside him, Liam let out a long, slow breath, his eyes distant and thoughtful. "It's crazy, isn't it?" he murmured, his voice soft and contemplative. "Everything that's happened, everything we've been through. Sometimes I feel like I'm going to wake up and find out it was all just a dream."

Ethan chuckled, reaching out to take Liam's hand in his own. "Trust me, babe, if this is a dream, I don't ever want to wake up."

Liam smiled, a soft, tender thing that made Ethan's heart skip a beat. But there was a hint of uncertainty in his eyes, a flicker of doubt that Ethan couldn't quite place.

"What's on your mind, Liam?" he asked, his voice gentle but probing. "I can see the gears turning in that pretty head of yours."

Liam hesitated, his brow furrowing slightly. "I just… I can't help but wonder what's next, you know? We've been fighting for so long, battling against the forces of evil and corruption. But now, with Novak gone and the DMA on our side… what do we do? Where do we go from here?"

Ethan felt a flicker of understanding, a sense of the same uncertainty and trepidation that he saw in Liam's eyes. But he pushed it down, forced himself to summon the cocky, unshakable confidence that had always been his armor against the world.

"We write our own story, Liam," he said, his voice firm and unwavering. "We take the future into our own hands and shape it however we damn well please. No more living in the shadows, no more carrying the weight of the world on our shoulders. From now on, we do things our way. Together."

Liam's eyes widened, a flicker of hope and excitement sparking to life in their depths. But there was still a hint of hesitation, a touch of doubt that lingered at the edges of his smile.

"But what about the fight, Ethan?" he asked, his voice low and serious. "What about the mutants who still need our help, the enemies that still lurk in the darkness? Can we really just walk away from all of that, pretend like it doesn't exist?"

Ethan sighed, running a hand through his hair in frustration. He knew that Liam was right, knew that they couldn't just turn their backs on the world and ride off into the sunset. But he also knew that they had earned the right to a little peace, a little happiness. And he was determined to seize it with both hands, to hold onto it with everything he had.

"I'm not saying we walk away completely, Liam," he said, his voice soft but intense. "I'm just saying that we find a balance, a way to fight the good fight without letting it consume us. We've given so much of ourselves, sacrificed so much for the cause. It's time we started living for ourselves, too."

Liam was silent for a long moment, his eyes searching Ethan's face for some sign of deception, of ulterior motive. But all he saw was love, and hope, and a fierce, unshakable determination.

"Okay," he said finally, his voice barely above a whisper. "Okay, Ethan. Let's do it. Let's write our own story, together. As partners, in every sense of the word."

Ethan felt a rush of emotion wash over him, a wave of love and gratitude and joy that threatened to sweep him away. He wanted to tell Liam how much he meant to him, how much he loved him with every fiber of his being. But the words stuck in his throat, the weight of them too heavy, too permanent to voice out loud.

And so instead, he simply leaned in and captured Liam's lips in a searing, passionate kiss, pouring every ounce of his love and devotion into the press of their mouths. Liam melted into the embrace, his arms coming up to wrap around Ethan's neck as he deepened the kiss, his tongue tangling with Ethan's in a dance of desire and need.

When they finally broke apart, both of them were breathless and flushed, their eyes dark with want and their hearts racing with anticipation. Ethan rested his forehead against Liam's, a soft, contented sigh escaping his lips.

"Move in with me," he whispered, his voice hoarse and raw with emotion. "Stay here, with me, in this place that we can make our own. Our sanctuary, our home."

Liam's eyes widened, a flicker of surprise and joy passing over his face. "Are you serious, Ethan? You really want me to move in with you?"

Ethan grinned, a cocky, self-assured thing that made Liam's heart skip a beat. "Of course I'm serious, you idiot. I wouldn't have asked if I didn't mean it. I want you here, with me, every day and every night. I want to wake up to your face and fall asleep to your heartbeat. I want to build a life with you, Liam. A real, honest-to-God life."

Liam's smile was blinding, a radiant, joyful thing that lit up the night like a supernova. "Yes," he breathed, his voice shaking with emotion. "Yes, Ethan, of course I'll move in with you. There's nothing I want more in this world than to be with you, to make a home with you."

Ethan let out a whoop of joy, sweeping Liam up into his arms and spinning him around in a circle. Liam laughed, the sound bright and carefree as he clung to Ethan's shoulders, his face buried in the crook of his neck.

And there, in the warmth and safety of each other's arms, they knew that they had found something rare and precious. A love that could weather any storm, a bond that could never be broken.

They were Ethan and Liam, the Arcana and the firefighter. And together, they could face anything the world threw at them.

Thank you and Please Leave a Review!

Dear Readers,

As we come to the end of this wild and whimsical journey with the first book of the Major Arcana Series, I want to take a moment to express my deepest gratitude. Thank you for joining us on this adventure filled with laughter, love, and a touch of the supernatural.

It's been an absolute joy to share this story with you, and I hope their antics brought a smile to your face and warmth to your heart. Writing their tale has been an incredible experience, and I'm so grateful for the opportunity to share it with all of you.

If you enjoyed our story, please consider leaving a review. Your feedback means the world to me, and it helps other readers discover our book and join in on the fun.

Thank you again for your support, your laughter, and your love. Here's to many more adventures together!

With heartfelt appreciation,
Ken Sanchez

About the Author

Ken Sanchez, the visionary behind spellbinding M/M romance-fantasy worlds where love and magic entwine in a mesmerizing dance. With a heart devoted to the art of LGBTQ+ romance and an unbounded imagination,

Please sign up for my newsletter to get my new releases and get some freebies! And join my Facebook group for more updates! Linktree link is below!

You can connect with me on:

https://linktr.ee/kensanchezbooks

Also by Ken Sanchez

Enchanted (Willowbrook Book One)
In the enchanting town of Willowbrook, a young man named Benjamin discovers a remarkable power—the ability to bring stories to life. When he encounters a reclusive Beast named Adrian, cursed to shift between a fearsome ice dragon and a human form that freezes everything he touches, their destinies entwine.

As Benjamin and Adrian navigate a treacherous journey filled with love, friendship, and the transformative power of stories, they must break Adrian's curse to save Willowbrook from an eternal winter. With the town's magical essence slowly fading, time is running out.

Stormweaver (Willowbrook Book Two)

In the enchanted town of Willowbrook, where supernatural forces intertwine, a storm is brewing, threatening to shatter the delicate balance between magic and reality. Weather witch Dominic Reed seeks solace in his bakery, Glimmer, but his haunted past and tumultuous family dynamics refuse to fade.

Enter Christian Belgrade, heir to a vampire coven, whose scarred history and possessive nature are eclipsed only by his mysterious powers. When their worlds collide at Christian's club, a revelation unfolds, setting off a chain of events that will test their strengths, unravel their vulnerabilities, and force them to confront the shadows that lurk in the magical underbelly of Willowbrook.

As the connection deepens between Dominic and Christian, they must navigate the treacherous waters of Elder Eros Grim's vendetta and Dominic's malevolent stepfamily. Will love be enough to weather the storm that threatens to consume them, or will the secrets of their pasts tear them apart?

Shadowplay (Willowbrook Book Three)

When Peter Naps arrives in the enchanting town of Willowbrook, he's hoping to find answers to the questions that have haunted him for years. Plagued by mysterious gaps in his memory and a sense of otherness he can't quite shake, Peter is drawn to the town's strange energy and the whispers of magic that seem to call to him from every corner.

But as he delves deeper into the secrets of Willowbrook and his own forgotten past, Peter finds himself entangled in a web of danger and intrigue. Guided by cryptic clues and the enigmatic James Crane, a man with his own hidden agenda, Peter begins to uncover the truth about his powers and the forces that seek to control them.

With the help of a quirky cast of characters, including his fiercely loyal best friend Lyra and the mysterious librarian who seems to know more than she's letting on, Peter must navigate a treacherous landscape of shadows and secrets, where nothing is quite as it seems and the line between friend and foe is blurred. As he races to unravel the mystery of his own identity and the dark forces that threaten to tear Willowbrook apart, Peter will be forced to confront his deepest fears and most painful truths, to embrace the power that lies within him and the love that refuses to let him go.

Echoes of Destiny (Shadowguards Book One)
Eryx, a gifted musician, channels haunting melodies that echo his forgotten godly lineage. When a sinister encounter alters his reality, he finds solace in an enigmatic guardian named Alex, whose alluring presence sparks an inexplicable connection.

Unbeknownst to Eryx, Alex is Hades, sentinel of the Underworld. As he guides Eryx through their intertwined destinies, an undeniable attraction forms, challenging the fabric of their worlds.

Amidst mysticism in contemporary New York, ancient prophecies resurge with encroaching darkness. Their bond becomes a beacon of hope as Eryx's ancestry awakens and their love deepens. The duo embarks on a quest that will test their resolve, unravel hidden truths, and decide humanity's fate.

Light Redeemed (Shadowguards Book Two)

The line between mortal and divine blurs as an ancient threat resurfaces, determined to plunge New York into chaos. Eryx Ross, now fully embracing his destiny as Apollo's vessel, must navigate his burgeoning powers and deepening bond with the enigmatic Alexander Knight, the mortal embodiment of Hades. Together, they face an unconventional challenge that will test their love and the very fabric of their world.

Amidst the gathering darkness, Eryx and Alex's souls entwine on a cosmic scale, their love a beacon of hope against the sinister machinations of the Order. They rally allies both old and new, gods and mortals alike, to stand against the rising tide of evil. But the Order holds a terrifying trump card – a mimic with the power to steal magic – threatening to unravel all they hold dear.